*"G
again and drive you to my place."*

God, how he wanted to be with her, but she needed time, and he'd give her anything she needed.

"I don't get a kiss goodnight?" she asked with one raised eyebrow and a flirty tone in her voice. He liked it when she let her guard down and gave into this playful side of herself.

Two could play at this game. With a deliberately deepened voice, he asked, "Do you want a kiss goodnight?"

She tilted her lips down into a pouty frown. "I guess you don't want to kiss me." Bell tried to reach for the door.

Dane turned her to him and kissed her deeply. She caught on quick and matched her movements to his. They lost themselves in each other's arms. She squirmed toward the door. He leaned in closer, keeping his lips pressed to hers until the last second. She stood on the truck's running board, her hands planted on the seat as she leaned into the truck and smiled at him like he'd never seen her smile.

"God, you're beautiful."

Her laugh would play in a loop in his mind for the rest of his days.

"Goodnight, Dane."

By Jennifer Ryan

HER LUCKY COWBOY
WHEN IT'S RIGHT
AT WOLF RANCH
DYLAN'S REDEMPTION
FALLING FOR OWEN
THE RETURN OF BRODY MCBRIDE
CHASING MORGAN
THE RIGHT BRIDE
LUCKY LIKE US
SAVED BY THE RANCHER

Short Stories
CAN'T WAIT
(appears in ALL I WANT FOR CHRISTMAS IS A COWBOY)
WAITING FOR YOU
(appears in CONFESSIONS OF A SECRET ADMIRER)

ATTENTION: ORGANIZATIONS AND CORPORATIONS
HarperCollins books may be purchased for educational, business, or sales promotional use. For information, please e-mail the Special Markets Department at SPsales@harpercollins.com.

HER LUCKY COWBOY

A MONTANA MEN NOVEL

JENNIFER RYAN

AVONBOOKS

An Imprint of HarperCollinsPublishers

This is a work of fiction. Names, characters, places, and incidents are products of the author's imagination or are used fictitiously and are not to be construed as real. Any resemblance to actual events, locales, organizations, or persons, living or dead, is entirely coincidental.

AVON BOOKS
An Imprint of HarperCollins*Publishers*
195 Broadway
New York, New York 10007

Copyright © 2015 by Jennifer Ryan
Excerpt from *Everything She Wanted* copyright © 2016 by Jennifer Ryan
ISBN 978-0-06-233495-4
www.avonromance.com

All rights reserved. No part of this book may be used or reproduced in any manner whatsoever without written permission, except in the case of brief quotations embodied in critical articles and reviews. For information address Avon Books, an Imprint of HarperCollins Publishers.

First Avon Books mass market printing: September 2015

Avon Trademark Reg. U.S. Pat. Off. and in Other Countries, Marca Registrada, Hecho en U.S.A.
HarperCollins® is a registered trademark of HarperCollins Publishers.

Printed in the U.S.A.

10 9 8 7 6 5 4 3 2 1

If you purchased this book without a cover, you should be aware that this book is stolen property. It was reported as "unsold and destroyed" to the publisher, and neither the author nor the publisher has received any payment for this "stripped book."

Sometimes all you need is one person to see you for who you really are to know you're loved.

PROLOGUE

Bowden Ranch, Montana
Eleven years ago

Dane was flying.

One moment he was riding his horse across the far reaches of his family's land, the next his horse reared up and kicked his massive hooves in the air, spooked by some unseen threat. Dane let loose the reins and fell sideways, hoping the horse didn't trample him. Dane's left foot hit the ground first, his ankle twisting painfully as his body slammed into the packed dirt and weeds. His shoulder hit next, breaking most of his upper body's fall, but his head smashed into a jagged rock. Pain exploded through his head.

Hombre galloped away. Alone now, Dane rolled and lay flat on his back, staring up at the canopy of tree branches overhead. The sound of the rushing river next to him added to the thrashing heartbeat in his ears. He rubbed his hands over his eyes, hoping that cleared his spotty double vision. His left hand came away wet and sticky with blood from the gash swelling on his head.

He closed his eyes tight, his hands falling limp on his stomach. When he opened them moments later, he stared into a pair of dazzling blue eyes. The young girl's dark hair hung down, covering most of her pale face as she stared at him. The most beautiful girl he'd ever seen.

"Are you okay?"

Such a soft, sweet voice. Where had she come from? No one lived out here. He liked the peace and quiet. The solitude.

"I must be dead. You're an angel."

Those ethereal eyes went wide with surprise. "Trust me, I'm no angel." She filled those soft words with as much shock and disbelief as showed on her pretty face.

Calling her a liar probably wouldn't make her like him.

She crouched, opened her hand, and set a long blue feather on his chest before touching her fingers to his aching head. The sting made him hiss in pain. Definitely not dead. Which meant she was real. Despite his prone body and inability to think clearly, one thing came through loud and clear. He wanted to know this girl.

"I need to stop this bleeding."

He must have torn his T-shirt when he hit the ground. She ripped a piece free, walked to the edge of the river, and dipped it in the icy water. His vision blurred. He closed his eyes and moaned when she pressed the cold cloth to his head.

"There now. You'll be okay."

At fifteen, the last thing he wanted to do was ask for help, but his head swam and his ankle throbbed in time to his heart and the headache pounding in his head. No way he'd get home on his own. "My ankle hurts. Please, you have to get my dad. Find one of my brothers."

Her soft hand settled on his chest over his heart.

She snatched it back, like touching him burned her. He missed the sweet contact.

She reached for his foot and carefully pulled off his boot. He tried to bite back the groan, but it burst from his tight lips when the pain shot up his leg. Not cool to look like a wuss in front of a pretty girl, but with his head busted open, he was in bad shape.

She ripped his shirt again and used the long strip to bind his ankle. It actually felt better.

She sat beside him, her hands clenched in her lap. "I shouldn't be here. I shouldn't have touched you. I'm sorry."

He didn't understand her distress. He tried to sit up and comfort her, but he fell back to the ground, his eyes closing as blackness swamped his dizzy mind.

A hand settled on his shoulder and shook him. He groggily moaned and tried to open his eyes. The bright sun blinded him until his father leaned over and blocked the light as he stared down at Dane.

"Dad?"

"Are you okay, son? Is anything broken?"

"My head hurts. Ankle, too, but nothing is broken but my pride. I fell off my damn horse."

"Okay, now. I'll get you home. Can you get up?"

"I think so." Dane pressed his hands down at his sides and rose to sitting. The wet piece of fabric fell from his head and landed on his bare belly, along with the blue feather that fluttered into his lap. "Where is she?"

"Who?"

"The girl."

"Dane, no one is here."

"She helped me. She's got to be around here somewhere."

"There's no one for miles."

"How did you find me?"

"Your horse came home without you. I know you like to ride along the river, so I followed your trail." His dad cocked his head, his eyes taking on a thoughtful gleam. "I did think I heard you whistle for me."

"I passed out."

"Must have been the wind in the trees."

Dane didn't think so. He pinched the end of the feather between his thumb and index finger and stared at it. He scanned the riverbank and out toward the hills. He didn't see her anywhere. He didn't understand the way his chest went tight and the sadness that overtook him. Nothing but his regret that he didn't get to thank her or say goodbye. He never got her name.

His dad held out his hand. Dane took it. His father pulled him up, and Dane stood on his good leg. He tested out his twisted ankle. The slight pressure sent a bolt of pain up his leg.

"How's your vision?"

"Better."

"You did a good job using your shirt to bind that ankle and staunch the bleeding on your head."

"I didn't. She did."

His father eyed him, shaking his head side to side. "Dane—"

"I'm telling you, Dad, there was a girl. She helped me."

"Okay, son. I believe you, but I didn't see anyone out here with you. I don't know where she could have gone. We're in the middle of nowhere."

Which was the reason Dane liked it out here so much. Still, how did she get out here, and where did she go?

He lifted himself up into the saddle and grabbed the

reins on the horse his father brought back for him to ride. He kept his eyes trained, searching the entire area the whole way back home, but he saw nothing, no one.

Dane went back to the spot beside the river more than a dozen times, looking for his dark-haired, blue-eyed angel. He never found her, but he'd never forget her either.

CHAPTER 1

Las Vegas, Nevada
Pro Bull Riders World Championships

Bell loved everything about her first rodeo. The cowboys in their Wranglers and chaps. The beautiful horses. The excitement that built with every second of the ride. The lights in the arena and the roar of the crowd as they cheered for each competitor. She'd never seen such a spectacle.

She thought the same thing when her plane flew over the Las Vegas strip the other day.

Her half sister, Katherine, grabbed her arm when another bull burst out of the chute. The crowd's cheers turned to an ominous "Oh" as the rider flew off the massive animal and landed on unsteady legs, making a run for the fences when the bull turned and rushed his way. Katherine's husband, Tony, waved his arms along with the other rodeo clowns to distract the beast from going after the retreating bull rider.

"He's so sexy," her sister said about Tony, finally letting go the death grip she had on Bell's arm.

Bell smiled at her vibrant sister, wondering how the

hell they got here. Bell had tried to get out of this trip to Las Vegas and, of all things, the Pro Bull Riders World Finals. She might be from Montana, but she'd never been a ranch girl.

Two years ago, Katherine moved to Montana and Tony's ranch. She visited her grandmother's house—Bell's purgatory—and discovered the family secret—a half sister from an affair her father had years ago. The look on Katherine's face changed from shock to dawning understanding about all those angry snippets of hushed-up conversations between their father and her mother. For Katherine, it finally all made sense. Angry about being kept in the dark, she'd apparently contacted their father in California, demanding answers. Only one was given. Bell might be Katherine's half sister, but she was not family. Flabbergasted by their father's response, Katherine went against their father's dictates and continued to contact Bell.

While Katherine had known nothing of Bell, their grandmother had rejoiced in sharing all the details of Katherine's blessed life, torturing Bell with the fact she was nothing more than an unwanted burden. Katherine had been the chosen one. Bell, the whisper behind one's hand. The skeleton locked in the family closet. Never to be seen again.

Somehow Bell ended up here, sitting beside the woman who had the life Bell had once dreamed about. Katherine had grown up in a beautiful home surrounded by love from both her parents. She'd been the golden, spoiled child.

Bell's life had been anything but charmed. Her whole family hated her, including the grandmother who'd raised her. A religious zealot, she'd told Bell every day that she was nothing but a sin, a spawn of evil, something to be hidden away from civilized, God-fearing people. Even her own parents had recognized the evil in her and cast her out. She should be grateful her grandmother had taken pity on her and raised her, trying every day through prayer to convince God to save her from her wicked ways.

She'd lived in hell under her grandmother's rigid dictates, enduring her sharp, bitter tongue. Because once she'd known kindness.

Before her grandfather died, he'd taken a keen interest in educating her and sparking her interest in gardening and raising chickens. She'd never forget the day he brought her outside to the new coop and asked her to hold out her hands and close her eyes. She cupped them in front of her, closed her eyes, and thrilled at the anticipation rising inside her. He set something fuzzy in her hands. When she opened them, she squealed with delight at the bright yellow chick he'd given her and the ten others flitting about her feet.

She remembered his kind smile and the playful way he'd tug her hair when she did something well. She wished she remembered him better. For him, she continued to take care of her grandmother. One good deed deserved another, though some kindnesses were harder to repay than others. And her grandmother made it extremely difficult to this day.

Why the hell did Bell agree to come here? She and Katherine had nothing in common. Polar opposites, Katherine's optimism clashed with Bell's realistic outlook on life. Their awkward conversations and interaction proved the divide between them might never be bridged. Still, Katherine plugged on, trying and trying to connect with Bell, despite Bell's reluctance to open up. No one in the family ever wanted her. She didn't understand why Katherine cared, so she kept things polite but distant. Until Katherine begged her to take this trip with her and Tony. Bell gave in to that nagging voice in her heart, telling her to stop pushing Katherine away, let her in, and try to forge a relationship with her one and only sister.

So she'd flown in with Katherine and met Tony at the hotel after he drove his bulls in for the competition. She planned to make the most out of her short vacation and try to get to know Katherine better.

The crowd cheered again, and Bell silently admitted she had another secret reason for coming. A chance to see *him* again.

"Our last rider of the night," the announcer began. "A man who needs no introduction. Dane Bowden!"

The crowd went wild, rising to their feet, fists pumping in the air, cheering, "Great Dane. Great Dane. Great Dane."

Bell sat on the edge of her seat, heart in her throat, eyes locked on the man she hadn't seen since that day his horse threw him by the river. He climbed up onto the gates of the chute, pulled off his black Stetson, and gave a single wave to the crowd, flashing that devilish grin she remembered from her childhood. Everything in her went still, the crowd and noise fell away, and all she could see was the man she could never forget.

Geared up in his safety vest, chaps, spurs, and signature black Stetson, Dane climbed over the rails and into the bucking chute to take his position on the beast's black back. Twelve hundred pounds of pent-up, raging bull beneath him, he slipped his hand beneath the flat braided cord, pulled the rope over his hand, secured his grip, and held on for dear life. Eight seconds to decide where he'd land between victory and death.

It sucked that he had a tear along the thumb in his favorite pair of deerskin gloves, but he tried not to let it throw him off his game. Someone had been messing with him, his gear, and his truck for the last two weeks, but nothing could stop Dane today. He'd always been able to put everything aside, focus, and reach for that thrill and the win. This was his last championship ride, and he meant to go out a winner. He'd promised his parents and brothers he'd come home, run the family ranch, give up his wandering ways, and settle down to a normal—boring—life.

Yeah, right after this ride.

He'd tame this black beast tonight, then deal with the one within when he settled back home in Montana. Tonight, he'd ride under the Las Vegas lights.

Dane nodded, the chute door opened, and the bull bucked and reared. Dane held tight, one arm in the air as the bull twisted and the crowd went wild. He sank his spurs into the bull's side, held tight with his knees, and moved with Black Cloud. The bull kicked, reared, and spun around. Blake held tight for another round. Time to get off this ride, collect his winnings, and go out number one. The spot he'd been chasing these last years had always seemed one place out of his grasp. With three big brothers, first always seemed out of reach. He'd been second this whole year. Might as well be last. Tonight, he'd finish first. A champion.

The buzzer sounded eight seconds. Done. Victory. Dane smiled as the crowd cheered.

There are two great athletes in every ride. The two-legged one won this time.

Dane tried to dismount, but the bull spun at the last second and caught him in the side before his feet hit the ground. The rodeo clowns moved forward in his peripheral vision, but not in time. Black Cloud turned, rammed his head into Dane's chest, and sent him flying again. The impact pushed the air and his mouth guard out of his mouth. He bit the side of his lip and tasted blood. Sideways in the air, his left foot touched the ground first, then his body slammed into the dirt. His head bounced with the impact, making his vision spark and blur, but not before he saw the bull's body swing over the top of him in slow motion, his massive hooves coming down at Dane's legs, snapping his left leg bones like twigs. The flesh tore along with his jeans. White-hot pain shot through every nerve like lightning. Dane's heart jackhammered in his chest and ears. The bull rammed him again with his huge head, sliding Dane several feet along the dirt. The fierce pain shot through him, stealing his breath. His heart slammed into his ribs.

Shit. This can't be it. I can't go out like this.

So many things he wanted to do with his life. Instead of the past coming back to him, flashes of all he'd never do ran through his mind. He'd never run his own ranch. Never get married. Never have children. Never know the kind of love and happiness the rest of his family had found.

Damn if fate hadn't swung the rope, lassoed his life, and yanked him from victory toward death.

Overwhelmed with pain, his body went numb. A

collective gasp went up from the crowd, and the lights went out.

The minute Dane shot out of the gate on the back of Black Cloud, Bell's heart slammed into her ribs again and again. Her stomach tightened with anticipation and dread all mixed together. She prayed he won. She prayed he didn't get hurt.

God, he looked magnificent. His big body swayed back and forth as the animal bucked and tried to toss him off. Dane held tight. She admired his strength and determination, the focus he showed in his intense gaze. Arm in the air for balance, his fist clenched in triumph at the sound of the buzzer. The huge smile that spread across his face said it all. He'd won.

She breathed a sigh of relief and smiled with him. The bull twisted and caught Dane off guard. She sucked in a gasp and her heart stopped. Dane's big body flew through the air. The bull hit him hard, then crushed Dane's leg under his sharp hooves. Blood spurted from the compound fracture. Her medical training kicked in. She didn't hesitate; she jumped out of her seat and shimmied down the row past the other stunned spectators. Then she ran down the stairs, jumped the short wall, ran the few feet to the seven-foot fences, and climbed over them. She didn't stop when the security guard yelled, or when the two rodeo clowns tried to grab her. She headed straight for the man bleeding out on the ground. She skidded to a stop on her knees beside him, pushed his chaps up over his thigh, and tore open his jeans to reveal the splintered tibia and fibula sticking out of his slashed skin. She hated to move his messed-up leg, but necessity and saving his life prompted action. She stuck her hand down his boot, grabbed his ankle with her hand to stabilize it, and pulled his boot off with the other so she could see the full extent of the damage. The bull continued to stomp and twist in her peripheral vision. She straightened Dane's leg, panic rising to her throat when he grunted in pain, but she didn't stop. She pulled back the torn skin, found the squirting artery, and pinched it closed with her finger and thumb.

"Look out!"

Bell glanced up just in time to catch the swing of the bull's hindquarters up toward her head. She spread her knees, leaned back, and lay her shoulders to the ground between her feet. Despite her quick movements, she still caught a hoof to her forehead. Just a graze, but unfortunately, she let go of Dane's artery. The bull's hooves landed in the dirt inches from her arm. A horse and rider drew close, trying to distract the out-of-control animal. She pulled herself up and covered Dane's body with hers, a hand over his face and head as the bull charged, head down. The horse and rider knocked the bull to the side, but not before she got slammed in the shoulder, rocking her and Dane back before the rodeo clowns drew the bull's attention. Black Cloud ran off for the exit gates like nothing had happened.

Her head throbbed where she'd been hit, blood trickled down the side of her face, and her vision blurred and cleared a few times. The pain in her shoulder pulsed down her arm. She ignored it all and focused on her dying patient.

Covered in dirt and dust, she rose up, found the spurting artery again, pinched it off with her fingers, and checked Dane's leg, waiting for the arena to clear so the paramedics could get to them.

Damn, he'd lost a lot of blood.

The way he'd been tossed around and slammed into the ground, she bet he had a concussion, possibly some bruised or broken ribs, maybe a spine injury.

"Dane, are you okay?" Tony sank down beside her on his knees.

"He's out cold."

"That was my bull he was riding. Shit." Tony's gaze met hers. "Bell, your head."

"You need to back up and let the paramedics in," she ordered, no time to talk or worry about herself. Dane needed them to save his life.

"How the hell did you get down here so fast?" Tony asked.

She didn't know. She'd seen the injury, and the compulsion to get to Dane, to save him, had overridden every other thought, as well as her common sense.

That bull could have killed her.

A rush of fear washed over her, but she let it go and focused on Dane and keeping her fingers pinched onto his torn artery.

"We'll take it from here," a dark-haired paramedic said, dumping his gear in the dirt.

"I'm Dr. Bell. I'm an orthopedic surgeon out of Bozeman. I need a clamp to pinch off this artery."

The medic handed over the instrument. She fixed it to the artery just above her fingers and let go, knowing time was of the essence. The knock to her head made her thinking slow, but she tried to keep her focus, relying on her ER training to get her through and think step by step.

"We need to stabilize this leg. Get a neck brace on him. Check his vitals. Run a line."

The paramedics cut Dane's shirtsleeve to his shoulder, revealing the blue feather tattoo on the inside of his forearm. She read the words below. "An angel watches over me." She sucked in a startled breath.

"IV's in, Doc. How's the leg look?"

Bell refocused her attention on his mangled leg. "Scissors." She held out her hand and accepted the instrument. She cut off Dane's sock and slit the leg of his pants up to midthigh, spreading the bloody material wide to get a better look at his leg. She didn't like the looks of his foot. She pinched the skin near his big toe. Man, the guy had some big feet. The skin turned white and took several seconds to turn pink again. Not enough circulation.

"We need to move," she coaxed the paramedics, who worked to stabilize Dane's head in a collar. "I need a splint, some bandages, gauze. Come on. Move."

She'd spent six months in the ER. Controlled chaos. With trauma victims, every second mattered.

"What're his vitals?"

"Breathing is shallow, but steady. Clear airway. BP one twenty over seventy-seven. Heart rate eighty-nine."

"Dr. Bell, what the hell are you doing here?"

She glanced up and caught Gabe and Blake Bowden standing over the paramedics. They'd flown in from Montana to see their brother ride. At one time or another they'd both brought in a woman to the Crystal Creek Clinic for her to treat. They didn't know her. Not really. But she knew all about them. She'd grown up right next door, but they'd never known it.

She plunged ahead, not taking the time to answer. "Does Dane have any allergies to medication?"

"None," Gabe said.

"Any surgeries or illnesses in his past?"

"He had his tonsils out when he was a kid. A torn ligament and muscle in his shoulder repaired two years ago. Laparoscopic surgery on his knee three years back," Gabe added.

"Is he taking any medications?"

"Not that I know of. Blake?"

"Maybe some ibuprofen. It's been a tough couple days of competition. He's sore, but in good health. He probably went out drinking last night, though he doesn't usually have more than two beers when he's competing."

"Any drug use?"

"No," Gabe and Blake said in unison.

"You're sure. A little pot, maybe some coke when he's out partying?"

"No," Gabe growled, protective of his little brother.

"When was his last tetanus shot?"

"Who knows? It might be on file at the clinic," Blake said.

She irrigated and cleaned the wound with sterile saline–soaked gauze pads, then she packed and wrapped the wound. She and the paramedic put Dane's leg in a splint and secured it so they could move him. Done, Bell grabbed Dane's good leg. One of the paramedics took his head, the other his shoulders, and they rolled Dane to his side, sliding the backboard under him so one of the guys could strap him down.

"Light." She took the penlight from the paramedic and checked Dane's pupils. All good. She unstrapped his chest protector and pulled it free. She ran her hands over his ribs and checked for any broken bones. Nothing. She rubbed the heel of her hand over Dane's chest, checking for a cognitive response.

Please, you've got to be okay. Usually she didn't know the patients she worked on. This man held a special place in her mind and heart. Even if he didn't know it.

"Dane. Hey, Dane. Can you open your eyes and look at me?"

He let out a halfhearted moan and tried to open his eyes. Relief washed over her from her head down, loosening her tense muscles.

"Good, Dane. We're taking you to the hospital now. You're going to be fine."

She helped the paramedics get Dane on the stretcher. She took his feet, and they took each side near his head, walking off across the arena to the waiting ambulance. For the first time, she became aware of the crowd of people around them and in the stands. Sound, muted, returned to the world around her as a hush remained over the crowd, waiting to see if Dane would give them a sign he was okay. Unfortunately, with the beating he'd taken, it wasn't likely he'd wake up anytime soon. He was stable for now. She'd done what she could for his leg. They needed to get him into surgery.

"Dr. Bell, how is he? Is he going to be okay?" Gabe asked from beside her, his words tentative and filled with concern and a touch of fear.

"He's got a torn artery and a compound fracture. He needs surgery. They'll have an orthopedic and vascular surgeon ready when we get to the hospital."

"You're a surgeon. What's your assessment?"

She hated to even say the words. "He might lose the leg, but a good surgeon can stabilize the bones, repair the surrounding muscle and tissue damage, and give him a fighting chance to save the leg." She tried to stay positive, even though his chances weren't that good unless he got the best care possible. Out of her control. She wished she could do more. "He's young and in remarkably good shape. He's critical, but stable. His chances are good."

They loaded Dane into the back of the bus. Bell jumped in, despite the looks she got from the paramedics.

"You call it in. I'll keep him stable."

The paramedic got on the radio with the hospital to relay Dane's vitals and other information so the trauma team would be ready when they arrived.

Before they closed the back door, she looked at Gabe. "Get to the hospital. You'll want to be included in all the decisions. Once we get there, his care is out of my hands. You need to talk to the surgeon before he does anything. Ask for specifics."

The doors closed, cutting her off from saying anything more. Bell didn't want to say it, but Dane's catastrophic injury might be too far gone to save the leg. Dane needed an advocate. Someone to push the doctors to do everything to save the leg—as long as Dane remained stable.

Bell took Dane's hand and squeezed. "You're in for one hell of a recovery no matter what happens. You need to fight."

Dane's eyes fluttered open. He whispered something behind the oxygen mask. She pulled it away.

His deep brown eyes held her gaze. "My leg hurts. You have to get my dad."

He'd said those words to her years ago, down by the river. Another time. Another state. Another girl. She wasn't that castaway anymore.

"Dane, you're going to be okay. Do you know what day it is?"

"Friday? No, Saturday? Where's my dad? Get one of my brothers."

"Gabe and Blake are on their way to the hospital. They're right behind us."

"Are you an angel? You disappeared?"

That made her smile. She placed the oxygen mask back over his nose and mouth. His eyes closed again, but he held tight to her hand. A nice strong grip that gave her hope he'd be okay.

She traced her finger over the feather tattoo. An angel. Ask anyone in her family, and they'd probably tell you she'd been sent by the devil. Her overzealous religious grandmother told her as much practically every day of her life.

The ambulance pulled into the ER entrance. The crew pulled Dane from the bus and rolled him inside the ER. The trauma team waited for his arrival, including the orthopedic surgeon.

"Dr. Bell, I'm Dr. Patterson. What's your assessment from the scene?"

Bell filled in the doctor, giving him the details of Dane's injuries while the trauma team quickly took X-rays to see if Dane had any other broken bones. Moving fast, they needed to get him upstairs to the OR.

"I'll take a look as soon as they have him prepped, but it sounds like there's no salvaging that leg," Dr. Patterson said, so matter-of-fact that it sparked her temper.

"You can save it. It will be an effort, but I'm telling you it can be done."

"The bone splintered and broke into multiple pieces. We're talking more than a plate or two. It'll be a miracle if it heals and he doesn't have a permanent limp, or worse."

"He's an athlete in the prime of his life."

"He's a bull rider, hardly an Olympic sprinter or skier."

Her anger flashed again. Her heart beat faster, and she fisted her hands so she didn't wring his neck for dismissing Dane and his talent so easily. "I'm not going to argue the strength and skill it takes to ride bulls and broncos. I'm telling you, his leg is salvageable. You can do the job."

"I'm telling you it's probably not worth it with the amount of bone, tissue, and vascular damage."

"And I'm telling you to save his leg." Gabe stepped up beside them in the middle of the hectic ER. "If she says it can be done, then you better do it."

Bell made the introductions. "Dr. Patterson, Gabe Bowden. Dane's older brother. Next to him is his brother Blake, and this is Ella, Gabe's wife."

"Mr. Bowden, as I've discussed with Dr. Bell, the trauma to your brother's leg is extensive. He's in critical condition. We don't even know if the artery and vessels can be repaired."

Gabe glanced down at her.

She read the command in his eyes to give her opinion. "It can be done."

"That's an optimistic view from a doctor barely out of medical school." Dr. Patterson's snide comment didn't faze her. She'd heard a lot worse when correcting or schooling a colleague much older than her twenty-six years.

Ella stepped in front of Gabe and took over like the CEO she was. Bell admired the young businesswoman's confidence. "Dr. Bell may not want to correct your ignorant assumption, but I will. She graduated college at eighteen, medical school at twenty-two, and is a fourth-year orthopedic surgical resident at Bozeman Hospital and Surgical Center. I bet she outscored you in school and can outperform you in the operating room. So here is what is going to happen. You are going to get your boss in front of me and allow Dr. Bell in that operating room with Dane. If not, I will flood this hospital with the many lawyers I have at my disposal. Under no circumstances does my brother-in-law leave here without his leg—attached. Am I clear?"

"Mrs. Bowden, she doesn't have privileges here or in this state, no matter her qualifications."

"I'm sure exceptions are made for specialists. She is the specialist Dane needs. I won't say it again. Make it happen, or I will."

Gabe and Blake stood behind Ella like a wall of muscle backing her up. They glared at Dr. Patterson, who only took a second to walk over to the nurse's station and pick up the phone. He didn't look happy. Based on the grimace on his face, whatever he was saying to his boss tasted sour.

"Dr. Bell, you're covered in blood." Gabe whispered the words with a gentle tone.

For the first time, she held up her hands and stared at her bloodstained fingers. Her jeans were wet and sticky with Dane's blood.

"I'm sure one of the nurses can find me a pair of scrubs." In fact, one of the paramedics and a nurse came up, rolling a cart of supplies and a wheelchair.

"Have a seat, Doc. Let's fix up that head wound," the nurse said.

"I'm fine."

Gillian, Blake's wife, touched her shoulder. "When the adrenaline wears off, you'll realize you've got a four-inch gash across your forehead and into your hair that's going to hurt like hell in a second when you allow yourself to feel it. Let them clean it up."

Bell touched her fingers to her head. Sure enough, they came away sticky with her blood mixed with Dane's. She winced and hissed in a ragged breath. The anger waned from dealing with Dr. Patterson, and the pain became a part of her reality. It throbbed along with her rapid heartbeat. She needed to take a few deep breaths and calm down if she was going to be of any use to Dane in the OR.

"You got kicked in the head by a bull," Blake said. "Take a minute to get yourself looked at by the medical staff."

"You nearly got killed saving Dane's life," Gabe added.

Bell fell into the wheelchair, reality sinking in. Her mind filled with visions of that bull still trying to attack Dane and the lengths to which she'd gone to protect him. She could have been killed. Her stomach soured and dropped in her gut. She pressed her hand to it, trying not to think too closely about what motivated her to do it.

She touched her forehead again. *Can I do this surgery in this condition? Yes.* Her vision was clear, and so was her thinking. The surgical plan had already taken shape in her mind. She could do this. For him.

"Come on, we need to hurry. They're taking Dane upstairs in two minutes," the nurse coaxed.

"Sorry about this, Doc, no time for subtlety," the paramedic said. He cleaned the wound with quick and effective, if not delicate, strokes with the saline-dampened swabs. "This needs stitches, but we'll close it up with some butterfly bandages for now."

Great. Stitches. Usually she was the one giving them, not getting them.

The nurse dumped a pair of scrubs in her lap. The paramedic worked fast to clean her face, ignoring the water dripping onto her ruined shirt. She went with it, mentally preparing for the surgery ahead. *If* they let her operate on Dane. Even if they only let her into the surgical suite, she'd keep an eye on the surgeons and make sure Dane got the care he needed.

She appreciated his family's confidence and support. After all, she'd taken care of both Ella and Gillian over the last months, but none of their injuries compared to Dane's.

"Let's go. You've been approved for surgery by hospital administration," the nurse said. "That's one hell of a lady to get them to move this fast."

Bell stood and followed the nurse, noting the feral gleam in Dr. Patterson's eyes. Not the first time she'd stepped on a man's ego.

Gabe and Blake stepped in front of her. Though words weren't necessary, she read the worry and fear in their eyes as Gabe spoke for both of them. "Please, whatever you can do for him."

She touched her hand to Gabe's forearm. "I will do everything I can to save his leg. You need to be prepared if I can't."

"I know you can do it," Gabe said.

"Do what?" Katherine asked, stepping up beside the group. She and Tony must have followed the Bowdens to the hospital to pick her up.

"I'm headed into surgery. It'll be a few hours. Go back to the hotel. I'll take a cab back when I'm done."

"Surgery, Bell? Look at you. Your head."

"I'm fine. I have to go. It's already been nearly half an hour."

Bell ran after the nurse waiting for her by the elevator. She got in and caught a last glimpse of Blake, with Gillian at his side, and Gabe with Ella. Bell wondered whether anyone would show up at the hospital and demand the best care for her if something happened to her.

She stared at her sister with her husband, Tony. She barely knew the woman. Jealousy still shimmered in her heart every time she looked at Katherine. The daughter her father wanted, cared for, loved. The one he kept—not the mistake and shame he hid away.

The elevator doors closed, but she held the image of Dane's close family in her mind. She vowed she'd do everything in her power to keep her promise to them—to Dane.

CHAPTER 2

Dane woke up by degrees, assessing the many aches and pains, from his toes up to his throbbing head, as he took in the dim room. Gabe slept in a chair beside him, Ella on his lap, her face snuggled into his neck. Dane squeezed his eyes shut on the too-sweet picture they made and rolled his head on the pillow. Everything ached. He found Blake on his other side, passed out, arms folded across his chest.

He raised his hands, noted the IV lines going into both arms. The slight movement made his ribs ache. He pressed his hand to the bandage around his chest, took a shallow breath, and let it out on a soft groan.

"Six are bruised. One has a hairline crack. It'll heal in a few weeks," someone whispered from the end of the bed in a soft, soothing voice. Odd, but that voice eased his mind and warmed his heart.

He glanced down the length of him to find the owner of that sweet voice, but his gaze locked on his leg, suspended in a sling from the ceiling. Everything came back to him. The bull tossed him in the air like a rag doll, hit him in the side, and he fell hard. The crushing, agonizing pain that shot through him when the animal landed on his leg, snapping it like boys did pencils in class to impress girls. The blood. The dark-haired, blue-eyed angel that came out of nowhere. He brought his fingertips to the feather tattoo on his arm.

A hand settled on his other foot. He felt that touch in every fiber of his being and focused on it rather than the nightmare in his head.

"You're fine, Mr. Bowden."

"My leg?"

"Two plates, nine screws, an innovative wire mesh to hold the smaller pieces together. Dr. Ford repaired the extensive tissue damage and your torn artery. It'll take a couple months, but you'll heal. You won't be able to walk on it for several weeks, but you'll get by on crutches. You're very lucky to be alive."

Dane finally focused on the woman. Stunningly beautiful, she slowly removed her hand from his foot. He missed that simple touch like he missed the rain in the heat of summer. With her head slightly turned away, she never quite looked right at him. Her beautiful denim blue eyes softened before her gaze fell away again.

"I remember you. Do I know you? Have we met before?"

Ella cupped his face in her hands. She leaned down and kissed him on the forehead, blocking his view of the woman. "You're awake. How are you?" Ella asked.

"Sore."

"I'll get you some pain medication and leave you with your family."

"Thank you, Dr. Bell," Ella said as the doctor walked out the door.

Dane stared at Ella and Gabe standing over her. "Dr. Bell? From Montana?"

"Yes. Do you know her?" Gabe asked.

"No. Just that you guys said she helped Ella and Gillian. What is she doing here?"

"Saving you. You nearly bled out in the middle of the arena," Blake said, scrubbing his hands over his face and digging his fingers into his eyes.

"Someone want to tell me what the hell happened after I got dumped on my ass."

"Dr. Bell was in the stands, watching with her sister, when you got hurt. Tony Cortez is her husband."

"Dr. Bell is married to Tony?" Why that pissed him off, he didn't know, but it did. A lot.

"No. He's married to her sister, Katherine."

Relief shot through Dane. Again, why? He didn't even know her. Memories floated, but didn't stick. He remembered her, but from where? Just last night, or another time? Another place? Could she be the girl he'd seen by the river? He couldn't be sure it wasn't wishful thinking and his drug-induced haze. The drugs and pounding headache made his mind fuzzy.

"Black Cloud is Tony's bull." Dane put at least one of the pieces together.

"Yes. Doctor Bell knew time was critical. She rushed from the stands and got to you, stopped the bleeding for the most part, and rode with you in the ambulance to the hospital," Ella explained.

"Then Ella threatened the surgeon on staff with a battalion of lawyers if he even tried to amputate your leg." Blake shook his head.

"What? It was that bad?"

"You were critical and the damage to your leg was extensive, but Doctor Bell assured us that with a good doctor, your leg could be saved," Gabe said. "The surgeon here didn't agree with her, so Ella made the hospital grant Dr. Bell special privileges to operate on you. She and the vascular surgeon worked nine hours to save your leg."

"So, what? I'm all good now?"

"Barring any complications from infection, yes. But you'll need to stay off it for a few weeks, then you'll have some rehabilitation and physical therapy once it heals. You'll probably have a limp," Ella added, concern in her voice and eyes.

"I don't care about a fucking limp. I've got my leg."

"They're pumping you full of antibiotics." Gabe tapped the bags hanging over him. "We can take you home in a couple of days once they move you to antibiotic pills. Meanwhile, enjoy the painkillers. If you're hungry, I'll sneak you in a burger later." Gabe clamped a hand on his shoulder, and the relief in his eyes touched Dane deeply.

"So, did I miss anything else while I was out?"

"You won," Blake announced.

The smile crept across Dane's face reluctantly. The sound of the buzzer went off in his head again, and the adrenaline shot through him as he remembered that fleeting moment of victory last night. Winning the PBR championships, the money, paled in comparison to keeping his leg, but it made him damn happy.

"You did it." Gabe squeezed his arm. "You're the three-million-dollar man."

Yes. He'd won the last of the money to hit that mark he'd set for his retirement from the circuit. He wanted to go home with the money in the bank to set up the ranch the way he wanted. To make his mark, the way his older brothers were making theirs. Enough money to get him started and a buffer to get him through any lean years. Start-up money and a safety net.

Holy shit, I did it. I won. I survived. The relief hit him like a crashing wave.

A nurse knocked and came in, carrying a syringe. "May I have your name, please? It's protocol."

"Dane Bowden."

She checked his armband, then shot the syringe into his IV line. The rush hit him all at once.

"Damn, what did you give me?"

"Dilaudid. That should help with the pain. I gave you half the max dose. If that doesn't keep you comfortable, let me know. I'll give you another half dose. It may make you sleepy. Is there anything else you need?"

"Can you ask Dr. Bell to come back? I need to talk to her."

"I'm sorry, she left. I can call her if you'd like."

"Is she coming back later?"

"She'll be back to check on you this evening, but she didn't give a specific time. The orders on your chart are to contact her if there is any change in your condition." The nurse stood next to his leg. "Can you wiggle your toes for me?"

Dane did so, but it hurt like hell. He grimaced in pain. Ella took his hand and squeezed.

"Great. Can you feel this?" The nurse tapped each of his toes with the tip of her pen.

"Yeah. I can feel that." The relief overwhelmed him. Until now, he'd only been aware of the pain. He wiggled his toes again. The pain made him more aware of his foot and the fact that he still had it.

"Dr. Bell warned not to overwork the muscles right now. You need to keep your leg and foot as still as possible. The tissue damage was extensive, and she wants you to give it time to heal."

"Why isn't she here to give me all these instructions?" The sharpness to his words made the nurse narrow her eyes and frown.

"Dane. She's been up all night with you. She probably went to get some sleep," Gabe said.

"She's literally been watching over you and that leg all night to make sure the artery repair held and your toes stayed pink," Ella said.

"Would you like me to call her?" the nurse asked again.

"No. No, I'll talk to her when she comes back."

"Rest. I'll be back to check on you soon. Use the call button next to you if you need anything."

The drugs worked their way into his system, relaxing him as the pain ebbed. An image of the dark-haired doctor, her hands clasped as she stood by his feet, popped into his head. That image transformed into a young girl sitting beside him, her hands tangled together in her lap. Her unforgettable blue eyes. The ones he woke up to moments ago. The same ones he'd stared up at as a teen when he'd fallen from his horse by the river on his family's ranch. The girl who was there one minute and gone the next.

He held his arm up, stared at the blue feather tattoo, and remembered it all. Then and now.

An angel watched over him.

He needed to talk to Dr. Bell—the woman who saved him—again.

CHAPTER 3

Dane lay in bed, sore and bored out of his mind four days into his hospital stay. His mind wandered back two days to the press conference. Reporters with their notepads, recorders, and cameras had stood at the end of his bed, recording a piece for the TV news and to post on the PBR website, since he'd missed receiving his awards after the competition. The PBR reps had held the huge World Champion trophy above his head. As he'd held his bonus million-dollar check, the buckle, and the title, showing off for the cameras, his brothers and their wives looking on from the corner of his room, he'd wondered why all of a sudden he cared about the empty spot at his side and in his life.

After the press conference hit the airwaves, a stream of buddies from the rodeo came by to visit the last two days, along with several women. Winning the championship and the money brought the buckle-bunnies out of their burrows, looking for a treat from him. Not going to happen. Over the last few months he'd started to realize he wanted something more than a good time for a night or two. He thought he'd been living the good life; all the while, his brothers had found something he'd never thought he'd wanted but now thought more and more about with each passing day—a woman to love, who loved them back with a fierceness and an intensity that everyone, including him, could see.

He'd never left an unhappy woman in his rearview mirror. Still, lately, he thought about all those women, compared them to Summer, Ella, and Gillian, and wondered if he let *the one* get away because he'd been chasing a dream and not a life.

He stared at his leg, his toes poking out of the bandages and brace, and thanked God he was still alive and in one piece. Or at least several tacked back together, thanks to his elusive doctor.

The nurses assured him that Dr. Bell said his injuries were healing and the looming threat that his artery would burst lessened each and every day. Still, he wanted to hear it from her. He needed to talk to her about his recurring dreams. The day, so long ago now, when he'd seen a girl with her eyes, who everyone swore didn't exist.

"Hey, man, where did you go?" Tony asked from Dane's bedside, pulling him back to reality.

Lost in thought, he hadn't heard them come in. Tony's wife stood beside him, with apology and sympathy in her eyes as she took him in from head to feet.

"Sorry. The meds make my mind drift. What's up?"

"I spoke to Gabe. He said you were feeling better today and that it might be a good time to visit. Man, I am so sorry about what happened."

"Nature of the game. Not your fault, or the bull's. Shit happens."

"Not like that. You could have been killed. Bell, too."

Dane cocked his head and studied Tony's wife. "Katherine, right?" She nodded. "Gabe and Blake told me your sister was in the stands. She saved my life."

"She certainly did," Katherine said, pride and dismay in her hazel eyes. Not blue, like her sister's.

"How the hell did she get into the arena so fast?"

"She came out of nowhere," Tony said. "One second me and the other guys are trying to distract the bull away from you, and the next, she's hauling ass to your side. She held your artery closed, even when the bull tried to kill you both again."

"What?"

"It's all over YouTube," Tony said.

"It is?" This is the first he'd heard of it.

Tony pulled out his phone, touched his finger to the screen, and turned it in Dane's direction.

Dane nearly lost his breakfast when he saw Dr. Bell climb over the railing, pass two cowboy clowns on the run, and skid on her knees to a stop beside him. The blood spurted from his leg, but she didn't hesitate to find the artery and pinch it closed. If that wasn't enough, the bull came at them, knocking her and him several feet across the dirt. She didn't flinch. He did now, and his stomach went tight with dread. He knew the outcome, but seeing it still made his insides knot.

"What the hell was she thinking?"

"She wasn't," Katherine said. "If she was, she would have known better than to risk her life like that."

"Katherine," Tony said, an edge to his voice. "She saved Dane. If our bull had killed him, well, I couldn't live with myself."

"Still, she should have waited until they moved the bull away. I finally have a chance to get to know her, and she does something crazy like that."

Odd. If they were sisters, why did Katherine have to get to know her?

"This is the best part. That woman has nerves of

steel," Tony said, his eyes glued to the tiny screen and the drama of Dane's life playing out for the hushed crowd.

The bull swung around in a circle right over him. Dr. Bell literally laid her back in the dirt, her shoulders between her feet. He didn't know how she bent that way. When she rose up again, her head was bleeding.

"Wait. Go back."

Tony rewound the video. Dane watched it again, this time watching as the bull's hoof grazed Dr. Bell's forehead. "She nearly had her head bashed in." The disbelief in his voice was just a glimmer of the denial swamping his brain. It couldn't be. She didn't just save his life; she'd nearly gotten killed because of him. He owed her his life. As he watched her and the paramedics tend to him, he vowed he'd pay her back or spend the rest of his life trying. She'd given him a second chance at life. Until this moment, when he saw the reality of what happened, he'd thought he was lucky to survive that ordeal. Luck hadn't saved him. She had. Again.

Dane glanced out the window next to the door and down the hall. Dr. Bell stood with her head down, reading his file. She licked her finger and turned one of the pages, her eyes narrowed in concentration. He loved her short, dark hair. Nearly black. Nothing like Katherine's honey blonde. Odd, they looked nothing alike. No resemblance at all.

Katherine stood at least five-eight. Golden skin to match her hair. Not heavy, but a woman with curves. Dr. Bell, on the other hand, had a porcelain complexion that contrasted to her dark hair. Not as tall as Katherine, probably five-six, she had a more athletic frame. Lean muscles and soft curves. She certainly filled out a pair of jeans nicely. The V in her red T-shirt showed off the swell of her breasts. Those blue eyes stood out as truly her best, most striking feature.

Bell sensed him staring and turned to face him. He felt the impact of her gaze in his chest when it went tight. He held his breath, falling into the depths of that blue sea filled with worry and something he couldn't identify.

How the hell did she get under my skin this way?
Why the hell does she act like she doesn't know me?

She flipped his chart closed and walked toward him. He couldn't take his eyes off her. She moved with purpose and ease all at the same time.

Without taking his eyes off her, he asked, "Is she okay? Is that why I haven't seen her these last few days? She's not well."

"She's fine," Tony assured him. "She's only got a couple days of vacation left, so she and Katherine have been taking in the sights before we head home. Of course, Bell will fly with you."

"She will?"

"Your sister insisted. Your family doesn't want anything to go wrong when they move you, so Bell agreed to ride back with you to make sure you're okay."

His family and the nurses kept him up to speed on his condition, always stressing that he was okay and on the mend. Nothing to worry about. Now he wasn't so sure. If he needed a doctor on the flight home to look after him, maybe he wasn't in the clear.

"Seriously, I'm glad you're feeling better," Tony said. "You'll be back riding bulls in no time."

"Not going to happen. Bell said his leg won't support that kind of physical work again," Katherine said.

That got Dane's attention. He took his gaze from the woman approaching his door and stared at Katherine.

"Um, sorry, I thought you knew."

"I have yet to speak to your elusive sister about my leg."

"I'm afraid that's my fault. I guilted her into leaving the hospital. She works so much. We were supposed to use this time to get to know each other better." Katherine's steady gaze looked over him to the woman walking toward them. Dane didn't understand the sadness and regret in Katherine's eyes.

Tony wrapped his arm around his wife. "It's okay. You'll find another opportunity to spend time with her."

"She's so apprehensive. It took me a month to coax her into coming here with us."

Dane turned to the window again and frowned. "Oh shit."

Four women he knew from various places, who always showed up at the rodeos looking for him or another winning cowboy for some fun, blocked Dr. Bell from coming to his room. Gabe, Blake, Gillian, and Ella razzed him unmercifully about the string of women lining up at his door to see him over the last few days. He didn't feel any kind of special bond with any of those women who came to see him, then or now. Except for one. She saved him.

Maybe she saved him from continuing down the same path he'd been on, the one he'd thought he loved but had turned into a habit rather than a real life worth living.

Oh God, he needed to get off the pain meds if he was thinking like this. Actually, maybe it was a good thing. His brothers and parents had been hounding him to take a look at his life and decide what he wanted for his future. Until now, he'd balked at giving in to their demands that he come home and settle down, stop living his life with reckless abandon. Maybe he should stop thinking *that* life meant settling for less, when it really was the life he wanted. He'd nearly lost his life. He'd almost missed seeing his niece Lily grow up and Gillian and Blake's baby come into this world. He'd almost missed finding someone to share his life and have children of his own with.

Hell, he'd almost missed the best part of life.

Up until now, he'd been chasing dreams, money, women, and the thrill of the ride. Nothing compared to what his parents had and his brothers found with their wives. The connection he shared with his family. Knowing they'd put their lives on hold to be with him here. That kind of love meant everything.

Dr. Bell risking her life to save his meant something. That kind of risk and sacrifice deserved a reward. He meant to find out what it was she needed and give it to her. It was the least he could do for all she'd done for him.

A real man pays his debts, and he owed her big time.

Shit. First he needed to save her from his overzealous, if not adoring, fans.

Bell stopped short in front of the wall of blonde women blocking Dane's door. Five-six, she felt like a dwarf looking up at the five women who towered over her. She felt like the odd man out at a 1980s-rock-hair convention. The ladies' long blonde hair, in varying styles of waves and stick-straight, hung down to the middle of their backs. Lean and curvy, they stood before her, looks of anticipation and simmering anger in their hazel to brown eyes. The man had a type. A very definite type.

The exact opposite of her.

Why did she care, anyway?

Men fell for leggy blondes with big boobs all the time. Such a cliché.

They did not choose brainy women with short-cropped dark hair, who looked more like a swimmer than an exotic dancer. Let's face it, she was no man's fantasy. In the few instances guys actually paid attention to her, she was the friend they confided in about the girl they really liked.

"Are you Dane's doctor?" one of the women asked.

"Yes, I am."

"Can I see him?" pink blouse asked.

"I want to see him first," white tank top demanded, hands on her denim-covered hips.

"He'll want to see me," black skirt that barely covered her ass said, stepping in front of the other women. "I'm his fiancée."

"The hell you are." White tank top took a menacing step closer to black skirt and glared. "We've been seeing each other for months."

"Bullshit. We had dinner last week," blue shirt piped in for the first time.

"You're not wearing his ring," white tank top pointed out.

"It's being sized," black skirt shot back.

"You're a lying bitch," pink blouse accused.

The women closed in on each other. Bell rolled her eyes and stepped in the middle. "Listen up. I'm going to check on Dane. He's got a couple of friends visiting at the moment, and his family is due back soon. You may all visit with him, one at a time, after I've finished my examination and so long as he isn't overtired."

"Dane. Tired. Honey, that man can go all night," white tank top said, licking her lips.

All the women got this far-off look on their faces, thinking about their nights with the same man. She shook her head in disgust.

Why did they want someone who wanted all of them and cared for none of them?

How did being with so many women prove that he was a man? To her, a real man loved one woman. Then again, she couldn't fault Dane. At least he hadn't married one woman and stepped out with a dozen more. Black skirt said he'd asked her to marry him, but like the other three women, Bell didn't quite believe it. Dane didn't seem the kind of man to settle for one, when chasing after four was a hell of a lot more fun for him. Of course, any man that looked like him didn't have to chase many women; they flocked to him. Case in point, the bevy of blondes standing outside his room.

Yesterday, three others had been standing around his bed, fawning over him. He'd given them polite smiles and called them all honey, but none of it seemed genuine. Instead of going in to check on him, Bell left to join her sister at the spa for a facial and a massage. Both good things, but Bell didn't know how she and Katherine were supposed to get to know each other better when they spent practically the whole time with goo on their faces or someone rubbing their backs, neither of them saying anything to the other.

Setting aside thoughts of arrogant, women-chasing men and her family troubles, she addressed the horde. "I'll be right back. Try not to kill each other."

Bell opened the door to Dane's room and stepped in, smiling at her sister and Tony.

"Hey, Bell, we were wondering if you'd make it past Dane's Dames," Tony teased.

Trying her best to be professional, she held back the smirk. "Uh, yeah, about them. Your fiancée would like to see you."

Dane's eyes went wide with surprise a second before his lips pressed into a tight line. "None of them is my fiancée. Send them all away."

"As you wish. I'm sure the next group will be along shortly."

His eyes narrowed on her. Did she see a glimpse of regret and shame in those dark eyes? Impossible. Men weren't ashamed of having fun. No, if they felt anything close to that, they pushed it away and shoved the annoyance out of their life for something better. That's what her father did when his affair went public. To keep his pretty wife and young daughter, he ruthlessly pushed Bell's mother out of his life, then dumped his unwanted burden—Bell—on his mother, a woman even he couldn't stand.

No surprise Dane wanted the annoying women yelling at each other in the hall out of his sight.

"Right. Well, I'll toss them out as soon as I have a look at you. Katherine, Tony, if you wouldn't mind leaving me with my patient, I'd appreciate it."

"Bell, what time do you want to go to dinner tonight? It's our last night in town," Katherine said.

The ever-present plea in her voice always set something off inside Bell. She was never quite sure what Katherine wanted from her. Sure, to forget the past and be friends, sisters, in the here and now.

Bell mustered up her resolve to spend yet another dinner listening to Katherine and Tony's plans for their ranch in Montana, the family they couldn't wait to start, and all the wonderful things they wanted for their future. Right. Katherine and her perfect life. Every wonderful thing that came out of her mouth made Bell want to rant about all she'd endured, all she'd been denied growing up, which Katherine took for granted.

"I'll meet you back at the hotel in an hour. We can decide where we'll go from there."

"Why do you call her Bell?" Dane asked out of the blue.

Bell caught the startled look in Katherine's eyes. Her sister turned away to look at Dane. "She's always been known as Bell."

A simple enough answer, but not entirely true. Yes, she'd always been known by "Bell" because her parents had been so horrified by the scandal that neither of them had given her their last name. No, her mother, in all her Miss Kentucky glory, didn't want to tarnish her already rusted tiara by acknowledging that Bell was her illegitimate daughter by a man she tried desperately to snare into marrying her when he was already married. Oh, her mother didn't know that at the time. Hell, she barely knew the man's name when she fucked him in a conference room during a fund-raiser for some cure for some disease. No, her mother targeted the man being honored that night with some award for his outstanding research on a new drug. Not the first one he'd been instrumental in creating. Not the last either. The man was a genius. Too bad that night he thought with the wrong head, impregnated Bell's very young and calculating mother, and got caught by the chairperson of the committee throwing the party in his honor. The scandal rocked the scientific community and her father's marriage, but like all things that are kept out of sight, she remained out of mind for the next twenty-six years and counting.

"You call her by her last name?" Dane asked, pressing the issue.

Katherine glanced at her, wondering if she'd explain. Not going to happen. Bell had long ago stopped trying to explain something not worth her words.

"Let's take a look at your leg."

Tony took Dane's hand and held it tight. "I'm sorry, man. Really. I know it's only a matter of time before a bull rider gets hurt, but I hate that it was my bull."

"Don't worry about it. Your sister put the pieces back together. I'm grateful she was there."

Dane stared at her, but she focused on his chart, reading over the nurse's notes from yesterday. Didn't mean she didn't feel that penetrating stare.

"Feel better soon," Katherine said to Dane. "I'll see you at the hotel, Bell."

"See you there," she answered.

The door closed behind Katherine and Tony. The silence in the room stretched as she read over how much medication Dane had been receiving and when. His pain levels had decreased. The length of time between doses had increased. All good signs.

"Why won't you look at me?"

Startled by his deep voice and the question, she looked up and caught his questioning gaze.

Sticking to business, she asked, "How are you feeling this morning, Mr. Bowden?"

"Dane."

She waited for his answer.

"You saved my life. Can't you even say my name?"

"Dane, how are you feeling?"

"Confused."

Worried about his concussion, she moved to the side of the bed, took her penlight, and leaned over him. She checked both eyes and his pupil reactions.

"Are you experiencing any dizziness? Blurry vision?"

"No."

"Headache?"

"No. My head is fine. Well, better."

"Can you elaborate on your confusion? Are you experiencing any memory loss? Do you have difficulty remembering things, or thinking of the right words?"

"No. I can't seem to figure out why you stand there acting like you don't know me, when we met eleven years ago."

She remembered every detail. She'd seen him fall from his horse and gone against her grandmother's strict command that she not speak to anyone, let alone let them see her outside. She'd lost her outside privileges for three months after Dane had come to her house looking for her.

"I didn't think you'd remember me."

"I thought I fucking lost my mind after you helped me and disappeared. Where did you go?"

"Home."

"Where was home? What were you doing out in the woods in the middle of nowhere?"

"I lived next door to your ranch with my grandmother."

"You're a Warwick?"

"No. But she's my grandmother."

One side of his face scrunched in confusion. "That doesn't make sense. There was never a girl living next door."

"How is your pain level today?" She changed the

subject. She was his doctor. Not his hidden-away neighbor. Not his friend.

"Fuck my pain level. I want to know why I never knew that crazy woman with the crosses in every window and on every door of her house had a girl living with her."

"She didn't want anyone to know I exist."

"Why?"

"Well, like most people, she wanted to hide the family shame."

"Why the hell would she be ashamed of you?"

"Mr. Bowden, my background really has no bearing on your injuries or taking care of you, so let's get back to you."

"No. I—"

"Mr. Bowden, if you don't want me to continue as your doctor, I'm happy to turn you over to another orthopedic surgeon. I'm supposed to be on vacation. I took your case because I know your family."

"You took my case because you saved my life and refused to let that fucking butcher hack off my leg because he didn't want to take the time to fix it right. Look at you. You've got stitches across your head. Ella said your shoulder is black and blue where you got hit. You laid yourself over me and protected me when that damn bull came after us again. You stayed with me after I got thrown from my horse until my dad came to get me all those years ago. You stayed with me all night after you spent nine hours in surgery fixing my leg. Don't stand there and tell me that you did all that because you know my family and it's your job. It's something more."

"Mr. Bowden—"

"My. Name. Is. Dane."

"Dane."

His eyes went soft, and he sighed out his relief. Whenever he saw her, something flickered to life in his chest. It flared now, when he heard his name from her lips. Why? Because she said his name. What did he care what she called him?

"I don't know what it is you expect me to say."

"I want you to tell me what happened after I fell off my horse all those years ago."

"I took care of you the best I could until your father came looking for you. When he arrived, I saw him take you home."

"You didn't stay and tell him what happened. You hid."

"Yes."

"Why?"

"So I wouldn't get into trouble."

"Why would you get into trouble for helping me?"

Bell wrapped her arms around her middle. "Because I wasn't meant to be seen."

He narrowed his eyes. "Why? Because you're some family shame? That makes no sense."

She rolled her eyes. "Believe me, it did to my family."

"Is that why your sister calls you by your last name?"

"Bell is my first."

"Why do you use your first name as your last name?"

She sighed and glanced up at the ceiling, trying to hold on to her patience. "Dane, this has nothing to do with your injuries. My past, my name, are none of your concern."

"They are when you saved my life twice."

"I hardly saved you after the horse threw you."

"Bullshit. He found me because he heard you whistle for him."

Caught, she rolled her lips into her teeth and didn't say anything.

"Why did you hide?"

"I've said all I'm going to on the matter. Now, if you'd like to discuss your injury, I'm happy to do so. Otherwise, I'm supposed to have dinner with my sister."

"You look nothing alike. Why is that?"

"Okay then. Which of Dane's Dames would you like to see first?" She used the term Tony used earlier. "Or shall I send them all in, and you can take your pick from the litter?"

"Why won't they just go away?" He held his hands together, raised his arms, and pressed the backs of his hands to his forehead and closed his eyes.

"One thinks she's your fiancée. The other three call dibs. I'm sure the horde that came in and out yesterday feel the same way."

"Do you have any idea how it feels to nearly die and wake up and find all these women coming to see me, and I find that I don't care about any of them? Yes, they're friends. Mostly a bit more than acquaintances. I like them. I've had my fun and so have they, but not one of them is here because they're concerned about my welfare. They know about the money, and what it means for my new future. A future I have because of you. You saved me, but you can barely stand the sight of me. Why? Why would you risk your life for someone you don't know or care one bit about? In fact, the way you look at them, then me, tells me you certainly don't approve."

Why did he care so much? Why did it seem so important that she like him? Because she saved him. That connected him to her. That's all it was. Right?

"Mr. Bowden, it is not for me to approve or disapprove of how you choose to live your life. I don't dislike you. I barely know you."

"My name is Dane." The words came out on a weary exhale.

Reading his need for her to understand his confusion about his life, where he'd been the day before his accident and where he was now as a person, she reluctantly gave up one of her secrets.

"I used to watch you ride by the river. I envied you that freedom. I wanted to ride your horse and feel the wind in my hair." *I wanted to ride away and escape my lonesome life.* "I'm the reason your horse got spooked that day. I'm the reason he threw you. I saved you in that arena, yes, because I'm a doctor and saving people is what I do. But I saved you because I'd hurt you once. I'm sorry for that. I owed you. I became a doctor because of you."

"You never owed me anything. I didn't control the horse. It's my fault I got thrown. You certainly didn't have to risk your life in that arena to save my life."

"Be grateful I did. You would have bled out. Gabe and Blake told me you're moving home."

"With this leg, I can't rodeo anymore. Besides, I promised my family I'd settle down and run my dad's ranch. He's traveling with Mom, and my brothers have their own families and lives. It's left to me, or my father sells. I don't want to see that happen."

"Just because you settle in one place doesn't mean you have to settle, or change who you are."

Dane cocked his head and studied her. "I never thought of it that way." He'd been pressured to return. He wanted to, but he didn't want to be told to do it and when. He wanted to do it on his terms. Well, fate stepped in and made it impossible for him to do anything else right now.

"That leg will need plenty of time to heal, but once it does, you'll still be able to ride horses. You'll have to be careful. It won't take an impact like before, but you'll get by."

"Thanks to your handiwork. How did you become a surgeon so young?"

"And we've circled back to me again."

"I still have so many unanswered questions."

She wrapped her arms around her middle again. "None of which matter."

"They matter to me."

She huffed out a sigh. "What's important is that we're getting you up and out of this bed today. I want you to stand and move as much as you can. Lying in bed all day is not good. We worry about blood clots."

"My toes are tingling again. The swelling keeps coming back."

"The nurse noted that the ice helped last night."

"Yeah, but it's a pain in the ass to try to sleep when your leg is frozen."

"Better frozen than gone."

"Trust me, I'm not complaining. I wiggle my toes, feel the nurse pinch my skin, and I am so damn happy I can feel it every time."

"Good. If you continue to progress today and tomorrow, I'll send you home the day after that. You'll have follow-up visits with me, and you'll need to go through some extensive physical therapy. Under no circumstances are you to put any weight on that leg for the next two weeks. The shattered bones need time to mend."

"How long until you think I can walk on it again?"

"We'll see. The damage was extensive. You tore a couple of muscles. That will take time to heal and build the muscles back up again. You're in remarkably good shape. I'm sure you'll recover fully. The hardest part will be reining yourself in from overdoing it. You don't want to cause more damage. The last thing you want is for something to happen and you lose the leg anyway. It took a lot of convincing for the hospital to let me operate on you. It took a hell of a lot of creative thinking to put you back together, so don't mess up all my hard work."

"I'll do everything you say, Doc. I swear. My brothers had a long talk with me about what you told them. I may be all right now, but I could still lose the leg if I'm not careful."

"So long as we avoid an infection, I think you'll be okay. You will let me know if you have any numbness or pain. If you spike a fever, you need to get to a doctor immediately."

"Believe me, I will. I'm not taking any chances this goes south."

"Good. Now, how are your ribs?"

Dane shifted uncomfortably in the bed. "They ache, but nothing I can't handle."

"Okay. I'll check on you again later this evening."

"After I'm asleep, right? That's when you like to come by."

She frowned. "Believe it or not, I've been here about every three hours over the last few days. I can't get into your room for all the honeys you've got at your bedside."

He gave her a cocky smile. "Well now, honey, if you wanted them gone, all you had to do is say so."

That insincere comment set her off. "Let's get one

thing straight. I'm your doctor. So turn that smile down. I'm not one of your Dane's Dames. I don't answer to 'honey,' and I don't compete for a man who finds every woman special while they're in his sights."

That stung deep. Probably because the daggers coming out of her eyes hit the bull's-eye. "Hon . . . Dr. Bell, I didn't mean anything by it. I'm sorry."

"A minute ago you wondered how all these women showed up to see you but weren't here because they cared about how you are. You might consider that none of them really care because you never really mean it."

She walked to the door but stopped when he called her name.

"Dr. Bell."

She turned and glanced back at him.

"Are you okay?" He cocked his head to indicate her head.

She touched her fingers to the line of stitches. "I'm fine. Just a scratch."

"You operated on me with that gash and a concussion. I'm asking because it matters. Are you okay?"

"It didn't really hit me until after it was all over, but yeah, I'm fine."

"I saw the video. I've never been more scared in my life than seeing that bull come after you and hit you, even though I knew how it turned out."

"I'm sure flying off that bull and getting hit was scarier."

"You're wrong."

She opened the door a crack, but he stopped her again.

"Hey, Doc, I still want those answers. Someday I'll get them from you. Until then, anything you need, just ask. I owe you for saving my life, and I pay my debts."

"You don't owe me anything."

"We both know that's not true. Do you still live at your grandmother's place?"

"Yes," she answered reluctantly.

"If I came calling to say my thank-you in person, would your grandmother still tell me you don't exist?"

"Probably. And there's no need to call on me. Set up an appointment at my office. Your sister Ella has all the information."

"Keeping everything professional."

"There is nothing personal between us."

He cocked one eyebrow. "Says the girl who admits to spying on me."

"I wanted your horse," she shot back, trying to deflate his ginormous ego.

Dane chuckled, and her stomach tied in knots. His deep voice resonated someplace deep inside her. That laugh made her want to join in. She'd always loved that about him. Every time she saw him, whether riding with his brothers or alone, he always had a ready smile that made him seem so happy and in on the fun. She'd never been in on anything. She'd always been alone. The outcast and outsider. Even in college, she'd been the youngest in her classes. Much smarter than the other students—and her teachers. Her poor social skills meant she said things that made others feel less smart. Being a girl made it all worse when she showed up older guys and men. They didn't like that. Which meant they dismissed her, because they couldn't impress her. Women did the same, because they didn't want to look less than next to her, too. They wanted to stand out and get the guys. They always did.

"So, do you want me to send in the parade of blondes?"

He frowned. "No." He stared out the window at the four women talking back and forth at each other, none of them listening to the others, if the heated glances and hand gestures told the tale. "The thing is, I don't want to hurt their feelings any more than it appears I have. You see, I never see more than one girl at the same time. I like to keep things casual, but I'm not a total douche bag. If they all come in here, demanding to know which one of them I choose, when the answer is none of them, I'm going to have to do some fancy dancing to get myself out of this crap. And why the hell do they want me in the first place?"

Bell tried to hold back the laugh. After all, this wasn't funny, but seeing a guy who had a line of women coming in and out of his room the last few days and didn't know what to do with all of them made her laugh. "You don't know what they want from you? Are you serious?"

"Maybe it seems obvious to you, but seriously, what is it?"

"You want my honest assessment?"

"Lay it on me, hon—" He caught her narrowed gaze. "Doc."

"Not one of those women ever said they love you. Not one of them asked me how you were doing. They're out there comparing notes to see which of them you paid more attention to. They're one-upping each other, recounting personal details about your time together to show the others that you favored them more. None of them actually believes you care for them. How could you, when you regard them as single-use women?"

"What?"

"Disposable."

His lips pressed into a tight line. "Harsh. I'm not that bad."

"Yes you are. Even you admitted that to me and yourself ten minutes ago. You just don't want them, or me, to point it out, because then you have to do something about it. Easier to ask me to send them away, you fly home to Montana, and your problem is solved. Let's face it, none of them is going to chase you across several states, because they know they'll get the cold shoulder you pull out when you're done. They're hoping you're in need of a sexy nursemaid now that you're laid up. You pick one of them, they'll spend the next days or weeks trying to convince you how much they care about you and want to be with you. That will get old for you real fast, because you are in no condition to do the one thing you always do with them."

"What's that?"

Yes, that smirk would drive her crazy. In a good way. If she spent any length of time with him. Which she wouldn't. Other than checking up on his recovery progress, she had no reason to see him. He had no reason to want to see her. The thought kind of made her sad, because despite the fact he was a womanizing man whore, she liked him.

"Sex." Even though the topic made her uncomfortable, she'd learned as a doctor to be frank. Dane needed a good dose of truth. As his doctor, and because he'd asked, she'd give him a big dose.

"I kind of expected you to sugarcoat it, or at least beat around the bush."

"Why? You hold no special value to it, like you hold no special value to them. One thing is required to have the other. That is the only link between them. There are no special feelings, no connection you share other than your body connected to theirs for as long as it takes you to find satisfaction and move on to the next conquest."

"I guess your diagnosis is that I'm a womanizing asshole who wants nothing more than sex." He frowned and looked embarrassed. The truth stung.

"Maybe that's who you were. Now that you've had this near-death experience, you've discovered that's not who you want to be. It's up to you. Maybe that's your past standing in that hallway and walking through the revolving door that has been your life up until now. Maybe you want something new and different for your future. Who knows, given a few weeks' recuperation, you're back up on your feet, or at least crutches, and you'll be back to chasing every blonde Betty in Montana."

"Maybe I'll find the one woman worth settling down for."

"Why do men always think they have to settle down to stay with one woman? Why can't you find a match to who you are?"

"I'm damn glad you're one hell of a surgeon, but you might have missed your calling as a psychiatrist."

"Nothing I said hadn't already occurred to you. Just remember one thing."

"What's that?"

She stared him right in the eye. "Everything changes."

"Don't I know it." Dane stared at his leg and wiggled his toes because he could.

"You've been through a lot. Your leg won't be exactly what it used to be. You're moving back home, but that isn't going to be what it used to be, since you'll be taking over your family home alone. The business your father ran isn't the business you'll continue and expand.

Nothing in your life is the same as it was days ago. Take the time you need to figure out what you really want in all the facets of your life. Concentrate on getting better and spending time with your family."

"I hate lying around in this bed doing nothing."

"Well, I'll just send in the Barbies, and they'll keep you busy."

Dane groaned. "Doc."

"I'm sorry. That was uncalled for."

"But true. Seems I need a good dose of that along with some more pain meds." He shifted in the bed, trying to get comfortable.

"I'll get your meds. What would you like me to do about the ladies?"

He laughed under his breath at that term. "Send them in. I made this mess, I'll clean it up."

"I'll send them in two at a time. I'll start with blue and pink shirt. They seem to be the most mellow."

Dane looked out the window. "Wait. No. Send her in." He pointed to a new arrival. "Her name is Brandy. She's a friend."

"Bachelorette number five it is."

Dane grabbed her arm. "No, Doc. She's an actual friend."

Bell stared down at his hand on her skin. He released her, but she got the point. He wanted her to understand that some women did matter. Brandy mattered to him. Funny, the touch sent a shaft of heat through her, but the fact that woman mattered to him left her cold.

"Okay. Your family will be here soon. I'll let the others know you're not up for more guests."

"Thanks, Doc."

Bell opened the door. The ladies moved forward, anxious to get into the room. Bell stood her ground, blocking the entrance. "Brandy, Dane would like to see you. Please come in." The other four ladies expressed their disappointment in a collective huff that turned to pouty frowns all around.

"Dane, honey, I came all this way to see you, sugar," black skirt called out.

"Dane, baby, I miss you," white tank top shouted.

Dane adjusted his position in the bed and groaned in pain. Maybe he laid it on a bit thick, but it gave Bell an excuse to dismiss the ladies. "I'm sorry. He's in a lot of pain. I can only allow one visitor before his family arrives. You'll have to come back another time."

Brandy moved forward as the other girls left down the hall in a huff. "Uh, Doctor, is he okay? His leg, it looks really bad."

Bell stepped back into the room with Brandy and caught Dane's look.

"Told you."

Yeah, okay, this one was a friend. She actually cared about Dane's health, not necessarily his wallet. At least on the surface. Bell's heart sank. She tried to ignore the surge of jealousy. What did she want with a man like Dane anyway? What the hell would he see in her? She definitely wasn't his type and didn't want to be either.

"Brandy, it's so good to see you. Where's Kaley?"

"At home with my mom. I drove in from Arizona when I heard about your accident. Are you okay?"

"Doing better, thanks to Dr. Bell. She put me back together."

"I'm so glad. I was really worried."

"You must have new pictures. Show me." Dane looked up at her. "Doc, you got to see this little girl."

Brandy beamed with pride. "He's a sucker for all girls."

Bell smiled. "I got that from the line he's had out the door."

"That's Dane for you. There's always a line, but sometimes he manages to be a good guy."

"Hey, I'm sitting right here."

"You know what I mean. You know when to put aside your fun to help out a friend."

"How are things with Rowdy these days?"

"He's my ex," Brandy explained for Bell's benefit. "He didn't get that nickname for no reason. He's come around a few times, but I've stuck to my guns like you told me. You were right, if I give him an inch, he weasels his way back into my life. I can't have that. Not anymore. Not with Kaley." She pulled up the picture on her cell and handed it to Dane.

He smiled and traced the little girl's face. "She's grown so much."

"Like a dandelion. I don't know what I would have done without your help, Dane. The money you send means everything to me. If something happened to you . . ." Her words came out choked up.

The money he sent? Was the child his? Bell didn't ask. Not her business. But with the way he lived his life, one woman after another, it very well could be that he'd gotten at least one, if not many, of them pregnant. These things happened. She was living proof.

Dane took Brandy's hand. "Hey now, honey, I'm fine. Good as new, thanks to the doc. I'll be going home in a couple of days. You can contact me at my family's place. You know the number. You've got my cell. Anytime you need me, I'm there."

Bell felt like an intruder. These two were definitely friends. Probably even more. "I'll let you two catch up. Dane, I'll have the nurse come back with your meds."

"You said you'd get me out of this bed today."

"The physical therapist will be here in an hour. Do not put any pressure on that leg."

"Is there any way I can take a shower?"

"No. But the nurse can give you a sponge bath."

"You sure you can't help me out with that?"

Yep, that smile would charm an eighty-year-old woman into doing his bidding. The heat flashed in her gut again. Damn hormones. "I'm on vacation."

Bell walked out the door, trying not to smile about the sly flirt.

Dane appreciated Brandy driving in from Arizona to see him. He'd met her four years ago on the rodeo circuit, and they'd become fast friends. He loved her sweet, funny personality. She used to be a world-class barrel racer. At the time, he and Rowdy were good friends and comparable competitors. Rowdy took one look at Brandy racing around the ring and fell head over heels for her. Rowdy and Brandy and Dane and a fourth went out on many double dates. Rowdy and Brandy always together, Brandy teasing Dane about his latest date.

The first year was filled with cheering each other on in competition and dinners out with lots of laughs and good times. Then Rowdy suffered a minor back injury after a hard fall from a bull. He drank away the pain and Brandy's affection. His quick temper turned volatile, his sharp words followed by a hard shake, a slap, and worse. When Dane saw the bruises on Brandy, he made it clear that if Rowdy touched Brandy in anger again, Dane would pay him back in kind. Rowdy, resentful of Dane's continued success, distanced himself and isolated Brandy. They showed up less and less often at the rodeos. Dane gave up trying to get through to Rowdy, but he maintained his friendship with Brandy, checking in with her often to make sure she was okay.

"What's going on with you and the doctor?" Brandy asked, giving him a knowing smile. Like Bell, she thought he needed to tame his wild ways.

Dane deflected that loaded question. "What is going on with you and Rowdy? I recognize that look on your face and the bruises on your arm."

Brandy pulled down her shirtsleeve, covering the dots of bruises on the inside of her arm where Rowdy's fingers left their mark. Dane didn't let her see his anger, but damn, he hated to see those marks. He hated the man even more. Real men did not hit women.

"He comes around sometimes. He wants to see Kaley. When I refuse, he gets physical."

"Which is why you need to keep him away from you and your little girl." Dane read the indecision in her eyes. "No matter how much he pleads and begs and tells you he's a changed man, Brandy. They're all lies. He gets to drinking, and you know the outcome. He's hurt you too many times for you to ever believe he'll change. You can't take the chance he hurts Kaley."

"I'll never let that happen. I've learned my lesson. I won't let him back in my life."

"Has he said anything more about getting a lawyer and visitation rights?"

"Doesn't matter if he does. I made sure he won't get them. Well, not easily anyway."

"What did you do?"

"What I had to do to protect my daughter." Brandy's voice held the conviction he wished he heard more often. He wished she'd use that tone with Rowdy. Maybe then the asshole would leave her alone.

Too many times, she didn't stand her ground. Since she got pregnant with Kaley, she'd found her courage. If she couldn't stand strong for herself, she'd stand strong for her little girl. Dane wished for more for their sake, but he couldn't do more than he already did for them. They weren't his business. Unless she asked for his help, he needed to stay out of it.

Brandy stayed and talked to him about Kaley and all the cute new things she did each and every day. At a year and a half, she was giving Brandy a run for her money, literally running all over the place, playing with one thing or another. Brandy beamed, her joy so evident in her smile and words.

Dane loved hanging out with Gillian's little brother, Justin, whenever he made it home for a visit. Now he'd have a niece or nephew to add to the mix when Gillian gave birth. He wished he was better and could drive back to Montana on his own and stop in Colorado and visit Caleb, Summer, and their new little baby, Lily. Happy for his brother, he wanted to see the little girl that made Caleb light up in all the pictures they sent him.

He wanted that kind of happiness for himself. He wished he knew how to get it. He'd never found it with any of the women he'd dated. Of course, he'd never been looking for it. He'd never put in the time and effort to get to know any of them in any kind of deep or meaningful way, to see if they could cultivate something more than a hangover.

The physical therapist showed up at the same time his family did.

"I've got to get on the road and back to Arizona,"

Brandy said. "I needed to see for myself that you're okay." She leaned over and gave him a hug. He might have held her a little longer than usual, thankful he had a good friend like her in his life.

"I'll be fine. Take care of yourself and your little girl."

"I will."

Dane hated the sense of dread that came over him every time he let Brandy out of his sight. He held her hand and gave it a squeeze. "Brandy, no matter what he says, no matter what he does, do not let him back into your life. When you look at him, you want to see the man you fell in love with. I want to see my old friend. But he's changed. He's not that guy anymore."

Brandy squeezed his hand back and gave him a reassuring smile. "I'll call you. Stay out of trouble and listen to your doctor."

"Trouble finds me," he teased, hoping trouble didn't go looking for her.

CHAPTER 4

Finally that bitch was home. Rowdy had waited for nearly two hours. She never got home this late. She better not have been out with some guy when she should have been home, taking care of his kid.

Instead of getting out of the car, Brandy sat in the front seat of her old Honda, texting on her cell. He jumped out of his truck and stumbled, catching his balance at the last second. He grabbed the door handle and pulled her car door open, leaning on it with one hand, the other planted on the roof as he bent over her and held himself up at the same time.

"Where the fuck have you been?"

Brandy gasped. Her eyes went wide. She pressed her phone to her chest. "Oh my God. You scared the shit out of me. What are you doing here?"

"Waiting for you to get your ass home."

"By the smell of it, you either just came from a bar, or you've been drinking in your truck. Either way, you're not supposed to be here."

"I can go wherever the hell I want."

"Yeah, but you always end up here, even though you know I don't want to see you."

He grabbed her arm and tugged. "Get out and give me a hug."

She pulled back, leaning farther into the car. "No. I've told you time and time again. We are not together anymore. Go home and sleep it off."

"Can't we talk?"

"I've said everything I have to say."

Her cell phone chimed with another text. She held it against her chest, her gaze down on her lap.

"Where have you been?"

"Work."

"Liar. I checked at work. You didn't have a shift tonight. What are you hiding?"

"I'm not hiding anything."

The cell phone chimed again. This time, he didn't grab her; he snatched the phone from her hand. He took two steps back, swiping his finger over the screen to read the texts.

Brandy came out of the car, yelling, "Give that back. You have no right to look at my private messages."

She tried to grab the phone, but he held it over his head. She jumped for it. All he did was laugh and give her a push to get her to back up. She landed on her ass on the driveway and stared up at him with that look on her face.

"What? You did that all on your own."

"You pushed me."

"You came after me."

She stood and held out her hand. "Give me my phone, or I'll go inside and call the cops."

He pretended to hand it over, but he snatched it back and laughed until he saw who sent the texts. "Dane. You're fucking Dane."

"It's none of your business who I talk to and see."

"Where have you been? Did you drive to Las Vegas to see him?"

"No."

Brandy: Just got home.
Dane: Thanks for coming. I'm glad we got to talk.
Brandy: Me too.
Dane: Kaley is getting so big. I miss my girl.
Brandy: She misses you. Come visit.
Dane: I will soon. If you need anything, call me.
Brandy: Get better soon.
Dane: Send more pics of Kaley.
Dane: Sweet dreams, honey.

Rowdy felt his simmering temper flare to life like a living thing. His whole body tensed.

"Kaley is my child. Not his." He bit out the words he shouldn't have to say.

Stupid bitch cheated on him. Maybe she said she wasn't with him any longer, but she didn't mean it. Back then, she'd never meant it. She'd always come back to him. Until that asshole started sneaking around with her behind his back.

Brandy bit her bottom lip. "She's mine. You don't get to see her because you can't control your temper."

"She's my child. Not his."

Brandy shook her head. "No. She's not. She's Dane's. You know that."

"How do you even fucking know who her father is, you whore? You'll fuck anyone, including that fucking show-off, who thinks he's God's gift to women. You're nothing to him. He's got a different girl in his bed every night. Everyone knows that."

"He's not that bad," she defended the asshole.

"Are you in love with him?"

"He's a good friend. He takes care of me and Kaley. All you do is make things worse."

Rowdy took three steps toward her. She backed away. She was always trying to get away from him.

"Brandy!" her mother yelled from the stoop. "Come inside."

"She's not a child. She'll be in when we're done."

"You're done, Rowdy. Take one more step toward her, and I'm calling the cops."

He glared at the old woman, noticing the phone in her hand. She'd do it. Wouldn't be the first time he spent the night in the drunk tank.

"I want to see Kaley."

"It's after ten. She's in bed," Patty snapped. "You go on home now. Brandy, it's been a long day. I could use your help with your father."

"Yes, Mama." Brandy held her hand out. "I need my phone."

He slapped it into her hand but held onto her and the phone. "You mean nothing to him. I love you, Brandy. If you'd just give me a chance, I'd show you how good we could be together again."

"Please, Rowdy. Let me go."

"Never. You and Kaley are my girls."

Brandy jerked her hand and phone from his. "No, we're not." She rushed to her mother.

"Yes, you are, Brandy," he yelled as Brandy and her mother ran into the house. "I'll never let you go. You're my girls!"

CHAPTER 5

Bell walked into Dane's room and stopped short when he looked up and smiled. Her heart actually stuttered. Damn the devil for giving him that too-charming grin. She felt the zap of it buzz through her and she tried to ignore it, as well as her instinctive need to smile back and hope the smile he gave every woman meant more when he smiled at her.

That was the problem with a guy like Dane. You'd never really know how he felt because he treated every woman the same. She didn't want that. She didn't want a relationship at all. They were messy. Complicated. Too much work and trouble. Right?

How would she know? She'd kept men at arm's length her whole life. She never fit in at school, where everyone was so much older than her. She didn't get people her own age because she'd been so far ahead of them in school. She didn't fit anywhere, so she stayed on the outside, always looking in, analyzing everything people said and did. Always hiding who she really was because she wasn't like any of them.

"Hey, honey, how was dinner with your sister last night?"

Case in point. She looked behind her, then back at Dane, one eyebrow raised. "Is one of your Dane's Dames here? You can't possibly still be calling me 'honey.'"

"Uh, sorry, Doc. I didn't mean anything by it."

"Yeah, I know. You never mean it to any of them either."

Funny, he actually looked sorry for saying it to her. She dropped the subject, worried she might have hurt his feelings. They'd had that talk about him changing his life. He'd meant it that he regretted his past. He'd had a lot of fun, but what had it really gotten him? Lonely lying in a hospital bed.

"Dinner was good. Who doesn't love an all-you-can-eat buffet?"

"You. I've seen you walking around with your Greek yogurt, fruit, and salads. Look at you, the epitome of tone and fit. Runner? Swimmer?"

"Both." Huh, the man paid attention. *Yes, to every woman.*

"Figures. So I guess flowers and a huge box of chocolates wouldn't be enough to say thank you for all you've done."

"Isn't that what you get a woman for Valentine's Day?"

"I guess. I don't do Valentine's Day."

"Right. That might mean something."

"Exactly. See, you get me, Doc."

Yeah, she got him. "While I like to live a healthy lifestyle, chocolate is a food group and should be enjoyed as often as possible."

"Like sex."

"Excuse me?"

"Well, it's not a food group, but it should be enjoyed as often as possible."

"Not in your condition. How are the ribs?"

"Trust me, honey, nothing would stop me from having sex. The ribs are sore, but manageable."

She ignored the "honey." The man couldn't help himself. Still, she didn't know what had gotten into him this morning. Was he trying to piss her off?

"The physical therapist said you did well on the crutches."

"I zipped around the corridor and nurse's station, no problem."

She'd heard all the comments from the nurses about Dane's good looks, hot body, and ever-ready smile. They recounted the woes everyone had over not being the one to give him a sponge bath last night. He'd actually asked for privacy and done it himself.

"Is Brandy going home with you today?"

"Why would she do that?"

"You'll need someone to help you at home until you can move around better."

"I'll get by. My brothers and sisters will look out for me. My mom and dad will be there for a couple of days when I get home, but then they're off to Paris for a couple of weeks."

"Paris. Wow. I bet they're excited."

"Mom loves Ella's apartment there. It's their second trip."

"Must be nice to have such a rich sister with an apartment in Paris."

Dane shrugged. "I guess. She makes Gabe happy, and that's all that matters."

She didn't expect that answer from him.

"So, Doc, are we out of here or what?" Dane leaned up, turned on the bed, and let his legs dangle over the edge. He sucked in a breath, trying to stave off the pain.

"What hurts?"

"Ribs. Leg. My back. Take your pick."

"What's your pain level?"

"Irritable and ready to go home."

"So, like a six?"

"Seven."

"When's the last time you got your meds?" She flipped open his chart to look it up.

"Doc, come on. After five days, I want the hell out of here."

"You didn't have any pain meds this morning. Why?"

"They make me groggy. If I can't get up and stand on my own, you won't let me out of here."

"Dane, that's not true. Besides, you're not leaving here on your feet. You're leaving and staying in a wheelchair for at least a week while those bones and your torn muscles mend. I made that clear. The physical therapist made that clear."

"I can't sit around on my ass all day doing nothing."

Clearly something else was bothering him. She cocked her head and studied him.

"Stop looking at me that way."

"Tell me what it is."

"What? It's nothing. I want to go home."

"Before, you weren't ready to go home and start your new life. Now, you can't wait. What's changed?"

"Nothing. I'm tired. That's all. How's your head? Are you good?"

Again she studied him, trying to read whatever he didn't want her to see. "I'm fine. But you're not."

"I want to go."

"Not until you tell me what's bothering you."

"You. You're bothering me. I can't stop thinking

about you." He blurted out the words, then covered his face with both hands and scrubbed them over his face. His hands dropped to his lap, and he bent his head and spoke to the floor. "I can't stop seeing that video in my head. You. The bull. He almost killed you."

Drawn to his worry and concern, she put her hand over his and squeezed. "I'm okay. Nothing happened to me."

"Nothing happened to you. Look at you, Bell."

Her name came out soft and filled with such tenderness that tears stung the backs of her eyes. She blinked them back. He'd caught her off guard with his concern. That was all. It didn't mean anything.

"Dane, really I'm fine. The stitches look bad, but they're really nothing. Don't worry about me. Concentrate on getting better."

"I have the chance to get better because you risked your life to save me. Don't think I forgot how much I owe you."

"It's done. Over. You don't owe me anything. It's my job. The reality of what's happened to you is settling in. Given time, you'll get better, and you won't think about it so much."

That's all this was, his mind trying to deal with a traumatic event. His feelings and emotions rose to the surface now that he was able to process the events with a clear head.

"I will find a way to pay you back."

She took her hand away. Too personal. Too close to feeling less like a doctor offering comfort and more like a friend consoling another. They weren't friends. They'd just shared an experience that had been traumatic for both of them. Now, it was over, Dane was going home, and she'd go back to her mundane life.

"I'll get your meds. You'll need them to get through the flight. Do not get out of bed until the nurse comes with the wheelchair." She looked over her shoulder when the door opened, and smiled at Gabe, Ella, Blake, and Gillian. "He's all yours, guys. Cheer him up. He's far too melancholy for a rodeo champ."

Dane frowned at Dr. Bell's back. He'd seen the look on her face when he'd called her honey on purpose just to get a rise out of her, and the way her face and eyes had gone soft when he'd called her Bell. He didn't know why he did it. Something inside him wanted to see the real her. The one she didn't hide from everyone, including her own sister. He'd seen her, the real her, just for a second when he'd said her name.

For the first time, a woman meant something to him. He only wished he could figure out why she meant something, and what that something was. Even when she was gone, he thought about her, wondered what she was doing, and when she'd be back. Anticipating her return nearly undid him last night and this morning. He needed to see her. Why? Reassurance that he was really okay? Nope. It ran deeper than that, and he didn't want to dig deep. He wanted it to be something easy. Not complicated and complex, because that meant more changes. More responsibility. More permanent.

The need to make her see him as something more than the rambling rodeo cowboy, going from town to town and woman to woman, surged through him. He didn't know how to get her to see him as someone different than that guy other than to actually be the guy he wanted her to see. But who the hell was that? He didn't know, because right now he couldn't see past getting out of this bed, out of this hospital, and back home. Doing all those things meant they'd go back to their lives and he'd be separated from her, and that was the last thing he wanted, which made him surly and do stupid things like call her honey just to get a rise out of her.

She messed with his mind. He wanted it to stop.

Was he focused on her because he didn't want to face what came next? This next phase of his life, which he'd barely had time to actually plan past winning the championship and earning the money he needed and wanted for his future. He didn't know what that future actually included or looked like.

"Missing your horse already," Blake teased, slapping him on the shoulder and bringing him out of his tumultuous thoughts. "Not to worry, I've got all three of them and your truck downstairs."

"What?"

"I'll drive them back to Montana."

"Shit. I didn't even think about it."

"Mind's in a haze with all those painkillers," Gillian said. "Don't worry, Blake and Gabe made all the arrangements necessary for you to go home."

"What do I owe you for the plane ticket?" Dane asked Gabe.

"Nothing. Ella took care of it. She chartered a flight for us."

"Ella, no. I'll take care of it."

"It's already done. No way could you sit on a commercial flight with your leg like that." Ella pointed to the black brace.

He wiggled his tingling toes. The circulation coming and going with the swelling worried him. Dr. Bell assured him it would get better. Ice and time. The ice he didn't mind. The length of time it would take him to get back to his old self did. He hated sitting around doing nothing. He felt useless. He needed to do something. Too much time to think had gotten him nowhere but stir-crazy.

"So, are you taking me back to Wolf Ranch to recover?"

"No. You're going to your place," Gabe said.

"My place? Mom and Dad's place, you mean?"

"No, your place. Mom and Dad bought a three-bedroom house on a couple of acres on the outskirts of Crystal Creek. They moved into it this past week."

"Wait. What? That's not what we had planned."

"Do you really want to live with your parents?" Gillian asked. "They planned to buy something in a couple of years but moved it up when the perfect property came up for sale."

"Why?"

Gabe grabbed his shoulder. "Because, my whiny little brother, you were so reluctant to come home and run the place. Now that your options are limited, they wanted you to have the place to do what you want to do."

"I don't get it. I thought Dad wanted to make some of the improvements we talked about and do it together."

"You don't need Dad's help with the ranch. He's happy to turn it over to you," Blake said.

"But what about you guys and Caleb? We're supposed to split the land."

"Why? Caleb is happy in Colorado with Summer and Lily. I've got Wolf Ranch," Gabe said. "Blake has his place with Gillian and Justin at Three Peaks. We're good, man. We're happy. Of course, you'll have to settle up with Mom and Dad on some of the expenses. They're not letting you totally off the hook, but the ranch is yours. It's what they want. It's what

Caleb, Blake, and I want for you. We want you home, man. Safe and sound with a fridge full of beer when we stop by."

"Often," Ella said.

"You're the first on the babysitting list," Gillian said, smoothing her hand over her still flat belly. "Justin wants to hang with his brother, too."

Dane shook his head. He loved that kid. It made him smile every time the little guy told people they were brothers. He missed his family when he was out on the road. He both liked and hated hearing all the fun they had when they got together. He missed them. He missed being a part of their everyday lives. The last few times he'd taken over for Gabe at Wolf Ranch, he'd felt at home, satisfied with the work, but he'd wanted it to be his, not one of his brother's. Not his parents'. He wanted his own. He never expected his parents to make it permanent and move out and buy another house, leaving him everything.

The thought made him pause and rethink his plans again. He wouldn't be going back to living in his old room under his parents' roof. The house was his. The business was his. Shit. That put a whole new spin on things. It's what he wanted, but not what he'd originally thought—and fought against—for the last few years. This was the real deal. He'd be responsible. For everything.

His father and brothers no longer saw him as the kid they had to protect and help. Sometime in the last few years, they'd finally seen that he'd grown up and become a man, capable of taking care of himself and doing for himself. He'd always had their love, but now he felt he had earned their respect.

How the hell was he supposed to take over the ranch

and house in his condition? With this chance and their confidence in him, he couldn't fail now. Not when he hadn't even begun.

He looked up at all their expectant faces, and it hit him. They'd help him. Like he'd always chipped in to help them. Not because they didn't think he could do it but because they understood that when he could stand on his own two feet, he would.

"Bring Justin by anytime. He can be my gofer. Lord knows, I'm going to be practically immobile a while longer."

"That's right," Dr. Bell said, his chart and a bag under her arm as she pushed a wheelchair into his room. "Ready to go?"

"More than ready." Yeah, he couldn't wait to get home to *his* place. The home he grew up in but would make his own now. The house and land right next door to hers.

Gabe and Blake each grasped one of his arms, helping him stand and balance on his good leg. Thanks to Ella and Gillian, he had sweats, a T-shirt, and a new pair of tennis shoes, though he only needed one. He was ready to get home and crash on the couch, watch TV, and get some much-needed sleep. The hospital was too loud. The nurses came in constantly to check his blood pressure, take blood, and generally make sure they woke him up when he finally fell asleep. Too many people stopped by to see him. He appreciated it, but right now, he wanted to be left alone to think about what his brothers said about him taking over the ranch, what happened to him, and what he was going to do next.

Dane hopped forward and turned, then Gabe and Blake helped him settle into the wheelchair. Dr. Bell carefully lifted his bad leg and set it on the stand to keep his knee straight and take the weight off it.

She checked his toes and the new bandages under the brace. "Looks good. Here, take these."

He took the pills from her outstretched hand and popped them in his mouth. A nurse handed him a cup of water. He drank down the water and the pills, hoping they'd take effect soon. The throbbing pain in his leg and ribs got worse with every breath he took. He shouldn't have stopped the pain meds altogether. He hated that he needed them, but he didn't have a choice. No way he'd get through the trip home without them. He'd have to be careful. He'd seen too many friends start on the pain meds after a hard ride and never get off them. He didn't want to go down that road. Not that he had a problem. But that's what happened sometimes— you took one because you needed it, then you needed two to take the edge off, and the next thing you knew, you couldn't live without them.

He thought of Rowdy and his drinking. The damage his addiction had done to his life. Brandy's. Kaley's if Brandy didn't keep him away.

Bell handed the bag of medication and instructions to Gabe. "Put these in Dane's things." She checked her watch. "Make sure they're on the plane with us. He'll need another pain med in four hours. If we're delayed, I don't want him to go without the next dose." She looked down at Dane. "It's not good to just stop taking them. You need to taper off gradually. No alcohol or other drugs with them. You don't want to mess with drug interactions or more side effects."

"I'm all good, Doc. I'll follow your directions."

"If these pain meds aren't enough, call my office. I can reevaluate your pain levels and find a better solution. If you experience anything strange with your leg—tingling, muscle spasms, persistent pain, a fever—you call my office."

"Give me your number, and I'll call you."

"My office number is on the prescriptions. Your family has my business card."

"That's not the number I want."

"That's the only number you're getting. Now, let's go. While you may think I've been at your beck and call here, I actually have other patients I need to get back to."

Bell walked out of his room ahead of everyone, but not before she heard Gabe say, "Give up, man, she's out of your league."

"Never going to happen. I owe her."

"Trust me, you'll pay up when you get her bill," Blake teased.

They said their goodbye to Blake in front of the hospital. He climbed into Dane's truck at the back of the lot and drove out first. Dane watched the truck and his trailer disappear.

"What happened to the back window?" Bell asked.

"Some asshole busted it out, stole my gear, and tossed it in a Dumpster at the arena. Lucky for me, security found it."

"Did you talk to the officials?" Gabe asked. "Sounds like someone tried to sabotage your chances at the championship."

"They tried, but I still won."

"You got lucky," Ella said.

"An angel watches over me."

Dane caught Bell staring at the tattoo on his arm. Her gaze locked with his. He gave her one of those mischievous grins that sent a ripple of warmth over her skin. She looked away, trying not to get caught in the illusion he created so easily that she meant something to him.

"Has anything like that happened before?" Gabe asked.

"A couple of times. Nothing major. Nuisance kind of stuff. Nothing I couldn't handle. The damage to the truck was the worst of it. Now that I'm retired, I'm sure whoever was doing it will leave me alone."

They piled into the rented SUV. Bell sat in the far back, watching and listening to the family. They got along so easily. Ella and Gillian talked about Gillian's pregnancy, decorating the nursery, and a horse that Gillian was rehabilitating at Three Peaks Ranch. Gabe and Dane talked about cattle, what Dane thought of doing some crossbreeding between the two ranches, and Dane's having to upgrade the old family home now that he was moving in alone. Bell felt like an intruder and a voyeur. Definitely the outsider in the tight-knit group.

"Hey, honey, did we lose you back there?" Dane asked from the front passenger seat.

"You left all your honeys back at the hospital and arena," she reminded him.

The sigh he gave her made her want to smile, but she held it back. Ella and Gillian had no trouble laughing at Dane.

"He calls everyone honey," Gillian said.

"Not you and Ella. He calls you by your names or 'sis,'" Bell pointed out.

Ella turned and stared back at her. "You're right. He does. Interesting."

"Oh God, please don't start analyzing me like the doc did," Dane pleaded. "It's bad enough she calls me on it every time I slip."

"About time someone called you out on the dismissive way you treat all those women you have no trouble sleeping with but can't seem to carry on a conversation past 'Hey honey, wanna come back to my room?' " Gillian smacked Dane's shoulder when he groaned.

Gabe busted up. Dane punched Gabe on the shoulder, turned in his seat, and glared at Ella and Gillian.

"You guys really think I'm that bad?"

"Do you know any women who aren't blonde and can talk about anything besides how hot you are?" Ella asked.

"Well, that is my favorite subject." Dane took laughing and rude jibes from his brother in stride. "The women who matter and actually care about me and not the fat payday I just got were in the room with me. The others I sent on their way."

"That's sad," Gillian said. "The only women you care about are your sisters."

"You aren't the only women I spent time with while I was laid up."

Bell thought of Brandy and her little girl, Kaley. Yes, Dane could be serious. Carry on a conversation with a woman. Care for her. Dane and Brandy had a tight bond.

Then Bell thought of the conversation she'd had with Dane about his future. She'd seen his sincerity. His thoughtfulness in thinking about his life and the changes he wanted to make. She'd seen a real need to take this second chance and do something with it. He'd let his guard down and shown her a piece of who he really was.

Before the others could keep razzing Dane, she asked, "Who's going to take care of you the first week or so that you're home?"

"You mean you're not coming to stay with me?" Dane teased.

"Don't worry, we're all taking turns making sure he stays off his leg. Mom and Dad stocked the fridge and got the house set up. They'll meet us there when we get home," Gabe said.

Ella looked over her shoulder. "We'll make sure he follows that long list of instructions you gave us."

"It's important that he keeps taking all the antibiotics until they're gone. Same time each day is best. Keep up with the pain meds and the physical therapy exercises."

"And seeing you once a week," Dane added.

"Just until I see that the smaller bones are healing and there's no infection. Then, we'll spread that out a few weeks."

"I'd like to see you more than once a week."

Everyone in the car went quiet, reading more into his words than he'd meant. *Face it, Bell, he's just flirting with you the way he does with everyone else. Right?* So why did Gillian share a look with Ella? Were they as surprised as Bell was by those simple words?

She didn't answer him. She left it alone and thanked God they'd arrived at the airport. She'd never flown on a private plane. Probably never would again. She got out of the car after everyone else and stared at the small plane just outside the hangar. Gabe helped Dane out of the front seat and into the wheelchair, putting his leg up again. Bell studied Dane's face for any sign that he was in too much pain to be moved, but he seemed fine and stared back at her with an odd look in his eyes she couldn't read. She went to the back of the SUV and grabbed her suitcase and satchel. She rounded the car to follow Ella and Gillian to the plane.

"Gabe, take Bell's bags for her," Dane called to his brother.

Gabe walked toward her, rolling a big suitcase behind him.

"I've got it," she said, appreciating Dane and Gabe's manners, but perfectly capable of stowing her own things on the plane.

Gabe pushed Dane to the plane's short staircase into the cabin and stopped. Dane planted his good foot on the ground, took Gabe's outstretched hand, and pulled himself up. Off balance, he almost fell over. Ella reached out and steadied him. Unable to use the crutches Gillian carried, Dane turned and sat on the third step. He braced his hands on the step behind him, pressed up on his palms, and pushed with his foot until his butt landed on the step above. He crab-crawled up the steps, his wide shoulders barely fitting through the narrow doorway, until he sat in the plane's cabin. Then he turned, took Gabe's hand, and rose back up on his good foot.

"Well, that was humiliating."

"I could have carried you in like a baby," Gabe said.

Dane shoved him aside and fell into a seat, gently setting his bad leg on the seat across from him. Bell stepped over his outstretched leg and took the seat next to his foot, tossing her satchel next to him on the seat across from her.

"Are you okay?" Ella asked Gillian in the row behind Dane's seat.

"Fine. Just tired and ready to go home and sleep in my own bed."

"You all right, sis?" Dane called over to Gillian.

"Stop fussing, both of you. I'm fine."

"All right, folks, we're ready to taxi out. Buckle up.

We'll get you up in the air and on your way home to Montana. The bar and galley are stocked with drinks and snacks, as Ms. Wolf requested. If there's anything you need, just let us know," the pilot said, taking his seat next to the copilot.

Bell watched out the window while the plane taxied out to the runway. Dane watched her. She didn't acknowledge his intense stare. She didn't know what he was looking at or for. Better to let it go. They'd be back in Montana, she'd go back to work, and she wouldn't have to think about the way he made her feel.

She felt him in a way she didn't understand. It was like some dial inside her tuned into him. Now all she focused on was his breath, his movements, and the way he took up the space across from her.

Unable to resist any longer, she turned and looked at him. He didn't seem fazed that she'd caught him staring. In fact, he stared harder.

"What?"

"I like your hair."

Self-conscious, she reached up and touched her fingers to her short style. She liked the pixie cut, with slightly longer bangs that swept over her forehead. She could sweep them back for a different style. Either way, it took her less than ten minutes to do her hair. When she had to put on a cap for surgery, she came out looking pretty much the same as when she went in. With her hectic schedule, she didn't have time to do her hair, and tying it up in a ponytail when it was long got old real fast.

"Uh, thanks. It's easy."

"It suits your face."

"Thanks," she said, drawing out the word, wondering where he was going with all this.

"You have no idea how pretty you are."

She didn't know what to say. She didn't consider herself pretty. In fact, she never really thought about her looks. She focused on the things that mattered. Her education and training. Doing her job. Anything but herself, because when she looked too deep, all she found was the hurt she hid from everyone. Better they focus on who she'd become instead of the abandoned and lonely girl inside.

"If this is as smooth as you get, bro, give it up now," Gabe teased.

Bell's cheeks warmed. No way was he flirting with her. This was something different. He looked at her like some puzzle to solve. He didn't get her, so he needed to solve whatever questions still lingered in his mind.

The plane's engines revved. She felt the vibration rush through her. She didn't mind flying, she'd just done it so rarely that it made her nervous. More nervous than the man across from her. They sped down the runway and took off. Bell kept her focus on their rise into the sky out the window beside her. Dane kept his focus on her.

"Where'd you get those blue eyes? They're nothing like your sister's."

"We have different mothers."

"Does your mother have dark hair?"

"Light brown."

"What about your dad?"

"Do you want a genetics chart for my mother and father to show you how two people who are complete opposites produced a dark-haired, blue-eyed girl?"

"If it'll get you to answer the question, yeah."

"It's not such an oddity."

"It's not odd. It's stunning."

That caught her attention. She turned from the window to look back at him, but she caught Gabe and Ella, sitting next to each other across the aisle behind Dane, smiling at her.

"What do you do when you're not working at the hospital or clinic?" Dane asked.

"I'm always working." To prove her point and stop him from asking more questions, she opened her laptop and pulled up the medical journal article she'd been working on since taking Dane's case.

She typed for ten minutes before he interrupted her again. "What are you writing?"

"An article about the way I fixed your leg and the innovative wire mesh I used to hold the bone fragments in place to heal."

"Really?"

"Really."

"Can I see it?"

She hit save and handed him her laptop.

Dane read for a few minutes, his eyebrows drawn together in concentration.

"I need a medical dictionary for every other word in this thing. How do you write like this? Nothing makes sense."

She smiled and took her laptop back. "I'm writing this for other doctors to use as a guide for what I did to your leg. If you have a full recovery and have even eighty percent use of your leg, that will be amazing, considering most doctors would have amputated, thinking the damage too severe. Granted, much of the credit goes to the vascular surgeon who repaired the artery. Without the blood flow, it wouldn't matter what I did with the bones."

"How smart are you?"

Defensive, she snapped, "Smart enough to put you back together."

"So, what, you're a genius?"

She didn't like talking about it. People didn't embrace different. They liked normal. Familiar. Knowing she was smarter than them put them on guard, or turned them away. Yes, they thought it fascinating, but still, they looked at her like she was different in some negative way. They thought she thought she was better than them. She didn't think that. In fact, she wished she was normal. She wished she wasn't smarter. She'd wished a lot of things over the years. Nothing about her, nothing she did made the people she'd wanted to think her special take notice.

"Come on, Doc, go ahead and say it. You're a genius."

"Yes."

"So how much of a genius are you?"

"You want a quantitative value?"

"Have you been tested?"

She pressed her lips together, remembering her professor's face when he'd looked at the results in astonishment.

"Twice. In college, when I was seventeen."

"Damn. You started college at seventeen?"

"No. That was my last year of college. I graduated about the time I turned eighteen."

"Man, you are really smart. So, what's your IQ?"

"There are different types of tests with different scoring. If you go by the convention most people use—like Albert Einstein had an IQ of about 160—then mine is higher."

"How much higher?"

"What does it matter?"

"How much higher?" Dane coaxed.

"A lot."

"What is the quantitative value of a lot?"

"Twenty-nine."

"You have an IQ of one eighty-nine?"

"Something like that. The tests aren't truly accurate for determining a person's intelligence because there are many types of intelligence. Still, that's the norm that most people are familiar with, so you can extrapolate what you'd like from it."

"I extrapolate that you've got one hell of a brain."

"My father and grandfather were both geniuses. My grandfather never attended school past the third grade, but he read every book he could get his hands on. He taught me to read by the age of three. We used to play word and math games together."

"Why didn't he go to school?"

"He was needed on the family farm."

"Where did you go to school? You didn't go to school in town. I would have remembered you."

"My grandfather taught me before he died, when I was six. After he died, I studied on my own until I went to college."

"Are you serious?"

As Gillian passed by Dane, she grabbed hold of his seat. She pressed a hand to her head before she sank to her knees and fell to the floor.

"Gillian!" Dane yelled, leaning forward and reaching for her.

Bell dumped her laptop on the floor, jumped over Dane's outstretched leg, and reached her first. Gillian tried to press up on her hands, but she fell back down and moaned.

"There now, take it easy. You're going to be okay.

Let's go real slow and just roll over." Bell helped her roll to her side and over to her back. Tears welled in Gillian's eyes. Dane rested his hand on Gillian's leg. Ella and Gabe stood in the aisle at Gillian's feet.

"I got dizzy," Gillian explained.

"Okay. Let's check you out. We'll make sure you're okay before we get you back up." Bell looked to Dane. "Hand me my satchel."

"Is she going to be okay?" Dane asked, concern and fear in his eyes.

Bell took her satchel, set it on the floor beside her, and pulled out her blood pressure cuff. She slid it under Gillian's arm, wrapped it around, and secured the Velcro. She pulled out her stethoscope, putting the head on Gillian's arm and the earpieces in her own ears. She pumped up the cuff and let the air out slowly.

"How far along are you in your pregnancy?"

"About ten weeks. I'm not even out of my first trimester. Am I going to lose the baby?" Gillian's voice trembled with that whispered fear.

"Your blood pressure is normal. One twenty over seventy-nine. How is your morning sickness?"

"I'm queasy in the morning, but I never actually get sick."

"May I touch your stomach?"

"Yes. Is it bad?"

"Doc, come on, is she going to be okay?" Dane asked, his hand securely gripped around Gillian's as she looked up at him with watery eyes.

"You probably got up too fast, but let's make sure. Are you having any cramps?" Bell tried to keep her voice calm. Right now, it didn't seem like anything more than a dizzy spell.

Bell dipped her hand just inside Gillian's pants and

felt her belly, testing for any signs her uterus tensed for a contraction. Nothing.

"No cramps. Other than the sour stomach in the morning, I'm usually good through the day. Tired. Sometimes I can't keep my eyes open in the afternoon."

"All perfectly normal. When's the last time you ate?"

"I, uh . . ." Her gaze locked with Dane's. "I didn't eat this morning. My stomach hurt when I got up, so I waited to eat something. We went to the hospital to get Dane. Blake said he'd get me something, but we got busy getting Dane to the plane, and I forgot."

Bell smiled. "Okay. There you go. You need something to eat. Ella, please get me a glass of juice. Apple if you've got it. Orange might be too acidic for her stomach right now. Find some crackers or pretzels to start. Maybe some protein. A piece of cheese, or something."

"On it right now."

Bell slipped her hand under Gillian's head. "Let's try to sit up and see how you do. Any dizziness or cramping, you let me know."

"Okay."

Dane held her hand and gave it a squeeze. "You trying to kill me, little sis? You can't scare me like that. I'm in no condition to give Blake the news you fainted."

"I did not faint."

"You kinda did," Gabe teased.

Ella handed over the glass of apple juice. Bell helped Gillian raise it to her lips, but Gillian's hands shook so badly that she couldn't hold it alone. Gillian sipped at it, then drank deeply. Bell remained sitting on the floor behind Gillian's back. Ella sat at her feet, and Gabe had taken the seat next to her on the other side of the aisle from Dane. Ella held out a platter of cheese and cold cuts and set a basket of crackers and tiny bread rounds on Gillian's legs.

"Let's have a picnic," Ella said, trying to ease the tension as everyone focused on Gillian.

"I'm fine. Really. No one needs to tell Blake what happened." She chewed on a bite of cheese and cracker and let out a relieved sigh. "I'm feeling better already."

"That's the sugar in the apple juice working its way into your system. Keep eating." Bell pressed her fingers to Gillian's pulse at her wrist.

"Is she okay?" Dane asked again.

"She's fine. Her pulse is a bit rapid, but she'll calm down once she's had some food and a minute to relax."

Gillian pressed Dane's hand to her cheek and smiled softly. "I'm fine. I'm sorry I scared everyone."

"You took ten years off my life," Dane responded, squeezing Gillian's hand. "You need to take care of yourself. If you needed something to eat, why didn't you say so? We'd have stopped to get you something, sis."

"I was so worried about getting you on the plane, I forgot."

"Taking care of that baby is more important than anything right now."

"It's nice you feel that way, but really, I'm fine. I think Dr. Bell was right. I just needed some food and a little sugar to make me feel better."

"When you wake up in the morning, try a few crackers and some water. They should settle your stomach. Get up slowly in case you are dizzy. Then eat a good breakfast. It doesn't have to be big, but something to get you going in the morning. Sometimes smaller meals throughout the day are better for the nausea than eating a big meal." Bell checked Gillian's pulse again. "Much better."

They shared the snacks and drinks Ella served everyone. Gillian and Bell remained on the floor of the cabin. When Gillian felt better, Bell helped her up and to the restroom, which was where she'd been headed in the first place. When she came out, Gabe wrapped his arm around her and led her to the seats behind Dane's. Ella had set out a pillow and blanket so Gillian could curl up and take a nap for the rest of the flight. Gabe settled next to his wife, and they snuggled close, keeping an eye on Gillian. Bell returned to her seat, stepping over Dane's leg again. He took her hand before she sat. She turned, trying not to bang her head on the plane's roof.

"Thanks, Doc."

"No problem."

"I mean it. You're great in an emergency."

"She's fine. It happens all the time to pregnant women."

His warm hand held hers. They stared at each other, the moment stretching. She slid her hand free, her palm sliding over his calloused one. She liked the rough feel of it against her skin. She took her seat and a deep breath, telling herself she needed it to calm her nerves after the incident with Gillian, but knowing the rapid beat of her heart had everything to do with the gorgeous, rugged man across from her.

He leaned forward, grabbed her laptop off the floor, and handed it to her. She took it and caught her breath when he laid his hand on her knee and squeezed.

"Relax, Doc. Put that away and take a break. You deserve it."

"I need to get it done now and turned in. I'm back to work tonight."

"Tonight? But you've barely had a moment to yourself, what with taking care of me and following your sister around to all those things you didn't want to do."

"How do you know I didn't want to do them?"

"Come on. You're the only girl in the world who rolls her eyes over shopping at The Forum at Caesars Palace or going for a massage."

"It's not that I don't like those things. The point of the trip was to get to know each other better, but she picked the one place I'd never go, to do all the things I don't particularly like. Besides the massage."

"So, you're not a shopper or gambler?"

"Not really."

"I'm glad you took the gamble and came anyway. You took the worse odds on fixing my leg, and I won big."

"You can stop thanking me. I get it. You're grateful."

"I don't think you know how much."

She didn't have an answer for that. His intention to thank her only made her uncomfortable. She'd done her job.

"It's more than you doing your job. You went above and beyond for me. That speaks to the kind of person you are. You've got guts and integrity." Sensing her discomfort, he shook his head and changed the subject. "If this trip was to get to know your sister better, what would you have done? Since you feel she went about it the wrong way."

"Not the wrong way, just not in a way that lent itself to open conversations. As much as she wants us to be friends, she holds everything back, afraid that if she says or does the wrong thing, it will all be over."

"If she said the wrong thing, would you shut her out of your life?"

"I'm the one who has every reason to be upset. Not her."

"Defensive," Dane pointed out. "Maybe she feels she can't be herself around you because you've got all those reasons you keep to yourself to be upset."

"Who's analyzing who now?"

"I'm just saying. I'm close to my family. You are obviously not. So far, I know that you and Katherine share the same father, but nothing else. There's a story there."

"One better left untold. Some skeletons are better left buried and forgotten."

"You haven't forgotten it."

"No. But I've moved on with my life. I wish everyone else would, too."

"So, you don't really want a relationship with your sister."

"Leave it alone, Dane. What I want, I'll never get."

"What's that?"

"Why do you care?"

"You fascinate me. I want to know."

She sighed and stared out the window with no intention of answering him. But the whispered words fell from her lips anyway. "I want them to see me, not what I represent." *I am Bell. Not a mistake. Not some bad thing that happened.*

Dane leaned forward and whispered back. "You're an amazing woman. If they can't see that, it's their loss. I know that doesn't make it better, but it's true. I'm sorry I ruined your vacation with your sister. Who knows, given time, she'll see in you what I see."

"You barely know me."

"True, but I'm working on it."

"Why?"

"I like you. You saved my life and risked your own to do it. While there are a lot of people in my life, I believe only a handful of them would do that for me. Those are the people worth knowing. I hold onto those people because they care, and they make me want to care for them."

"Like Brandy?" she asked, wishing she could take it back when he smiled, catching on that she was interested in his relationship with the other woman.

"Brandy's a lot of fun. Before Rowdy turned into an asshole from hell, they were inseparable. She loved him, and he adored her. We spent a lot of time hanging out and playing cards and pool, killing time between rodeos. She used to love to razz me about the women I dated. She saved my butt a few times, warning me away from someone even when I didn't see the subtle hints that they were nothing but trouble. But she's just a friend that I help out. While she cares about me, she's more interested in what I can do for her. I'm okay with that setup, because some people need help. I don't think she'd have jumped into that arena to save my life, but I don't fault her for that. She's barely able to keep her life together."

"Are you going to miss it?"

"What? The glory days?"

She couldn't help but smile back at him this time. The man had a way of disarming her, drawing her in and making her a part of his fun whether she liked it or not.

"All of it. The rodeo. Bull riding. The lifestyle."

"There is nothing like the adrenaline rush of riding a bull. I don't know why people do drugs, chasing that high, when all they have to do is grab a rope, hold on, and ride one of those out-of-control beasts. It's addictive. I don't know if I'll be able to give it up or find something else to replace it." The worry that he'd turn to drugs to chase that high must have shown on her face. "Don't worry, Doc, I've never been into chemically induced illusions of happiness. Not my style. As for the lifestyle. I won't miss sleeping in my truck and dirty, run-down motels. I won't miss the bars, playing pool and cards, and drinking to kill time. I won't miss hearing about what my brothers and their wives are up to on the phone, when I get to be there in person and experience it with them. I won't miss long drives from one place to the next. And yes, I won't miss a different woman every week or so who scratches an itch but never makes me feel better because at the end of the day, I'm still alone with my thoughts in the dark just like you said.

"While I am still trying to come to terms with what happened and the fact that this damn leg is going to make my life difficult for the next month or more, I am looking forward to being home with my family and friends and the place I love to be.

"I liked what you said about not settling down for a woman but finding one who fits me. Maybe all I'm looking for is what you're looking for. Someone to see me.

"The reason I make you nervous, Doc, is because I see far too much of who you really are, and I like you. For some reason, you've become too used to people not liking you for whatever reason. You're too smart. You're someone your grandmother didn't want to exist. I still can't get over that one. I'm sure you can't either. You want people to see through all of your past. All I'm asking is that you do the same with me.

"I am not that guy you think I am, despite the stream of women coming to see me. I don't think women are disposable. I think they're fun, kind, intelligent people who know their own minds and do what they want to do for their own reasons. I never took advantage. If they wanted to play, I was up for the game. I never hurt anyone. That's not who I am."

"I never thought you were."

"Yeah, you did." He tilted up one side of his mouth. "Don't worry, Doc. I gave you every reason to think that on the surface, but you looked deeper and saw the truth. Those women had a good time. I had a good time. No one got hurt. I never made them any promises, and they didn't want any. When I told you I'd pay you back for what you did for me, you believed me, because you know I take that very seriously. I'm not some heartless bastard. I'm just a guy who's decided that my youthful adventures, while fun, are in my past. It's time to get serious about my future. I've got a lot to live for and a second chance to make my dreams and plans a reality. Thanks to you."

Bell didn't know what to say to that. No one had ever really opened up to her this way. Sure, patients tended to unload their feelings and fears to her, but not like this. She knew Dane. In a way. But she never expected such a strong man—a man who knew his own mind and heart, who did what he wanted when he wanted because he could—to open up and speak with such honesty.

Yes, the man had a way of disarming her, pulling her in, and making her care. She felt like some kind of bond had been forged between them. More than the words he'd said, it was the sincerity and openness with which he'd spoken that touched her deeply. She'd never had a friend who would tell her secrets and share her most private thoughts. Dane had shared his with her, and it meant something and connected them in a way she'd never felt. She liked it, but didn't know what to do now. It made her nervous and scared to open herself to him in the same way.

They sat across from each other for the rest of the flight in silence. Both of them aware of the other so close and the pull between them that made them glance over just to see if the other one felt it, too. That silent conversation that said so many things she wasn't aware of and felt so new to her. Was it new—or at least different—for him?

She hoped so.

The plane landed, and they all got out. Dane did the same crab crawl down the stairs, then took Gabe's hand to stand up at the bottom, where he fell into the waiting wheelchair. A black SUV complete with driver waited nearby to take the family home.

Ella walked over to Bell and embraced her. "Thank you for everything. You have no idea how much we appreciate everything you did. Saving Dane. Spending your vacation with us at the hospital. I, uh . . . Would you be interested in a business proposition? I have a project I've been thinking about for the last few months. I didn't really know where to focus it, but now I do. I've got some great ideas for helping out Crystal Creek. I want to be a real part of the community. With your help, I think we could do something that is really needed."

"What do you have in mind?"

"I'll make an appointment with you, and we'll discuss it in detail. I'd like to put some money into the clinic."

"Really? That's wonderful. So many times we don't have the supplies or equipment we need and have to send patients to the hospital in Bozeman."

"Exactly. I think with your expertise, my resources,

and the community's involvement, we can turn that place into what everyone wants and needs."

"I'm on board. I'll put together my ideas. Whenever you'd like to discuss it, I'll be ready."

"I hoped you'd say that. It will be a big project. We'll probably spend a lot of time working on it together. I don't have many friends here, aside from Gillian, so I'm looking forward to getting to know you better."

"Me, too," Gillian said, stepping in to give Bell a hug. "Thank you for keeping me calm on the flight and taking care of me. I really appreciate it."

"My pleasure. You take care of yourself and that baby. If you need anything, come down to the clinic. We'll take good care of you."

Gabe took his turn to say goodbye and hug her. "Thanks for everything. Can we take you to your car?"

"No. I'm fine. I left it in the long-term lot. After the flight, I'm happy to walk across the airport to get there. You guys go home and get some rest. It's been quite a week."

"Yeah, for all of us," Gabe added.

"I'll see you all later. Take care," she said to Dane.

"What? No hug for me?" Dane said.

"I'll see you back at my office in a week." She turned and started to walk away.

"I'll be there. I miss you already."

That stopped her in her tracks. Five steps away, her back to him, she set her satchel on the top of her suitcase, turned, and walked back to Dane. She leaned down, wrapped her arms around his shoulders, and squeezed, inhaling his woodsy scent and something that was uniquely him. She released him slowly. Reluctantly. Her body stopped of its own volition. She stood, bent over him, their faces inches apart. The something inside her that didn't want to let him go pulled her in until her mouth hovered an inch from his. His breath washed across her lips. Hers caught in the back of her throat. The moment stretched, her gaze locked with his smoldering dark eyes.

His fingers caressed her cheek. The soft touch startled her. She took a step back before she gave in to the urge to kiss him, hold him closer, and press her face into his neck or run her fingers through his thick dark hair. She turned and took a step away, but he grabbed her hand. She didn't turn around, but glanced back over her shoulder.

"Thanks, Bell. For everything." He turned her hand and studied it, his warmth seeping into her skin and spreading through her whole system. "You have an amazing head and heart and hands. You put those all together and you save lives. That's an amazing thing, Bell."

Again, he left her speechless, unable to say anything to his softly spoken words that held so much sincerity.

Dane squeezed her hand, then released it. It didn't seem possible, but she felt even lonelier without that connection to him.

She walked back to her luggage, pulled out the suitcase handle, and rolled the bag behind her, trying not to focus on Dane's gaze locked on her back—or maybe her ass, knowing him.

A week seemed like a long time to go without seeing him. She missed him already, too. She didn't think she'd ever missed anyone. Not like this. She'd missed not having the family she wanted. She'd missed having the things her sister had and took for granted. But she'd never missed an actual person, let alone a man, until now.

CHAPTER 6

Dane hated the sight of the temporary ramp going up the steps to his childhood home. He vowed he'd be out of the wheelchair and walking again soon. He had things to do. Plans to implement. A woman to repay—and get to know better.

He couldn't get her off his mind. She stayed there like a ghost haunting his thoughts. Just when he thought of other things, she popped up and became a part of them. Like coming home to this house. Her grandmother's place was right next door. Okay, so right next door was a hell of a long way away, but she'd be there when she wasn't working. He wondered if she'd ever come here to see him. Ride the horses. She'd said she'd wanted his horse all those years ago when she'd spied on him.

"What is that smile?" his mother asked, walking out the front door with his dad right behind her.

"I always smile at pretty women, you know that, Ma."

He loved that his mother blushed, even when her son complimented her. "You save that for someone special. I'm three out of four for happy marriages for my boys. I'm looking to make it four."

"Yeah, well, first I've got to get my ass out of this chair."

"Watch your tongue, boy," his father scolded, not really meaning it. They did this kind of thing, and it felt so damn good to be home and with them again.

"Sorry, Dad." He hugged his mother and shook his dad's hand. "I missed you guys."

"We would have come, but Gabe and Blake assured us you were in good hands. By the time we got ready to be on a flight down, you were out of surgery and everything was looking okay."

"Mom, it's fine. I understand. Gabe told me you bought a new place."

"Well, you bought us a new place. Come inside, and we'll talk about it."

His father grasped the handles at his back and pushed him up the ramp and through the front door. Ella, Gabe, and his mother followed. Everyone remained quiet when he stared at the empty house. Well, empty of his parents' things. They'd bought him a new sofa, area rug, chair, side tables, and a coffee table to go with a monster flat-screen TV. Every other room he could see from the foyer sat empty. Hollow, like his gut felt, knowing everything had changed and this wasn't the house he grew up in anymore. This was his house. He lived here. Alone.

He didn't like it. This huge place should be filled with a family. He'd been alone on the road, moving from one town to the next, staying in one-room motels. Enough space for him—and sometimes a guest. But this place should be filled with the love and laughter and happiness he remembered from his childhood. It echoed in his mind but seemed absent from the cavernous rooms.

"If you don't like the living room furniture, say so now, and we'll return it. Otherwise, I hope you like it. I tried to get something you'd be comfortable with and would last you for years to come."

Dane stared up at his mother. "I like it. Thanks. I'm just surprised. I didn't know what to expect when Gabe said you were leaving me the house and ranch. I didn't really put it all together that you and my past moved out."

"This is the future you wanted, son. Your own ranch. We talked about my retiring. I wanted to do it sooner," his father said, "but I waited for you to make your mark on the rodeo circuit, earn the money you wanted, so you could come back here your own man. You didn't expect to come back in this condition and under these circumstances, but we are so glad you're home."

Dane took in his father's words. His dad was grateful that he'd agreed to come home and take over the ranch. It was a load off his dad's mind, and now he could travel with his mom without worrying about the business. Dane hadn't expected that, but it made it easier on him to take over and do what he wanted without worrying about stepping on his dad's toes.

"So am I. I'm just a bit confused. When did you guys do all this?"

"We found the property about six weeks ago. We didn't want to bring it up before your big day. We are so proud of you, son."

His father's praise hit Dane right in the heart. "Thanks, Dad. But it didn't exactly work out the way I wanted." He stared down at his outstretched leg in the brace, thinking of the stitches down his leg and the plates, screws, and wires holding his bones together.

"You performed well and won. What happened after was a tragic accident. You don't know how scared we were for you. Thank God Dr. Bell got to you in time," his father said.

"Oh, she got to him, all right," Gabe teased.

His mother and Ella shared a look and one of those mysterious smiles that says so much.

"I owe her my life."

"Is that why you stared at her all the time?" Ella asked.

"Drop it." He didn't want to get into it with all of them. Yeah, he liked her. He wanted to get to know her better, but she saw a side of him he didn't much like anymore either. Could he convince her his interest was more than getting her into his bed? He hoped so, because when she'd given in and hugged him goodbye, he'd wanted to kiss her like he'd never kissed another woman in his life. It had taken every ounce of self-control he possessed not to crush her to him, take her mouth, and taste her. She smelled like a field of wildflowers. Fresh and sweet.

He liked talking to her. She said what was on her mind and she didn't mince words, even when she gave him her honest opinion. She spoke the truth, even when he didn't want to hear it.

Thanks to her and that damn disastrous ride, he'd taken a good long look at his past and decided he wanted something better for his future. He wanted her. The girl who haunted his dreams but was a very real presence now. She'd gotten inside of him all those years ago. Now that he'd actually met and talked to her, he wanted more. Time to figure out what this feeling pulsing in his chest and coaxing him to call her right now just so he could hear her voice really meant.

I'm losing it.

He never thought he'd turn into one of those guys

who chased after a woman. Women chased him. Damn if he didn't want to steal his brother's truck, go see her, spend more time with her, and just be with her.

Why? What was so special about her? Was it just the fact that she'd saved his life?

Everything inside of him said no. Something more pulled at him.

"Well, come into the kitchen. I've made a light meal. We'll catch up," his mother said.

"Ella and I are heading home. I need to check in with my ranch foreman. Ella's got some calls to make for work. We'll catch up with you and Dad later. Dane, I'll be by the day after next to take you to physical therapy. Gillian will be by tomorrow to help you out." Gabe handed over his bag of meds. "Take those like the doc ordered. Get some rest."

"Thanks for staying with me. Ella, I can't thank you enough for chartering the flight and threatening lawyer hell on the hospital to get them to save my leg and let Dr. Bell operate on me. I owe you big time."

"No, you don't. We're family. You know how important that is to me. You are important to me. I love you. Be good. Stay off your leg. Rest. I'll take you to see Bell for your next appointment. I want to talk to her more about my plans for the clinic."

"I want to hear about them, too."

"I thought you might like it if she spent more time in town at the clinic rather than at the hospital in Bozeman." Ella winked at him. "Unless of course you'd rather the distance."

"Hell no." All eyes turned to him. Maybe he shouldn't have answered so quickly or definitively. "Ah, it'll be nice to see her at the clinic. I hate driving all the way to Bozeman for anything."

"Especially a beautiful woman." Gabe clamped his hand on Dane's shoulder and squeezed. "Nice try covering, though."

"Shut up. Take your wife home."

Gabe and Ella said their goodbyes. Dane sucked it up, ignored the pain in his ribs, and wheeled himself through the empty dining room into the kitchen. His mother had laid out a platter of cold fried chicken, a bowl of potato salad, fresh fruit, and some rolls. The kitchen didn't seem quite so cozy without all his mother's decorations. No crockery filled with cooking utensils. No fruit crate plaques on the walls. No blue-and-cream gingham curtains on the windows. No breakfast table next to the windows in the alcove. Just the wood stools lining the breakfast bar along the island where the food sat on the counter.

His mind started redecorating. The tile countertops were old and outdated. Maybe new granite in a light tan to complement the maple cabinets. New handles and knobs in brushed silver to go with the new faucet his father put in last year. Too modern for the way the kitchen looked now, but with a few changes in the room, he'd make it work.

Paint. The whole house needed a fresh coat of paint. Inside and out. He could do some of the work himself once he was on his feet again. Right now, he'd hire someone to come in, clean the place up, make some minor repairs and restorations, and make this place his.

"What color are you planning to paint the kitchen?" his mother asked, walking into the room with his dad.

"Maybe off-white or a pale yellow. Depends on the color of the new countertops."

His mother smiled. "I didn't think it would take

you long to get over the fact we moved out and moved you in."

"You'll want new carpet upstairs," his dad said. "It's been too many years since we redid anything up there."

"That's an easy fix. I'll hire someone to do it."

"About the house, son. Your mother and I are giving it to you, but we expect some compensation. We talked in general terms about this when you said you planned to come home after the championships."

"Dad, I've got the money to pay you for this place. You don't have to beat around the bush. What do I owe you?"

His father grabbed a folder off the counter and handed it to him. Dane opened it and found the real estate papers, which indicated his buying the property at a hefty discount and repaying his parents for the furniture they bought to get him started. He added up the total for both and frowned.

"Dad, this is nowhere near what I expected to pay you."

"That is a fair price. It's the money your mother and I feel comfortable having you pay for a property we would have left to you four boys anyway. Your brothers agreed you should get this property."

"They agreed to this." Dane pointed to the papers.

"All of it. Like you want to do, they've made their own way and don't need your mother and me to support them or give them anything."

"If you understand that about me, then let me pay you what this property is worth."

"What we're asking is more than we ever paid in the first place. It's enough for us to live on the rest of our lives. We've helped each of your brothers over the years in some way. You never asked for help, even when things were tough for you in the beginning. You're smart. You save your money. You plan. This is our chance to help you, even though you don't need it. We are so proud of you for all you've accomplished. We know you'll make a good home here. You'll run your business well. You'll make this place yours. That's what we want for you, Dane." His dad put his hand on Dane's head like he used to do all the time when Dane was a kid.

Dane took his dad's words to heart. They wanted him to let go of the past and make this place his. He wanted to do that, too, but having his parents' blessing made all the difference. He didn't need to feel guilty for mentally redecorating even now, planning what he wanted to do in the stables and on the land. They'd turned it over to him, entrusted him with their home and land and legacy with no qualms about what he did with it. They knew he'd do them proud. He'd certainly spend his life trying to live up to their expectations, as he always had.

His mother handed him a plate. His father took his seat at the bar beside his mother. They ate in silence for a few minutes. Dane savored the fried chicken. His favorite. He'd missed his mother's cooking.

"Dane." His mother had a look in her eye. She wanted to ask him something but didn't want to overstep. He could only guess what she wanted to discuss now.

"About Dr. Bell. Maybe you want to settle in here and get things running the way you'd like before you pursue other interests."

"Are you warning me away from the doc? I thought all parents wanted their kids to grow up and date doctors."

His mother and father shared one of those looks that says so much between them but Dane couldn't quite read. They knew something he didn't.

Interested in what they were hinting at, he asked,

"Dad, why did you let me believe I'd hallucinated her all those years ago? You knew she lived next door, didn't you?"

"Not at first," his father answered. "The scandal happened years ago, then died down, and I hadn't really thought about it in years."

"What scandal?"

"Mrs. Warwick's son had an affair with Miss Kentucky not even two years after he married and had a daughter with his wife. Bell is the result of that one-night stand."

"Bell's sister, Katherine, is married to a buddy of mine. I don't know Tony well, just in passing at the rodeos. His bull is the one who took me down."

"Their small ranch and yours sandwich the Warwick land."

His father said, "yours." It hit Dane all at once. The responsibility of owning and running a business on this land. The small herd of cattle his father kept, the horses in the stables, and everything else. All his now.

He thought of the layout of the property in connection to the Warwick land that bordered it. The Warwicks had a huge chunk of prime grassland, a river snaking through most of it and onto his property. Mrs. Warwick didn't have any animals on the land. Nothing but pristine wildlife. Untouched for decades, except for her tiny cabin house and vegetable gardens.

If he remembered right, Tony Cortez and Katherine's place was much smaller. Maybe a thousand acres. Not enough space to run even a medium-size operation. But maybe that would change with Tony's bull doing so well in the championships. They'd get some major stud fees and possibly buy more land. Or run cattle on Katherine's family property. Where Bell lived.

"Dr. Bell's father was, is, a big deal in the pharmaceutical industry. He's quite smart and developed a couple of drugs that help save lives. The affair caused an uproar for him personally with his wife and in his family, but professionally, it was nothing more than a blip. Still, when he discovered the affair produced a child, he made what I will graciously call poor choices."

"What do you mean?"

"His wife refused to take the child. She had her own daughter and was trying to hold onto her marriage. She didn't want another woman's baby. Dr. Warwick didn't want a reminder of what he'd done tearing his family apart. He didn't want to have to explain the child at the company picnic." The anger in his father's voice surprised Dane. Family was everything. A child was a blessing. That Dr. and Mrs. Warwick didn't want Bell pissed Dane off just as much as it did his father.

"Why didn't Bell's mother keep her?"

"The girl he got pregnant was all of nineteen with her whole life ahead of her. She wanted to marry a rich man who'd take care of her the rest of her life. She thought she'd found the perfect catch. She didn't want a child, she wanted a means to an end. When she didn't get it, she didn't want to spend what she thought were the best years of her life struggling as a single mother. She handed the baby, Bell, over to Dr. Warwick. The very same day, he handed Bell over to his mother to raise."

"Why isn't she 'Dr. Warwick'?"

"I don't know. Not for sure. I can only guess they wouldn't allow her to use the family name she'd tarnished."

"She didn't tarnish anything. Being born is not her fault. Her father and mother had the affair. They did wrong. That has nothing to do with Bell." Dane felt sick, thinking about Bell telling him her grandmother still wished she didn't exist. Who could say such a thing about an innocent child?

"That's not how her family thinks."

"Their thinking is wrong. She's an amazing person. She's a genius."

"It runs in the family. Which is why, when I contacted the authorities about Bell being hidden away in that house, they didn't take her away to someplace better."

"What are you talking about? When did this happen?"

"Right after your accident. You insisted you saw a girl out there. In the middle of nowhere. If you really had seen someone, she had to have come from the Warwick spread. I went over there and talked to Mrs. Warwick, who insisted no such girl existed. Bell walked out of the chicken coop not knowing I was there. The fear on her face when she saw me unsettled me. Mrs. Warwick went off, threatening all kinds of crazy punishments, from making Bell recite the Bible ten times to taking away her books."

Dane's stomach soured. His heart ached with sorrow. "I imagine for someone as smart as Bell, isolated from the world, her books were very important to her," he said, thinking of a little girl locked away from everyone and everything.

"Her grandmother threatened to take away her outside time. She was only allowed outside for two hours a day. Most of that time she spent working in the garden and cleaning out the chicken coop. Sometimes she disobeyed her grandmother and strayed further from the cabin to the river, where she saw you.

"Anyway, the authorities checked out the house, her, and determined her basic needs were being met."

"Right. She had food, water, clothes, and a roof over her head." Dane felt sick.

"All those things. Including the education her grandfather started before his death and Bell continued after on her own, since her grandmother refused to send her to school. A social worker gave her a test to verify her grade level. She finished it in twenty minutes and didn't miss a single answer. They determined she'd surpassed what she'd have learned in high school."

"So no one did anything about her being alone out there."

"No. The law says you have to provide for the child. You are not obligated to love them."

"What aren't you telling me?"

"The social worker tried to take Bell's hand. Bell flinched away. The social worker thought she'd been abused. Hit."

"Not the case though." Dane hated where his mind went. The awkward way Bell hugged Ella and Gabe goodbye. The look on her face when she hugged him. Like she hadn't known if she'd done it quite right. Even before that. The way she'd stared at him before she'd come to him. He hadn't been able to decipher it then. Now he thought he got it. She'd wanted to hug him but hadn't felt she deserved it. Like maybe doing so would be a very bad thing.

"Bell had never been touched from the time she was able to do things for herself. Her grandmother told the social worker not to touch the demon. Human contact of any kind would only allow the evil in Bell to seep into them. Infect them. She'd felt it every time she'd had to care for Bell as a baby. The evil hadn't been very strong, but it grew worse as Bell got older, so her grandmother stayed as far away from Bell as she could at all times."

The rush of rage made Dane fist his hands. "Holy hell. You've got to be kidding me."

"I wish I were, son. The social worker couldn't take Bell, but she did give Bell the information she needed to save herself."

"She told Bell that with her smarts she could go to college," Dane guessed.

"Bell didn't have access to a computer, a phone, TV, any modern things. Just her books. The social worker told Mrs. Warwick that Bell should go to college and that she'd qualify for scholarships and grants. Mrs. Warwick couldn't wait to get rid of her, so she allowed the social worker to help Bell get into college."

"Bell said she still lives there."

"Maybe in some limited way. She spends most of her time at the hospital. I heard in town that Mrs. Warwick suffers from diabetes, so I imagine Bell checks on her often," his mother said.

"Why the hell would she do that after the way that woman treated her?"

"Because up until she left for college, she'd only ever known that life." The disgust and pity in his father's eyes matched the jumbled feelings running through Dane. "That woman is the only person she knew until she walked onto a college campus at the age of fifteen."

Dane shook his head, unable to put words to everything he felt inside. He wanted to go to her, hug her close, and let her know she wasn't something to be hidden away but a woman to be celebrated for all she'd overcome, all she'd endured, all she was today despite how her family wronged her. How could they treat another human being so poorly? Dane didn't get it. He wanted to punish Mrs. Warwick for being a backward-thinking lunatic. He wanted to kill her father and mother for abandoning their own child.

"Why didn't you tell me she was real? All this time, I thought I imagined her." He let his gaze fall to the tattoo on his arm. His father frowned down at it, too.

"I felt sorry for her. I didn't want her to be in any more trouble than it seemed she was in. I tried to help her, but I may have made things worse. At least in the short term. She seems to be doing well now."

"She's a phenomenal doctor."

"Yes," his father said, but his tone hid a deeper thought.

"What else?"

"Nothing. She's really changed her life."

"But."

His father and mother shared another of those looks.

"Just say it. I'm going to be seeing her a lot over the next couple months while my leg heals. I'll figure it out eventually."

"People talk," his mother said.

"Yes, they love to run their mouths about things they know little about." Dane hated gossip. More often than not, people spoke out their ass, with more embellishment than actual facts. He'd been the subject of a lot of gossip over the years. Look at his reputation. He'd earned about half of it, but the rest was nothing but pure speculation and jokes at his expense about the number of women he slept with and his sexual prowess. Some of it made him laugh. He was a guy, not superhuman. He hadn't much cared until he'd had the very open and candid conversation with Bell in the hospital and seen the disapproving look in her eyes when she'd felt he dismissed all those women as nothing more than something he used for the night and discarded at the light of day. It wasn't really like that, but he understood now why she'd turn her nose up at him. Her father had done that to her mother, and she'd suffered the consequences while they'd gone on with their lives like nothing happened. She thought that's how Dane was, too. Not so. He liked the women he dated. If a baby came out of one of his affairs, he'd man up and take care of his business—his family.

He liked kids. He loved spending time with Gillian's brother every time he came home. He'd like to have kids of his own someday. A family to fill this too-empty house again.

"She's not like the other women you know." Nice of his mother to be diplomatic.

"Yes, she has a job that doesn't require her to take someone's order, smile, and shake her ass to get better tips. Come to think of it, she barely smiles at all. She's all business. Heaven forbid you call her honey and forget that she's a doctor."

"Dane, think of her background. Her father treated her mother with little regard for her feelings or the fact she was carrying his child. Bell's whole family hid her away like some awful secret. She was treated like a demon in her own home, never touched or loved or cared for with any regard for her feelings or well-being."

"I'm sorry, Mom. I forgot to take my pain meds. My leg and ribs are killing me. I wasn't thinking clearly and said something stupid."

"That's exactly what I'm worried about you doing with her. You need to keep things with Dr. Bell on a professional level. She's your doctor. She'll take care of your injuries."

"I know she will. She's great at her job. Probably the best in her field."

"Which hasn't been easy for her."

"Why do you say that?"

"Think about it. She went to college with kids who were four to seven years older than her, and she outperformed all of them. That didn't exactly make her popular. She entered medical school with people far older and more experienced than her and showed them up, too. She's never learned to interact with people in a normal way because her whole life has been an awkward interaction between her and people much older. She didn't go to her high school prom, or even date a high school boy. When she went to college, she wasn't old enough to drive, let alone go to a keg party at some frat house. Imagine what college must have been like for her after living the way she did with her grandmother. Imagine what her life is like now, trying to relate to people when she shares very few experiences with them because she either didn't experience them at all or she did so at a much younger age than everyone else."

"The reason she's so awkward around her sister."

"The reason she's awkward with everyone, sweetheart." His mother took the empty dishes to the sink. She turned back to face him. "If what Gabe hinted at is true and you like her, the best thing you can do is treat her with kindness. Understand where she came from and that she is not like any other woman you know. If you trifle with her, Dane, you could really hurt her."

He almost said he never trifled with women, but his mother would hear the lie even he couldn't pull off.

"That girl is all alone in this world. She may have people, but they are not her family," his father said.

"It disgusts me the way that man treated her and still calls himself a father. Her grandmother is a messed-up, mean-spirited woman who should never have had the privilege to raise a child. That she didn't completely ruin that girl, well, I don't know how she didn't. She sure did try hard enough to make Bell believe she was no good."

"It's not like you guys to warn me away from women, or even ask about who I'm interested in, so why do it with her?"

His mother glanced at his dad. "Tell him."

His father sighed. "When I saw Bell come out of that chicken coop, she dropped the eggs onto her toes, completely terrified I'd come to kill her."

"Why would she think that?"

"Because her grandmother yelled at her that she'd spread her evil, tainted you, and the devil had taken you."

Her grandmother should be shot for all her cruelty. "Ah jeez, are you serious?"

"Bell thought you died because she touched you."

"I passed out," he snapped, letting his anger show.

"I told her that. Her grandmother spouted a bunch of lies about her being responsible. I will never forget the look on Bell's face and the sadness that came into her eyes. She dropped to her knees in all those smashed eggs, clasped her hands together, rose her face to the sky, and begged God to take her instead."

Dane's stomach tightened and sank along with his heart. His chest ached with every breath he took, and it had nothing to do with his cracked and bruised ribs.

"As smart as she is, son, she was still just a little girl influenced by the only person in her life and the ones who refused to see her. Now she knows that she isn't evil, but her past still makes her who she is now."

"Someone who is nothing like anyone I've ever known. Someone who ran into that arena despite the danger to herself to save my life. Someone to whom I owe every breath I take and every beat of my heart."

"You've thanked her for that. Gabe did so on behalf of the entire family as well. Our gratitude has no bounds," his mother added. "We wanted you to be aware of who she really is. When you see her, be mindful of what we've told you. She deserves nothing but the best from this family."

A warning from his mother if ever he'd heard one. The thing was, he wanted to give Bell his best. He'd never felt he needed to do that with anyone else. He hoped he had it in him to do, say, and be his best for her, because no way he would keep things professional when this had always been personal—for both of them.

CHAPTER 7

Bell set her book aside and picked up her ringing cell phone. She checked the caller ID and sighed. Her answering service. Must be about one of her patients. This late at night, it couldn't be good.

"Hello."

"Dr. Bell, this is Claire, with AnMed. One of your patients insists on speaking with you. Mr. Bowden states you operated on him recently, and he's reinjured his leg."

Bell's heart stopped. If Dane did something to his leg, he could lose it. Fear washed through her. She leaned forward in her chair, ready to get in her Jeep and rush to his place to help him.

"Is he on the line?"

"No, Doctor. He left his number for you to call him back."

"Give it to me." Bell wrote down the number and hung up on the answering service without so much as a goodbye or thank you. She dialed Dane's number, stood, and dug her car keys out of her purse.

"Hello."

"Dane, what's happened? Did you fall?"

"I'm fine."

Bell stopped in her tracks, her hand on her bedroom doorknob. "What's the matter, then?"

"I wanted to talk to you."

"Are you hurt?"

"No. Well, I am in some pain, but I took my meds as you instructed."

"I don't understand. My answering service said you'd hurt your leg."

"Yeah, about that. I'm sorry. I lied."

Angry, she asked, "You lied?"

"What are you doing?"

Her confusion only grew with his evasiveness. "I'm not clear why you called me. Do you need medical help?"

"I'm sure I do, but that's not why I called."

Bell began to think maybe he did need his head examined. He made no sense. "Maybe you should tell me why you called so I understand what this is about."

"I want to talk to you."

"Okay. Do you have a question about your injuries?"

"No. Um, this is actually harder than I thought."

"Dane, if you're not hurt, and you don't want to ask me about your injuries, what is this about?"

"You."

"Me?"

He let out a sigh filled with frustration. Her agitation built the longer he took to get to the point. She hated when she missed social cues that others picked up on so easily.

"Uh, did you have to work late tonight?"

Bell narrowed her eyes and sat back in her chair again. "I got home about an hour ago. Why?"

"What are you doing now?"

She checked the clock beside her. Nine-thirty at night. She wondered what he'd been doing. "How many pain pills did you take?"

His deep laugh rumbled through the phone. "I'm not doped up, Doc. I had dinner with my parents after Gabe and Ella dropped me home. I took one pain pill and my antibiotics after I ate. My parents went home and left me alone in this big empty house. I couldn't stop thinking about you, so I called your office number. Now I've got your real phone number."

"Ah, okay. I still don't get why you called me."

"So I can talk to you."

"About what?"

"We've covered this, Doc. I want to know about you. How's your head?"

"Oh, it's fine. No more headaches. The concussion is healed. Even my shoulder is feeling better."

"Good. That's good."

"Okay, then. Have a good night. I'll see you at your appointment early next week."

"Doc, I'm not done talking to you."

"Oh. Um, okay."

"Did you have dinner?"

"Yes."

"What did you have?"

"A salad at the hospital cafeteria."

"My mom made fried chicken, potato salad, and fruit salad. She's a really great cook. How about you?"

Bell held the phone in front of her and stared at it, trying to figure out this strange phone call. She put it back to her ear. "I'm an okay cook, but I mostly eat out because I'm usually working."

"You didn't have to cover the clinic tonight?"

"No. One of the other doctors took the shift."

"Do you like working there?"

"It's a nice change of pace. I like keeping my skills current, working with the varied patients that come into the clinic with their many injuries and illnesses. It fills up my time."

"Why do you need to fill up your time? Don't you like to do anything but work?"

"Um, why are you asking me all of this?"

"It's called a conversation, Doc. I'm trying to get to know you better."

"Why?"

"Because I think you're an interesting woman, and I want to."

"Why?"

"Do you have any friends?"

That made her heart sink. She'd never been good at personal relationships. Inevitably, people found her weird. Most of the time, they stopped talking to her, thinking she wasn't interested in them or the conversation. Most of the time, she didn't know what they were talking about and couldn't contribute. She didn't understand the references to TV shows or pop culture. She'd never seen TV or listened to songs on the radio until she'd gone to college. Even then, it had all seemed so strange to her. She thought attending a smaller college in Oregon, and then medical school at the University of Washington in Seattle, wouldn't have been such a culture shock. She'd been wrong. Everything had seemed so different from her life in Montana. The psychologists she'd seen at both schools tried to give her tools to cope. It helped, but she'd still been out of place without the background and experiences others took for granted.

She'd dedicated her life to learning everything she

could in her classes and becoming a doctor so she could support herself. As soon as she was able to pay off the last of her student loans, she'd move into her own place. She hated being here with her grandmother, but she felt obligated to care for her—despite the woman's relentless antagonism—because of her grandfather.

"I, uh, work with lots of nice people." Casual acquaintances were more her speed. She kept things about work. Sometimes she asked questions about them when she caught snippets of conversations they had with others. Like whether Heather's sister enjoyed her vacation to Hawaii, or if Becky's daughter had gotten over her recent flu bug.

"Do you ever hang out with any of them? Go to dinner? To a movie?"

"Uh, no. Sometimes I sit with colleagues in the cafeteria." She defended herself. The longer this conversation went on, the more socially inept she felt. Both on the call and in her life. Why did he point these idiosyncrasies out?

"I'd like to take you to dinner sometime. When I can actually drive again."

"Why would you want to do that?"

"Same reason I called you tonight. To get to know you better. What's your favorite food?"

"I don't know."

"It's a simple question. You have to like something more than your salads and Greek yogurt. Chinese? Italian?"

"Pizza," she admitted. Her first night at the college campus, she went to the cafeteria. She didn't know what a lot of the menu items were. Corn dogs. Chicken nuggets. She'd never heard of such things. Then she'd seen the pizza with the melted cheese. God, it had looked so good. Smelled even better. The first bite hooked her.

"A girl after my own heart. I bet you ate a ton of pizza at college. It's kind of a prerequisite, right?"

"I guess so."

"What's your favorite topping?"

"All of them. Depends on my mood. Sometimes it's pepperoni with black olives and mushrooms. Other times it's chicken with spinach, bacon, tomatoes, and garlic sauce."

"You almost lost me on the chicken on pizza, but that actually sounds kind of good."

"There's this brick-oven place by the hospital. I love going there. They make the best pizza."

"We should go together when I'm up on my crutches. I want to try one of those chicken pizzas."

"Don't you have something else to do?"

"Like what?"

"I don't know. I'm sure there are a dozen women you'd rather spend your time with."

"None of them is you. Blake should be home with my horses and truck in a couple of days. You said you wanted my horse all those years ago."

"Are you going to give it to me?" She didn't think that's what he meant, but she couldn't help asking him. She loved seeing the horses on her drive home.

"If you want him, he's yours. He's a bit of a spoiled brat, but he loves a good long ride."

"What would I do with a horse?"

"Ride it."

"I don't know how to ride a horse."

"What? You live in Montana. How . . . never mind. Sorry. I wasn't thinking. I'll teach you to ride. You'll love it."

"Why did you say sorry?"

"Uh, I forgot your grandmother doesn't have any horses or cattle on the property."

"Right. Nothing but me and her here. That's what you meant. You had dinner with your father. What did he tell you?"

"Nothing." The word came out too quickly.

She didn't believe him. Bell had given Dane her version of what happened after his accident all those years ago. She'd left out what happened when his father had come calling. Looking back, she felt like such a fool for the way she'd reacted. She hadn't known any better. Now she did. The embarrassment rose up to her throat, choking her.

"You're not a very good liar."

"I'm sorry for what happened." He sounded sincere, but she heard and felt his pity.

He knew what happened with his father. What a complete idiot she'd been. Maybe he even knew about her parents and how she'd ended up with her grandmother.

"I don't want or need your pity, Dane. I'm not that little girl anymore. I have a new life. A different life."

You lie to yourself as much as you lie to him. Your life may be different, but in many ways nothing has changed. She might eat pizza, but she ate it alone. She did most everything alone.

"Bell, you make it damn hard to get to know you. We're just talking here. You tell me something. I tell you something. It's a conversation."

"You haven't told me anything." Why did she say that? She should hang up. He'd called her under false pretenses. No reason for her to carry on with this ridiculous conversation, telling him things he didn't need to know, or that mattered in the first place. He'd get bored. See she was nothing like the other women he knew, and he'd move on. A novelty in his life, he'd find someone more interesting and forget about her.

"What do you want to know?"

"Why you're doing this?"

"I like you. I want to know more about you. It's that simple and that complicated, Bell. I know you don't get it. I'm not sure I do either at this point. I want to be your friend. Is that so hard to believe?"

"Yes. It is." She didn't realize she'd said the words out loud.

"Well, believe it. Friends know things about each other. They talk about their day. Since I spent most of mine with you and we've caught up on our evening, I'm moving on to things I don't know about you. Like what's your favorite color."

This seemed ridiculous, but she'd play along. For now. Because she'd never had a close friend but had always wanted one. "Blue."

"Like your denim blue eyes?"

She smiled. People often commented about her eyes and their contrast to her hair. She'd never heard them described like that. "Pale blue, actually. Like the sky."

"Might make a nice paint color for the house?"

"Do you plan to paint?"

"I came home to a practically empty, four-bedroom, three-and-a-half-bath house that my parents lived in from the day they were married until two days ago. They haven't painted in years. Not exactly my taste either. Since I've got some time before I can start working the ranch, I thought I'd spend it working on the house."

"Your leg . . ."

"Needs time to heal. When I'm a hundred percent—hell, even fifty percent—I'm good with my hands. I could do all the work myself, but I'll follow your orders and stay off my leg."

She gave in and treated him not like her patient but like a friend she'd never had. "Sky blue would be pretty in a bedroom or bathroom. It would be really pretty on the ceiling of a white bathroom. I always wanted to paint my bedroom ceiling that color."

"Almost like being outdoors while you're inside."

"Exactly. What's your favorite color?"

"Green. Give me fields of green and I'm happy."

"So long as you're up on horseback."

"I love to ride. It's in my blood."

"What else do you like to do?"

"Play poker with my brothers. Pool at the bar. Hang with my buddies. Ride bulls. Have fun."

"That I already knew."

"But Bell, I never had fun at someone else's expense. It's not fun to hurt someone. I'd never do that to anyone. I wanted you to know that much about me."

"Dane, I saw the look on your face when those four women showed up to see you. You didn't want them to all come together. You didn't want to hurt their feelings by picking one over the other. You didn't want them to hurt each other by telling tales about you. I don't think you set out to keep all your relationships casual. You moved around a lot. You didn't want to get tied down. None of them ever made you change your mind about sticking it out.

"I went to college. I saw the way people hooked up without any expectation of anything more than having a good time together. I understand that not all relationships are long term or permanent. So relax. I don't think you're a bad person for dating women you had no intention of marrying.

"I guess with all that practice, you know what you like and what you don't want. There's something to be said for that. When and if you decide you want a relationship, at least you'll know what it is you want in a partner."

"As you said, it's not settling down so much as finding someone who is my match. I'm glad you understand. It must have been strange for you to be on a college campus and see all those rowdy people hooking up, partying, and living a different kind of life than you were used to, or could participate in."

"Quite the eye opener. Let's just say I got an education in more than academics."

"Did you live in the dorms?"

"No. I rented a room from an older woman off campus."

"Definitely more your speed."

"I guess so. She worked nights. I went to school all day while she slept. It worked out to be a good arrangement. We passed each other in the evenings. I stayed up late reading and doing my homework."

"Was it hard to adjust to college life?"

"I tried to take it all in, but everything overwhelmed me. I'd never been inside a classroom. I didn't know the procedure for doing homework. I'd never used a computer. Being smart helped. I learned things quickly. My professors were told that I'd need extra help. Each of them had a meeting with me and went over what I needed to know and how to do things. They all had student assistants. I used those people a lot to answer my many questions. I embarrassed myself more times than I can count, but I got through it."

"Now you're a computer wizard, a mad scientist, and a hell of a doctor."

She laughed. "Something like that."

"What was your favorite class?"

"Psychology. I learned a lot about people in that class. I'd never had access to any kind of books like those. Why people do things interested me."

"You had a lot of questions about the people in your life and all the different people you discovered at school. You needed a way to sort it all out."

"I spent a lot of time during the semester with my psychology teacher. She was really great. I still keep in touch with her." She didn't admit to having seen the psychologist on a regular basis throughout those years. He didn't need to know how hard it had been to cope.

"You impressed her with your insights, right?"

"I didn't have the same background as others, so my perspective on things was fresh and different. She enjoyed listening to my take on different topics. We collaborated on a paper."

"You got published with your professor."

"Several of them. I loved school. I thought I might want to be a teacher, but socially that would have been difficult for me."

"Why? You're nice. You listen to people. You work with patients."

"That's different. The doctor-patient relationship is very short and exact. I assess them, diagnose them, fix them, and send them on their way. There is nothing personal, and only my medical knowledge is of importance. It's the personal stuff I have a hard time sharing. I can't believe I'm talking to you about any of this."

"Why? We're friends."

"One conversation makes us friends?"

"This one does. Besides, this isn't our first personal conversation. We had those other ones in the hospital and on the plane. You may not be good with other people, but you're great with me."

"It's late. I'm tired. I must be out of my mind to encourage you."

"No encouragement needed. I called you. As much as I want to keep talking to you and listening to your sweet voice, my meds have kicked in, and I'm exhausted."

"You've had a long day. You're still healing. You need your rest."

"I'm comfy on my new couch. I think I'll crash here instead of trying to make it up the stairs on my own. I still haven't seen the bedroom furniture my parents got me."

"Didn't you already have a room at home?"

"Yep, but everything was from my childhood. I'm too big to be sleeping in a twin bed anymore. My feet hang off the end. It was okay for the few times I crashed here when I came home, but they wanted me to have something new now that I live here full-time. New bed. New life. Thanks to you."

"I had nothing to do with the bed, or you choosing a new kind of life."

"I have a life because of you, Bell. I'm so glad you're real and a part of my new life. I can't stop thinking about you. I wish you were here."

"I'm going to blame those little gems on your meds."

"Not the meds. Just you. So, will you have dinner with me?"

"I don't know if that's a good idea. You're my patient."

"Don't make me get another doctor just for a date."

"That's just it, Dane, I'm not just a date. I'll never be the woman who is just a date. Get some rest. I'll see you next week."

Bell hung up and sighed, staring at her cramped little room with the floor-to-ceiling books stacked so tightly together that she couldn't see the walls. Her grandfather had hoarded the books. She loved them as much as he had. She wanted to open another now and lose herself in another world. Too bad the only world she wanted to be a part of was Dane's.

Dane gripped his phone so tightly his fingers ached. He wanted to chuck it across the room. Instead, he tossed it on the new wood coffee table beside him and stared up at the ceiling.

Frustrated she didn't get it, he smacked his fist against the back of the couch. "Fuck."

Didn't she see how hard he was trying to get to know her? Didn't she see how much effort he'd put into talking to her tonight? Wasn't it enough that he'd gone out of his way to get hold of her? She had to know that meant something. Right?

No. Because she'd never dated anyone. She'd never had a relationship with a man.

Wait. Hold it. Shit. She'd never had a relationship with a man.

Well, damn, that put a whole new spin on things. He hadn't thought of it in those terms. He understood her background, but he hadn't put it into the context of dating her. Like his mother said, she'd never gone to high school, been asked to a dance, gone on a date, or worked her way through all those awkward teenage moments of a first kiss and . . .

Has she ever had sex?

That thought stopped him in his tracks. Could she possibly be in her midtwenties and still be a virgin?

He felt protective of her. He didn't want some other asshole coming into her life and having all those experiences with her. He didn't want anyone to hurt her because they didn't understand where she'd come from and how much she'd overcome.

He admired her hard work to change her life. He wished it had been normal, but he wanted to give her better. Yep. She made him want to be better for her. Could he be her friend, date her, introduce her to things she'd gone without all this time, and not fuck it up? Not mess her up even more?

He reached over his head, turned off the new wrought-iron lamp, and lay in the darkness, contemplating his options. Only one would do. He wanted her in his life. He wanted a real relationship with her. He'd figure out a way to make it happen and hope he didn't make too many mistakes. It would be a new experience for both of them.

CHAPTER 8

Bell took the chart from the holder on the door and read the name. Dane Bowden. Just that was enough to make her stomach and heart flutter with anticipation and bring up all her memories of the calls they'd shared over the last week. He contacted her every night at nine-thirty, just like that first night. They spent a few minutes, a half hour, an hour, and sometimes longer on the phone. They talked about their day, their childhoods—though he gave up far more details about that than she did. He told wonderful stories about growing up with his brothers. Fishing and camping trips. Riding horses. School with his friends. High school sweethearts and heartbreaks. Big details and little ones. He shared them all. Every one of them she soaked up, drawing closer and closer to him.

Dangerous territory.

In the back of her mind, she questioned why he pursued her. What made him want to talk to her? Why did he choose her to share these pieces of himself with?

He said he wanted to have a relationship with her. But what kind of a relationship? A romantic one?

She sucked it up, took a deep breath to calm the butterflies in her gut, and knocked on the door.

"Come on in," Dane called.

She opened the door and steeled herself to see him again. Did the man have to be that good-looking? She saw all kinds of people, but none as handsome as him. No one had that dazzling smile.

"Hey, Doc. You made it."

"Sorry I'm late. I got held up at the hospital for a consult in the ER." She glanced at his sister. "Ella, so nice to see you."

"You, too. I'm your next appointment."

"I saw that. Are you okay?"

"Fine. I just wanted to talk to you about my Crystal Creek Clinic project, so I made an appointment."

"Uh, okay." Bell turned to Dane and noticed there wasn't a wheelchair in the room. "How did you get here?"

"Ella drove me in. Why?"

"No. I mean, where is the wheelchair?"

"I can't stand that thing. Gave it up two days ago." He pointed to the door and the pair of crutches leaning against the wall.

"You're using your crutches already?"

"Moving makes me feel better. Sore, but in a good way."

"What did your regular doctor have to say about your ribs?"

"I don't have another doctor. You're my doctor."

"Dane, you're supposed to see your general practitioner to oversee your case."

"I'm seeing you. You're the only doctor I want and will see. So you check me out. Tell me what you think."

She pressed her lips together to stop the smile. The

man got to her every time. Smart, he used the double meaning of his words to say one thing and mean another. She liked his quick wit.

She shook her head and resisted the urge to scold him like a little boy who couldn't take this seriously.

"Raise your arms until it hurts your ribs." She waited and noted that he didn't flinch but raised his arms all the way up. "Not bad. How's the pain level?"

"My ribs ache, but not that bad. They've gotten a lot better."

She moved and stood in front of him.

"You smell good," he said.

Ella laughed. "Give her a break, charmer. Let her do her job before you flirt with her."

"I like flirting with her. She can still check me out."

"I give up," Ella said, leaning back in her seat.

Bell rubbed her fingers over Dane's cracked ribs. He flinched and pressed his arm to his side to get her to stop.

"Okay, Doc. I'll be good."

"How much have you been up and using the crutches?"

"Not that much."

"He was in the stables feeding the horses, using one crutch," Ella said.

Bell frowned and narrowed her eyes.

"Ah, come on, don't give me that face. I'm fine."

Mad and scared for him, she grabbed the X-ray off the counter and slipped it into the light-box holder.

"You're fine? Are you sure about that?" She turned the light-box on and watched his face register the shock when he saw the plates, screws, and wires holding his shattered bone together. "Now tell me that you're fine. Tell me that if you stumbled on that one crutch and put your foot down to take your weight, you'd be fine. That the bone I spent hours repairing is strong enough even with all my hard work to support your two-hundred-pound frame."

"You told me, but I really had no idea."

"Now you do. I told you to rest. Let the bone and muscle heal. But you can't do what you're told. I'll bet your thigh muscles ache from overcompensating for the other muscles in your leg."

"They do."

"Well, at least you're honest about that."

"I swear, Doc. I'll be a better patient."

"No, you won't. Lucky for you, the bone is healing well. You've had no fever or infection. While that does not give you permission to ignore my directive, you haven't done any further damage."

"I swear, Bell, I've been very careful."

He'd switched to using her name, hoping she'd understand and not scold him again. He got it now. Seeing the proof of the damage changed things for him.

"Careful isn't good enough, Dane. You need to rest that leg. Have you been icing it?"

"Every night."

"The swelling should be better. Let's take a look."

Dane swung sideways and rested his leg on the table. Bell undid the straps and opened the brace. She didn't move his foot, ankle, or leg, but carefully undid the bandages over his stitches.

"Have you been changing the bandages and cleaning the incisions?"

"Yes, twice a day just like you instructed and the nurse at the hospital showed me."

"These look good. I'll take the stitches out. That should help with the itching."

"Thank God. Finally, some progress."

"You are making progress, but it's going to take weeks to heal completely. I feel like I'm repeating myself. I say the same thing to you over and over, but you don't listen."

"You won't have to again. I swear."

"You better, or I'll call Gabe and have him take your crutches away from you," she threatened.

Outraged, he sucked in a breath and glared. "You wouldn't."

She raised one eyebrow. "Wanna bet."

"Ella, make her stop," he pleaded.

"Do what she says, and she won't sick big brother on you." Ella gave Bell a firm nod.

"Why are you feeding the horses? Don't you have someone to do that?"

"Blake stops by and helps out. I've got two guys working on the ranch, but I wanted to work. Hell, I wanted to do something besides sit on my ass all day."

"One more week. Then I'll reevaluate the bones. Then maybe . . . maybe I'll let you start walking on it. What I mean by that is I'll let you begin putting pressure on it while using the crutches. You will not take off on a 5K run."

"How about I take you for a ride?"

"What?"

"Horseback riding."

"Let's stick with walking on your leg for now."

Bell's gaze dropped away, a hint of fear in her eyes. Horseback riding frightened her. He'd help her get past that, but not now. When he was better and she wasn't worried about him and getting on a horse. All he wanted to do was spend time alone with her. A chance to really get to know her and for her to get to know him.

"I'd love it if you came to my place. I'll make dinner. We'll watch a movie."

She wrapped her arms around her middle. "I'm working every night for the next week at the clinic." The hesitation in her voice gave him hope.

"Come for breakfast."

She laughed and shook her head. "Can we do the whole doctor-patient visit? Let's get that done."

"You're killing me, Doc, and making me look bad in front of my sister."

"You've really lost your game since you fell off that bull," Ella said, deadpan. "It's sad, really. What would all your buddies say?"

"Kiss her and get it over with," he suggested.

Bell took a step back and put up her hand. "I am not kissing my patient."

"I'm just teasing," he said to reassure her. "Take these stitches out, then we'll go to lunch."

"You're incorrigible."

"I love it when you use those big words."

She rolled her eyes, but he got her to smile again. As much as she resisted, she liked the attention. If she didn't, he'd stop. Well, he'd try to convince her in a different way.

She set the tray of supplies on the table between his legs and pulled on her latex gloves.

"Man, that is really something." Dane stared at the long scars down his leg.

"They'll fade over time."

"There's a spot down by my ankle. It tingles sometimes, but when I touch it, it always feels numb." He rubbed his finger over it.

"Nerve damage. The feeling might come back over time."

"Right. I need to let it heal and see what happens, right?"

"I know you're frustrated and bored, but you need to find something to do that doesn't require you to walk or stand."

He rolled his eyes and sighed out his frustration. "Right. I'll spend my days binge watching *The Walking Dead* and *Breaking Bad*."

"Uh, okay."

He cocked up one side of his mouth. "You have no idea what I'm talking about, do you?"

"No."

"Do you own a TV?"

"No."

"What do you do in your spare time?"

"I read. I hike. I take care of my ailing grandmother." Not her favorite thing to do, but the woman did raise her. She was sick and required Bell's care. She'd provided for Bell out of family obligation. Bell returned the favor. Not out of love or devotion but out of human decency. Despite how she'd been treated, Bell's conscience wouldn't allow her to turn her back on the only person who'd kept her. "I work."

"Have you ever been to a movie?"

"All the time. I love movies. No commercials. Like a book, I want the story to flow without interruption."

"Who do you go to the movies with?" The question sounded more like a demand. The feral look in his eyes took her aback. Why did he care?

"I go alone."

"You go alone? To the movies?" Dane and Ella glanced at each other, a mix of sadness and disbelief.

Yes, she was one of those rare oddities who sat alone at a restaurant table and in the middle of the theater.

She'd learned to ignore the pity stares and enjoy herself. She didn't want to hide away anymore.

Embarrassed by their stares and pity, she re-dressed his leg and strapped the brace back into place. Better to turn this meeting back into a patient visit and steer clear of her personal life. Every time he pointed out all the things she didn't do like other people, it made her feel even more isolated and lonely.

She tried to make friends, but it never turned out well. Inevitably, she made some social faux pas. She missed references to things she didn't know about. The jokes would start. How can someone so smart be so stupid? Of course they said it behind her back—mostly—but she got it. Too sensitive, she usually couldn't stand to be the butt of other people's jokes, because they felt threatened by how smart she was—academically.

"Hey, Doc, I lost you." Dane's deep voice pulled her out of her head, where she got lost often.

"Uh, sorry. We're all done. How are the pain meds holding up?"

"Fine. I've got them spread out to five hours apart."

"If you actually rested, you'd spread that out even more. Let me know if you need a refill." She turned to face Ella. "Would you like to take the meeting into my office?"

"Sounds good. Dane, you can wait in the lobby if you don't want to listen to all this stuff about the clinic."

"And miss out on staring at the doc some more? No way. Let's go check out the doc's office."

"It's nothing special."

"Let's see." Dane slid off the table onto his good leg and hopped over to the crutches.

Bell stopped beside him. "Wow, you're really tall. I don't think I've actually stood beside you."

He stared down at her from his six foot height to her much shorter five-six frame. "You're a little bit of a thing, but I like that."

"No, you don't. You like tall, leggy, busty blondes."

"I used to like them. I have better taste now."

Bell rolled her eyes, passed him, and walked down the hall. Ella followed her with her own expressive eye roll and wink. Maybe he shouldn't say things like that to Bell, but he loved seeing the expression on her face. Every time, for just a split second, she believed him—or at least wanted to believe him.

He waited every minute of the day for the clock to strike nine-thirty so he could call her, hear her voice, listen to her tell him about her day. Over the last six days, she'd gotten more comfortable. The awkwardness dissipated but never quite disappeared. She kept parts of herself closed off because she was always afraid to say the wrong thing. When she did, he politely corrected her or steered her to the proper term or jargon. She made him smile when he used a reference to pop culture that went right over her head. She amazed him with her knowledge about, of all things, tomatoes. Off the top of her head, she'd named a dozen different varieties, their taste, growing season, size, hybrid versus heirloom, and various colors. All because he'd told her the tomato on his sandwich tasted bitter and underripe. Next year, he planned to get her to help him start a garden and plant some of those tomatoes. When he asked her how she knew so much, she told him she read a book about it once. One of her grandfather's. She barely remembered the man, but the few memories she shared with him were filled with love and adoration for the one and only person who'd been kind to her as a child.

In Las Vegas, she'd worn casual clothes. Jeans, T-shirts, even a pretty blouse. Here, she kept things to business attire. He loved her deep purple slacks and cream top. She chose bright colors that set off her eyes. Light makeup in a soft pink. Nothing showy. Natural. She didn't need anything more. Today, she'd combed her bangs back into curls and spikes that gave her an edgy look but still made her face look soft. God, that face. He thought about her all the time. He couldn't get her off his mind. She didn't look anything like the other women he'd dated. She'd been dead-on about that, but she appealed to every one of his senses. She smelled like wildflowers and hand sanitizer. He loved looking at her soft curves and watching her walk with that purposeful stride. She really had no idea how pretty she was, or how she drew every man's eye. As they passed another patient, he smiled, and Bell nodded her acknowledgement. Dane glared at the guy. He looked away immediately.

He loved listening to her voice in person or on the phone, even when she lectured him. He liked that she didn't hold back the truth—about anything.

He'd love to get his hands on her. The few times she'd touched him to check out his injuries, she'd worn gloves. What he wouldn't give to have her put her bare hands on him. He'd kiss her. Finally discover how she tasted. He spent far too much time fantasizing about making love to her, knowing that she didn't have anyone else in her life that she connected to on that level. Not just the physical, he wanted to share that bond two people felt when they came together and made love. With her, it would be different.

A voice inside warned him not to get too close. He didn't want to hurt her. He didn't want her to think she was just another conquest, but he wanted her more than he'd ever wanted another woman. He wanted her in a way he'd never experienced with anyone. Dangerous ground for a wanderer like him, especially now that he'd settled back home on the ranch. If this went south, if he screwed it all up, he'd have to see her again eventually. He didn't know if he could live with himself if he hurt her. By accident, or on purpose.

He entered her office behind Ella. Bell closed the door next to the windows that looked out onto the main office space. Another set of windows dominated the wall behind her desk and chair. She took her seat, and Ella took one of the chairs in front of her. Dane leaned his crutches against the wall, pulled out the other chair, and sat down.

Her diplomas hung on the wall next to Ella. "Bell Brittany."

Bell's gaze locked with his.

"So they gave you a first and middle name but couldn't bother to give you a last name?"

"Apparently my mother never made it past the Bs in the baby name book."

"Oh, Bell." Ella reached over and put her hand over Bell's on the desk.

Uncomfortable, Bell slipped her hand free. She clasped her hands together on the desk and stared at Ella, waiting for her to begin the meeting.

"You didn't have parents, honey, you had a sperm donor and an incubator," he said.

She glared at him.

"What?"

"He does it without thinking," Ella answered.

"What do I do?"

"Call every woman honey."

"This again."

Bell sighed. "Ella, about the clinic. I spoke with Dr. Sheldon. He mentioned that you've got quite a project outlined for updating the facility. He held back the details."

"I asked him to, because I wanted to go over them with you in person. Here's the thing. Since I've moved back, I've wanted to do something to give back to the community. You were one of the first people I met here. You took such good care of me, I thought why not start with the one place everyone in town needs. The clinic. Not just someplace they can go for minor illnesses and injuries but a place that can service the community."

"You want to turn the clinic into a hospital?"

"On a small scale, but yes. I'd like to add a surgical suite. Maybe two. Rooms for patients to stay for observation or extended medical care for a week tops. Serious conditions that require round-the-clock doctors and nurses on staff would still need to go to Bozeman. Mothers could have their babies closer to home. I'm thinking an overall general practice with minor surgeries performed on-site."

"The building we're in now won't accommodate what you have in mind."

"No, but the old feed store and warehouse on the outskirts of town is a perfect space to renovate."

"I don't think it's available anymore. I pass it every morning on my way in to work. Someone is already working on the buildings."

"I am." Ella took out a folder from her tote bag and set it on Bell's desk. She pulled out a folded paper and spread it wide to cover the majority of the available surface. Dane leaned in, along with Bell, to get a better look.

"The building has been gutted. The electricity and plumbing are being done now. What do you think of the layout? I worked on it with Dr. Sheldon, but I'd love your take on the overall project."

"Well, I love that you've got birthing suites across the building from the surgical suite and recovery rooms. You've got the scrub room on this side of the first surgical suite, but quite far from the second one. You might think of moving it between the two rooms with a door leading into each room. If you make the room a bit bigger, we can store some of the surgical equipment in there, too." Bell pointed to the section between the surgical suites. "If you put it here, you'll have more square footage. This smaller suite will gain room on the other side where the scrub room is now. It's a better use of space and allows for a better flow from room to room if there is an emergency and doctors and nurses have to move between them."

"Okay, I didn't think of that. Dr. Sheldon didn't mention it."

"He's a general practitioner with years of experience, but not in an emergency room or surgery. At the front of the building, you could section off the waiting room and add an additional door. Here." Bell pointed to a window on the drawing. "Add a wall here and create two rooms. The smaller one will be for sick patients who may be contagious. The other side for injured patients or follow-up visitors. Shift the reception desk thirty degrees to the right. Put in a half wall that keeps patients separated but allows for the receptionist to have full view of both rooms."

"That's a great idea."

"If it's possible, you might want to add a couple cots in the locker room. If a doctor needs to stay for a double shift, they'll need a place to grab some sleep for a couple of hours."

"Do you sleep at the hospital?" Dane asked.

"A lot. Mostly it's the ER staff that stays over, but I cover shifts once in a while. Other times, I sleep at my desk at the clinic."

"Bell, that's no way to get a good night's sleep," Dane said.

"The cots will be a lot more comfortable."

"I'll pay for the damn cots." Dane shook his head at Bell. She deserved better than a chair, a cot, that damn tiny cabin she lived in with her grandmother.

"You'll earn enough money for those and a lot more at the charity benefit I'm holding in two weeks." Ella's bright smile hinted that she'd left something out.

"What are you talking about?" Dane asked.

"I've put together a charity benefit and invited a lot of influential people from the surrounding communities. I'm looking for investors, but I'm also looking for the community to donate their time and money to make this a place they feel a part of and comfortable coming to for all their needs. To raise money, I'm holding a charity dinner and bachelor auction. I've got ten of the most eligible bachelors in Montana ready to take their lucky ladies out on a date at this swanky restaurant I got to donate dinner for two for each couple."

"What does that have to do with me?" Dane asked, dreading the answer.

"You, my professional bull riding champion, are my most sought-after eligible bachelor."

"No way. Not going to happen."

"Are you really going to say no to me? To the community? To Dr. Bell's new cots and the facility that will be a wonderful place for her to work and run?"

"Wait. What?" Bell asked, her eyes wide.

"That's what I wanted to talk to you about. In addition to your input on the new facility, I wanted to offer you the position of chief surgeon."

"But there are other doctors who are more qualified, with many more years of experience."

"I've spoken to several doctors at the hospital, here, and at the clinic. They all reluctantly state that you are the best choice. You've got the medical training, knowledge, and practical experience to do the job. You work an amazing hundred-hour week between the hospital and the clinic. Every week. The vacation you took to Las Vegas is the first vacation you've ever taken. Ever. That's inhuman. I'm offering you a sixty-hour week. You'll be closer to home. The clinic will be less than half the drive you make now from your grandmother's place. I don't know what your current salary is. You may take a hit going to the new clinic for a short time, but as the clinic gets up and running and taking more patients, you'll earn more money."

"It's not about the money. I always thought I'd work in the hospital."

"Are you happy doing that? Does what I'm offering you interest you at all? Maybe you have another idea, something I haven't thought of that we could come to a compromise on. I don't want to lose you altogether. The community has come to count on you at the clinic. With you onboard for the project and playing a larger role, it's my hope that the town will embrace this new project."

"It's a good idea," Dane added. "So many times the people living in and around Crystal Creek can't get the care they need because of limited resources. This will make things a lot easier for the residents. It'll save on ambulance trips to Bozeman for less-serious injuries and illnesses."

"Does that mean you're my most eligible bachelor?" Ella pleaded with her eyes.

"Can't I just write you a check and take Doc out to dinner?"

"I expect you to write me a check and do the auction. If Dr. Bell wants to buy you for the date, that's up to her."

"Oh, no. I'll write you a check, but I am not bidding in an auction for Dane or any man. No way."

Ella laughed at Bell's horrified expression. "From the sound of things, I think all you'd have to do is say yes to get a date with Dane."

"That's all any woman has to say." Bell pointed out the cold, hard fact that used to be true but wasn't anymore.

"Hey."

"What? Am I wrong?" Bell cocked up one dark eyebrow, an I-dare-you-to-contradict-me look in her blue eyes.

"Dead wrong. The only woman I want to see is you. I wish you'd believe that." With his past, he didn't blame her for being skeptical. Still, he'd never had to pursue a woman this hard. He'd never taken his time to get to know someone the way he tried to do with her.

"It's kind of hard to believe."

"Then I'll just have to keep trying to prove it to you until you believe me."

"Is there any way to call him off?" Bell asked Ella.

"No. Once they get something into their heads, it's hard to deter them. Enjoy it. He's never gone out of his way for any woman."

Dane needed to thank Ella for throwing him a bone. She saw it. Bell didn't.

Damn, it was hard to change his life. If he walked into a restaurant or bar right now, in ten minutes he'd have a woman on his arm. In half an hour, he'd have her in his bed. Not bragging. Fact. He'd done it more than a dozen times.

Nice of him to point out the glaring problem in his life. He had no problem getting a woman, but he didn't know how to keep one.

He'd never had a real long-term relationship. Dating the same girl for months in high school wasn't the same as doing it as an adult with the intention of leading to a lasting relationship. He'd never had one of those with a woman, but he wanted it with Bell. Bell had never had a boyfriend, so this was new for both of them.

"Ella, I can't do the auction. If this is in two weeks, I'll still be on crutches. How will I make this date happen? I can't drive. Hell, I can barely walk."

"You can use the car service. With your name attached to this, we'll get tons of bids."

"Can't you find anyone else to do this?"

"I've found several men, but no one with your reputation."

"That's just it, I'm trying to overhaul my reputation." He cocked his head in the doc's direction.

Ella smiled. "I mean your rodeo reputation and star status in these parts. That alone will bring people in. Men to meet and mingle with you. Women for a chance at a date with you. Please, Dane. I need your help."

"Fine. One date. I'll eat dinner. I'll be charming. But that is it."

"And you'll write a check."

He rolled his eyes. "As long as you use the money for what Bell wants."

"Deal. Now, Bell, please take some time to think

about my offer. This thing is coming together quickly. I'll get your suggestions over to the architect and put them in place."

"One other thing. The second set of prints showed the building where the doctors will have their offices. They'll each have an office and two exam rooms."

"Yes. Do you want to change something there?"

"No, it's just that . . ."

"What?" Ella asked.

"It'll probably add a lot of cost to the construction, but you might want to think about adding a covered walkway between the two buildings. Maybe make it wide enough to add a few picnic tables for the staff to have lunch, or visitors to sit and wait in the spring and summer. When it snows, it will be easier for the staff to go from building to building. If we examine someone during office hours and they need further testing, they can walk over without having to go through the parking lot. It will make things easier for disabled and elderly patients."

"I hadn't thought of that. I'll add it to my list." Ella grabbed a blue sticky note from Bell's desk. She jotted down Bell's suggestion and stuck it to the blueprints over the spot where the walkway could be built.

"Well, it was nice to talk to you. I'll think about your offer and get back to you," Bell said, resorting to her professional demeanor when she was uncomfortable with the more personal stuff.

"Talk to Dr. Sheldon about the plans for running the clinic. See if it is something you really want. Your role will be different than it is now. It will expand. I hope I haven't overstepped by implying that I think you're not as happy as you could be as just a surgeon. Maybe that's why you cover for the doctors at the ER and at the clinic. You want a more rounded doctor experience than specializing in one thing. You don't seem to be the kind of person who settles for routine but looks to constantly expand her knowledge and experience. This is your chance to do both on a daily basis."

Bell didn't respond but pressed her lips together and stared off in contemplation. Dane hoped she took the job. She'd work closer to home. No more driving into Bozeman on the treacherous roads in the winter months. She'd be closer to him.

"I'll get this one out of your way before he asks you a third time for a date," Ella teased.

"I think he's up to a hundred and eighteen."

That made Dane smile. She might actually be keeping count. "What number do I have to get to before you say yes?"

"I'm your doctor. You're my patient."

"Here I thought we were friends. I'll call you later tonight. Bell Brittany."

"Please don't call me that."

The sad look in her eyes made him agree. "Okay, Bell. Thanks for checking on my leg and ribs."

"You're welcome. I'll see you in a week."

"If not before," he said, touching his hand to Ella's back to get her moving out the door so he could grab his crutches. "I like your office. It's you."

"How do you mean?" Bell scanned the space, a slight frown on her pretty face.

"Neat. Orderly. Elegant with a touch of country. The outdoors inside with all the plants." Pots in varying sizes filled up the room with their glossy green foliage. "Filled with books." The built-in bookshelves were stacked with all kinds of books. Medical, nonfiction biographies and how-to's, along with fiction. She liked mysteries and thrillers. With her sharp mind, she probably enjoyed the intricate and twisting plots.

"I like books."

"If only I could get you to like me that much."

Ella stood, waiting down the hall for him; he hesitated, then went with his gut. "I like you that much, Bell."

He turned to go, but Bell grabbed his forearm. He glanced down at her fingers wrapped around him. One finger traced the tattoo on his arm. He felt the sudden spark, then the heat rush through his veins. She snatched her hand back, her eyes wide with recognition that she'd felt it, too. She folded her arms around her middle. He wanted to feel her skin pressed to his again.

"I, uh, will see you next week." Her gaze fell to the floor.

"You said that already."

Her head snapped up and her eyes locked with his. She hesitated, but took a deep breath and said, "I do like you."

He smiled, because his chest felt so full of happiness that it rose up and filled his face. "Was that so hard to admit?"

"Kinda."

"I'll call you later. Have a good lunch. Don't work too hard, Doc."

"Dane?"

"Yeah?"

"You have a nice smile." Her arms tightened around her waist. Admitting that to him wasn't easy for her.

"I like yours, too, but I think you've got the prettiest eyes I've ever seen. I like it when you look at me and see me."

He hobbled down the hall to Ella on his crutches. He wanted to look back and see if Bell watched him, but he didn't dare. They'd shared something for a moment. He'd take that small victory and quit while he was ahead.

"She likes you," Ella said when they got into the elevator.

"I'm working on it."

"She's not what I expected for you."

"I think I said something similar to Gabe about you."

Ella chuckled. "So you did."

"She's been in the back of my mind for years. I thought about her all the time. Probably why I dated women the exact opposite of her. No one who looked like her ever measured up. Now I can't stop thinking about her."

"I'm happy for you, Dane."

"But?"

"I wonder if you've got the stamina to see this through. She's not like the other women you know. She's not going to jump into your bed, or easily leave once you're over it."

"What if I told you I'd think less of her for jumping into my bed, despite the fact that's exactly where I want her?"

"You like her because she's not like the others."

"I'm trying something new. Getting to know her on a deeper level."

"You've got no choice. If you want her in your bed, that's the only way you're going to get her there."

"No, that's the only way I'm going to get her to want to stay there." The elevator doors opened, but Ella didn't step out. She stared up at him. He gave her the honest truth. A truth he'd finally realized over the last six days he'd spent talking and getting to know Bell.

"She's not a woman you ever get over."

CHAPTER 9

Rowdy would never get over Brandy. He loved her. Why couldn't she see that? He'd proven it to her time and time again, and still she kept him at arm's length. Always on the outside, hiding things from him, never telling him anything about Kaley. His fucking daughter. Not Dane's.

He took another swig from the fifth of whiskey, recapped it, and stuffed it under the truck seat where he always kept it. He watched. He waited. She should have come out of the hotel ten minutes ago. Done with her cleaning up after other people, making beds they'd spent the night fucking in, sponging down bathrooms where they'd left their towels on the floor for his woman to pick up. He hated that she worked this shit job. She should be home, taking care of his kid.

The glass door swung open. She stepped out and raised her face to the sun. Her golden hair glowed. She looked damn good in her tight jeans and white T-shirt. He rubbed his hand over his aching cock and shifted his balls. Damn, but he wanted to fuck her from behind, her hair fisted in his hand, her head pulled back, her tits shaking as he pounded his dick into her.

He got out of the truck, swiping the back of his hand across his lips. "Brandy," he called, stopping her in her tracks as she headed for her car.

Her eyes went wide and her lips pressed into a tight line.

Why wasn't she ever happy to see him?

"I don't have time to talk to you right now. I'm running late."

Dismissed again, his anger boiled in his gut. He closed the distance between them, even though he had to take a few extra-long strides to catch her as she backed up. He wrapped his arms around her waist and pulled her close, letting her body rub against his hard cock.

"Come on, baby. Let's go someplace and talk. I miss you." He leaned in to kiss her neck, but missed when she kinked her neck to keep him away. "Don't be like that. Give me some sugar, baby."

"No. Let me go, Rowdy. I don't have time for your shit right now. I need to stop off at the pharmacy and get my dad's medication."

"I'm just asking for a few minutes of your time," he pleaded.

"For what? A quick fuck so you can scratch an itch. I'm not your girl. I'm not your baby. We're done."

"We'll never be done. You and me, we love each other."

"I don't love you anymore, Rowdy. You need to move on."

Stunned she'd say such a thing, he let loose his hold, and she bolted for her car and jumped inside.

Furious she kept taking off on him, he ran for his truck, climbed in, and followed her. He caught her at the light and yelled out his open window, "Pull over, Brandy, we need to talk."

"Leave me alone."

He blew through the stop light right behind her. She sped up. So did he. He honked at her to get her to pull over. She didn't, and his anger flashed. He pulled into the clear oncoming lane and honked again, steering closer to her to get her to stop at the curb. She turned to miss him, but sped up and got ahead of him again. He hit the gas, pissed off and feeling surly, and slammed his front end into hers. She swerved, nearly lost control, and slammed on the brakes, her right front tire practically up on the curb. He hit the brakes and came to a stop, his truck blocking her in. Now he had her. She couldn't get away.

He got out. She sat in the front seat, her phone in her shaking hands. He rushed her and pulled the door open. She screamed, "No, Rowdy, please, leave me alone."

He grabbed her arm, took the phone, and pulled her out of the car.

"Stop this. Please," she pleaded.

He pushed her up against the side of the car, pressing her into it with his body to keep her from running away. She struggled, pushing against his chest with her hands. "What the fuck do you think you're doing?" he snarled.

"Me?" Her voice rose. "You ran *me* off the road. You hit *my* car. You're drunk. Again." She squirmed to get free, but he gripped her arm hard to make her stop. She yelped, then stopped and settled down.

"I had a couple of drinks." He shrugged like it was nothing. Because it wasn't anything. He could hold his liquor.

"A couple too many."

"Why the hell are you always nagging me about that? I know my limits."

"You're drunk and driving. You could have killed me." She smacked him on the shoulder with a flat hand.

He pressed his hands to the hood of the car on each side of her shoulders, letting the weight of his body hold hers. He caught sight of the photo of Kaley on her phone screen. He must have hit something to make it come on. He stared at the photo for a moment and thought of everything he wanted and everything they'd lost these last months.

"How did it all fall apart?" he asked, genuinely perplexed that she didn't want to be with him, when he tried so hard to do right by her. It all went to shit sometimes because she pushed. She flirted with other guys. She never did what he wanted or said.

"Rowdy, you know why I don't want to be with you."

He swiped his thumb over the phone screen to see more pictures of his little girl. Instead, he read the text messages that came before and after the photo she sent to Dane.

He's why she couldn't be with him. Some friend Dane turned out to be, stealing his girl.

"You're still fucking that asshole."

Brandy planted both hands on his chest and shoved him back. He lost his balance, his head spun, and he stumbled. She ran for it down the street.

He didn't think, just went after her, grabbed her arm, spun her around, and swung. The blood spurted from her mouth when his fist smashed into her beautiful face. She fell to the ground, her head thumping against the asphalt, her cheek scraped and bleeding from sliding on the pavement. Limp. Lying in a heap. Knocked out cold.

Like a bucket of ice water dumped over his head, he realized with stunned disbelief what he'd done. He kneeled beside her and patted her face. "Brandy. Wake up. Wake up!"

She didn't move. Fear stole his breath. He checked up and down the street. No one in sight. He couldn't leave her lying in the road. She'd come to, call the cops, and he'd end up in jail. Again. Not fucking going to happen. He'd take her to his place. They'd talk. She'd see reason. She'd forgive him again. She always did, because she knew he didn't really mean it. Sometimes he lost his temper. If she'd cooperate, damnit, this wouldn't happen.

He pulled her up and over his shoulder, then rushed her to his truck just as another car turned the corner. Keeping his back to it so they didn't see his face, he got Brandy inside before the vehicle drove by. He ran around to the driver's side, gunned the engine, and tore out of there, his tires squealing. He checked the rearview mirror, hoping no one else saw them leave. He'd forgotten to close her car door.

"Fuck!" He slammed the heel of his hand on the steering wheel. The sting went up his arm. He looked down beside him and smacked Brandy in the head. Her head rolled, but she didn't wake up. "You fucking bitch. You ruin everything."

He pulled the bottle of whiskey from under the seat and took a long pull, letting the liquid burn its way down his throat to his gut. He shut off everything inside of him and drove, no real plan in mind. He thought about what he'd say to the bitch sleeping beside him. She was either going to come around to his way of thinking, or this was the last fucking time he tried to get her to see how much he loved her.

He pulled into the driveway at his place on the outskirts of town. He needed to feed the horses and do some chores, all the things he'd neglected following Brandy around, trying to get her to see reason.

She moaned and rolled her head sideways, pressing her hand to her swollen face. Startled, she sat up and turned to face him. She glanced around. "How did we get here?"

"You passed out."

She moved her jaw side to side and pressed her hand to her cheek. "You knocked me out." Her voice trembled. Tears filled her eyes, then spilled over.

"You won't listen."

She grabbed her phone off the dashboard, where he must have tossed it when he'd gotten in, grabbed the door handle, and tried to get out. He grabbed her by the hair and pulled her back. She screamed, reached back to his hand to get free, and pinched the skin at his wrist, twisting painfully, making him let go. She turned and slapped him across the face. The sting surprised him and sent a tidal wave of rage rushing through his veins.

What happened next didn't register past the red haze in his mind until he looked down and found his hands wrapped around her throat, her eyes wide and lifeless. His fingers ached from squeezing so hard.

Her limp hands lay over his. He wished she'd stop biting her nails. He liked a woman who had pretty hands. Brandy didn't.

He let loose her throat, ignoring the angry red marks on her neck, and traced his finger over her brow, pulling a lock of golden hair away from her face. He sank back into the driver's seat and stared out the window at his overflowing mailbox hung next to his front door.

So many things he needed to do that he'd put off far too long. Only one thing left to do now. Make that cocksucker pay for stealing his woman. He'd let that asshole get away with showing him up far too long. Dane always got what he wanted. Not this time. Rowdy would take everything from him. Then he'd come back here, get Kaley, and they'd live a good life together. He'd take care of his little girl. No fucking way that dickhead took her, too.

Some methodical part of his mind took over. He drove out of his driveway with a sense of purpose. He'd take his time. Find the one thing Dane cared about and couldn't live without. Then Rowdy would take it away and let Dane feel the depth of loss Rowdy felt now. Right before he killed the bastard.

CHAPTER 10

Bell walked out of the locker room at the hospital, teetering on her new high heels. She loved the black beaded straps that crisscrossed her feet and went around her ankle. Not her usual style, but she wanted to look nice next to Ella, who had style and poise. She always seemed so put together and chic. The best Bell came up with was a deep amethyst dress with a tight bodice, square neckline, and cap sleeves. The skirt dropped from just under her breasts down to her knees and swished when she walked. She should have gotten more sensible shoes. Her feet would ache by the end of the night.

"Dr. Bell, do you have a minute?"

"I'm sorry, Tim, but I'm on my way out." Dr. Hamberg worked in the ER. She'd covered for him last week when he'd needed a night off to take his wife out for their anniversary.

He swept his gaze from her hair to her feet. His eyes snapped back to her hair. She'd taken a bit more time, curling the top and slicking back the sides. She loved the edgy look. She'd seen a model with something similar in one of the dozen magazines she'd scoured, looking for a stylish dress, shoes, and hairstyle she could match in real life.

"Uh, you look really great."

"Thank you. If you'll excuse me."

"I guess you can't cover for me tonight."

"No, I'm sorry, I've got plans."

"You never go out. Ever. What's the special occasion?"

"A fund-raiser for the Crystal Creek Clinic."

"Right, you work there on your days off."

She never had days off. Maybe she should take some. Go shopping for more stylish clothes. See a movie. She hadn't been in months. Find a new restaurant. Try her hand at dating. She'd been on a few dates in medical school, but never more than two with the same person. Too focused on her studies, feeling like an outcast when the other students were older than her, she'd given up on her personal life. Stick with what you knew and were good at.

"Well, have a good time."

"Thank you. I hope you find someone to take your shift."

"Probably better if I stay here—my wife is home with the flu."

"You'd probably be okay if you got your flu shot."

"Oh, I got it, but that's not going to help me survive my cranky wife." He smiled and walked away down the hall.

"Bring her home some soup from Martin's Café. She'll appreciate it."

Tim turned and nodded his head. "Score some points for all the long hours I work."

"Make her feel better and get a smile."

"I love it when she smiles."

Bell walked out the hospital side door to her Jeep in the doctor's parking lot. Tonight, she didn't exactly look the part of a woman who drove a Jeep. She smiled, liking this new facet of herself.

She drove through downtown to the hotel where the event was being held. She didn't know what to expect when she got there, but it certainly wasn't all the banners advertising the occasion.

She drove to the hotel entrance and sprung for valet parking. Easier than having to find a parking spot amidst all these other guests. This way, she didn't have to walk so far in her heels.

She entered the lobby with several couples. The ladies looked lovely in their cocktail dresses, the men in their dark suits. Apparently, she'd missed the memo about wearing one of those little black dresses. She drew stares from the men and women. Self-conscious, she smoothed her hand down the skirt, hoping she hadn't missed the part that everyone was to wear black.

She followed the noise and the other people to the huge ballroom. At two hundred dollars a plate, she hadn't expected this many people to attend. The place was packed. Alone, she smiled as she passed people, hoping to spot someone she knew—namely, one of the Bowden family. Preferably not Dane. The man didn't know when to quit. She wasn't his type. They had little in common.

Liar.

They actually had found a lot they had in common on their long phone calls.

Which you take every night because you like talking to him.

Food seemed to be the one thing they always found common ground on. Dane had traveled across several states and had discovered many good restaurants, not always on the beaten path. She liked to find those small restaurant gems, too. She loved hearing him talk about his horses like they were his children. Each of them had their own personality. She hated to admit how much she'd like to go to his place and see them up close. She'd love to learn to ride. Too bad she had no intention of giving in to that desire with Dane. Or any other desire. No way.

She wasn't going to end up like her mother—a man's cast-off one-night stand.

Ella and Gillian spotted her from across the room. They looked lovely in their dresses, their hair done in pretty styles. Gillian glowed in a gorgeous turquoise-and-cream dress that hugged her curves and made her hair color shift from blonde to red. Ella wore a midnight blue gown that sparkled with a silver sheen. She'd pulled her light brown hair up into a simple bun with spiral tendrils framing her pretty face. Bell was grateful she wasn't the only one who'd chosen to wear a color. The three of them stood out amongst most of the guests. Several other ladies dared to wear red, pink, and golden-hued dresses, but they were definitely the minority.

"Bell, you look beautiful. Where did you find that dress?" Ella asked.

"A boutique I pass on my way to my favorite restaurant for lunch. The designer opened it about six months ago. I've always wanted to go in and buy, but mostly I window-shop. The window displays are amazing. Kind of trendy chic with a touch of elegance."

"You've got to take me. I love the simplicity of your dress. It has just enough flair in the details in the sleeves and neckline. It's stunning. Of course, on you anything would look great." Ella's compliment went right to Bell's heart.

She'd never had a girlfriend, but every time she was with Ella and Gillian, they seemed so laid back and easy to get along with. They never looked or spoke to her like she was different.

"You did something different with your hair. I love that style," Gillian said. "I wish I had the guts to chop my hair short."

"Don't you dare." Blake stepped up to his wife and handed her a drink. "I love your hair long. Bell, you look fantastic. Dane's eyes are going to pop out of his head when he sees you."

"Where is bachelor number one?" Ella asked.

Blake used his beer glass to point out Dane, standing amidst a horde of blondes with legs that went on for miles, all dressed in short black dresses.

"He's like one of those bug zapper lights. He attracts every blonde in a hundred-yard radius," Bell commented.

Everyone cracked up. She hadn't meant to say that thought out loud. Dane heard the ruckus and fixed his penetrating gaze on her. She felt the stare heat her skin as he scanned her from head to foot. A smile spread across his face and lit his eyes. She couldn't help smiling back, because when he looked at her that way, damn if she didn't feel beautiful.

"Told you," Blake said. "Three, two, one. Here he comes."

Sure enough, Dane broke free of the crowd of ladies around him without so much as an "excuse me." The women stared at his back, disgruntled frowns and glares on their overly made-up faces. Bell had gone for subtle makeup, letting the dress color enhance her blue eyes, along with a soft lavender shadow and black liner and mascara. She'd painted her lips a shade darker than her natural color.

She stood out, but for all the right reasons tonight. She pulled off the look and felt her confidence grow with each step Dane took in her direction, his eyes locked on her.

"That is a man on a mission," Ella said.

"Look out, Bell, here he comes," Gillian added.

"There's no getting away," Blake said. "He will hunt you down."

Her stomach knotted with anticipation. She'd never had a man look at her the way Dane did. Yes, she believed he wanted her. For what and how long, she didn't know.

Unable to take her eyes off Dane, she tried to decide what she liked best about his new look. His tailored suit fit his wide shoulders and lean waist to perfection. Not even his uneven gait and crutches took away from his determined stride. He'd shaved the usual scruff from his square jaw and combed his dark hair back into a sophisticated style. The man looked like a magazine cover model. He'd sell a million copies with all that arrogant male magnetism. She wasn't immune to his good looks or his charm, but she tried to be for her own sanity. Giving in to him would only end in disaster. For her. He'd move on with any one of the blonde Bettys snarling behind him.

Dane's heart stopped cold when he saw her standing there, looking so damn beautiful, then his whole body went hot with the wave of lust that shot through him. Every time he'd seen her in the past, she'd been in either casual clothes, work attire, or, during their last appointment, scrubs. Nothing prepared him to see her in that dark purple dress, her hair done up in a funky style that contrasted her sweet personality and hinted at a wilder side he wanted to get to know better. The woman constantly surprised him. He liked that about her.

"Hey, gorgeous. Purple is definitely my new favorite color. You take my breath away."

"I bet you say that to all the girls," she shot back.

"Only to the ones who deserve it. So far, that's only you."

The skeptical look in her eyes frustrated him. Nothing he ever said to her went down smooth. She always winced, like it left a sour taste in her mouth. He'd have to try harder to get her attention and make her believe him.

Well, he had her attention. The heat in her eyes nearly scorched him when she stared at him hobbling across the room. He wanted to be off these damn crutches. Hard to pull off strong and confident with a busted leg. He'd stick with arrogant, but it only put her off. She'd call him on being cocky. So he was left with trying to be himself and hoping that was enough.

"You look so different tonight." She studied him like some unknown infectious disease under a microscope.

"I ruined a perfectly good pair of pants looking this good." He glanced down at the cut-off pant leg he'd tucked into the top of his black brace.

"Totally worth it," Ella said, smiling at him.

He hoped Bell thought so, too. He wanted to kiss her, hold her hand, and pull her close to his side so every man in the room knew the gorgeous woman belonged to him. She'd probably jab him in the gut if he tried. Not that he could pull it off smoothly with the crutches tucked under his arms, holding him up. The last thing he wanted was for her to knock him on his ass.

Not that she really would, but still, he didn't want to give her a reason to push him away.

Gabe joined the group, holding two whiskeys on the rocks, with a glass of wine for Ella clasped tightly between his fingers. Gabe handed Dane one of the whiskeys.

Bell glared, her pretty mouth dipping into a disapproving frown.

"What?" he asked.

"Nothing."

"I haven't had any pain meds in three days. My ribs are good. My leg is better. We covered this the other day at your office."

"Did I say anything?"

"Yes. With just one look."

That made her smile.

"Bell, your sister just arrived." Ella pointed across the room to Katherine and Tony standing just inside the entrance.

"Excuse me. I'll go say hello."

"I'd hoped you'd make the rounds with me and speak to potential investors about the clinic," Ella said.

"Of course. Just give me a few minutes."

Dane shoved his drink into Gabe's chest, giving him no choice but to take it back. He grabbed the crutches' handles and went after Bell.

"Go get her," Blake said behind him.

Damn right.

He caught up to her a few seconds after she reached her sister.

"Katherine, you look lovely," Bell said, leaning in to give her sister a friendly hug.

"Bell, you look amazing. That dress is fantastic on you."

"She's the most beautiful woman in the room, but you're a close second." Dane complimented Katherine, who smiled even as her sister glared up at him.

"Why aren't you with your family?" Bell asked him.

"I want to be with you."

Tony coughed to cover a laugh. "Dane, man, good to see you up and around. How's the leg?"

"Getting better every day, thanks to the doc."

"So, you two are seeing each other?" Katherine asked.

"No," Bell said. "Yes," he said.

Bell glared at him.

"What? I saw you the other day, last week, tonight."

"We are not dating."

"Only because you refuse all my invitations to go out together. I'm left with making appointments with you at your office and calling you every night. Apparently in your book, that's dating."

"You talk every night?" Katherine asked, a soft smile on her face when she glanced at Bell. "That's wonderful. I'm so glad you've put yourself out there."

"We're not seeing each other."

"I'm seeing you. I'm just waiting for you to catch up." *Or give in.*

"So, Bell, are you really going to give up your practice and work full-time at the clinic?"

"I'm not giving up my practice, I'll just be moving it to Crystal Creek. I'd still have admitting privileges at the hospital."

"You decided, then? You're going to take the job?" Dane hoped so. Maybe then she'd have time to go on a proper date with him.

The surprise in Bell's eyes told him even she hadn't meant to say it quite that way. Maybe deep inside she'd decided, but she just hadn't made the conscious decision to put her words into actions.

"I, ah, have been thinking about it. I like that I won't have to commute to work so far, and I can practice medicine on a wider scale. Hip and knee replacements get tedious after a while."

"Not enough busted-up cowboys coming into your office?" Tony asked.

"Some, but I'd like the challenge of working on a variety of cases."

"With your smarts, you'd be great at it."

Katherine's compliment took Bell off guard. Her eyes went wide, and she opened her mouth to say something but closed it again.

Dane studied the two sisters. Even up close, he couldn't find any resemblance between them.

"Are you a certified genius, too?" he asked Katherine.

She snorted out a laugh and cocked her head. "I'm no slouch in the brains department, but Bell hit the genetic lottery with her dark hair, blue eyes, and mega brains. She takes after our father in that way. He's amazingly smart and accomplished, just like her."

Katherine caught herself and looked away from Bell.

"Some things we inherit from our parents," Dane said. "Others are just who we are. Like Bell's kindness, strength, and generosity. She's got amazing heart. She'd never turn her back on anyone. Look at the lengths she went to to save me."

The tension between the two sisters became palpable. They barely looked at each other and stood an unnatural five feet apart. The silence grew deafening.

"How are the improvements on the house coming? Did you finish the spare bath?" Bell asked Katherine to break the silence.

"Just in time. I wanted to tell you in person. We're expecting." Katherine beamed with excitement. Tony wrapped his arm around her shoulders and hugged her to his side, smiling down at his wife.

"That's fantastic," Bell said, her eyes filled with joy. "There must be something in the water. Dane's sister-in-law Gillian is pregnant as well. His brother Caleb and his wife, Summer, had a little girl in September."

"Congratulations," Dane said to Katherine. He shook Tony's hand.

"An uncle," Tony said. "Are you looking to finally tame your wild ways now, too?"

"Nope. Looking for someone who wants to be wild with me." He pointedly looked at Bell.

She rolled her eyes and shook her head. "He'll always be wild."

"Amen to that," he responded, making her smile again.

"If you want wild, Bell is not your girl. She's steady and down to earth," Katherine said.

"Boring, you mean." Bell frowned.

"I think Bell just hasn't had a chance to explore all the possibilities of who she is and what she wants. Yes, she's a dedicated doctor, but that doesn't mean she doesn't have other interests. She loves the outdoors. She's a food snob," Dane pointed out.

Bell smacked him on the arm. "I am not."

"Okay, she's a food connoisseur." He cocked up one side of his mouth and gave her an it's-the-same-thing look. "She's well read in a variety of subjects. If given a chance and an opportunity to try new things, I bet she'd do so with excitement and interest. She's got this thing for the different regions and histories of Italy. A food tour of the country would probably be right up her alley."

Bell laughed under her breath. "I'd actually love that."

"You should do it," he suggested, knowing she'd do it alone and probably enjoy herself because she was used to doing things alone. But he'd like to do it with her.

"When is the baby due?" Bell changed the subject back to the original topic.

"July seventh. We've got so much to do. I can't wait to get started on the nursery."

"Will you find out the sex of the baby, or do something neutral?" Bell asked.

"I'm such a planner, I need to know. I want everything to be perfect. Mom and Dad can't wait for their first grandchild. Mom already bought a ton of toys and picked up a bunch of baby furniture magazines."

Katherine caught herself and snapped her jaw shut. "Sorry, Bell."

"Don't be. It's wonderful news. I'm sure your family is very excited."

Your family. Not Bell's. He'd always wanted to ask her if she had any contact with her father or mother. By the way the two sisters acted and spoke, no. Sad. Unfortunate. Katherine seemed close to her parents. Bell remained the outcast. More like a castaway, destined to spend her life isolated from the people who should have been her safety net.

"Bell, Ella is flagging us down. You promised to schmooze the moneymen."

"Right. I'll see you at dinner," Bell said. "I believe we're at table two."

"Bell, I'm sorry," Katherine said again.

"You didn't do or say anything wrong. Stop apologizing for something that you didn't do and can't be changed. I'm happy for you. I can't wait to meet my niece or nephew."

"You mean that?" Katherine bit her lip, unsure.

"Absolutely. I'll see you in a little while." Bell gave her sister a warm smile, but it didn't quite reach her eyes. She spun on her toes and walked away.

Dane trailed after her.

"Thanks," Bell said.

"Does it make you mad to hear her talk about her parents that way?" he asked.

"Why would it?"

"Because the father she's talking about was never a father to you."

"She lives her life, and I live mine. She thinks they intersect somehow and gets uncomfortable when she brings him up. The thing is, my life took a turn when I was born and never crossed theirs again. Does it hurt? Yes. Sometimes it does. But I try to remember that what happened to me has nothing to do with her."

"Still, you're jealous sometimes, even pissed off."

"I'm entitled to my feelings, but she doesn't deserve for me to take them out on her."

"No way in hell I'd be generous enough not to spew my resentments at her."

"I reserve them for the people who deserve them."

"I call bullshit."

She stopped in the middle of the room, people all around them staring at Dane, the champion bull rider and hometown celebrity, and turned to face him with narrowed eyes. "Excuse me."

"Bullshit. You resent the hell out of her. That's why in the last two years the two of you haven't gotten any closer. I have enemies I talk to with more warmth than the two of you have with each other."

"We have nothing in common."

He bent and stared her right in the eye to call her out. "You choose to keep her at arm's length. If she doesn't know anything about you, she can't report back to your father anything that will make him hate you more."

Bull's-eye. A flash of anger narrowed her eyes.

"Who asked you?"

"Just calling them like I see them. It's nothing you don't already know."

"Dane! It's so good to see you, you sexy man." A blonde sidled up to him and wrapped her hand around his biceps, then leaned in close, her breast pressed to his arm, and kissed his cheek.

Unable to move without hitting the woman with his crutch, he stood immobile, watching Bell's eyes flash with more resentment. She sighed, like this was an inevitability she'd been expecting. He had to admit that since he arrived, he'd run into several women he'd slept with and a dozen more who'd like to sleep with him. None of them appealed, and the one woman who did looked like she wanted to deck him.

It took him a minute to remember the woman's name. "Claire."

"Karen."

"Sorry. It's been a long time." Not long enough in his book. If he remembered right, she'd been pushy and possessive after the couple of times they'd seen each other. "I'd like you to meet Dr. Bell. She'll be the chief surgeon at the new clinic."

"Is that right?" Karen kept hold of his arm. He gently removed her fingers and took a step back. She frowned, but he ignored it.

"Yes. She fixed me up in Vegas. She works at the hospital here in Bozeman."

"That's nice."

Right. Karen didn't want to hear anything about Bell. All she wanted was his attention. It pissed him off that both she and Bell ignored his feelings for Bell. He'd have to do a better job of showing everyone, and especially Bell, that she was the only woman he wanted.

"If you'll excuse us. My sister is waiting to talk to Bell."

"By all means, Dane, stay and talk to your friend." Bell's tone said she believed that's where he wanted to be. He'd have to prove her wrong.

"I'm sticking with you, Bell."

Karen eyed him and Bell, trying to figure out if they were together or not. He made it seem that way, but Bell kept her distance. Didn't Bell know all she had to do was draw closer to him and he'd be at her mercy? No. Because Bell didn't believe she held that kind of appeal to anyone, let alone a man.

"Karen, so nice to see you again."

He pushed forward on his crutches to get Bell moving down the aisle again. They joined Ella, who expertly led Bell into conversation with several groups about the clinic and their plans. He got waylaid by several more women, but remained close to Bell's group. He tried to be polite, make small talk, and generally give the impression he wasn't interested in any of them. Bell's sideways glares started to tick him off. Then he realized she wasn't actually angry at him but jealous. Why would it bother her if he talked to other women otherwise?

Normally, he might have played it up, but with Bell that wouldn't work. She'd take it to mean his feelings for her were superficial. They weren't, so he began to use his crutches and her to block women from hugging and touching him. He remained politely dismissive when they tried to draw him away for a drink, or to talk privately. Ella and Gabe noticed. Bell must have, too, because she glared less and less and stood beside him, never actually touching him or making anyone believe they were a couple, but not so far away that anyone could stand between them. Progress.

Bell found herself grinding her teeth every time a new woman came up to Dane and flirted outrageously with him. Every touch to his arm, peck on the cheek, hug that lasted a bit too long made her gut tighten and sour with dread. The anger built with every woman's eyes dipping to the huge championship belt buckle Dane wore and a suggestive "It's so big," said with high-pitched awe.

Over the last hour though, she began to notice something strange. Dane didn't engage the women with any outward sign he was interested in them. He didn't flirt back. One beautiful woman after another came by to speak to him, and not once did he stare at their over-abundant cleavage, comment on how they looked, or anything to show he appreciated their charms.

He didn't call a single one of them honey.

He caught her looking at him after the last woman left, and he cocked his head. She smiled for the first time since she arrived, genuinely happy to be with him. Why was she so critical of everything he did? Because she wanted to know if his interest in her was real and meant more than the satisfaction of yet another conquest. If a conquest was all he wanted, he'd had ample opportunity to take any one, or more, of the women he'd spoken to tonight to bed. Still, he remained by her side, talking to the people about what a great doctor she was, how she'd be a remarkable asset to the clinic, and how she'd be perfect to ensure the clinic ran efficiently and was fiscally responsible, while providing the best care possible for the patients. He truly admired her skill as a doctor and a potential administrator of the clinic. His praise made her insides flutter and made her feel important and accepted. He made her feel special.

The more she thought about the job, the more it appealed. She liked the possibilities of all if offered for her future. One of those possibilities was potentially seeing him.

Standing this close to the man made the flutters melt into a ball of heat that radiated out to every cold corner of her body. She'd never felt this kind of attraction and desire, but seeing him all dressed up, his wide shoulders a reminder of his strength and sculpted muscles, made her want to draw even closer. His smile made her heart flutter. The way he talked about her gave her even more hope that this thing between them was growing and evolving into something worth taking a chance on.

"Dr. Bell, I'd like to introduce you to some of my friends," Dane said, using her title with everyone. She appreciated that he kept things light and on business for now. When they were with his family or alone, he always called her Bell. It had been days since he'd slipped and called her honey. Some habits were hard to break, but he'd done so, if tonight's encounters with other women were any indication. "These are the Kendrick brothers. Rory, Ford, and Colt. Their place is halfway between my place and Wolf Ranch."

"Rory, Ford, so nice to see you again. Colt, how's the arm?"

"Good as new, ma'am." Colt pulled the sleeve up his

arm to show off the long scar. "Barbwire snapped loose and sliced me open. Dr. Bell sewed me up."

"She did the same and more for me. Mine involved power tools and screws," Dane said, indicating his leg. The brothers laughed with him. The Bowden and Kendrick families went way back.

"It's my heart that's killing me now, Doc." Colt put a hand to his chest. "You can't look that good and still shoot me down. Let's get a drink."

Bell smiled, her cheeks flaming pink.

"Put me out of my misery and say yes this time," Colt begged.

Dane frowned. So, Colt had asked her out before. Anger raced through his veins. He wanted to crack Colt over the head with his crutches.

"Watch it, little brother, you're stepping on Dane's toes. You're about to end up on your ass," Rory warned.

"No disrespect, Dane. I had no idea you were seeing the doc."

"Now you do," Dane staked his claim. No way he let a Kendrick steal his woman. Even he wasn't blind to their good looks and appeal.

Bell's mouth dropped open, but she didn't tell any of them that she and Dane weren't seeing each other.

"Well now, boys, don't all fight over one woman. She's a pretty one though. Sweet thing, you want to trade up from these yahoos, I'm all yours." Grandpa Kendrick slammed his meaty hands down on Rory's and Ford's huge shoulders.

"Hello, Sammy. How are you?"

"I got this ache between my legs. What's your recommendation, my sweet Bell, a brunette or a blonde?"

Bell laughed and smiled, delighted by the old man. He never failed to shock her. Which he meant every time. "Dane seems to have cornered the market on blondes. Stick with brunettes."

"You're the best of the bunch," Sammy said, giving her a wink.

"Which is exactly why I'm with her," Dane said.

"That's because you've gone through all the blondes," Rory teased, earning a furious glare from Dane.

Sammy laughed and smacked Dane on the back. "Looks like someone finally came to his senses and is looking for quality, not quantity. You boys should do the same."

"We're not looking for anyone," Ford answered for all the brothers.

Sammy shook his head and refocused on Bell. "How's that old bat that calls herself your family?"

"The same."

"It'd take Niagara Falls to wear down that woman's sharp tongue."

Bell went to the old man, put her hands on his chest, and leaned up to give him a kiss on the cheek. She caught Dane's wide, surprised gaze out of the corner of her eye.

"Thank you, Sammy, for the new chicks. You know how much I love the docile Dorkings."

"Just my way of thanking you for taking such good care of me, sweet thing."

"I appreciate it. You take your medicine like I told you, and you won't have to come see me quite so often."

"I like coming to see you."

"I know you do. I like seeing you, too, but I'd rather you visit me at home than at my office."

"When did you two start hanging out?" Dane asked. The Kendrick brothers looked just as surprised.

"Sammy and my grandfather were close friends.

When he passed, Sammy kept coming over to visit with me. He tells wonderful stories about my grandfather and his boys." Bell smiled at Rory, Ford, and Colt. Dane wanted to punch all of them bloody for smiling back at her that way.

"This little sweet thing is a light in my life. I tell you. If any one of my grandsons was good enough for her, I'd have set them together long ago, but I'm keeping her for myself."

"Thanks, Granddad. Real nice." Rory rolled his eyes, used to their grandfather's outrageous behavior.

"We better sit down to eat. You guys are up soon for the auction."

"What the hell are you talking about, old man?" Ford eyed his grandfather.

"Didn't I tell you? I entered you all for the bachelor auction."

"The hell you did." Rory fumed. "Is that why you got us to dress up and come to this shindig?"

"Anything for that Ella Wolf. That girl sure is pretty. Smart, too. She's helping out my sweet thing with her clinic."

"Jeez, Granddad, don't you think you should have told us?" Colt scolded.

"Why? You're here. There are lots of pretty women. They'll bid to get a date with you, and maybe I'll get a great-grandchild by the time I die."

"You've got to stop with the grandchildren business. None of us is married, let alone seeing anyone." The anger in Rory's eyes glossed over the glimpse of resignation Bell caught before he shook his head and stared up at the ceiling.

Grandpa Kendrick wanted a great-grandchild and made no bones about getting one. Soon. He talked about it all the time and told her during their visits how reluctant his grandsons were to settle down and start a family. She wondered if they knew he was plotting to get what he wanted, despite his grandsons' apprehension. She couldn't wait to see if the auction sparked anything for the men, or if their grandfather would take his matchmaking to the next level to see his grandsons happily married and making babies. She thought it kind of sweet the way he good-naturedly plotted behind their backs to get them to do what he wanted. He had their best interests at heart, which showed in the way all three men shrugged off the fact they were about to be auctioned off to a room full of eager women.

Really good-looking men. Not quite as handsome as Dane.

There you go again, comparing others to him.

Still, no one really stacked up to Dane. Not even the ruggedly gorgeous Kendrick brothers.

Sammy leaned down and kissed her on the forehead. "See you, sweet thing. This one gives you trouble, you let me know."

"He's always giving me trouble. He doesn't listen to a thing I say."

"She never cuts me a break," Dane complained.

"Good." Sammy smacked Dane on the shoulder. "You need a woman like that."

Dane nodded. "I guess I do, because I'm a glutton for punishment when it comes to her."

Sammy laughed and smacked Dane on the back again. "Teach her how to be happy."

"I'm working on it."

Bell's mouth hung open as the Kendricks walked away. "Well."

Dane bent close. "He's right, and you know it."

Bell rolled her eyes. "Whatever. I'm starving. I need to find my sister and our table."

"It's this way."

"Don't tell me we're sitting together."

"Ella wants me to play my part as her most eligible bachelor, and I want to sit with you. She gets her way, and I get mine."

"Right, except that you'll be going out on a date with one of the blondes who can't stop hanging on your arm."

"My hands have remained on my crutches the whole time, and my eyes are glued to you in that dress. I wish you'd see what is right in front of you."

She stopped short of their table and put her hand on his arm. "Dane, I'm sorry. That wasn't fair. You've been a perfect gentleman all night. I did notice."

"Whether we came together or not, I'm here with you, Bell."

"I see that, too. I'm trying to get used to it." She squeezed his arm, letting him know she meant it.

"Let's sit and eat. You can tell me all about you and Sammy Kendrick."

She laughed. "Jealous."

"He got a hug and a kiss. You let him call you sweet thing, but I call you honey, and you shoot daggers out your eyes."

"You know there's a difference."

"Which is why I've changed my behavior. For you. That should count for something."

"It does." It made her heart swell and reach out for him even more. It made her sprout dreams of them together. She could be the woman on his arm, the one every other woman wanted to be. She'd never thought she'd be that person to anyone. She'd never thought herself a desirable woman, but he made her feel that way.

He looked down at her hand on him and smiled. She took her hand back, and they walked the few steps to their seats. He touched her shoulder to stop her from pulling out her chair. He set his crutches aside and pulled the chair out for her. She sat, and he helped push her in before taking the seat beside her.

"Oh my God, that is so much better."

Dane laughed. "Are your feet killing you in those pretty shoes?"

"They are lethal weapons."

"Yes, they are. They make your legs look killer."

The compliment made her blush. He gave her one of those dazzling smiles she liked so much. It warmed her insides more than the flush on her cheeks. Another thing he'd done to please her. He hadn't given that smile to anyone else tonight. Oh, he'd been pleasant and smiled, but not at this wattage. No, he reserved that for her tonight.

"Bell, Dane, are you ready for dinner, too?" Katherine asked.

"I'm starving," Dane replied, his eyes on Bell, letting her know without words the only thing he wanted was her. A shiver danced over her skin. She liked this. Him flirting with her, letting her know in every way that he wanted her, that she appealed to him.

"Ever since I found out I'm pregnant, all I want to do is eat," Katherine confessed.

Bell felt the resentment rise that her sister had a wonderful family and a baby on the way. Dane's hand settled over hers on the table. Her instinct was to pull her hand free, but then she felt the heat of his skin against hers. She didn't move; she simply let that warmth spread up her arm and into her heart. She glanced over at him sitting beside her. He forked up part of his salad and put in his mouth, smiled, and chewed like he touched her every day. His eyes held understanding, which she took in and let settle in her heart.

She turned back to her sister, who stuffed half a roll in her mouth. "It's the hormones and the growing fetus. You should eat when you're hungry, but watch the added sugar and salt."

Katherine laughed. "The sugar is the hardest. I crave chocolate like you wouldn't believe."

"That is definitely the hormones."

"A friend of mine craved watermelon and cherries through her whole pregnancy . . ." Katherine rattled on about her pregnancy, plans for the nursery, and what she was going to do about working at the marketing firm. Her sister might not be a genius, but she was pretty darn good at her job, and she liked it a lot.

Dane jumped in, talking to Tony. They covered everything from rodeo bulls to cutting horses and everything ranching in between. At one point they got into a heated debate about NASCAR racing. All the while, Dane kept his arm draped over the back of Bell's chair.

Dane groaned loud and long when Ella stood on the small stage at the podium and began the bachelor auction.

"I'd like to thank everyone for coming tonight and donating to this worthy cause. I'll announce the winners of the spa retreat door prize in just a little while. Right now, ladies, I have assembled ten of the most eligible bachelors I could find, including this year's Pro Bull Riders world champion, my brother Dane Bowden."

A cheer went up from the crowd, from men and women. Dane's popularity knew no bounds. The men all wanted to talk to him about bull riding and winning. The women wanted to sleep with the sexy cowboy. Bell wanted something she'd never had from anyone. For him to think her special.

Dane raised his right hand to salute the crowd. His left hand remained at the back of her chair. His fingers brushed along her shoulder in hypnotic circles. She turned and looked at him. He smiled for the crowd, then looked down at her, and the smile kicked up another notch. Unable to keep herself from getting caught up in his fame, she smiled back at him. The man had done something phenomenal and won an astronomical amount of money doing it. He risked his life every time he got up on those bulls, all to secure his future—and, let's face it, for the thrill of the ride. He'd competed. Won. And ended his career the best at what he did. He had to be so proud of himself. Sure, that last ride ended badly, but not until he'd held on and won. He'd held on during the surgery, and even now, when he struggled against his nature and took things slow and easy through his recovery. The same way he was taking things slow and making them easy on her while she decided if she trusted him.

That's what this came down to. Did she trust him? So far, he hadn't given her any reason not to. Not really. The other women from his past were just that. His past. Since he'd met her, he'd stayed true to the fact he wanted to see her and only her.

"You okay, Bell?" His eyes narrowed with concern as Ella called the first bachelor up for auction to the stage. The applause grew and the women whooped and whistled for the handsome banker.

"I just figured something out." She was special to him. Why else would he do all this? He didn't have to, with dozens of women here tonight who'd accept his attention without questioning his motives the way she had all night. If he wasn't serious about her, he could be with any one of the other women who'd flirted outrageously with him tonight. But he wasn't. He stayed with her, even though she'd been difficult and made him work for it.

She tried to think of how to tell him what she was thinking, but she couldn't come up with a way to say it that didn't make her sound odd.

"What is it, Bell? You know you can say anything to me."

"I trust you." Wow, she really meant it.

"Then tell me what you figured out."

"That."

"What?"

She put her hand over his on the table and squeezed. "I trust you. You've never lied to me, or did anything that contradicted anything you said."

"Uh, okay. Why would I?"

"You wouldn't, because that's not who you are."

He turned his hand and held tight to hers. "I'm glad you think so."

Bachelor number two went up to the stage after number one got a two-thousand-dollar bid. Dane shook his head at the raucous crowd.

"Let's hope all the ladies bidding get a man before I get up there."

Bell laughed. "Even if they already have one, most of these women are here for only one reason: a shot at one night with you." The thought turned her stomach. She didn't want him to go out with any of them. She wanted him to stay with her.

"They won't get anything, because I'll be with you."

"What do you mean? No, you won't." The thought made her sad.

"Come on, Bell, friends don't let friends go on dates they don't want. You're going to bid and save me from these women. You can't let me get dragged away like that guy." Dane cocked his head toward the stage, where bachelor number five got pulled off by his tie, straight into a rather large woman's breasts for a hug. Good-natured, the guy smiled and hugged the woman, playing things up for the crowd.

"I don't know. They kind of make a cute couple. He seems happy," she teased.

Dane let his head fall back, and he sighed out his frustration. "Please, Bell, save me from all these women and my sister's madness in making me do this. I don't want to go to dinner with anyone but you."

The sincerity in his voice got to her. She didn't answer but let him hang, thinking she'd feed him to the she-wolves. The Kendrick brothers went up before Dane. Cody played it to the max for the crowd. Not surprisingly, his brothers didn't want to be outdone by their little brother, and they played to the crowd of women, too, slipping off their suit jackets and flexing for the ladies. Cody undid his dress shirt and showed off his six-pack of abs.

"Now that's what I'm talking about." Katherine slapped Bell on the arm, smiling up at the stage.

"You want to see some muscles, Bell, I've got all you need," Dane told her.

The memory of seeing all of them splayed out on the operating table sent a shiver up her spine. "I know. I've seen them all. Including that very interesting half-moon scar on your hip." He eyed her, wondering how she knew that. "We checked you out extensively during surgery to make sure you didn't have any other injuries. I peeked," she admitted.

"Anything else you found interesting besides my ass?"

She hid a smile and tried to pull off serious. "Doctor-patient confidentiality. You understand."

"We're talking about me."

"I'll never tell," she teased even more. It was so easy to rile the man when she allowed herself to engage him on this level. "Though I would like to know how you got that scar."

"I'll tell you over dinner if you save me from this."

"The *man* doth protest too much, methinks."

"What?"

"*Hamlet*."

He narrowed his eyes at her, not getting it.

"Perhaps you protest going up there, but really, you like all the attention."

The Kendrick brothers went for over three thousand dollars each. Not surprisingly, Colt went for the most money.

"And now, ladies, let's hear it for my brother, Pro Bull Riders world champion, Dane Bowden."

The crowd went nuts.

Dane didn't stand. Instead, he leaned in and whispered in her ear. "Please, Bell. I really do want to go to dinner only with you." He leaned back and looked her in the eye. "I'll pay whatever you bid."

"Go up there. They're waiting for you."

He still didn't move.

"I'll bid, but only because I was going to make a donation anyway."

He kissed her on the forehead, stood to another round of applause, grabbed his crutches, and worked his way to the stage. The five steps up took him extra time, but he made it and stood next to Ella. She covered the microphone and said something to him. He shook his head and hugged her close. They both turned to the cheering crowd.

Ella opened the bidding. "Okay, ladies, this is a bona fide cowboy through and through. The man rides bulls, trains cutting horses, and runs his own ranch. He may be a little banged up, but that's never stopped him from having a good time." Ella gave him a sideways glance with an apology in her eyes. Dane eyed her back and frowned. Didn't matter if he didn't want her playing up his rowdy side; the crowd went nuts anyway, shouting out bids. "Two thousand."

"Twenty-five hundred."

"Three thousand."

Bell better get in there before she couldn't afford to pay. "Thirty-two hundred."

"Thank you, darlin'," Dane called from the stage, giving her a wink, playing his part for the crowd. She caught the look of thanks he cast her.

That "darlin'" was supposed to let people know he wanted to be with her, but it had the opposite effect. More bids came in all the way up to eight thousand dollars.

"Ten thousand," Katherine called.

Ella hit her gavel on the podium. "Sold for ten thousand."

"Katherine, I can't afford to pay that," Bell said under her breath.

"Don't worry. I have the money. You didn't want anyone else to go out with him. Now they can't."

"Where did you get ten thousand dollars?" Her sister didn't have that kind of money. She and Tony made a decent living, but with a baby on the way, they couldn't afford to donate that kind of money. It dawned on Bell the second her sister's gaze fell away. Her stomach went tight. Her shoulders tensed.

"He gave you the money." *He* being their father. He helped Katherine all the time. Why not? He could afford to on his outrageous salary. Granted, he was one of the top scientists in his industry. She didn't like it one bit that his money indirectly helped her with the clinic. Katherine's idea, no doubt. Their father wouldn't lift a finger or give her a dime to help her. He'd certainly never cared about her well-being. Now he'd indirectly paid for her to go out with Dane.

"Bell, it doesn't matter where the money came from. It matters that the money is going to a very good cause. The clinic is important to the community."

Bell tamped down her anger. "You're right. It's for the clinic."

"I'm sorry if I've upset you."

"You haven't. It's a generous donation. I thank you for doing it. Really. I appreciate it."

Katherine touched her shoulder. "I think the two of you are really good together. He's not exactly the kind of man I pictured you with, but he seems to genuinely like you."

"I believe he does."

"Then stop pushing him away if that's not what you really want. Men like the chase, but you got to let him catch you eventually, or you'll bruise his ego and he'll give up."

"Bell, you saved me." Dane took his seat beside her again.

"Katherine did. She's making the donation."

"Well, thank you, Katherine."

"No problem. I want my sister to be happy, so don't mess this chance up," she warned.

Bell smiled and shook her head. Okay, maybe her sister did mean well even if she went about it the wrong way. Katherine should leave their father out of it.

"From now on, Katherine, let's keep things between you and me."

Katherine pressed her lips together and nodded. "Deal. I really am sorry if I upset you."

"I'm fine."

Dane touched her neck with his fingertips to get her attention. She turned to face him. "What happened?"

"Nothing. The money came from my father for the donation. I overreacted. That's all."

Dane frowned. "I can make the donation instead of Katherine if it makes you feel better."

"Let it be. She planned to make the donation anyway, but she used it to get you out of a date with the blonde Bettys."

"You like that name for all of them."

"It suits."

Dane held up the envelope with their dinner gift certificate. She tried to take it, but he drew it away from her grasp.

"Hey, I've been wanting to try that place out."

"Great. I'll take you. What night do you want to go?"

"I agreed to get you out of a dinner with another woman. I never said I'd go with you."

"Come on, Bell, go to dinner with me. Please." The sincerity in his voice touched her heart.

Her sister's words came back to her. If she kept pushing him away, would he really give up? Why did she keep doing it? Because she needed to know he wouldn't give up? "I have to go. I have an early shift in the morning. I need to get some sleep."

"You didn't answer me."

"It's not a no, it's just not a yes yet."

"I'll take it, and I'll walk you out."

"You don't need to do that. Rest. After all the standing and schmoozing we did, your leg must be tired of supporting all your weight."

"I'm fine, Doc." He rose from his chair and grabbed his crutches. "Let's say goodbye to Ella and the rest of the family first. Katherine, Tony, nice to see you guys again. I'm sure I'll see you soon."

"See you, man. Have fun on your date," Tony said, winking at Dane.

Dane shook his head.

"I'll see you both soon," Bell said to her sister and brother-in-law. "Drive home safe. Katherine, take it easy on the buttered rolls. Eat more spinach and broccoli."

"Great. Now I'm hungry again."

"I see the dessert tray headed this way. You can have mine, too."

The appreciation in Katherine's eyes made Bell laugh.

She and Dane made their way over to say goodbye to his family.

"Seriously, Bell, that was a generous donation for the clinic. Dane's definitely not worth ten grand," Ella teased.

"Hey. That hurts." Dane mock frowned at his sister and took the ribbing that ensued from his brothers.

"Katherine will give you the check. She made the donation."

"We'll talk soon. We raised more than I expected. Maybe we can move a few more pieces of equipment from the wish list to the buy list."

"Sounds good. I'll see you soon."

Dane endured the jibes from his friends and the pouts from the ladies as they made their way out of the ballroom, grabbing their jackets at the coat check. They walked through the lobby toward the front doors, but Dane stopped her.

"Hold up, Bell. I need to drop something off."

She followed him to the front desk. He pulled out a bunch of key cards from his suit jacket pocket and handed them to the lady behind the desk.

"I don't need these."

Dane turned to go, but Bell asked the lady, "How many are there?"

"Four." She held them up like a poker hand for Bell to see.

Dane stood with his head down between his shoulders, holding onto his crutches, waiting for Bell to scold him again.

"Not bad, Mr. Bowden. That's better than decent." She let her approval show in her words. "Do you even know the women who stuffed those in your pockets?"

"One of them. The other three I've met but don't really know."

"Wow."

"You're mad."

"Not at all." She thought about the way he'd practically begged her to bid on him so he didn't have to go out with those women. "Really, I'm not mad at all. I can't blame them for trying. You've made your point."

"I'm afraid to ask, but what point is that?"

"You're done with that kind of lifestyle. Those

women, and others like them, hold no appeal for you. If you wanted to be with any one of them for the night, all you had to do was walk me to valet and go back in and take any one of them up on their offer. Instead, you handed over the keys in front of me because you're trying to be honest with me as best you can while still letting me see all of who you are."

"You analyze things far too much, but I'm glad you get it."

They walked outside. Dane handed over the valet ticket she pulled from her purse, along with a huge tip. They stood beside each other while she waited for her car. He walked her to the driver's side and helped her inside while the valet held the door.

"I had fun tonight."

"I'm glad you came," he said. "I'll call you tomorrow night. Maybe you'll agree to our date."

"Do you need a ride home?"

"My ride is right behind you."

She checked the rearview mirror and spotted the black SUV and driver.

"Ella didn't want me to drive with my leg, so she had the car service pick me up."

"Tell him you've got a ride, and I'll take you home."

"I'm way out past your place."

"It's not that far. I'm happy to do it."

Dane waved the car forward so he didn't have to walk the distance on his crutches. The driver rolled down the passenger window.

Dane handed in another big tip for the guy. "Thanks for the ride in, but I've got a ride home. You can take off."

"Thank you, sir. Enjoy your evening."

"Thanks. I'm enjoying it immensely," Dane admitted.

Bell rolled her eyes, knowing the driver thought Dane was going to get lucky, and Dane knew she knew that. It made her uncomfortable.

"What?"

"Get in before I leave you here. And turn down that smug smile."

"You love my smile."

She hated to admit, even to herself, how much she did.

Dane stowed his crutches in the backseat and took the few steps to the front seat on both feet. He opened the door and got in.

"How's the leg feel when you put your weight on it?"

"It hurts, but it's getting better. I need to start using it before I lose too much muscle."

"You'll get there."

She drove out of Bozeman and headed toward home. It would take an extra forty minutes to drive Dane home, but she didn't mind. She loved driving at night in the country. The stars were out and beautiful. They drove for a long time in silence.

"Are you glad no one else won the bid to go on a date with me?" Yes, Dane was fishing, but his softly spoken words held a note of how much her answer mattered to him.

She tried to keep things light. "Do you really need me to answer that?"

"Yes."

His earnest response surprised her. For all his appeal to other women, he needed to know he appealed to her. The same thing she'd needed to know, and he'd made her feel, tonight.

Maybe she had pushed him away one too many times. "I got really nervous and upset when the bids went higher than I could afford to spend. I didn't want anyone else to go to dinner with you despite the fact I know that's all it would have been for you."

He brushed his fingers across her cheek in a soft caress. "Was that so hard to admit?"

"For me, yes. I'm not good at all this personal stuff. You've been very patient and understanding when I get things wrong."

"You never get things wrong."

"Half the things you say, I don't understand."

"We're even there. Sometimes I don't get what you're talking about. You can be intimidating at times."

"Why? You're really smart. Even when I talk about things that probably don't interest you at all, you always listen and ask questions. You're inquisitive, like me." She took a deep breath and admitted, "You intimidate me when we're alone."

"Bell, nothing is going to happen without your consent. I'd never push you in that way."

"I feel like you're waiting, and I'm holding you up."

"Some things are worth waiting for. You aren't holding me up. It's been a long time since I did the whole get-to-know-you-before-anything-physical-happens thing. This is new for me in so many ways, and I'm enjoying getting to know you while we both let the physical attraction simmer. Don't think I don't see the way you look at me sometimes, or the way you catch your breath when I get too close."

"You get too close on purpose."

"Because I like the way it makes me feel as much as you do when you don't move away. That's part of getting to know you, too, Bell. Understanding who you are and how you react to me."

Dane held out his hand, palm up. She laid her hand

over his. His fingers linked with hers and closed around her hand. His warmth seeped into her. She liked his rough skin against her smoother palm and the sheer size of his hand engulfing hers.

He brought her hand to his lips and kissed the back of it.

"I had a great night with you, Bell. That's enough for me right now."

"You're a good date. You stayed by my side, picked up the conversation when I didn't understand some reference to rodeo or TV, and you acted like I was the only woman in the room, despite how many women came up to you and dropped their keys in your pocket."

"Not all of them did that."

"No. It was about a one-to-twenty-five ratio, considering you met about a hundred women tonight. Excluding me, of course."

"That's what I like about you, Bell. You do the math, add it all up, and figure out the result. But you got the equation wrong."

"How so?"

"It was a one-to-one-hundred ratio."

"How do you figure that?"

"I only wanted one woman out of those hundred, and I ended up with her tonight. I like those odds and the outcome."

She squeezed his hand to let him know she appreciated not only the sentiment but also the compliment he hid in that statement, done in terms she got. In the way she spoke.

She pulled into his driveway twenty minutes later. The light on the porch came on.

"You should move the motion light to the end of the porch and face it toward the front door. That way the bugs will be drawn away from the door and fewer will get into the house."

"I never thought about that."

"It makes better sense."

"Do you want to come inside?"

"I have to be up at five-thirty. My first surgery is scheduled for seven."

"I hate it that you drive into work that early in the morning."

"It's not that bad. I love to watch the sunrise."

"Thanks for the ride home. I'll talk to you tomorrow." Dane opened the passenger door but didn't get out. Instead, he turned toward the beam of headlights and the sound of a car pulling into his driveway. "What the hell?"

"Who is that at this time of night?" she asked.

"Sheriff's deputy."

"What in the world do they want?"

"We're about to find out."

Dane grabbed his crutches from the backseat of the car. He waited by the open passenger door in the pool of light cast by the car's interior light.

"Dane Bowden?" the officer called, approaching with caution.

"That's me. What can I do for you?"

"Is Brandy Hubbard with you?"

"No, sir. Dr. Bell is in the car. We just arrived home."

"Dr. Bell, would you step from the vehicle and come around the front to stand beside Mr. Bowden."

Bell shut off the engine, got out of the car, kept her hands in plain sight, and walked in front of the vehicle like he requested. She stood beside Dane. He put his arm around her to ward off the cold November night.

"Were you in Arizona today, sir?"

"No. What's this about Brandy? Is she okay?"

"Where have you just come from?" the officer asked without answering Dane's questions.

"The Hilton in Bozeman. We attended a charity benefit for the Crystal Creek Clinic, put on by my sister, Ella Wolf. You can call her to confirm if you like."

"What time did you arrive at the hotel?"

"I don't know, around three this afternoon to hang out with my brothers while their wives oversaw the setup for the benefit."

"Where were you before that?"

"I got up this morning around six. Checked in with my guys taking care of the horses and cattle while I'm laid up. Had breakfast alone inside, watched the morning news, and left for Bozeman around ten. I picked up my suit around eleven at the dry cleaner's. I ate lunch at a fast-food place, then went to physical therapy from one until two. I headed over to the hotel, went up to my brother and his wife's room, where I hung out with both my brothers until it was time to get ready for the benefit."

"Do you have receipts for the cleaner's and lunch?"

Dane pulled out his wallet, the receipts and cash stuffed inside. He went to the hood of the car and dropped the cash, then sorted through the six or so receipts until he found the ones he needed. He handed them over.

"When is the last time you saw Brandy Hubbard?"

"She came to see me in the hospital in Las Vegas on October twenty-eighth. Why?"

"She's missing. Her mother filed a missing person's report this evening."

"How long has she been gone?"

"She left work around two this afternoon but never returned home."

"It takes forty-eight hours before you can file a missing person's report," Bell pointed out. "What circumstances led to the police taking the report early?"

The officer eyed Bell. Dane was grateful for her sharp mind. He could barely think at the moment, but she connected the missing pieces that didn't fit the scenario the officer outlined.

"A patrol officer found her car two miles from where she works with the keys still inside, her purse on the seat, the driver's side door open, and a few drops of blood on the pavement."

"What the fuck?" Dane ran his hand over his head, trying to think. "Was she in an accident and possibly wandered away confused, or something?"

"The vehicle had some front fender damage, but nothing inside the vehicle indicated she'd been hurt in an accident."

"In other words, the blood was too far from the car to make it seem plausible she hit her head on the steering wheel, windshield, or side window. You think she walked or ran from the vehicle and was injured away from the car."

"Yes, ma'am. Maybe you missed your calling as a detective, Dr. Bell."

"Have the police questioned Rowdy Toll? If someone laid a hand on Brandy and bloodied her, it most likely was her ex."

"The police have been unable to locate him at this time. They checked her phone records and found recent calls and texts from him and you. What is your relationship with Brandy?"

"They're thinking this is some love triangle," Bell pointed out.

"Only in Rowdy's fucked-up head. Brandy and I are friends. That's all," Dane clarified for the officer and Bell.

"When is the last time you spoke to her?"

"Yesterday. She texted me. She wanted to know how I was doing."

"May I see the texts?"

Dane pulled his phone from his pocket and pulled up the texts.

Brandy: How are you?
Dane: Better. Up on crutches.
Brandy: Good news. Glad to hear it.
Dane: Send pictures of my girl.
Brandy: She misses you. Here you go.

Dane stared at the picture of Kaley sitting on the sofa with a stuffed bunny hugged close to her face. Kaley smiled around her thumb stuck in her mouth, her bright blonde hair up in two pigtails.

Dane: I love that pretty girl. Everything okay?
Brandy: Not lately.
Dane: Come for a visit.
Brandy: Mom needs me here.
Dane: Do you need help?
Brandy: A couple hundred would help.
Dane: On its way.

"Do you send her money often?" the officer asked.

"When she's short. Maybe once a month, every other month. Depends."

"But you're not seeing each other?" The officer eyed him, one eyebrow raised.

"I told you, she's a friend. What about Kaley? Is she with Brandy's mom?"

"Yes."

"Are they looking for Rowdy, too?"

"Yes. I received a phone call to check you out."

"You've done that. I've proven I couldn't have been with her today. Those texts prove I don't wish her any harm. Now call the Arizona police back and tell them to find that woman-beating-bastard before he kills her."

Bell grabbed his arm before he took another step closer to the officer. "Dane, he's just doing his job."

"She should be home with her daughter. You're wasting time standing here talking to me. I didn't do anything to her. I've been stuck here, sitting on my ass." He pointed to his leg. "They need to find that asshole. I told her time and again to stay away from that fuck. I told her, one of these days he'd lose his mind and kill her. Please, you've got to find her before it's too late."

The officer handed back his phone. "If you hear from Brandy, please let us know."

"If you find out anything, I want to know."

"I'll see what I can do, Mr. Bowden. Thank you for your cooperation."

Dane stood beside Bell, watching the officer drive away.

"I'm sorry, Dane. You must be so worried. I had no idea about her past."

"Rowdy never could take no for an answer. He wanted her and didn't care if she didn't want him. Things were good sometimes. Until they weren't. She kept going back, because she remembered the man from those good times. Hell, she'd fallen in love with that man. Hard to reconcile he was the same man who hit her when he got drunk and jealous."

"Did you two ever, you know?"

"Once," he answered honestly. "She was sad and lonely one night after a fight with Rowdy. I missed home and had been on the road far too long without company. I teased and joked with her to make her laugh. One thing led to another, and we ended up in bed. We both woke up in the morning with a hangover and a bad case of regret. We were friends before that night and didn't want to ruin a good thing, so we never spoke about it. We both forgot it ever happened so we could still be friends."

Bell nodded and wrapped her arms around her middle. To ward off the cold, or to comfort herself, he didn't know. He took a chance and rubbed his hands up and down her arms to warm her up.

"Bell, I swear, nothing ever happened again after that night. I don't harbor any feelings for her other than being a good friend."

"Why do you send her money?"

"She lives with her parents. Her father had a stroke a year ago. The medical bills are more than she and her mother can handle. Sometimes she runs short and needs money to buy food and diapers. I help her out when she needs it. Which is another reason Rowdy hates me. I apparently stomp on his manhood every time I provide for his family."

"Why doesn't he take care of Brandy?"

"Because he's an asshole, who thinks he can control her by keeping her destitute. He spends his money on booze and video games and dragging his ass to rodeos, where he always loses. It's a wonder he hasn't gotten himself killed."

"I'm sorry, Dane. The last thing you need right now is me questioning your motives."

"You can ask me anything you want."

"Do you want a hug?"

"Hell, yes." He tossed the crutches aside and pulled her in close. She rose up on her toes and wrapped her arms around his neck. Her head pressed to the side of his and her chin sat propped on his shoulder. Even better, her whole body ran down the length of his. He desperately tried to remember she offered only comfort, so he took it in and tried not to think the worst had happened to Brandy.

"It's going to be all right."

"I wish I had your optimism, Bell. I'm worried it's already too late." He sucked in a huge breath and sighed it out, holding her close. "Damn, but you smell even better than you look in that dress."

"I need to go, but I hate to leave you with this bad news unresolved."

He hugged her tighter, then let her loose to stand in front of him, his hands on her shoulders, his fingers lightly caressing her soft neck.

"You should have worn a heavier coat."

"Look who's talking."

"I'm always too warm when I'm around you," he admitted. Right now, his blood ran hot for her, despite his mind being occupied with thoughts of Brandy. "Go home, Bell. Get some sleep so you're fresh for surgery tomorrow. People are depending on you. I'll be okay. Nothing I can do tonight anyway but wait and see what the cops find out now that they're looking at the right person again."

"They'll find her."

"I hope so." But would it be too late?

He bent and grabbed his crutches. Bell helped him get them under his arms. She reached up and touched the side of his face. He leaned into her palm and soaked up her comfort again. It helped knowing she cared.

"Call me tomorrow if you hear anything."

"I'll call you tomorrow no matter what," he said, knowing he'd need to at least hear her voice in order to stay sane. He'd definitely need another hug.

CHAPTER 11

Bell snagged the ringing phone from the stack of books on the table by her favorite chair and fell onto her stomach on the bed. Anxious, the butterflies in her belly took flight. The rush of anticipation made her light-headed.

"Hi, Dane."

"What's up, Doc?"

"What's with the strange voice?"

"Bugs Bunny holding a carrot like a cigar, talking to Elmer Fudd."

She didn't get the reference.

"We need to schedule a Looney Tunes marathon. You can't possibly go through life without watching cartoons."

Ah, now she got it. "Don't you think I'm a little old to watch cartoons?"

"You are never too old for cartoons. Besides, when you have kids, you'll be forced to endure an endless stream of them."

"If I let my kids watch TV."

"Harsh. You can't deny them Looney Tunes laughs. Seriously, that's child abuse."

Sometimes Dane acted like a big kid, but deep down he just liked to have fun. He made her want to have fun. He never made her feel uncomfortable about the things she didn't know. Instead, he explained them and moved on. He didn't belittle her idiosyncrasies. He thought them appealing.

"Any word on Brandy?"

"Nothing about her. Even worse, nothing about Rowdy. He never came home."

"That's not good. It only makes him look guiltier."

"He is guilty. Of what, I wish I knew, for Brandy and Kaley's sake."

"They'll find him."

"What are you doing?" he asked, changing the subject.

"I just finished a book."

"More rain-forest frogs?"

"Not tonight. A mystery novel."

"You're tired."

"Why do you say that?"

"When you're amped, you read things you're interested in learning about. Frogs. The Great Barrier Reef. Italian food by region. Last week you read some psychology book about patients with cancer."

"I have a patient suffering from bone cancer. I wanted to know how best to help him."

"Which is what makes you a great doctor. You're not just interested in his disease and how it's affecting his bones. You want to know how it's affecting his mind."

"The mind-body connection is well documented. The evidence is substantial. If I can find a way to keep his spirits up and help him with a positive attitude, that may help in his recovery."

"Absolutely. Look how well I'm doing."

"You are the epitome of a positive attitude, except when you just have attitude."

"Harsh. But true. I'm still frustrated this is taking so long."

"Patience is not your strong suit."

"Hey, I've been nothing but patient with you. Look at me, calling you every night. You haven't called me once."

"I don't have to. If it's nine-thirty, you're calling me." Bell smiled and stared at her dingy ceiling. "I like that you call me every night. At first, I wasn't so sure this would work out."

"You thought I'd get bored and move on after four days."

"Two, actually. But you didn't. Even when I have no idea what you're talking about, you still find things for us to discuss that keeps it fun and interesting. How else would I have found out you like to cook and you want to plant a garden?"

"You inspired me with all that talk of tomatoes. I found three types of peppers to plant. They range from mild to hot. I ordered the seeds. They should be here early next week."

"Look at you. You went from rodeo champ to farmer inside a month."

"I'm fucking going out of my mind, sitting around doing nothing."

"The physical therapist said you're coming along. The bone . . ."

"Stop. This is not doctor-patient time, it's let's-be-friends time."

"Sorry. So, what did you do today?"

"Worked on the house. It's coming along. Slowly. The kitchen countertops look awesome. The new carpet is thick and plush. It took me six hours to paint one room standing on one leg."

"Hire someone to do it. You can afford it."

"I need something to do."

"Which room did you paint?"

"I did the master bedroom earlier in the week. The master bath yesterday. Today, I did one of the spare rooms. I'm working my way from the upstairs down. It's made a big difference. The rooms feel different."

"Not like your parents' room but yours."

"Exactly. I'm calling this my transition period. Soon I'll have the house done, my leg will be healed, and I'll be back to working the ranch."

"You've got your ranch hands and Blake and Gabe handling it now, right?"

"Yes, Doctor. As ordered, I've stayed clear of doing the manual labor around here. Well, except for working on the house."

"Okay. You've been good."

"Do I get a reward?"

She smiled. Yes, definitely like a child, he needed to get something for behaving. "What did you have in mind?"

"Come outside."

She sat up on the bed, her feet planted on the threadbare rug. "What?"

"I'm sitting in my truck outside your house at the end of the drive. I miss you. Come out and see me."

She raked her fingers through the side of her hair and lay her hand on the back of her neck. "You saw me three days ago at the benefit."

"Too long, Bell. Get out here." He hung up on her.

Bell stared at her phone, completely taken off guard. He'd come to her house. In the few weeks they'd been back in Crystal Creek, she'd kept things as uncomplicated as possible. Yes, she took his calls, but that seemed the safest way to get to know the intriguing man without actually having to spend time in his company. He made her feel weird all over when he was near. She couldn't think straight around him. Her thoughts got all jumbled up between being his doctor and trying not to stare at his wide shoulders and handsome face. Sometimes he smiled at her and every thought left her head. He made her feel tingly and hot. She wanted to pull him close and smell the horses, hay, and woodsy scent he carried around with him like a second skin.

Should she go outside and see him?

Her grandmother would have a fit. Her meeting a man in the driveway. Such things were not done.

Why not? Who would really care what she did? Her grandmother. The woman didn't approve anything she ever did. Why did she always try to be so good and do the best at everything? No one cared. No one noticed. Every accomplishment she'd ever achieved had been met with indifference or criticism. She was tired of doing what she thought others wanted and not doing what made her happy.

Dane wanted to see her. He liked her. She liked him. Why not do what pleased her and not worry about what other people thought—people who didn't matter anyway.

She stood and caught her reflection in the mirror above her dresser. For the first time, she tried to see herself as a man would look at her. She tried to see what Dane saw. He liked her eyes. They did stand out against her dark hair and eyebrows. She tried a smile. She'd always thought herself passably pretty. Now she felt it. She had Dane to thank for that. He found her attractive. The man knew something about beautiful women. She'd never look like one of those Dane's Dames. She didn't want to look like any of them. She wanted to be her, the woman who drew his attention and had him calling her every night at the same time.

Her phone rang. The man who waited outside for her impatiently. She accepted the call and put the phone to her ear.

"You're taking too long. Stop thinking and come out here and see me." He hung up on her again.

She laughed. She couldn't remember ever laughing this much in her life. He was good for her. She liked the way he made her feel. The new things she'd been thinking about these last weeks. Like maybe she didn't have to spend her life alone with no friends. She liked spending time with his family. Maybe she'd given up too soon on others because she'd always been waiting for them to leave her, or criticize her and make her feel small. Like her grandmother. Well, not anymore.

She walked out of her bedroom and through the living room. About to open the front door, she stopped at her grandmother's voice.

"Where do you think you're going?"

"To meet a friend. I'll be back in a little while."

"Who is this so-called friend?" Her grandmother took another puff on her filterless cigarette, spewing even more smoke into the hazy, musty room.

"His name is Dane."

"Well, now. I knew you'd grow up to be just like your mother. Nothing but a whore."

"I'm nothing of the sort, Grandmother."

"Don't you sass me, girl. I see who you really are inside. Always have. You should pray for your sins. Pray He forgives you. Repent for all you've done and all you are. A man comes calling in the middle of the night for one reason."

Usually Bell would defend herself. Lay out her arguments to prove her point. Not tonight. Let her grandmother think whatever she wanted. Nothing ever stopped her from saying and thinking what she wanted anyway.

Bell opened the door just as her grandmother yelled, "You are nothing but a whore." She spotted Dane's red truck in the driveway, just beyond the circle of light cast by the outdoor lamp. She walked to the passenger side when he leaned over to open the door. She caught it as he pushed it open and smiled.

"Hi."

"Hey, pretty girl. Wanna go for a ride?"

"No. You shouldn't be driving."

"My left leg is the one busted up. I can drive now that I'm off the meds."

"I'm sorry, you're right." She stared at her feet and kicked a loose rock under the truck.

Dane stared at the top of her head. If he could, he'd get out, go to her, and wrap her in his arms and just hold her. She looked so beautifully broken.

"Climb on up. Have a seat. Let's finish our talk."

She surprised him and took the seat beside him, staring at the lonesome cabin. The place needed work. Or a bulldozer. No one had done any repairs or upgrades to the old place in the last twenty years.

"Your chicken coop needs to be rebuilt. That wood is rotting away to nothing."

"I read a couple of books on carpentry and building coops. It looks easier in the books than it is to actually do."

"Come now, Doc, you can't tell me you couldn't build one. You're great with your hands."

"Maybe in an operating room, but with my grandfather's tools, not so much." She sighed out more than her frustration over the coop and the tools.

Better just get it out of the way. If he was going to keep seeing her, eventually they'd have to talk about her grandmother. They'd talked about her childhood in general ways. Mostly from her perspective and all about herself. She never mentioned her grandmother, or the rest of her family, in anything more than general terms. Mostly it came out as a slip. Something that nagged at her but which she didn't mean to reveal. It's like they didn't exist. Or she didn't want them to. He understood, but he'd set out on this journey to be a good man for her by keeping things real and sticking to the truth.

This ramshackle of a place with the evil chain-smoking grandmother inside was her truth.

"Did I seriously hear your grandmother call *you* a whore?"

She wrapped her arms around her middle. She did that when he made her uncomfortable. He wondered how many times she'd wished for someone else to wrap their arms around her and make it all better. Like she did when she hugged him the other night.

"Yes."

"You told her I came to see you."

"For your booty call."

That made him laugh. "That just sounds weird coming from you, Doc."

Bell shook her head. "I need to stop trying to say things the way you do."

"First, I'd never say booty call. Second, when you get things wrong or use the wrong term, we laugh about it. It's fun."

"For you."

"Bell, I'd never laugh about anything you said or did at your expense. If I made you think that, I'm sorry."

Bell released her sides and clamped her hands on the edge of the seat. "It's not you. I let her get to me. Again. Every time. I don't know why I even try, or why I care."

"That's simple, Bell. You know the answer."

"She will never give me her approval. She will never accept me, or think anything I've done is good enough."

"And it hurts. To be rejected, ridiculed, made to feel like you're anything less than perfect."

"I'm not perfect."

"I think you are. You're an amazing doctor. You're kind to everyone you meet. You never say anything bad about anyone, including your family. They deserve it, but you don't stoop to their level. You hold your head high, because deep down you know the truth."

"What is that?"

"You're better than them."

She leaned her head back against the glass, turned her head, and stared at him. "Why did you come tonight?"

"Well, I came to make you smile. I'm not doing a very good job of it though."

"What is all over your hair and arms?"

Dane held his arm up to the dim light coming through the windshield. "Paint. I hadn't cleaned up yet when I called you."

She leaned in and took a closer look. "Is that light blue?"

"And some Cottage Cream."

She tilted her head. "Sounds lovely."

"It turned out great. You should come over and see it."

"Maybe I will."

"I think you'll like the master bath."

"Did you paint the ceiling blue?"

"You have to come and see for yourself."

She laughed. "You never give up, do you?"

"Not on anything I want."

"And you want me?"

"Yes." He gave her the honest answer and hoped she understood he meant he wanted her for a hell of a lot more than what he'd wanted from other women. Their kind of dating was taking a hell of a long time to get to what he really wanted. He sat beside her, damn uncomfortable with his dick throbbing and pressed to his fly. The thing is, he enjoyed their long talks. Waiting for her made it all seem more important. It sucked, but he'd go through this agony to know that when he finally had her in his bed, she'd know he cared about her and not scratching an itch.

"Why me?"

"I'll have to get you a book about chemistry. The biological kind."

"I've read two books on the subject, but I just don't get it. Pheromones and all that, I get. It's our biology coded to procreate. But the act of seeing someone, being attracted to them, falling in love." Bell shook her head, her eyes clouded with doubt.

"Do you find me attractive?"

Bell's gaze fell to his chest and arms, then back up to his face. She realized she'd been caught staring at his body, bit her lip, and looked everywhere but at him. "Uh, yeah. You don't need me to tell you how gorgeous you are. Every woman who's ever laid eyes on you has told you."

"Let's stick to you and me. Forget all them. I have."

"Right."

He touched his finger to her chin and made her turn to look at him. "I forgot about them the moment I met you. The only woman I care about and want to be with is you. Only you." He'd let some of his frustration out in his voice without meaning to, but she had to hear how much he meant those words and how hard it was for him to say them.

"Maybe it would help you believe me if you knew we both have something in common."

"What?" she asked.

"This is new for me and you. Can you cut me a small break and believe that what we have is different and new to me? I'm trying to do this right. I'll make some mistakes, probably have already, but I'm trying, Bell.

"If you find me attractive and like me, how about we try an experiment that will help you understand chemistry?"

"What are you talking about?"

"Do you trust me?"

"Not at the moment."

He laughed. *Yeah, she would say that.* "I'm asking you to trust me."

"Okay."

"Move closer."

She scooted two inches closer.

"Closer."

She shimmied over another two inches.

"Bell, come here." This time, he reached for her, placing his hand on the back of her neck and drawing her to him.

Their eyes locked. He leaned in and brushed his lips to hers in a soft stroke that demanded nothing and promised everything. He caressed his fingers over her short hair, let the strands slide under his fingers. She sighed and leaned into his touch. He pressed his lips to hers again, tilting his head for a more intimate angle. She watched him. He watched her. The surprise in her eyes turned to interest. He swept his tongue out to slide over her lips. She sucked in a breath and he took advantage, sweeping his tongue in to glide against hers. Just a taste was all it took to turn that interest in her eyes to smoldering heat.

He leaned back just an inch to stare down at her. "That's chemistry, Bell. That warm feeling spreading through you. The heat pooling in your belly. That need gnawing at your gut and racing through your veins. Your heart pounding in your chest and in your ears. That voice in your head saying, 'Do it again.'"

"Do it again." Her words were softly spoken, but held no less than demand in her plea.

He drew her close again. Maybe she pulled him in. Didn't matter. All that mattered was that her mouth met his in a kiss so shockingly erotic and sweet that he only knew her and the need he unleashed at her command. He pressed his lips to hers and slid his tongue deep into her mouth to taste and caress hers. She met his every move and took him under her spell. He tried to keep things tame. He kept his hands on her shoulders, his fingertips massaging her soft skin at her neck.

Bell tore her mouth from his and stared at him, wide-eyed. "This is kind of addictive."

"You're addictive." He pulled her back in for another long kiss. He loved that sweet sigh and sexy moan she made when she settled into his arms. He wanted to make her do it again. His fingers trailed down her neck. The shiver it elicited reverberated through him. He slid his hand lower and traced the top of her breast with his fingertips. She sucked in a surprised breath, then settled into the intimate touch. He took the kiss deeper, cupped her breast, and brushed his thumb over her tight nipple. She made that sexy moan again, arched her back, and offered up her breast for him to mold to his palm. He leaned into her, completely lost in her taste and the feel of her pressed against him and filling his hand. He wanted more. His elbow hit the steering wheel. He turned to bring her closer, but he banged his bad leg on the dashboard and grunted in pain.

Bell ended the kiss and pressed her forehead to his. "This is crazy."

He swept his thumb over her breast again. Her eyes flamed with desire.

"This is good." Different. Better than he expected or imagined. His whole body flamed with a need he'd never experienced. One kiss and she'd completely tilted his world and realigned it to hers.

"I should go."

"You'll have to let go if you want to do that." He glanced down at her hands fisted in his shirt, holding him to her. He wanted her to hold on. "Or don't."

She did let go and leaned back against the seat. He hated the separation, but he gave her space to breathe. He leaned back, too, trying to keep his hands from reaching for her again.

"I really had no idea. I mean, I've kissed a boy, but not like that."

He gripped her shoulders. "Wait, you kissed someone?"

She laughed. "I'm not as naïve and innocent as you think. I tried one other experiment."

"Who the fuck kissed you?" He wanted to kill whoever had touched her.

His outrage made her smile even more. "I was about

to graduate college. I was eighteen and tired of being the only girl who didn't know anything about sex. I went to a party, found a really cute boy about my age who I knew from one of my classes, and asked him to get me a drink. I drank one to his four. We ended up in his dorm room. A very quick few minutes later, I got the whole sex thing. He passed out, and I left completely unimpressed and wondering what everyone was talking about."

"That douche should be shot."

She cocked her head and stared at him, not getting the reference at all.

"He's an asshole who doesn't know how to treat a woman right," Dane snarled.

"Yeah, well, he got the job done."

"No. He didn't if you left there completely unsatisfied and not wanting to do it again."

"Really?"

Dane shifted and reached for her, sliding his hand up her neck to cup her face, his thumb sweeping along her jaw in a soft caress that made her eyes go soft. She caught her breath and her pretty lips parted, begging for his lips to touch hers again. "Do you want to kiss me again?"

"Oh yes," she sighed out. "I really do."

He leaned in close, his nose inches from hers. "Do you want to touch me?"

Her eyes dipped to his chest. Her tongue swept across her kiss-swollen lips. "Yes," she whispered.

"God, how I want to touch every inch of you. That's the difference between having sex and making love to someone you truly care about and can't wait to have close."

"Have you ever made love?"

Her softly spoken question made his heart stutter to a stop. She made him think. What the hell had he been doing with all those women? Lori in high school came damn close. He'd felt so much for her. He'd wanted her in a way that went beyond just sex, but the relationship went south when he'd caught her kissing some fan of the opposing high school football team. He'd really liked her. She'd stomped on his heart, and he'd never let that happen again.

Until now. He'd put his heart in Bell's hands. He hoped she didn't slice it to shreds with her scalpel.

"I thought I had, but now I don't think so. What I feel for you is so new and different. Never doubt that this is real, Bell. I'm not playing some game, or looking for some fun with a different kind of girl."

"Brunette."

"You know what I mean."

"Yes, I do." She leaned against his shoulder. He put his arm around her and drew her close. "I like this." She snuggled against him like a cat settling in for the night.

"I'm so glad you enjoy torturing me." She tried to pull away, but he held her close. "I'm kidding. Mostly."

"If you're uncomfortable because we didn't . . ."

"What?"

"You know."

"Say it."

"Make love."

See. Any other woman from his past would have said *fuck*. He loved that she took things seriously. She thought about the words she said and what they meant.

"I'll be fine. We're not there yet. You need more time to get to know me and unscramble your feelings from your overactive brain and all the thoughts you generate that boil down to one thing."

"What is that?"

"You want to be with me, but you're afraid of what that means. You think it means you're somehow like your mother. Deep down, you're worried that if you do sleep with me, I'll leave you in the morning, like I've done with other women in the past. I've never lied to you about who I used to be. I'm not lying to you now. I don't want you in my bed for a night. I want you in it every night.

"Maybe that scares you even more than all the rest. I'm not afraid to admit it scares me, too. I mean, am I capable of that kind of intimate relationship? I hope so. I've got some great examples to follow. My mom and dad. Gabe and Ella. Blake and Gillian. Caleb and Summer. They've created something worth having and keeping."

"I don't have any examples of couples that made it work and did it well," Bell admitted. "Look at my life. As smart as I am, I have no idea how to do this."

"I'm sure you've felt that way about a lot of things. You'll learn. So will I. We're in this together. Nothing and no one else matters, except what we say matters to us."

"You really mean that."

"Yes," he sighed out. "Now will you go to dinner with me?"

She turned, leaned up, and kissed him softly. "Yes."

Surprised by the show of affection, it took him a second to realize she'd finally accepted a real date with him. "It's about time. Pretty soon, I'd have to start seeing you about the complex you gave me that I'm not good enough for you."

"That is not true. I never thought that. I just don't want to be one of Dane's Dames."

"I really hate that term."

"It's not my favorite either."

"So, dinner tomorrow night. I'll pick you up at six-thirty."

"Perfect."

"Promise me, you won't cover a shift for someone to get out of seeing me."

"I promise. You, me, dinner, dessert that I'm not sharing, and more smiles and laughs."

"I like it when you smile. You should do it more often."

She tilted her head and looked up at him. "You make me want to smile. Thanks for coming over tonight."

"Nothing but selfish on my part." He pressed his hand to her thigh and squeezed. She stiffened for a second, surprised by his touch, but quickly settled into it. "I wanted to see you."

"I wanted to see you, too. I'm looking forward to dinner."

"Go inside before I kiss you again and drive you to my place." God, how he wanted to be with her, but she needed time, and he'd give her anything she needed.

"I don't get a kiss goodnight?" she asked with one raised eyebrow and a flirty tone in her voice. He liked it when she let her guard down and gave in to this playful side of herself.

Two could play at this game. With a deliberately deepened voice, he asked, "Do you want a kiss goodnight?"

She tilted her lips down into a pouty frown. "I guess you don't want to kiss me." Bell tried to reach for the door.

Dane turned her to him and kissed her deep. She caught on quick and matched her movements to his. They lost themselves in each other's arms. She squirmed toward the door. He leaned in closer, keeping his lips pressed to hers until the last second, when she got out of the truck and stood on the running board, her hands planted on the seat as she leaned in and smiled at him like he'd never seen her smile.

"God, you're beautiful."

Her laugh would play in a loop in his mind for the rest of his days.

"Goodnight, Dane."

"Night, Bell."

She jumped down, but he stopped her before she closed the door. "Hey, Bell, are you okay staying here?"

"I've lived in this house my whole life. Over the last couple of years, I've spent less and less time here. But my grandmother is ill. Eventually, I'll have to move her to an assisted living facility. She'll hate that."

"None of that excuses the way she treats you."

"No. And nothing will change the way she treats me."

"A good ass kicking will."

"Are you seriously thinking of beating up my grandmother?"

"I'm just saying it's not right. You don't need to stay here and take her abuse."

"Let it be. Be careful driving home."

"I'll be fine, but I like that you're concerned about me."

"I just don't want to have to piece you back together."

"But you're so good at it."

"Ha. Ha."

"I hope you're thinking about taking that new position at the clinic. You'd be a great doctor for this community."

"I already help out."

"I'd like it if you were closer to home. That commute to Bozeman, the hours you work, it must be a killer."

"It does get tedious sometimes."

"Get some rest, Bell. I'll see you for dinner tomorrow night."

Dane waited for her to go inside again. He tried not to react to her grandmother screaming, "You're nothing but a tramp." He unfisted his hands in his lap and grabbed the steering wheel.

He hated to leave her here and wondered how he could get her to live somewhere else. Maybe even with him.

Right, like that was going to happen when she'd only just accepted a first date. They were still a long way from moving in together. Still, the thought appealed. A lot. He'd never wanted to share his life with anyone. Now all he thought about was being with her.

CHAPTER 12

Bell jogged down the road toward Dane's place, completely lost in her memories of last night. Dinner out with Dane had been one of those turning point moments for both of them. Yes, they enjoyed each other's company. She loved being with him, but it was so much more. They'd shared a meal, their time, conversation, laughs, and held hands like they'd known each other for years. She'd fallen completely under his spell. She finally understood what it felt like to be in a relationship with a man. What it felt like to be cared for and liked and connected to another person. Whether it had been the candlelight, the wine, or just the man, she'd allowed herself to be in the moment and feel everything. Even now, the anticipation of kissing him again fluttered in her belly. He'd been right about the chemistry thing. They had it. As before, when she was close to him, she wanted to get closer, but now that feeling somehow amplified a thousandfold. Being close to him wasn't enough. She wanted to be with him all the time.

Which is why she'd taken the road to his house instead of going for her morning run on her property. Quite a distance, but she'd simply ask him to drive her home after she saw him. That's all she wanted, a look at his handsome face before she drove into town for her shift at the clinic. Maybe a few more of those kisses they'd shared last night in her driveway. Right before she'd gone inside and found her grandmother asleep, slumped in her favorite chair in the kitchen, a lit cigarette in her hand. She'd put the old woman to bed, making sure to check her blood sugar level and give her a shot of insulin. She'd checked her feet. One day soon they'd have to have a talk about possible amputation if her toes got any worse. Her grandmother didn't want to hear it, but she'd have to face the facts. She'd lose her eyesight completely before that happened. Between the diabetes and smoking, the woman was hell-bent on killing herself painfully and slowly.

Bell set aside her worries for her grandmother and picked up her pace, anxious to see Dane. He'd wash away all thoughts of her grandmother and make her smile.

Lost in the beautiful fall scenery, she focused on the trees with their gold and red leaves. Soon they'd have snow. Thanksgiving was next week. Maybe she'd spend it with Dane and his family instead of sitting alone in her room reading, or covering another shift at the clinic, taking care of grease burns on people trying and failing at deep-frying the turkey.

The wind whipped up again. She pulled her navy blue cap down over her ears to keep warm. She dug in and ran hard up the short hill. Her thigh muscles burned with the added effort. She caught a flash of silver behind the trees a second before a car pulled out, nearly hitting her. Thanks to her fast reflexes, she shimmied to the side, the car's bumper narrowly missing her thighs. She stumbled, twisted, and fell down hard on her hands. Off balance on the hill leading down into the trench, she rocked sideways and rolled down the hill, skidding on her hip and thigh the last five feet, tearing her jogging pants and scraping her skin painfully. Her foot caught on an exposed root, and she wrenched her knee when the rest of her rolled over. She put her hands out to catch herself and stop from landing in the ice-cold water at the bottom of the drainage ditch.

Tires squealed as the car peeled out and drove away. She took a deep, calming breath and tried to quiet her nerves and think. She rolled onto her butt and unhooked her ankle from the thick root. The pain hit her all at once. Her palms burned, her hip and thigh stung, and her knee felt like it might explode. Her ankle wasn't much better.

"What the hell?"

Tears stung her eyes, and a few slipped down her cheeks. She shook with fear and adrenaline. She ran her shaking hands down her thighs, trying to wipe away most of the dirt, but since she was covered in dust and debris, it didn't really help. She held her hands up and stared at the scrapes and blood. Not too bad. Not as bad as her side.

She glanced up the fifteen-foot drop and sighed. No choice, she planted her good foot on the ground and used her fingertips to help push herself up to standing. It hurt like hell to climb the embankment, but she made it, trying to keep most of her weight on her good leg and using her fingers to balance herself.

Exhausted and in too much pain to continue on, she sat on the side of the road, giving herself a minute to catch her breath and assess her injuries before she attempted walking again. A truck drove toward her. Fear made her body shake again, but she sucked in a deep breath, tried to remain calm, and waved her hands to get the driver's attention.

The truck stopped and Blake got out on the run. "Bell, what happened?"

The tears came in a torrent. She shook so hard her teeth chattered. Blake peeled off his coat and draped it around her. She pulled it close and let his heat seep into her.

"Are you okay? You need to talk to me, Bell."

"R-r-running. C-c-car came out of n-nowhere. Fell d-d-down there."

Blake stared over the edge of the road into the drainage ditch. "Damn, that's a long way down. How bad are you hurt?"

"Not bad. Sh-shock."

"Yeah, I can see that. I'm going to pick you up and put you in the truck. I was headed up to Dane's, but I'll rush you down to the clinic. They'll take care of you there."

"No. Go to Dane's. I'm f-f-fine."

"You don't look it."

"D-Dane's."

"Okay. Here we go." Blake lifted her with ease and carried her to his truck. She reached for the handle and opened the door. He set her on the seat and turned the heating vents toward her.

She reached up to brush the hair from her forehead. "I lost my cap."

"I'll look for it. Sit tight."

He closed the door. She pulled the coat tighter around her. Not that she needed it for more warmth; she just needed something to comfort her.

Blake walked up the road about twenty feet and grabbed her cap. He stood and stared up the road and down the hill. He walked farther up the road, took out his cell phone, and snapped a photo of where she guessed the car had come out of the trees. He took another picture of the skid marks on the road and another of the hill she'd slid down into the ditch. He shook his head and frowned, stuffing his phone into his back pocket. He walked back to the truck, his eyes on her. He opened the door and climbed in beside her.

"Feeling better?"

"Getting there."

"Anything broken?"

"Just scraped and bruised. I twisted my knee."

"Can you walk?"

"Not well. I need to clean these cuts and scrapes and assess the damage."

Blake hit the gas, and they sped down the road to Dane's place. She couldn't believe how close they actually were. Maybe a mile or so. Blake skidded to a stop behind Dane's truck. He got out and came to her side just as she opened the door. He plucked her from the seat and carried her to the house.

"I can try to walk."

"You're a wreck, Doc. Relax."

Blake opened the door without knocking, kicked it shut with his foot, and carried her toward the light in the kitchen. Dane filled the doorway. His eyes went wide when he saw them.

"What the hell happened to you, Bell?"

He rushed forward, ran his shaking hand over her hair, and leaned down and kissed her forehead. Blake handed her over to him. She wrapped her arms around his head, buried her face in his neck, and let all the pain and fear out with her tears.

Dane hobbled back into the kitchen with her in his arms and leaned against the counter, holding her close.

"What the fuck happened?"

"I found her on the side of the road about a mile from your place. Looks like she was out for a run and a car ran her off the road."

Dane caught the look in Blake's eyes. Blake held something back. Something Dane probably didn't want to know but would ask about after he took care of Bell.

"Come on, let's get her to the clinic," Dane told Blake.

"No. I want to stay with you," she said.

"You're hurt, sweetheart. I need to get you looked at by a doctor."

"I am a doctor." She sniffled back the last of the tears, sucked in a deep breath to calm herself, and let it out on a ragged sigh. "I can clean the scratches and bandage them myself."

Dane glanced at Blake for his silent assessment. Blake nodded, agreeing with Bell.

"Run up to the master bath," Dane ordered Blake. "I've got a ton of bandages and ointment from having to redress my leg after the surgery."

"Just take me upstairs. I need to wash off all this grime and clean the cuts and scrapes with some soapy water."

"For all that, jump in the shower and wash off. I'll help you."

"I can do it myself."

Blake gave him a knowing smile. Okay, maybe he'd gone too far with that.

"Put me down," she ordered.

"I don't really want to." Dane hugged her close, but he let loose when she squirmed in pain. "Come on, Doc, let's take a look at you."

Dane walked out of the kitchen, limping on his brace

but standing on his own two feet once again. He finally could walk without the crutches. Just in time, too, to take care of Bell. She'd been looking after him all this time; now he got to return the favor.

"You are not carrying me up those stairs on that leg."

"I got you, Bell."

"No. Put me down. I'll walk up them myself before I let you hurt yourself."

Dane sighed out his frustration. He couldn't even carry his woman up the stairs to his room. That's right, she belonged to him. He still felt the fear in his gut when he saw Blake walk in with her in his arms. He hadn't known exactly what happened, but she'd looked a mess, and that had been enough to set his blood boiling in his veins. He wanted to find whoever hurt her, and pound them into the dirt. Six feet under.

Dane handed Bell over to Blake again. His brother carried her up the stairs like it was nothing. Dane frowned but sucked it up and followed Blake into his room. Blake set Bell on her feet just outside the bathroom door.

"I'll leave you two alone. Dane, meet me downstairs when you've got her squared away."

Code for *Hurry the hell up, I've got something to tell you*.

"Can you walk?"

"I think so." She took a step. She couldn't put her weight on her bad leg, so she limped the rest of the way, holding onto his arm to steady herself.

"Sit on the side of the tub. I'll grab the bandages and stuff." He found what he needed in the cupboard and turned back to her. She stared up at the ceiling.

"I love it in here. So bright and cheerful. The ceiling turned out perfect."

He'd finished the bathroom with her in mind. Cottage Cream on the walls, sky blue on the ceiling, and he'd redone all the towel bars and fixtures in brushed nickel. He added navy blue rugs and towels. He had to admit, it turned out well.

"Your suggestion." He set everything on the hamper beside her. The tear in her pants revealed the deep bleeding scrapes that were beginning to bruise. He grabbed both edges and tore the opening larger to get a better look. "That's bad, sweetheart."

"Once I clean it up, it won't look so ominous."

"The hell it won't."

Her hand shook when she reached down to brush away some of the dirt. He took her hand and turned it over, examining the heel of her palm. "Damn, that's not good. Look at your poor hands." She used them to heal people, and they were a bloody, dirty mess.

"Dane, stop. Let me take care of it. I'll be okay."

"I'm not okay seeing you like this."

"Come here." She reached up to grab hold of his neck and pulled him down for a kiss.

He went willingly, needing the sweet contact as much as she did. He held the kiss for a long moment, waiting for her to settle into him and relax. He kissed her several times, then leaned back and looked down at her upturned face, dirt smudged on her cheek, silent tears trailing down her skin. He brushed them away with his thumbs, and she opened her eyes and stared back at him.

"Let me help you."

He kneeled in front of her and took her foot. He set it on his thigh, undid her lace, pulled off her running shoe and sock, and gently set her foot back on the white marble tile floor. He did the same with her other foot, then stood and went to the walk-in shower, where he turned on the water to lukewarm. He went back to her and helped her pull her hoodie and shirt over her head. She didn't seem to mind being half naked in front of him in her sports bra and ruined pants. Still, he didn't want to make her uncomfortable.

"Can you get into that shower alone?"

"I think so. It'll be nice to get cleaned off."

"Good. I can't leave you alone in here, sweetheart. I'm afraid you might stumble or fall. So I'll close my eyes and turn my back and wait as long as it takes for you to soap up and rinse out those cuts."

"Okay." Her bottom lip trembled. The shock still hadn't worn off. Once the adrenaline left her system, she'd crash and need a good long nap.

Dane sat next to her on the wide tiled tub ledge and closed his eyes, listening to her peel off the rest of her clothes. To keep her calm and know where she was in the room, he asked, "What were you doing running on the road?"

"I thought I'd stop by and have a cup of coffee with you. I wanted to thank you again for dinner last night."

"I had a good time, too. I didn't want it to end," he admitted. "I'm still bummed you wouldn't share that double-chocolate cheesecake with me."

"I gave you a bite," she said from the shower stall. The sound of the water changed when it cascaded down her head and body.

Okay, she was in. Another few minutes, and he'd help her bandage those cuts and scrapes.

"I wanted more." With her, he always wanted more. Right now, he wanted her back in his arms so he knew she was safe and okay. "It's like ten miles to my house. You really ran all that way?"

"I like to run. And it's eleven point two miles to your house."

"Damn, sweetheart, that's a long run."

"You're worth it."

He hung his head, taking in that sweet admission. It was not easy for her to tell truths like that, so it meant even more when she did.

"I planned to ask you to drive me home. I guess you don't have a choice now."

"You're going to stay right here with me for a while so I can take care of you for a change."

"I'm supposed to work a shift at the clinic."

"I'll call them and let them know what happened. No way you can stand on that leg all day. You need to let it rest."

"Now you sound like me."

The water went off. The shower door opened. He waited to be sure she didn't slip and fall.

"I need your help."

The quiet plea made him open his eyes and turn to her. She stood just outside the shower, a dark blue towel wrapped around her dripping wet body.

"All of a sudden, I'm very tired."

"It's okay, sweetheart, I'm here." He went to her and snagged another towel off the bar on his way. He wrapped it around her shoulders and helped her the few steps to the toilet seat. He held her arms and helped her sit down, though she mostly just let her legs loose and fell onto the seat. He took the towel from her shoulders and draped it over her head, wiping the water from her short hair. When he took the towel away, her hair stuck up in spikes. He smiled, leaned down, and kissed her.

"You're the most beautiful woman I've ever seen."

Tears welled in her eyes again. "I'm a wreck, as Blake put it."

"You're going to be fine, sweetheart." He raked his fingers through her hair. Not satisfied, he grabbed his brush from the counter and swept her hair back from her face.

He used the towel to dry off her arms and legs. She pulled the towel wrapped around her away from her hip and thigh. He hissed in a breath. "Damn, sweetheart, that looks bad."

"Raw. Do you have some antiseptic?"

"Yeah, the stuff they gave me in the hospital." He found the bottle under the sink and handed it to her, along with several cotton pads. "That's going to sting like crazy."

"Yeah, I know." She clenched her teeth and got the job done.

He squirted out a generous amount of antibiotic ointment onto her outstretched finger. She spread it over the cuts with a hiss of pain that made his gut tighten. He winced for her.

He cut several bandages, which she used to cover the worst of the scrapes. He handed her the roll of gauze. She wound it around her leg and the bandages and secured it with the strips of tape he handed her.

"My clothes are ruined. I don't have anything to wear."

"Wait here. I'll be right back." Dane went into his room, opened his dresser drawer, and pulled out a gray T-shirt. He opened another drawer and found an old pair of dark blue sweat pants, then walked back into the bathroom. Bell's eyes were half closed. She sighed out her weariness when he handed her the clothes. "These should do for now."

"Thank you."

"It's the least I can do."

"Can you get me some ice for my knee?"

He glanced at her outstretched leg. "That's really swollen."

"I twisted it."

"Let's get you into bed, then I'll get you a bag of ice to put on that."

He turned and left her alone to get dressed. He closed the bathroom door, leaving it open a crack so he could hear her if she needed him. Walking over to the bed, he pulled his pillow from under the cover and dropped it on top. He snagged a soft blanket draped over the chair by the window and tossed it onto the bed, too.

Bell stood in the doorway, her hands braced on the frame, her hurt leg stretched out in front of her, his sweats dangling off her foot. His shirt went down to midthigh, the sleeves down to her forearms. "You look so damn cute in my clothes."

"I look like a dwarf."

"A cute dwarf."

"I need to lay down. I'm a little light-headed."

Dane went to her, lifted her right off her feet, and carried her to the bed. He gently laid her down and pulled the blanket up and over her.

"It's really sexy that you can pick me up like that and carry me around."

He leaned down and kissed her. "Just don't say that about my brother, too."

"It's not the same."

"Good." He brushed his fingers over her cheek and into her hair. "Tell me you're okay."

"I'm fine. Crashing after an adrenaline rush." She closed her eyes.

He pressed his forehead to hers and inhaled her sweet scent mingled with his shampoo and soap. It did something to his system to smell him on her.

He stood, but stopped from leaving when she grabbed his hand. "Don't go yet."

"I need to get some ice for your knee."

"Come back."

"I'm not going anywhere."

He went to the hall outside his room and called down the stairs. "Blake!"

"Yeah?"

"Ice for Bell's knee."

"On the way."

Dane went back into the room and sat on the bed beside Bell, taking her hand and linking his fingers with hers. He rested it on his thigh and stared at her. He didn't know what he'd do if something happened to her. They hadn't had enough time together. Not by a long shot. Hell, this was the first time she'd come to his house.

"Is it strange to have a woman in your bed you're not sleeping with?"

"No other woman has been in this house, let alone my bed, Bell."

"If it's not that, why are you staring at me?"

She hadn't even opened her eyes.

"Dane. Ice."

Dane turned just in time to catch the bag his brother threw at him from the door. "I'll meet you downstairs when you're ready."

Right. Blake still had something to tell him.

Dane grabbed the second pillow from under the covers, let loose Bell's hand, and pulled back the blanket covering her. He gently lifted her leg and stuffed the pillow beneath her knee. "This is going to be cold." The ice bag molded to her knee. The pillow helped hold it in place.

Bell's fingers wrapped around his arm, preventing him from standing up. He leaned down to her ear and whispered, "The answer to your question is, you're the only woman I want in my house and in my bed."

He kissed her cheek and pressed his forehead to hers. When he stood, she stared up at him. "Get some rest, sweetheart. I'll be back in a few minutes to check on you after I talk to my brother."

He walked to the door but stopped when she called to him.

"Dane."

He turned and closed the distance between them again. "Yeah?"

"You keep calling me sweetheart."

"You are mine."

"I like it." Her eyes fell closed again, and she snuggled into the bed and blankets.

He tucked the blanket around her, leaned down, and kissed her on the forehead. He stood over her, staring at her beautiful face. It took him a second to bring himself to leave her. He'd never forget how she looked in his bed. Exactly where he wanted her every day and night.

Blake met him at the bottom of the stairs. "How is she?"

"Passed out. Tired after what happened. The scrapes are bad. So is her knee, but she'll be fine. What aren't you telling me?"

"I called the sheriff's office. They just pulled up. That was no accident. Someone tried to hit her."

"No fucking way."

"Come outside. I'll show you and the deputy the pictures I took."

Dane hesitated to leave Bell alone in the house. The thought of someone hurting her on purpose made him furious and afraid for her.

"She'll be okay. Come on."

The deputy who had stopped by to question Dane about Brandy the night of the benefit stood by his car. He waited for them to come down and join him.

"What's this about, Mr. Bowden? I received a report about a hit-and-run."

Blake took his cell phone from his back pocket. "I was driving here to see my brother and help out on the ranch today. On my way in, I found Dr. Bell sitting on the side of the road, crying."

Dane groaned. He hated thinking of her out there alone, scared and hurt.

"She told me she was jogging and a car pulled out of some trees and nearly hit her. She scrambled to get out of the way and fell down a fifteen-foot embankment into the drainage ditch. She managed to get back up to the road on her own, but she's got some nasty scrapes and bruises."

"She twisted her knee and can barely walk on it," Dane said.

"Where is she now?" the deputy asked.

"Upstairs, asleep."

"I'll need to speak to her."

"Later," Blake said. "Take a look at these." Blake showed them the photos. "Now, if I'm sitting in a car inside these trees, I've got a clear view down the hill Dr. Bell was running up. The cover isn't that dense. Look at the ruts he left when he accelerated out of the dirt and onto the road. He left a bunch of beer bottles behind." Blake pressed his lips together and went to the photo of the street. "I think he saw her fall, thought he hit her, and peeled out of there. Those skid marks prove he left in a hurry. From his vantage point in the car, he wouldn't have been able to see down the hill where Bell fell." He brought up the picture of the steep incline down to the ditch.

"Damn, that's a far drop." Dane ran his hand over the side of his head. She must have slid most of the way down on her right side.

"I saw the skid marks on my way here. I'll go down and check out the scene. I'll still need Dr. Bell's statement. Do you know what kind of car? A truck maybe?"

"She said a car. Upset and in shock, she could have said car but meant a truck," Blake explained. "I passed five or six vehicles before I saw her."

"I'll bring her into town later this evening. I want her to rest for now," Dane said.

"I'll get started on the report and take some photos at the scene, too. Send me the ones from your phone. Include a list of the type and colors of the vehicles you can remember," the officer ordered Blake and handed him his card with his phone and email. Blake typed it into his phone and sent the pictures. "Thanks."

"Have you heard anything else about Brandy and Rowdy?" Dane couldn't help but ask, despite the fact information had been scarce.

"Nothing new."

Dane needed to call Brandy's mother and find out what she knew and see how she was holding up, taking care of Kaley and her ailing husband.

"I'll see you later this evening with Dr. Bell to take her statement. In the meantime, anything else happens, call it in."

Dane waited in the driveway while the deputy drove away. He stared at his brother, wondering who the hell would do something so reckless and hateful as to try to run down a woman jogging on the road.

"What the fuck happened out there?" Dane asked, wishing for a logical answer he'd never get.

"I don't know. I can only say what it looked like to me. Whoever was driving that car had to see her coming. If he didn't want to get caught out there doing whatever he was doing, then why not drive out and down the road at a normal pace? She probably wouldn't have thought twice about it."

"Unless she might have recognized them. She meets a lot of people at the hospital and clinic. Any one of them might have recognized her."

"Why run her down?" Blake asked. "She's the nicest person I know. She helps people. Who would want to hurt her?"

"I don't fucking know, but if I find out and get my hands on them, they'll wish they never did something as stupid as this," Dane vowed.

"Things are getting serious between you two, huh?"

"Not getting serious. They are serious."

"You're different with her."

"God, I hope so. I've tried damn hard to get to know her without screwing this up."

"You really like her."

"She's different. She makes me think. She makes me want to be better."

"All good things, bro. I'm happy for you."

"How come you didn't bring Justin?"

"He and Gillian went to breakfast with Uncle Lumpy."

Dane always laughed under his breath at the man's name. "You didn't join them."

"I came to see how you're doing and check in with your guys on the progress they've made with the fencing."

"It's all done. I finished the south pasture yesterday."

"Don't let the doc hear you say that. She finds out you've slowly been working your way back to running the ranch, she'll have your ass."

"Don't I know it. I only took care of about three hundred feet of fence. We're all good for the horses to arrive tomorrow." Dane couldn't wait for the twenty quarter horses to be delivered. With them and the ten his father had left for him to take care of and breed, he'd have the start of a good business, along with the three hundred head of cattle he had on the property already.

"We'll be here bright and early in the morning. I've assembled a good herd for you from several ranches."

"Thanks for all your help. I really appreciate it."

"No problem. I didn't think you'd be interested in the horses more than the cattle."

"I'll keep the cattle business going, but I need more of a challenge. Breaking and training horses will be just the thing I need."

"No breaking horses until your leg is a hundred percent."

"The ones you're sending me won't need to be broke. That'll be next year. I'll be all healed up by then."

"Go take care of your girl. I'll check on your crew."

"I can't thank you enough for everything, but especially finding Bell this morning and bringing her here. The thought of her left out on the road . . ."

Blake clamped his hand on Dane's shoulder. "I know, bro. I don't want to think about it either. She's tough. Had to be to grow up the way she did. She'd have gotten herself here on her own if she'd had to."

Dane didn't doubt it. "I'll catch you later."

Blake took off for the stables. Dane went back into the house and up the stairs. He stood in his bedroom's doorway staring at the beautiful woman sleeping in his bed. He needed to do something, whatever it took, to make her want to stay.

CHAPTER 13

"**F**uck!" Rowdy hit his palm on the Mercedes' steering wheel.

He loved this ride. Smooth. Fancy with all the gadgets. Still, he missed his truck. He pulled the bottle of whiskey from in between the seats and took a swig. He stared at his bag of coke on the passenger side floorboard. Luckily, it hadn't dumped out. He needed another fix after he'd fucked up killing Dane's new bitch. He thought he'd hit her, but now he didn't think so.

He kept his speed at the limit and tried not to look at any of the oncoming drivers. He didn't want anyone to notice him.

"Damn." He smacked his hand on the wheel again. "I almost had her."

He'd found Dane's place in the middle of nowhere and scouted it out the last few days. He'd even snuck up on the porch and watched Dane kicking back and talking on the phone, the TV on. He didn't catch much of the conversation, but he did catch his girl's name. Bell. He followed him the other night when he drove down to her place and sat out front kissing her in the front seat of his truck.

Rowdy waited for the clothes to come off and Dane to fuck her good, but instead, nothing happened. She got out and went back inside. Dane left with a smile on his face that Rowdy didn't get at all. He'd been turned down and left out in the cold. Still, the man drove away smiling. Which could only mean he really had a thing for the dark-haired bitch.

It became even more evident when Rowdy followed her to work the next day at the hospital. He picked her up again on her way home. She and Dane went to dinner together. Some swanky restaurant. Dane wore a suit. She wore a pretty blue dress. Rowdy watched them through the window, his rage boiling in his gut with every smile and laugh they shared. He had that once with Brandy. Dane took it away, moved on, and never looked back at the wreckage he left in his wake.

Well, if he wanted this Bell lady, Rowdy would take her away.

He'd missed this time. He wouldn't miss again.

CHAPTER 14

Bell woke up by degrees, starting with the aches and pains in her body. She opened her eyes and stared at Dane, sitting in the chair he'd moved from the window to the bed. He was reading a book, with his bad leg propped on the mattress next to her.

The relief she felt just seeing him watching over her washed through her and melted her heart. Drawn to him, she took him in, from the dark T-shirt stretched tight across his chest, shoulders, and massive biceps to his lean legs encased in denim. His hair was raked back, his eyes intent on the book. She longed to get closer to him and all his strength and the comfort he made her feel.

"See anything you like?" His deep voice resonated in her heart.

"It's strange waking up with a man, but I sure do like seeing you."

Dane dropped his foot to the floor, closed the book, and leaned forward. "I'll take it. How are you feeling?"

"Sore. How long have I been asleep?"

"A couple of hours."

"What are you reading?"

"A book about harvesting healthy grains. I'm thinking about working one of the fields. I need to get the soil ready and figure out the best type of grain to plant for our climate and growing season. I thought I'd talk to some of the people I know who grow grasses and grains and see what's worked for them, but I wanted to read up about it so I know what to ask."

"Smart."

"Yeah, I learned that from you. You read about everything. I thought I'd give it a shot. It passes the time while I'm laid up."

"That's quite a stack of books."

"I'd forgotten how much I like to read. I've been working my way through some mystery crime series."

"I'd like to borrow them when you're done."

"Sure. I called the clinic. They completely understood and asked another doctor to cover for you. Someone who probably owed you for always covering for them."

"Thanks for taking care of that, and me."

He set the book on top of the stack of others on the bedside table, then reached out and combed his fingers through her hair. "I'd like to take care of you all the time if you let me."

"I could really use a hug." She scooted back on the bed and made room for him. She patted the empty space beside her.

"You're asking for trouble."

"I need you to hold me."

His dark eyes narrowed on her, but he leaned forward and slid onto the bed beside her. He reached for her, wrapping his arms around her as she snuggled close to his chest. She let out a heavy sigh, completely at ease to be enclosed in his strong arms. In fact, she wanted to feel him against her even more and scooted closer. She smoothed her hand up his back over all the taut muscles.

"Be still," he grumbled.

She slid her hand down his back to his waist, dipped her hand under his shirt, and smoothed it up his warm, bare skin. God, the man felt so good.

"You're playing with fire, sweetheart."

Emboldened by the fact he'd said he wanted to take care of her and the sweet way he'd already done so after her accident, she said, "I'm kind of cold. Warm me up."

He rolled and pushed her to her back, then leaned over her on his elbow and stared down at her. All he did was allow her to reach her other hand around him. Now she ran both hands up his shirt and over his smooth skin.

"You're in no condition to play games like this."

"Who's playing?"

"I am not going to take advantage of you after you were hurt and scared this morning."

"I'm perfectly fine now. You are not taking advantage." She pulled her hands from his back and reached up to his face. She brought him down for a soft kiss. "You're doing that chemistry thing again." She kissed him, this time sweeping her tongue out to trace his lip and dive deep. She pulled back. "You know that thing where we both say, 'Do it again.'" She kissed him long and deep, dipping her hands back up into his shirt and kneading her fingers into his taut muscles. She dragged the shirt over his head. He shook out his hair and stared down at her. "Make love to me."

"You're sure."

"I have never wanted anything more in my life."

Dane hoped he had the strength to do this right and

not rush her. He'd never expected her to pull him into bed with her. Now that he was here, he meant to love her the way she deserved to be loved. He took things slow, kissing her until she melted into the mattress. Her hands swept up his back, down, around his sides and up his chest. She had strong, nimble fingers that stroked his body and enflamed his need for her.

She kissed her way along his jaw and down his neck. He dipped his hand inside the oversized T-shirt and spread his fingers wide over her smooth side, then inched his way to her breast and covered it with his palm. She sighed, and the hot air washed over his skin. She arched her back. He squeezed and kneaded the firm mound, plucking her hard nipple between his index and middle finger.

"More," she demanded on an exhale.

Oh, he had more for her. Lots more. He tore her shirt off over her head. He stared down at her creamy skin and pink-tipped breasts. Perfect. "God, you're beautiful." He dipped his head and kissed a trail down her neck and chest to her nipple, taking it into his mouth and sucking soft, then hard. Her fingers raked up his back and combed through his hair. She held his head to her breast, and he feasted on the bounty.

"Ah God, Bell, I want you so damn bad."

"I want you. Stop holding back."

She read him so well. He was holding back for her sake and his. He wanted this to last, but he felt the need gnawing at his insides.

"Now who is thinking too much," she taunted.

"You asked for it." He took her other breast into his mouth and sucked hard at the same time he smoothed his hand down her belly, under the sweats, and cupped her in his hand.

"Yes, I did."

He rubbed against her center, brought his hand up, and rubbed his fingers over her soft folds to her wet center, thrusting one finger deep. He pulled free and she raised her hips, seeking more. He gave it to her, sliding his finger back in, rubbing his palm against her clit. She moaned and made him want more of those sexy little sighs and groans she let loose every time he kissed, licked, sucked at her breasts and pressed his finger deep inside of her.

He kissed his way down her belly and pulled his hand free from between her legs. She stared down at him, nothing but trust and desire lighting her sparkling blue eyes. He hooked his fingers in her waistband and drew the pants down her legs. She never hesitated or stopped looking at him. Instead, she raised her hips to help him and settled back into the mattress. He smoothed his hands up her legs to her hips and back down her thighs. He replaced the caress with his mouth, kissing his way up one leg and down the other. She relaxed again. He shifted over her leg and lay between her spread thighs. He held himself above her on his hands and planted soft, wet kisses down the center of her belly, all the way to heaven.

"Dane?"

"Trust me." She'd never had a man love her like this. Well, he aimed to show her what making love was all about. He rarely did this with any woman, but with her, he wanted to share everything. He settled back on the mattress, planted his hands on her thighs, spread her legs wider, dipped his head, and licked her soft folds. With her on his tongue, he planted his mouth over her center and thrust his tongue deep. Her hips shifted and came up to meet his mouth. He loved her until she was writhing on the bed, rising up to the edge, but he didn't let her fall. He wanted to soar with her.

He kissed the inside of her thigh, and she squeaked out a protest that he'd left her on the brink of exploding in his arms. He rode that line hard but took a deep breath and tried to calm his body even as he undid his jeans and freed his swollen flesh. He pushed his jeans down his legs and pulled his good leg free. The brace hampered his movements, but nothing would stop him from making love to this woman and making her his. Forever.

He leaned up and kissed her hard and deep, reaching over to the bedside drawer and fumbling for a condom. He grabbed one, tore his mouth from hers, ripped open the package, and leaned to the side to slide it on. He rolled back on top of her. His chest met hers, and she pressed her breasts against him, her hips circling to find him and take him in. He settled between her thighs, pressed the thick head of his penis to her entrance, and joined their bodies in a long, slow glide that made him clench his jaw and close his eyes on the sheer pleasure that washed through him. She was so damn tight he needed to wait a few seconds for her body to adjust. She didn't wait at all. She rocked her hips into his, and he lost it.

Bell felt the shift in him the second she pressed her body along his. He pulled out and thrust deep, and she met him. That something shimmery and hot built inside of her again, gathering in intensity. She rocked her hips back when he pulled out and met him when he thrust into her again. His mouth crushed hers, his tongue glided in. She tasted herself on his lips and sucked his tongue. He groaned, broke free of the kiss, gave her a feral look, and buried his face in her neck as his body slammed into hers again and again. He shifted, grinding his hips to hers. She caught the wave of pleasure, spread her legs to accommodate his big body, dug her heels into the bed, grabbed his hips, and pulled him closer. The sweet friction their bodies created sparked something new. She found the spot that made it flame to life. Dane matched her moves. Her whole body went tight. That flame exploded with Dane's next deep thrust, and she held her breath as waves of heat and pleasure raced through her nerves. Dane pulled out and thrust deep again, his body tensing with hers. He shuddered against her. She wrapped her arms around his back and held him close.

He settled on top of her, his breath sawing in and out against her neck. She hugged him tighter, trying to figure out what this feeling inside of her meant. She felt so full. She didn't know what to say or do except hold onto him.

Dane felt the change in her. He felt it in him, too. He'd expected making love to her to be different. He hadn't expected it to be life-altering. He slid down her body, shifted to her side, and pulled her over to her side to snuggle against his chest. She lay facing him, her head tucked below his chin, her cheek pressed to his heart. She held onto him for dear life and he held her, giving them both time to figure this out.

"I've never felt this way about anyone," she whispered.

He wanted to reassure her, but he didn't know if he had the words to explain.

"I feel it, too. It's the connection you have to me now, sweetheart. I can't explain it except to say that you are so special to me, Bell, that I took a piece of you into me, and I gave you a piece of myself."

She looked up at him, her eyes bright with unshed tears. He didn't know what to say or do besides kiss her to seal the promise they'd silently made to each other to hold sacred the pieces of themselves they'd shared. He pressed his lips to hers in a soft caress that lasted only seconds but held all the feelings he had inside of him for this strange, beautiful woman who'd come into his life unexpectedly and changed it for the better in so many ways.

They lay there in the silence, holding each other, and settling into this next step of their relationship.

"Dane."

"Yeah, sweetheart?"

"I'm starving."

He hugged her close and kissed her on the top of her head. She'd come up with the perfect ice breaker for them to get up and move on after that cataclysmic event.

"You didn't get to have that cup of coffee. How about we go downstairs, and I'll make you a sandwich and a cup of joe. We'll sit on the couch and watch Looney Tunes."

"The 'What's up, Doc?' reference."

"You got it."

"Sounds good."

He released her and sat up beside her, untangling his jeans from around his brace. She didn't move beside him, so he glanced down at her. Bad idea. All that creamy skin over taut muscles and curves. His mouth watered, but he reined in his renewed desire.

"It's kind of weird knowing you've seen me naked," she said with a shy smile.

"Well, it probably won't make you feel any better to know I'm going to see you naked again. And again. And again. It's my new favorite thing."

"That just means I get to see you naked again. And again."

"And again. All you want, sweetheart."

She rose up and kissed his shoulder. Her hand smoothed down his side. Her finger traced the scar on his hip. "How did you get this?"

"I was seventeen and working with my dad, branding cows. I helped push them into the chute. One ornery cow got stuck. I jumped off my horse to help. She got unstuck and knocked me into the gate and a broken pipe. It stabbed me and left that half-moon scar."

"It's kind of cute."

"I'm glad you like it."

"I like you." She shifted, took his hand, and pulled his arm out to trace the feather tattoo. "When did you get this?"

"On my eighteenth birthday. I never forgot you, sweetheart." He reached over to the table, picked up a glass object, and handed it to her.

Bell traced her finger over the feather encased between two glass panes. "You kept it."

"Always, like the picture I have of you in my mind." Dane caressed her cheek, sliding his fingers into her hair and rubbing them against her head. "Reality is so much better." She leaned into his touch, turned, and kissed the tattoo on his forearm.

"I don't want to lose this feeling. I don't ever want to lose you," she confessed.

"You won't." He leaned down and kissed her softly.

She shifted on the bed, winced in pain, and set his treasure back on the table.

He laid his hand on her knee. "Is it bad?"

"No. It's actually much better. The ice took down the

swelling. You made everything else feel better." She gave him a shy smile.

He pressed his palm to her belly, leaned over, and kissed her softly on the lips. "I can't stand to see you hurt."

"I feel the same way about you. How's your leg?"

"Stop worrying about me. My leg is mending fine and you know it."

He turned back, pulled his jeans loose, and stuffed his foot down the leg. He shifted to the side of the bed, stood, and pulled them mostly up his hips. "I'll just be a second." He walked to the bathroom.

"You are one gorgeously built man."

He glanced over his shoulder at her lying naked on top of his bed, her dark hair mussed, blue eyes bright with appreciation as she stared at him. His gaze roamed down her toned body softened with curves he craved even now.

"How'd I get so damn lucky?"

"You smiled, and I was lost," she admitted.

"I've kept you with me all this time. From the moment you saved me after I fell from my horse at fifteen, I've been waiting for you to come back to me. And you finally did."

The soft, seductive smile she gave him settled into his heart. He couldn't live without this woman in his life. He didn't want to. He needed time to think about that. Let it settle in his mind, like it had settled in his heart.

CHAPTER 15

Bell grabbed the truck door handle and pushed the door open, while Dane opened his. Her head whipped toward him. "What are you doing?"

"Coming inside with you."

"Into my house."

"That's where you're going, right?"

She needed to change out of his shirt and sweats before he took her to the sheriff's office to give her statement about the accident, but she didn't want him to see where and how she lived. Her home was nothing like his spacious, clean, bright house.

"What's the matter, Bell? You've met my entire family. Don't you think I should meet your grandmother?"

"No."

"Why?"

"Because it's different, and you know it."

"Sweetheart, there is nothing and no one who will change my mind about the way I feel about you."

"Don't be so sure about that."

"You've seen my past. This is yours."

"No, this is my reality."

"It doesn't have to be." Dane slipped from the truck and closed the door.

No choice, she climbed down, closed the door, and met him at the front of the truck. He took her hand, and they walked to the porch together.

Bell took a deep breath and opened the door. As expected, the smell of stale cigarette smoke and dust assaulted her nose and turned her stomach even more than Dane's seeing this did. Dane scrunched up his face and looked down at her.

"Turn back now."

"After you, sweetheart."

She led him into the house, sidestepping the five-foot-tall stacks of junk her grandmother refused to throw away.

"This place would make a great episode about hoarders."

"I don't know what you're talking about."

"They have these shows on TV about people who are hoarders."

"That's not TV, that's sad."

"Yes, it is. Especially knowing this is how you live."

She leaned in and whispered, "I get rid of what I can. Mostly what is truly garbage. The rest I try to keep organized. It's a daily chore and fight with her."

"About time you came home." Her grandmother's gravelly voice came from the kitchen, along with the sound of her beloved *Wheel of Fortune*.

Bell walked to the arched opening.

"Look at you. The least you can do is brush your hair and wear proper clothes when you're in public. Don't need to disgrace me even more. What will people think of me?"

"The same thing I think, that you're a mean and

spiteful—" Dane clamped his mouth shut on the last word when Bell reached back and grabbed his wrist.

Her grandmother pulled her housecoat together at her breasts and stared, dumbfounded, at Dane.

"You brought him here? Into my home? You want to whore around, you'll not do it in this house."

"How you tune out the venom that comes out of her mouth is beyond me." Dane shook his head, his eyes scanning the piles of dishes, papers, and other debris littering every surface in the kitchen.

Her grandmother sat at the table, a lit cigarette in the ashtray nearly burned out and a new one lit in her hand. She took a deep drag and blew out the smoke. One of her favorite word search books lay in front of her, along with her electronic handheld poker game. She had several other types stacked beside her—Yahtzee, Slots, and *Wheel of Fortune*. A small TV set sat in front of her for only her to see. The buzz of the wheel spinning filled the kitchen as she watched her favorite show. Diabetes had made her vision so bad that she practically had to watch it with her nose pressed to the screen. Bell had never been allowed to watch. She'd never been allowed to stay in the kitchen longer than it took to make a meal and take her plate back to her room.

"It's a talent. Come on."

"You get out of this house right now."

"We're leaving in a minute." Bell limped to her bedroom along the corridor of crap she'd stacked up, making a path from her room to the kitchen that also split off toward the front door.

Bell pushed open her door, let Dane pass, and closed the door quickly.

"Holy shit."

She turned and caught Dane staring at her room.

Books stacked from floor to ceiling along the walls. At this point, she couldn't remember what color they were painted. Her clothes hung on a rack in the corner. A light blue matelasse bedspread covered her single bed. Her desk sat in front of the window, a single antique glass lamp on the corner, her laptop plugged in, along with her cell phone charger. Her reading chair sat in the other corner. A round table beside it held several books and a bottle of water. On the other side, her air purifier hummed and tried to keep up with the smoke that filtered into her room.

"It's like another world in here from out there."

"This is my space."

"Why do I smell oranges?"

"Orange oil in the bowl of potpourri on the desk. It helps mask the smell of smoke."

"Out there is a death trap, fire hazard, disaster. In here . . ."

"Is me. My books. My quiet refuge from her."

"Where did all these books come from?"

"Most of them were my grandfather's. The rest I've acquired since college."

"You've read them all." The awe in his voice made her smile.

She nodded. "Yes. At least once. Some, a couple of times."

She went to the closet door and opened it. She pulled out the top drawer of her dresser and selected a clean bra and panties. She found a pretty lavender tunic and a pair of yoga pants and turned to lay the items on the bed. Dane stared at her with such sadness in his eyes.

"You're amazing."

She bowed her head. "I didn't want you to see this place. I never wanted anyone to see this place."

"Why? I love this room. It's comfortable. Warm and inviting, just like you. I could live in this room."

"You can barely move around in here."

"You've packed it pretty tight with your favorite things, but I don't feel cramped. The ceiling needs to be painted and the roof needs to be repaired, judging by those water marks."

"I fixed the roof last winter."

"This place should be condemned."

"As I said, soon my grandmother will have no choice but to leave. Her eyesight is getting worse, along with her feet."

"I thought you'd never watched TV."

"Did that space look like two could sit and watch? That TV is as old as I am, but I wasn't allowed in the main house."

"She kept you in here? All the time?"

"I'd go out in the night and clean up and organize the mess out there. Mostly I threw out the trash and did the dishes. If I didn't, the smell was atrocious."

"It's not that great now." He closed the distance between them. "Say the word, sweetheart, and I will move you out of here. My place is huge. More than enough room for you to store your books. I've even got a whole kitchen for you to keep your snacks." He cocked his head to the shelf in her closet where she kept her groceries. Apples and oranges in a bowl, boxes of cereal she ate plain, bags of chips and pretzels, along with a couple boxes of multigrain crackers to go with her energy bars. A jar of peanut butter and single-serve jelly cups she took from restaurants sat next to a loaf of whole wheat bread.

So used to living this way, she never really thought of her sad reality.

"I think I need to get another scan of your brain. Your concussion must not have healed properly if you're asking a woman to move in with you."

Dane touched his finger underneath her chin and tilted her face up to his. "I'm asking *you* to move in with me."

"Because you pity me living here. Like this."

"No. Because I want you with me all the time." Dane cupped her face and stared down at her. "You don't have to say yes this minute. Think about it. The request stands. Whenever you're ready, you know where the house is. Walk right in and make yourself at home."

"I'm starting to think I don't know who you are."

"Yes, you do. Come on, let's get out of here."

Dane sat on the edge of her bed, distracting her with soft kisses and caresses while she tried to get dressed with him taking up the majority of the available space in her room. He took advantage, smoothing his hand over her belly when she took his T-shirt off over her head. Kissing the top of her breast over the clean bra she put on. Sliding his big hand around her side and over her bottom.

"We're never going to get out of here if you keep that up."

"I can't help myself."

She pulled her pants up her legs and shimmied to get them over her hips. Dane groaned, making her smile. She sat beside him and pulled on her boots.

"Let's get out of here."

Dane took her hand and led her back toward the kitchen.

"She'll infect you with her evil. The devil will return to claim his evil spawn."

Dane walked into the kitchen and stood over her

grandmother. "You give her every reason to leave, but she's stayed to take care of you because she's kind and generous beyond all measure. Say one more mean thing to her, and I'll make sure she's got more reason to walk out that door than she does to stay here with you. It's coming, old woman. How it plays out is up to you."

Dane took Bell's hand and walked her out the front door without a nasty comment from her grandmother.

"Dane, that wasn't very nice."

"No one says mean things to you and gets away with it. She needed a healthy dose of reality. Believe me, what I said was tame compared to what I'm thinking."

Dane held the door for Bell while she climbed back into the truck. He reached for her face, cupped her cheek, and leaned in for a soft kiss. He didn't say anything more, just closed her door, went around the truck, and got in on his side.

"You're moving much better on that leg."

"It feels a lot better. Two more weeks, and I'm free of this damn brace."

"But not free to go running all over that ranch and jumping off horses and such, thinking you've got full use of it."

"Right, Doc. You know, if you lived with me, you could lecture me all the time about protecting your handiwork."

"That's one for the pro column."

"It's in the con for me, but I can live with it. And you."

She didn't answer, but the idea of living with him took root and sprouted. Soon it'd bloom into a dream she desperately wanted to make a reality. Obligation held her back from saying yes. That and wondering if all the good she felt now would turn to bad if Dane got tired of her. Bored. What if he changed his mind? They'd only just begun to explore this new intimacy between them.

"Get out of your head, Doc. It's all going to work out."

"How do you know?"

"Because if I want it and you want it and we work at it, we can make anything happen."

She loved his optimism and held on to it for the long drive into town. He pulled into the sheriff's office parking lot and helped her out of the truck. He held her hand and walked beside her. The connection they shared pulsed between them. She felt a part of him and smiled when she caught their reflection in the glass door. They looked like a couple.

"We should go on vacation," Dane said out of the blue.

"Where?"

"Anywhere you want to go, sweetheart."

"I'll think about it. I've got about six weeks of vacation saved up."

"Damn, must be nice to get paid to take time off."

"I work like a demon."

"Well, according to your grandmother, you are one."

"I've apparently infected you, too."

"Let's hope there is no cure." The smile he gave her said he meant it. She believed it.

She gave her statement—what little she could tell the officer—in less than ten minutes. Dane sat beside her, holding her hand while they waited for the officer to check something out and get back to them.

The officer walked in, holding a paper. "I think we might have something on the silver Mercedes."

"Really?" Bell asked.

"A vehicle matching your description was carjacked from the doctor's parking area at the hospital you work at."

"Really?"

"Yes. The Bozeman PD are looking for the vehicle. So are we. Any reason someone would target you?"

"No."

"Have you pissed anyone off lately?"

"No. I work at the hospital and clinic, but nothing out of the ordinary has happened."

"Have you lost any patients? Maybe a family member blames you for a botched surgery."

"First, I don't botch my surgeries. Second, I haven't lost any patients. Complications and side effects from anesthesia and medication are common, but nothing stands out. Nothing that left a lasting effect on a patient's health."

"Okay, Doc, how about in your personal life? An ex-boyfriend who took the breakup personally."

"I imagine a breakup is very personal, but I haven't been involved with anyone." She turned and looked at Dane. "Well, except for him."

"I'll still need a list of the men you've dated."

"Okay. Dane Bowden."

The officer looked at him, eyes narrowed in confusion.

"She doesn't date. At all. It took me three weeks to convince her to have dinner with me."

"Seriously?" the officer asked Dane.

"Seriously. She's a brilliant doctor who has dedicated her time to helping her patients. She's nice to everyone she meets, even if they aren't necessarily nice to her. I can't come up with a single reason someone would target her."

"If it's not her, maybe this has to do with you."

Dane's eyes went wide with surprise. "Me? What the hell did I do?"

"You tell me. Is there someone you know who would go after her to piss you off?"

"If it's anyone, it has to be Rowdy Toll. He's jealous as hell that I'm friends with Brandy. Now she's missing. Come to think of it, I had some trouble the last weeks on the rodeo circuit leading up to the championships in Vegas. I thought it nothing more than rivals playing pranks."

"What kind of pranks?"

"Vaseline all over my ropes. Hiding my gear. Stupid shit. Someone even broke into my truck and tossed all my gear in a Dumpster right before the championships."

"Why?"

"Because it's a hell of a lot of money on the line. The thing is, the only times it happened, I'm almost certain Rowdy was competing, too. Nothing happened at any of the rodeos where he didn't compete against me."

"Since then, nothing out of the ordinary has happened?"

"Nothing, except Bell getting run off the road. I've been living back on my ranch, seeing Dr. Bell and sitting on my ass while my leg heals."

"The last report I received, they found Rowdy's truck abandoned at a truck stop in Wyoming. Seems to me he's either headed this way—"

"Or already here," Dane finished for him. "The thing is, Rowdy would be stupid to go up against me, and he knows it."

"Maybe that's why he's going after her."

Dane couldn't dismiss the possibility. "Rowdy had a tendency to get something into his head and not let it go. Like a dog with a bone, he'd chew on it for a good long time. If he thinks I had a thing going with Brandy, then he's lost his mind. I'm here. She was there. He should have been satisfied with that.

"If he is coming after me, you better find him before he does anything else crazy, because if I get my hands on him and find out he did something to Brandy and hurt Bell, I'll teach him a lesson he never forgets."

"Dane." Bell squeezed his hand.

"What? If this is all about him being jealous that Brandy and I talk on the phone and exchange text messages once in a while, then he's stupider than I ever gave him credit for being."

"Watch your back, Doc," the officer warned. "Be careful going to and leaving the hospital and clinic. Ask security at the hospital, or another doctor, to walk you to your car. Don't go anywhere alone. If this guy has fixated on you and Dane, he's dangerous."

Dane stood and pulled her up with him. "Keep me posted. You've got my number and hers. You catch this fucker, I want to know about it immediately." Dane gave her hand a tug. "Come on, Doc. Let's get out of here."

He settled her in the front seat of his truck and got behind the wheel, but he didn't start the engine. He stared out at the building in front of him. "I'm sorry, Bell. I never meant for this to happen."

"Of course you didn't. We still don't know if it's him. Even if it is, it's not your fault."

"Someone tried to kill you this morning."

"You couldn't have stopped or prevented that. Now we know to be careful. They'll find whoever did this. You never know, maybe Rowdy and Brandy went off for a lovers' tryst."

"The flaws in your optimism are showing. Brandy would never leave Kaley. She'd never leave her parents without telling them. Her father is sick, and her mother is struggling to hold on while the bills pile up. Brandy isn't someone who'd shirk all her responsibilities to run off with an asshole like Rowdy."

Bell scooted across the truck seat and leaned against his shoulder, wrapping her hands around his upper arm. "I know you're worried about me and your friend. It'll be okay, Dane. Whatever happens, don't blame yourself. Like you said, if he's stupid enough to go up against you, you'll teach him a lesson he'll never forget."

Yeah, Dane would kill the fucker if he hurt Bell again.

CHAPTER 16

Bell walked into the kitchen, grabbed the cigarette smoldering in the ashtray on top of three well-worn Bibles at her grandmother's arm, and smashed it out. She took the cinnamon roll her grandmother shouldn't be eating with her diabetes and dropped it into the trash.

"What do you think you're doing?"

"Trying my best to take care of you." Bell took the eggs from the fridge and cracked them into a pan on the stove. She broke the yolks and used the spatula to scramble them a bit, but not too much. Just like her grandmother liked.

"He'll leave you the first chance he gets."

Dane dropped her off at the house early this morning, reluctantly leaving her alone with her grandmother. Bell and Dane spent the last four nights together, wrapped in each other's arms and completely lost in the deep feelings they shared. She'd insisted on coming home today to clean the house of whatever crap her grandmother collected in that time and wash her clothes. She should take the keys to her grandfather's old truck and make sure her grandmother didn't go anywhere, but she didn't have the heart to limit her trips to town. Selfishly, Bell didn't want the chore of having to take her every week. She spent enough time with her grandmother, listening to her spew vile words and accusations. Still, with her eyesight getting worse, the time had come to do something drastic.

"He's free to do as he pleases, and he's still here. He likes me, Grandmother. He makes me happy. Don't you want that for me? After all that's happened, aren't I at least entitled to that?"

"No. You ruined everything. Since you arrived, my husband died and my own son refuses to come here. I have to go to Katherine's to see him. He won't even look at you."

"That's his choice." She hated that her father put his mother between them. All this time, she still felt like living here had been some form of punishment for her being born. "If you want to ask him here, I'm happy to leave so you can have the house to yourself. But let's get one thing clear—the reason he probably doesn't come here is because of all the stuff you cram into this tiny place."

"It's my stuff. You think I don't know you move things around and throw things away."

"I'm keeping the piles from toppling over and burying you alive. You should thank me."

Bell slid the eggs from the pan onto a plate. She poured a mug of hot water from the coffee carafe and plunked in a chamomile tea bag. Nothing would mellow out her grandmother, but the tea might dissipate her caffeine buzz from the three cups of coffee she'd already drunk.

Bell set the plate and mug in front of her grandmother. She grabbed the old papers and discarded food wrappers and napkins from the table and dumped them in the trash bin. Next to her grandmother she set down a book she'd picked up from the hospital gift shop. "I found a new one for you."

Her grandmother rested her hand on the book. She loved the hidden word searches. They kept her busy in between watching game shows on TV. Bell picked them up once in a while to make her grandmother happy. Not that anything ever really did.

"I miss him. He used to keep this place all fixed up."

"My father?"

She shook her head. "My husband. So handsome and smart. He left me far too soon."

"Yes, he did. I miss him, too. I don't have many memories, but I remember he was kind."

She frowned and glared at Bell. "He wanted you here. He never forgave our boy for what he did."

"I like him even more now."

"You'll leave here to be with him."

"If you mean Dane, yes, I will. For a chance to be happy and loved, I will leave here and hold on to him and everything he offers and the way he makes me feel. But I will make sure you are taken care of and your needs are met. It's better than you ever did for me."

"I put a roof over your head and food in your belly when no one else wanted you. I did my duty, the charitable thing."

"Would it have been so hard to say a kind word? Send me to school? Treat me like I was a human being and not Satan's spawn? I didn't sin. My parents did."

"You're just like him."

"Who?" She didn't think her grandmother was talking about her beloved, sinning son.

"Your grandfather. He wanted to punish your father."

"He was married with a child and had an affair. Isn't that one of the *you shall not*s in your Bible? Isn't it a sin to turn your back on your child?"

"And here you plan to turn your back on me."

"That's not true. I'm taking the one and only chance I've ever had to be happy. I will continue to care for your needs, but not at the expense of my relationship with Dane."

Bell walked out of the kitchen to her room and slammed the door. She stood with her arms banded around her middle and hugged herself close. Standing in that kitchen, feeling every day of her life with her grandmother weigh on her, she'd made her decision. She didn't want to feel this way anymore. Dane said the request for her to move in with him stood. The last days they'd spent together after her shift at the hospital had been some of the best days of her life. She didn't want to give that up. She didn't want to be here anymore. She wanted to be with the man she loved.

Thanksgiving was only a few days away. She'd tell him then. He'd be so happy. With Rowdy still out there somewhere, possibly out to hurt her and Dane, he'd want her at his place all the time. No, not his place. Their place.

Her mind sprouted dreams of how it would be. They'd eat their meals together. Watch more of those cartoons he loved and that made her laugh. She'd learn to ride his beloved horses and plant a garden in the spring on the small plot he'd pointed out as he'd teased her about planting peppers and tomatoes to rival the small garden she had here. She'd help him finish redecorating the house. They'd make it their place. Maybe one day, they'd get married and have a family. She'd be happy. With him. Their home. The life they'd make together.

She pulled her sweater off over her head, then found a T-shirt and her zip-up hoodie. She laced on her running shoes and grabbed her cell and headphones. She'd listen to some music and go for a walk. Her knee was better, but not enough for a run. She'd go to the river, find some inner peace, and figure out a way to tell Dane she was moving in with him on Friday.

CHAPTER 17

Rowdy's gut ached. He'd run out of cash and couldn't use his credit or debit card without getting caught. He'd broken into a house this morning when the old couple left to go to town. He'd stolen a couple bottles of booze, a six-pack of beer, a gas can, and a truck. He should have taken some food to go with the whiskey he downed.

Nothing but nerves. He'd never done anything like this. Not until Brandy. This would be the end. Dane would finally get his.

He knelt and set the six-pack by the chicken coop, checking out the tiny hellhole that bitch doctor lived in. What the hell was with all the crosses in the windows? No fucking way God saved that bitch from Rowdy's wrath.

Why the fuck she lived here boggled his mind. A big-time doctor should live in a ritzier house. She'd stayed with Dane the last few days, but not anymore.

He stood and swayed on his unsteady legs. He pulled the lighter from his pocket, flicked the roller, and stared at the flame. "Let it burn."

He grabbed three of the bottles from the carton and walked to the back of the house. He set two down, lit one, and tossed it through the back window. The bottle broke, making it less effective, but the flames rose up and caught quickly. Smoke billowed out the window and licked at the roof. He grabbed the other two bottles and a rag and ran to the other side of the house. This time, he found a rock and threw it through the window first. A woman yelled, "What the hell?" He lit the rag and tossed the gasoline-filled beer bottle through the broken window. The place went up in flames, and a scream broke the quiet outside, exciting him even more.

"Burn, bitch, burn."

He tossed the third through the old truck's open window and ran back for the coop. The rush of excitement pushed him on. He grabbed another bottle, lit it, and tossed it into the bitch's Jeep. It went up in seconds, black smoke rising into the air.

The chickens squawked and rushed to the back of the enclosure. He grabbed another bottle and lit it. He'd spilled some gasoline on his hand and jacket the last time he'd thrown the bottle. His arm caught fire as he tossed the bottle against the coop's wood wall. The straw went up, along with his arm. He shook it and patted it with his hand, but the damn thing didn't go out. He screamed, tore off his jacket, and wrapped it around his hand and arm to smother the fire. It worked, but his arm burned and hurt like hell.

"Fuck!"

He turned and stared at the destruction around him, mesmerized by the flames. He smelled the smoke and felt the heat. He closed his eyes, swayed, and let the rush run through him, dulling the pain in his arm and settling the vengeance in his heart.

He opened his eyes again and smiled. "Go fuck yourself, Dane."

CHAPTER 18

Dane tossed the last bale of hay on the stack inside the stables and pulled his gloves off. The wind whipped up and caught his hair, blowing it back. He needed to grab his cap out of the truck cab. He held his head up to catch the wind and took it in. God, it was good to be outside working for a change.

He thought of Bell for the five thousandth time in ten minutes. He hated that she'd gone back to her place, insisting he didn't have to stay with her every second. He worried about her while she was at work. He worried about her every moment she was out of his sight. But nothing happened in the last four days. He tried to convince himself Rowdy gave up with that last stunt, but Dane knew it was only a matter of time before Rowdy struck again.

Something caught his attention, but he couldn't quite put his finger on what alerted him to danger. He walked out past his truck toward the front yard, searching everywhere for a sign. One of his guys walked out of the barn. The horses in the nearby pasture whinnied and shook their heads up and down.

Dane smelled fire. He raised his head to the sky and

scanned the surrounding area, spotting black smoke rising from down the road.

"Rodrigo, get in the truck. That's got to be Bell's place."

Two more of his guys jumped in the back as Dane took his place behind the wheel and gunned the engine. He peeled out on the gravel and raced down the road to Bell's house. Rodrigo called in the fire. Dane could barely think past the fear rushing through his veins, tightening his chest, and choking off his breath.

She's safe. Those words became his mantra. He couldn't lose her now.

"I texted your brothers," Rodrigo said from beside him.

Dane saw the flames shoot into the air from the cabin's roofline. He thought of all that stuff piled high inside, of Bell stuck in that house, trying to wind her way through the narrow passages she'd made, trying to get out through the flames and the smoke. He thought of her sitting in her room, reading a book, smelling the smoke, maybe not knowing what it was until it was too late. She'd try to get to her grandmother. She'd open her bedroom door and face a wall of flames.

Every scenario that played in his mind ended only one way. Bell dead. The thought stopped his heart. He tried to tell himself it couldn't be. He'd get to her in time.

He pulled into her driveway and slammed on the brakes. The truck skidded to a stop. He leaped out and ran for the house, his heart in his throat, but several hands grabbed him from behind and held him back. He fought to break free and get to her. He needed to get to her.

"It's too late," a voice said from behind him.

"The house is a total loss."

"No one came out."

"I checked the back. There's no one there. Even the chickens burned."

Those ominous words echoed in his head.

"Noooo!" someone screamed. He screamed. This couldn't be. He never should have let her come back here this morning. He should have made her stay with him, where she was safe and protected. He should have stayed here with her and not gone home to work. How many times did she tell him to let his leg heal? How many times did he disobey doctor's orders? One too many times, and it cost him dearly.

He put both hands over his tear-filled eyes and raised his face to the sky, wishing, hoping, and praying this was all a bad dream.

Someone grabbed his shoulders and shook him. He let his hands fall and stared into Rory Kendrick's eyes. He hadn't realized the family drove over from their place when they saw the smoke, too.

Desolate. Unable to breathe without her. Empty in heart, mind, and soul. He didn't want to talk to anyone. He wanted to jump into the flames and join her in heaven, where they'd always be together. Forever.

"She's right there." Rory smacked Dane's jaw and made him turn his head to the right.

Dane couldn't believe his eyes.

Bell ran across the field in her jogging clothes, screaming for her grandmother as she headed straight for the house. Dane ran to her with no regard for his healing leg. He grabbed her before she got too close to the house, picking her up right off her feet and hugging her close, so damn thankful to see her alive and well. His shattered heart re-formed and started beating again. He took a deep breath, drank in her sweet scent, and thanked God, the universe, whoever, whatever kept her safe and alive.

"No! No. I have to get her," Bell screamed with such anguish that her grief became his.

"Bell, sweetheart, she's gone. The place is a total loss."

"No, no, no. I have to try."

He held her tighter as she fought to get loose and run into the burning building. He'd keep her safe. He'd hold on to her.

The roof collapsed and sent up a fireball of flames and sparks. Too close to the building, Dane felt the heat burn against his back. He walked with Bell in his arms, her feet dangling at his shins, back to his truck. Her whole body shook down the length of his. He set her on the driver's seat, facing him, and held her close, so damn thankful to feel her body pressed to his.

Red and white lights flashed as the fire trucks arrived ahead of his brothers. Blake and Gabe opened the passenger door and looked in at him. Dane shook his head to let them know Bell's grandmother didn't make it out.

Time passed without his being aware of it. His sole focus remained on the woman in his arms and her quiet tears that tore at his heart.

"Mr. Bowden, one of the other men said I should speak to you," one of the firefighters said from behind him.

Dane tried to let go of Bell, but she held on tighter. He peeled her off of him and cupped her tear-streaked face in his hands, kissing her softly. "You're okay, sweetheart. I'm not going anywhere." He pressed his forehead to hers and held her close. He looked into her anguish-filled eyes and let his heart speak. "I love you so damn much. If I lost you . . ." He crushed his lips to hers in a long, deep kiss, his hands pressed to both sides of her head. He tore his lips from hers and crushed her to his chest again. Her fingers and nails dug into his back, but he didn't feel the bite, just her sweet body pressed to him.

Dane released her with a reluctance that swamped his insides. Bell held on to him, even when he turned to face the firefighter and saw him holding a huge plastic bag with a cardboard six-pack holder and a single beer bottle with a half-burned rag hanging out of it.

The rage exploded from somewhere deep inside of him and engulfed his whole system. "You've got to be fucking kidding me. Is that what started the fire?" He'd seriously thought it an accident. Bell's chain-smoking grandmother had finally set the place ablaze. But no, that asshole Rowdy came here intent on killing Bell and burning her alive. Fuck.

"We found this next to what was the chicken coop. It's filled with gasoline. Our preliminary investigation indicates one was used on the old truck, the Jeep, the chicken coop, and tossed through the front and back windows of the house."

Bell pressed her forehead to his back, between his shoulder blades. Her hands gripped his sides. Dane didn't know what to say or do. He'd brought this threat and destruction into her life.

The fire smoldered as the firefighters used the tanker truck to hose down the area around the house to keep the fire from spreading across the dry fields. The truck and Bell's Jeep were already out. What a waste.

"We've called in a fire investigator and the sheriff's department."

"Your suspect is Rowdy Toll. The sheriff's department has a file open on him. He ran my girlfriend off the road with a stolen car when she was out jogging. Now he tried to kill her by burning down her house."

"Dane. Stop. I wasn't even here."

"Your car is in the drive. I thought you were inside." The fear he'd felt when he'd driven up and hadn't seen her outside zapped through him again and made his stomach and heart drop. "It's a good bet he thought you were in there. He came here to kill you, Bell. When I get my hands on that fucking asshole, I'm going to kill him."

"May I have your name, ma'am?" the firefighter asked.

"Dr. Bell. I lived here with my grandmother. Edna Warwick. She was inside when I left the house about an hour ago. I walked down the path through the field that leads to the river. I spent some time there, watching the water. The wind shifted, and I smelled the smoke. I thought she'd set the house on fire because of her smoking.

"I should have stayed here." She looked up at Dane. "You told me to stay put. Don't go out alone. If I'd been here, I could have saved her."

"Bell, no. He tossed a Molotov cocktail into your house. With everything she kept in there, the place went up like a tinderbox. You would have been killed."

Bell fell back on the truck seat, covered her face, and bawled her eyes out. Dane turned, grabbed her hips, and pulled her to him, picking her up by her shoulders and wrapping her in his arms.

"I got you, sweetheart. It's going to be okay. I'll take care of you. I'll keep you safe."

Gabe and Blake still hung out on the passenger side

of the truck. Gabe frowned and said, "We'll start working on the details." He cocked his head to Bell. "We'll get things squared away. I'll call in backup." Which meant he and Blake would call in their wives to figure out what Bell needed immediately. In the long run, Dane would take care of her.

Dane couldn't think of the details right now. All he knew was that Bell had lost everything. Her grandmother. Her few but treasured belongings. Her collection of beloved books.

"Hey," he called to Gabe as he stepped away to call Ella. Dane mouthed the word "books." Gabe nodded and started filling in Ella about what happened. Blake stood beside the Kendrick brothers and their grandfather, talking to them. Sammy Kendrick knew Bell well. He'd know what to do for her. Right now, the only thing Dane knew how to do was hold on to her and reassure her she wasn't alone.

"I'll take you home, Bell. We'll sort this out. I promise."

It took a couple of hours for the fire department to put out the fire and clean up their equipment. The Kendricks, Gabe, and Blake all went home. Dane's guys caught a ride back up to his ranch. Nothing more for them to do here. Dane and Bell spoke to the deputy from the sheriff's department about how the fire started, their whereabouts this morning, and the fact no one had seen anything.

No one knew where Rowdy hid out, or how he kept getting this close to Bell without getting caught. Dane's anger simmered, but he tried to remain calm for Bell's sake.

Just when he thought he could take Bell home, another car pulled into the driveway behind his truck. A guy in black jeans and a white dress shirt got out. Dane pegged him for another cop.

"Mr. Bowden, I'm Detective Viera."

"We gave our statements about the fire to the deputy." Dane cocked his head toward the man speaking to, and taking notes from, one of the firefighters.

"I'm not here about the fire. Well, not directly. I'm here about Brandy Hubbard. The sheriff's office told me you'd be here. I have some news."

"Did the Arizona police find her?"

"I'm afraid so. A woman hiking with her dog found the body."

Dane swore under his breath. "How did she die?" Dane choked out the words. He'd expected this news, but it didn't make it any easier. Bell's grasp on his arm tightened.

"Cause of death has not been determined. The body was burned in a remote area off the Soldiers Pass Trail outside of Sedona."

"Are you sure it's her?"

"Dental records confirm it. Her mother also identified a piece of jewelry she was wearing."

"An oval silver locket."

"Yes."

Dane glanced down at Bell. "She kept a picture of Kaley in it."

"Oh, that poor little girl."

"Mrs. Hubbard asked me to fill you in on what happened and let you know she'll contact you soon."

"Ah, why?"

"She didn't say. Because of what's been happening here, I agreed to deliver the message. We've tracked Rowdy's path here. He stole a Honda at a gas station in Wyoming after he dumped his truck. He's used the vehicle owner's credit card twice in that state, showing his path heading north."

"I know he's fucking here. Look what he did. He killed the woman who lives in this house. He tried to kill my girlfriend twice. Why can't you guys find this asshole?"

"The sheriff's department will protect Dr. Bell. They'll station a vehicle at your home if that is where she intends to stay."

"Damn right she's staying with me. That asshole won't get near her again."

"We're searching for Rowdy. We'll find him. The Mercedes isn't the only car we've tied to him in Bozeman and Crystal Creek. He's a desperate man. Desperate people make mistakes."

Dane closed his eyes and shook his head. "Two people are dead. Find him before he kills someone else. If you don't, I will."

"We're working on it. In the meantime, stay vigilant. Don't go anywhere alone."

Not much help, but sound advice. Dane knew what he had to do. Protect Bell at all costs.

The detective handed him his card. "Call me if Rowdy contacts you. Any information you provide is helpful."

Dane stuffed the card into his pocket. The detective climbed back into his vehicle and backed out of the driveway. Dane turned to Bell. "Let's go home. There is nothing else you can do here."

"They haven't found her body."

"They'll look tomorrow. That place is too hot to sort through, and they're losing daylight."

"What time is it?"

"Nearly five."

"How did it get so late?"

"You need something to eat, a shower, and some rest. We'll come back tomorrow. I promise." If she needed to be here when they pulled the body from the wreckage, he'd stand beside her and see her through the ordeal. "Scooch over, sweetheart."

He climbed behind the wheel. She stayed right beside him. He started the truck, put it in gear, and backed out of the driveway. Once he had them pointed home, he wrapped his arm around her and held her close. She sighed so hard that he felt it reverberate through his body.

He drove into his yard and turned off the truck. They stared through the windshield up at the house. "Welcome home, sweetheart."

She didn't say anything for a moment. Her words were soft and filled with regret. "Right before I went for my walk, I had a talk with my grandmother. I told her that I wanted to be with you. I wanted to take this chance at happiness and hold on to it and you as long as I can. I planned to ask if I can move in on Friday. Now if you don't say yes, I have nowhere else to go."

"Bell, never doubt that I want you here with me. No way in hell I let you out of my sight until this bastard is caught. So, yes, you're staying here in our house. I will do everything I possibly can to make you want to stay, because I don't want to ever lose you. Those minutes today when I thought you were gone were the worst of my life. I never want to feel that way again. So it's not that I have to say yes to you staying here, it's I need you here and in my life."

"I want to be here. I fought with her about it."

"You mean she said something vile and you defended yourself."

"I think I've spent my whole life defending myself."

"All that ends now. You're upset she's gone. I get that. It's a terrible thing that happened to her. You'll mourn her and the hope you'd held all these years that things between you could have been different. You can let go of that now, because life for you will be different. You'll be happy. While it may not feel like it right now, that is okay."

"I can't think about anything right now."

Dane opened the truck door, slipped out, and held his hand out to her. She didn't hesitate to take it. He closed the door and walked her up to the porch. Rodrigo stood off to the side of the house and gave Dane a nod that all remained quiet while they were gone. He let Bell into the house ahead of him. She stood in the foyer, staring at the half-empty house.

"I really need to buy some new furniture," Dane said.

"We'll work on it soon." She wrapped her arms around her middle and glanced over her shoulder at him. Shy. Her eyes asked him if she'd overstepped.

"What do you think about starting with the dining room?"

"And maybe do the other living room at the same time. A desk for me to work in the evenings, catching up on patient files."

"Bookshelves and a comfortable sofa we can curl up on together."

Tears welled in her eyes. He wrapped his arms around her. "It's going to be all right. Come into the kitchen, I'll make you something to eat."

"I smell like smoke."

"Food, then a shower. You haven't eaten all day."

He coaxed her through eating the simple meal he

made for her. Nothing but an egg, cheese, and bacon omelet and some toast. Dusk turned to darkness outside the windows as she sat at the breakfast bar in the kitchen, staring out the windows, shutting him and everything else out of her world.

He took her hand and pulled her out of her seat, leading her upstairs and into the master bathroom. She stood like a statue while he turned on the water taps and filled the oversized bathtub. Normally, he'd take pleasure in stripping her bare, but this was about getting her clean and relaxed so she'd sleep. She stepped in and settled back into the warm water. He grabbed the bottle of shampoo from the shower and a glass vase his mother left on a shelf next to the tub. He kneeled beside the bath, poured water over her head, added a dollop of shampoo to his hand, and scrubbed her hair clean, massaging her scalp until she sighed. He rinsed her hair and gently helped her lay back against the tub to relax again.

He stood to leave and said, "I'll be back in a few minutes."

She grasped his wrist so tightly that her nails bit into his skin. "Where are you going?"

He kneeled beside her again and ran his hand over her wet hair. "Just downstairs to clean up the kitchen and turn the lights out. We'll call it an early night. We both need some rest."

"You'll be back in a minute."

"Yes, sweetheart. Don't worry, you're safe here."

Dane hated to leave her, even for a minute, but he needed to check on things downstairs and with his guys. The haunted look in her eyes killed him.

His guys waited on the back porch. Two of Gabe's guys hung out with them.

"How's she doing?" Rodrigo asked.

"Not good."

Dan said, "Gabe said to let you know Ella and Gillian will be here tomorrow morning sometime. Scott and I will stay here until they find this asshole. Scott will take the front of the house. I'll take the back. We'll keep watch at night. Your guys can take the day shift."

"Thanks, Dan. I really appreciate this."

"No problem at all. Gabe said if you need more guys, he'll send a couple of the others over."

"I think we're good. I'll lock up on the inside. You guys keep watch out here. You hear or see anything, bang on the door and let me know. No way this fucker gets to Bell."

"Whatever it takes, man," Dan answered. All the other men nodded their heads in agreement.

Dane went over Rowdy's general description, made sure everyone was clear on what they were supposed to do, and how they were going to protect Bell. They'd all stick close to the house until Rowdy rotted behind bars. Or in a grave.

Dane went through every room downstairs, checking windows and locks and making sure the house was secure. He'd never worried about such things living this far out in the country. Now, he didn't think anything he did would be enough to keep Bell safe.

The bathroom light spilled into the master bedroom, highlighting Bell sitting on the edge of the bed, wrapped in a towel. She held the cordless phone from the nightstand in her lap.

"I called my sister. The sheriff contacted her earlier, but I wanted to tell her what happened myself. She's already contacted my father. He's flying in from California to make arrangements for my grandmother once they recover her body."

Dane sat beside her on the bed and put his arm around her. "Okay, sweetheart. You know you don't have to see him if you don't want to."

"I'm sure he has no intention of seeing me."

Dane didn't know what to say to her about that. The hurt in her voice made his chest ache. She'd been through hell her whole life, and now he'd brought the devil to her door.

"I don't have anything to wear."

He barely heard her whispered words.

"We'll take care of that tomorrow. Tonight, you can wear one of my shirts to bed."

"I'd rather just be close to you."

"Crawl into bed. Let me wash the smoke off me, and I'll join you in a couple of minutes."

"Did you lock up the house?"

"You have nothing to worry about, sweetheart. Not only did I lock everything but there's a man at the front door and back. There's a sheriff's vehicle parked just off the turn into the ranch. They'll keep watch all night."

"You set that up?"

"Gabe did. Not that I wasn't going to set up a watch myself, but Gabe sent over a couple of guys from Wolf Ranch to help out my guys. We'll split shifts until Rowdy is caught. You will be safe here. I promise."

Bell's lips pressed to his in a soft kiss, which she held and he sank into with a sigh. He needed her so much. She needed him. They'd get through this.

CHAPTER 19

The minute Dane slid naked into bed beside her, Bell reached for him. She needed to be close, take in his warmth, smell his skin, and feel his strength wrapped around her. She needed to feel something good and not all this empty numbness.

"Dane." She poured every request and need into just his name.

Understanding everything unspoken, he rolled her to her back, kissed her long and deep until her mind went blank. He didn't stop there. His hot, wet kisses trailed down her neck and chest until his voracious mouth found her hard nipple and clamped on tight. With his big body pressed along her side, she sank deeper into the bed and deeper in love with him.

His big hand caressed her side down to her hip and over her thigh in a sweep of heat that spread like a wave of lava. She ran her hands over his wide shoulders and down his back, digging her fingers into all those tense muscles. His hand swept up her thigh to her center, his fingers caressing until she couldn't help but moan. He pressed one long finger inside her. She rolled her hips and let go of everything but the feel of his big body next to hers and the pleasure he evoked, like a sorcerer casting a spell.

Her body hummed. Completely in tune with her, Dane shifted, grabbed a condom from the drawer, and tore it open with his teeth. She snagged it, sheathed him, and pushed him onto his back. She straddled his hips. He grabbed her sides, guiding her down on top of him. She took him in, filled herself up, and sighed out her relief at being this close and connected to him. She rocked forward, then took him back in slow. His big hands covered her breasts, squeezed, and shaped her to his palms. Eyes closed, she focused on everything her body felt. As all her inhibitions washed away, she let the power of seduction reign and gave herself over to loving this man.

The intensity in Dane shifted from giving her pleasure and holding back his release to joining her in the push and pull that became an erotic dance. They moved in unison. Her hips rocked to his thrusting deep. His hands gripped her hips and smoothed up her back. She leaned down for a searing kiss. His hands smoothed down and over her hips, pressing her center to his as he thrust deep and ground against her. That spell he cast exploded into a fireworks finale that made her gasp and pant as her body convulsed around his. Dane's whole body tensed and pulsed below her. When his hands relaxed on her hips, she fell on top of him, completely spent. His breath heaved in and out at her shoulder, his warm breath a soft caress that soothed her.

He wrapped his arms around her back and hugged her close. "That was something altogether different."

She lay with her face buried in his neck, her heart pressed to his, and whispered, "I love you, too."

He'd given her the words, but she'd held them back

until now, too steeped in her grief, when her world had shattered, to share something so wonderful. His love put it all back together. Though the cracks might still be there, she'd gathered herself in and found she was different, but better. She'd let go her past and found that elusive happiness she'd dreamed of having one day with this unexpected but oh-so-right man. He loved her. It didn't change who she was, or make her better. It made her feel real for the first time in her life, that somehow she was finally enough—just by being herself.

Dane rolled to his side, and she settled next to him. Face-to-face with him, wrapped in his arms, she stared into his dark eyes as he said, "I love you so much, Bell. Don't ever scare me the way you did today again."

Tears clogged her throat, but she held them back. She'd cried enough for her past. Now she wanted to celebrate her future and enjoy this moment and all of those to come with this man.

"I'll try not to. You have to stop running on that leg. Does it hurt?"

"You can't help yourself, can you?"

"I'll always take care of you."

Dane held her tighter. "I will always take care of you."

She fell asleep in his arms and woke to his smiling face the next morning.

"You're like a cat. Every time I tried to move this morning, you sank your claws into me."

She stared at her hand on his chest and the half-moon marks her nails had left. "I'm sorry. I guess I wanted you to stay with me."

"I'm happy to do so, but I've got some work to do before we head over to your grandmother's place and check on things. You need to call your office and have someone take over for you for at least a week. Maybe two."

"Dane, I can't put my whole life on hold until they find Rowdy."

"I'm not asking you to. I'm asking you to give me time to figure out how best to deal with this situation and for you to have the time you need to grieve and sort out your life. You lost everything in that fire, Bell. I'm sure it will take at least a couple of days just to buy you a whole new set of books to fill the shelves you need to buy for the living room."

Her heart felt lighter knowing how well he understood her. She wasn't worried about her clothes or other minor things. Her books had been her treasures. Her lifeline to a world she'd been kept from for too long. A world she'd thought existed only in books, in which she found solace even now. Her emotions were still so raw, but when she picked up a book and lost herself in a story, she gave her heart and mind the time they needed to heal while she discovered a new place, or person, and experienced a different reality.

"You said you have a ton of time saved up. Take it, Bell, give yourself permission and time to sort all this out in your head and in your heart."

"How is it that you understand me so well?"

"You're different. Everything about you interests me. I want to make you happy, so I pay attention."

"I'm not used to that. No one ever paid attention to anything I did."

"Get used to it. I am. I always will."

The doorbell rang three times. Bell tensed, but Dane smiled. "They're here."

"Who is here?"

"The family. Come on, put on some clothes and

come downstairs." Dane rolled out of the bed and pulled a pair of jeans out of the closet. He bent and stuck his legs into the jeans, tugging them up to his hips. She admired the view. God, the man had muscles. Long and lean, he took her breath away.

"Like what you see?" he said, smiling at her.

"Yes. I do," she admitted on a sigh. "It's hard to reconcile that as smart as I am, you make my insides turn to goo every time I see you naked."

"That's a good thing, sweetheart."

"Yes it is, but I'm a doctor. I've seen tons of naked people. But when I see you, I want you."

Dane planted his hands on the bed on both sides of her head and leaned down for a kiss. "I love how honest you are about everything. Don't ever stop saying and doing things with that much truth in them."

Like how she'd made love to him last night. She'd not only told him she loved him; she'd shown him with her open and uninhibited lovemaking. She'd shown him her heart and soul, trusting in him to see the truth she'd laid bare and to not break her heart.

The doorbell rang again. "Go get that before your brother kicks it in."

"He won't. He'll just think I'm up here making love to you."

The blush went up from her breasts to her forehead. Dane gave her one of those smiles she loved so much. "That smile might kill me."

"You'll die happy, sweetheart. I promise." He kissed her quick, spun and sat on the bed to pull on his leg brace, and left the room to answer the door.

She got out of bed and went into the bathroom. She didn't hesitate to jump in the shower and use Dane's things. She found a toothbrush in the drawer and brushed her teeth. Dane walked into the bathroom just as she finished brushing her hair with his brush. He held shopping bags in each hand and set them on the counter, pulling out a new brush, makeup, deodorant, lotion, and an assortment of other bathroom essentials, including a new hair dryer, hair spray, and gel.

"You didn't have enough time to go into town. Where did this come from?"

"Ella and Gillian are downstairs. I've been ordered to tell you to get dressed." He pointed to the jeans, blouse, underwear, and bra on the bed. "They're bringing in the rest of what they got you."

"The rest?"

"You lost everything you own yesterday. Ella is like the master shopper of all time. She met Gillian this morning, and they restocked some of what you need."

"I don't know what to say."

"This is what friends and family do for each other. Get used to it."

Bell stared at the clothes on the bed and the toiletries scattered over the marble counter. "Uh, I guess I'll get dressed."

"I'm jumping in the shower." Dane bent and pulled the straps free on his leg brace, stripped off his jeans, and stood before her gloriously naked. "You're staring again, Doc."

"Uh, hmm."

Dane's lips met hers in a long, soft kiss. "I love it when you're speechless. If I had time to erase every thought from your head again, I would." He smacked her on the bottom and shoved her toward the door. "Get dressed, or we'll never leave this bathroom and my brothers and sisters will come hunting for us."

That got her attention. They had company. "They'll be gone later, right?"

"And I will have you all to myself."

Yep, that wolfish grin melted her insides every time.

While he showered, she dressed. The clothes fit perfectly. She couldn't believe Ella and Gillian did so well on the sizes. The pretty dark blue blouse suited her feminine style and her mood for the day. Soft against her skin, the material clung to her figure and outlined her breasts. She turned to see Dane standing in the bathroom door, naked, dripping wet, running a towel over his dark hair. His eyes held a light of appreciation and temptation. She didn't move, afraid they'd both leap at each other and lose themselves in each other's arms. A distraction she'd enjoy but wouldn't stop her from having to face the reality of today. She needed to go back to her house and survey the destruction. She hoped they recovered her grandmother's remains today. Should she plan the funeral, or leave that to her father? If he took care of it, would she be invited?

"Go back to drooling over me. I don't like that somber look on your face."

Dane pulled on a pair of black boxer briefs, his jeans, and a dark gray thermal Henley.

"You look just as good dressed."

"The new clothes look great on you." He limped to the bathroom to grab his brace and strap it back on. The man healed quickly. The fact he couldn't rein in his activities probably accounted for his improved mobility.

"Your sisters are amazing, but they forgot shoes and socks."

"I'm sure they're in the bags downstairs. Come see."

"I'm going to have to go to the bank and DMV. My

purse was in the house. I don't have my ID, a checkbook, an ATM or credit card. Nothing I can use to pay them back."

"I already took care of it."

"What?"

"I paid them already. It's no big deal."

"It is a big deal. You don't need to buy me new things."

"Well, I did need to, otherwise you'd be naked right now, or wearing your dirty clothes. Besides those points, I wanted to do it for you."

"You knew they were going to go shopping for me?"

"Gabe didn't say so in so many words yesterday, but I guessed this is what he meant. Face it, sweetheart, you're a part of my family and this community. Once word spreads about what happened, people will be wanting to help you get back on your feet."

"I'm fine."

"You still need clothes. Don't suck the fun out of this for yourself or my sisters. They are happy to do this for you. You'll see."

Dane took her hand and led her downstairs. The stairs didn't slow him down anymore. He walked in the brace like he'd never been injured.

Bell stopped at the bottom of the stairs and stared at the stacks of bags on the coffee table and sofa.

Ella and Gillian stood behind the couch.

"Our condolences on your loss, Bell," Ella said, hugging her close.

"I'm so sorry for your loss," Gillian said, hugging her, too.

The tears filled Bell's eyes, but she didn't let them spill down her cheeks. Instead, she sucked back her sorrow and stared at the bounty before her. "You guys got all of this today?"

"We got to the stores right when they opened. I hope you like what we picked out," Ella said.

"It should be enough for two weeks. A couple of work outfits that you can mix and match. Jeans, slacks, T-shirts, blouses, sweaters. Oh, a new coat and a heavy sweater. It's navy blue. Ella and I got the same one in black," Gillian said. "We couldn't resist."

Ella picked up a bag and pulled out an ice blue blanket. "This is for you to curl up under and read a book. Feel it. Nothing is softer than this."

Bell took the blanket and held it to her chest, running her hand over the ultra-soft material. "I love it. Thank you."

"That's not all," Gillian said, pointing to the door.

Gabe and Blake walked through the door carrying a camel-colored chaise lounge. They placed it next to the side table facing the TV. A couple of guys walked in carrying boxes. They set them on the floor next to the chaise and went back out the front door.

"What's all this?" she asked.

"Well, you've got your blanket and a place to read. All you need is some books." Ella opened the lid of one of the three boxes and pulled out several books, then stacked them on the chaise. "We stopped by the bookstore in town and picked up a selection for you."

"Mysteries, a few romances, biographies, and nonfiction books about a range of subjects. Even a few gardening books. Dane said you liked those. I found one on tomatoes, like he asked."

Bell turned to Dane, one eyebrow raised in question.

"I kept my phone on vibrate last night. We shared a long series of texts early this morning while you slept."

She looked at everyone around the room and hoped they saw in her how much she appreciated everything.

"This is too much. I thank you for everything. No one has ever . . . I never had anyone . . ." She couldn't find the words. "It's more than I expected and ever hoped for, but I am so lucky to have friends like you."

Gillian took Bell's hand and pulled her around the sofa to the boxes on the coffee table. "You are not going to believe some of these shoes." Gillian flipped open several box lids. Ella, Gillian, and Bell got lost talking about all the purchases and oohing and aahing over the shoes. At one point, Bell caught Dane's eye and smiled. He and his brothers stood across the foyer by the dining room, talking in low tones. Probably about Rowdy and how they were going to keep her safe. She felt the target on her back, but she didn't worry too much. Not with the men looking out for her. Not with Dane looking out for her. She'd never had anyone care about her well-being and her happiness.

"Try these on." Gillian held up a pair of dark brown riding-style boots.

They'd definitely complement her outfit. Bell slid on a pair of socks, pushed her feet inside the boots, and zipped them up the side. She rocked back and forth in them, admiring the leather strap that went across her ankle with the silver heart and star studs across it.

"These are so comfortable and cute. I love them."

"We tried to mix the practical with what you'd need for work. Anytime you want to go shopping for more to fill out what we've got here, just give Gillian and me a call and we'll go with you," Ella said, smiling, like they did this all the time.

"I'd love that. I'd also like to take you two to lunch or out for dinner and drinks to thank you for doing this."

"Oh, we had a blast." Gillian touched her shoulder. Such a simple gesture of friendship, but it meant so much. Bell might have lost all her possessions, but what really mattered in her life was standing in this room. Her friends and Dane. She hoped one day they'd be family.

"We need to go," Dane said, pulling her from her thoughts. "Nice boots."

She stared down at them, then up at him. "I love them."

"They suit you. Ella and Gillian know your chic style."

"Yes, we do." Ella and Gillian both walked into Dane's arms and hugged him close.

"You think I'm chic?" she asked.

"Yes," they all said in unison.

He wrapped his arms around both of his sisters and pecked each of them on the head. "Thank you for making her smile. And saving me from taking her shopping." That cocky grin slipped when both Ella and Gillian nudged him in the ribs for being ornery. Just like real sisters. Like family.

She'd never had that either. Not really. Here she was a part of this. Included, not shunned and pushed aside and out of sight. Here, they took her into the fold and included her. They went out of their way to help her. She didn't know if her heart could take such overwhelming joy.

"We'll see you at Wolf Ranch for Thanksgiving," Gabe said, pulling his wife out of Dane's arms and against his side.

Blake took Gillian into his arms and stared down at her. "How are you feeling?"

"Good. Really good. I have all this energy today."

"The second trimester is easier. Your hormones have leveled off," Bell explained.

"Bell, grab your new jacket, or at least that heavy sweater. We need to go to your place. Gabe said the fire inspector and the coroner were already there sifting through the debris."

Bell picked up the thick sweater, pulled off the tag, and put it on. She took Dane's outstretched hand, and they followed everyone out to the trucks. She hugged everyone goodbye, thanking them all for their condolences and the shopping spree.

She settled in the truck beside Dane and leaned against his side. He waited for his brothers to pull out before they followed.

"You ready for this, sweetheart?"

"With you beside me, I can face anything." She meant those words. He gave her strength and courage, because if she stumbled, he'd catch her.

CHAPTER 20

Dane and Bell stood beside the truck while the investigators worked. With each layer they peeled off the pile of rubble in the kitchen section of the house, the closer they came to discovering Bell's grandmother's body. The tone and speed of the investigators changed about a half hour after Dane and Bell arrived. Everyone stood back and stared at the center of where they'd been digging.

Bell turned into his chest and hid her face. Her hands fisted in his shirt. He held her close but stared off into the distance while they lifted the body and zipped it into the body bag. The coroner rolled the gurney to the waiting van and loaded it inside the back. He came to them with solemn eyes.

"Dr. Bell, I am so sorry for your loss."

Bell let go of Dane and turned in his arms. He held her shoulders, offering her his support and silent understanding.

"Thank you for coming so early this morning. I couldn't stand to leave her out here any longer."

"I understand, but the hot spots kept flaring during the night. The site wasn't safe to remove her body. I spoke with Dr. Warwick last night. He should be here shortly."

"Here? He's coming here?"

"Yes. He wanted to ensure we recovered Mrs. Warwick and to take a look at the house and land. I understand he's meeting someone else here, too."

Bell turned in Dane's arms and grabbed his shirt. "We have to go. Now."

"Okay, but the Kendricks just drove in. Let's say hi and find out why they're here."

"Ah, sweet thing, I am so sorry for your loss, but good riddance to that devil woman. Here, hold on to this." Sammy handed Dane the wood box he'd been holding and pulled Bell into his arms for a hug. Bell held on tight to the old coot.

Dane caught Rory's nod for him to join him and his brothers a few feet away.

"What's up?"

"Colt and I are headed to your place," Ford said, standing next to his truck and talking under his breath so Bell didn't overhear. "Where do you want your new chicken coop?"

Rory slapped Dane on the shoulder and pointed to the back of Ford's truck. Sure enough, stacks of wood, chicken wire, a bag of feed, and two crates of chickens sat in the back. "Granddad wanted to do something for her to make your place feel like home. She took good care of her chickens. It's a shame the way they died."

"That's real nice of you guys. I've actually got a small fenced-in area just to the right of the toolshed by the stables."

"Sounds good. We're on it. Probably have most of it done by the time you get back," Colt said, climbing into the truck. Ford followed, and they pulled out of the drive.

"Dane, we have to go. Now." The fear and anxiety in Bell's voice alerted him to danger. This time it wasn't Rowdy but her father and sister's arrival, along with Tony, who was driving the truck.

"I need you to stay," Sammy pleaded, holding Bell by the shoulders. "You need to face your past. He needs to account for what he's done."

"He doesn't want to see me."

"He has no choice. Hiding from his mistakes doesn't erase them."

"That's exactly right. All I am to him is a mistake."

"No. His mistake was turning his back on you. Now he'll answer for it. Your grandfather made sure of it. For you."

"I don't understand."

"You will."

Katherine reached them first. Bell hugged her sister as she always did. Katherine held her tight, longer than usual. Bell gave into the comfort and held on to her sister.

Katherine released her. "Bell, I'm so glad you're okay. I was so worried about you. I wish we'd returned from delivering a bull to Tony's friend's place earlier last night."

By the time Bell called Katherine last night, they were still an hour away. Bell didn't mind they missed the fire and the aftermath with the police and fire inspector. Katherine didn't need that kind of stress in her condition.

"I'm okay. Still a little shocked and numb."

"Of course you are. I can't believe Grandmother is gone."

Bell didn't have any words. Instead, she stared at her father, who was talking to the coroner and signing some papers.

"He's taking care of the funeral arrangements. We'll have a church service in town, then a gathering at my house. Please say you'll come," Katherine pleaded. "This could be a chance to mend the family."

Bell didn't answer but studied her father. Light brown hair, almost blonde, swept across his brow, while the back was shorter. His eyes were the same hazel brown as her sister's. She saw the resemblance to her grandmother in his coloring, the shape of his eyes, nose, and mouth. At five-nine, he wasn't that tall for a man. Funny, she thought he'd be bigger.

He glanced her way but didn't smile. His face remained passive. His hands disappeared into his black slacks pockets. His crisp white tailored shirt looked as starched as his features.

Dr. Warwick walked toward Bell. Dane stood at her back, one big hand on her hip, silently letting her know she had his support. She leaned into him.

"You got this, sweetheart. You don't need him," Dane whispered close to her ear.

"Bell." Dr. Warwick glanced at Dane behind her and down at his brace. "I heard you've become quite the surgeon. You're making a name for yourself here. You should consider working in one of the larger, more prestigious hospitals in a big city. You'd do better both financially and professionally. The last thing you want to do is get stuck in a small town wasting your exceptional intellect and talent."

The man hadn't seen her since she was a baby, then he shows up and gives her career advice. Bell didn't quite know what to say, but acting like the last twenty-six years of her life hadn't been steeped in his betrayal and neglect wasn't okay with her. She deserved something more than his turning up his nose at her working in Bozeman and Crystal Creek. She deserved an explanation. A damn I'm sorry.

"My father did that," he went on. "Sunk his roots here and never flourished. You look so much like him. It's surprising really. DNA is a tricky thing. When you were born, and I saw your coloring, I accused your mother of trying to trick me. Well, the tests came back that she didn't. Still, I hadn't thought much that you looked like my father at the time. Seeing you now, the resemblance is definitely there."

Surprised he didn't know when to shut up, and that he'd compare her to his father, she said, "My memories of him are vague. He died when I was very young."

"That's right. I missed his funeral. I attended a symposium in Amsterdam, I believe. I was the guest speaker, so, you know, I couldn't get out of it."

No, he chose the limelight over his father's funeral. Clearly, he'd left this place and his family behind. Katherine only moved back after she met and married Tony. His family lived here, and Katherine had thought it an adventure to move from her lavish home in California to a ranch in Montana, close to her family roots. Life here wasn't quite as easy as she'd had it there. Snow in the winter, the distance from town, the isolation those two things created. Not the social life Katherine grew up taking for granted.

"Yes, well, Katherine said you'd see to Grandmother's funeral arrangements."

"And the property. Katherine and Tony will get the land to build onto their cattle business."

Bell's gut went sour. So easily he decided what would happen without asking her. Without even a discussion about what should happen to the home and land she'd spent her whole life on, while Katherine had only stepped foot on it a handful of times.

"What about me? Where will I go?"

"Katherine indicated you were staying with your boyfriend at the Bowden place."

"That is Dane's home. This is mine. You know, the place you sent me without a second thought. The place I was raised by a woman who hated every breath I took. The place I lived as the shame of this family and paid for your sins. The place I was hidden away from the world. Out of sight. Out of mind. This is my home. Not yours. Not hers."

"I'm sorry you feel that way, but you have no say in the matter. My mother put a roof over your head and cared for you, but the property belongs to the Warwick family. It will remain in my hands now, and in your sister's when I pass."

"I am a part of this family whether you choose to acknowledge it or not."

"I won't change my mind on this matter. You'll have to make other living arrangements. As there is nothing left here for you to take with you, this should be a simple matter of finding suitable lodging and replacing the items you've lost in the fire."

All very matter-of-fact and logical. Not a single sentiment or emotion. Nothing. Just the facts. What he said went.

"So that's it? The place burns to the ground, and I'm just supposed to leave and fend for myself?" Yes, she would live with Dane. He knew that, but that didn't mean Bell deserved to be told to get off the land she'd been raised on her whole life.

"It's not as if you don't have means and options," her

father said. "Really, Bell, you're a doctor. You make a good income and can afford to buy what you need."

"Just because I can buy what I need doesn't excuse the fact you're kicking me off the land that has been my home my entire life." She glared at her father. "If this land belongs to the family, then it belongs to me, too."

Katherine touched Bell's shoulder to show Bell her support as she spoke to their father. "Dad, Tony and I don't need all this land. We've got our place."

"You may not need it now, but over time Tony will expand his operation. You'll have the wealth and status that come with owning a big business. Bell will not get this land. It's for you, sweetheart."

Bell let loose some of the rage roiling inside her gut. "Tossing me away again like some unwanted piece of trash. I'm not irrelevant. I'm not invisible. You can't just dismiss me because I'm inconvenient and interfere with what you want." She stared down her father. "Even if you didn't want to acknowledge me as your daughter and be a part of my life, couldn't you have come here and split the property between us. Couldn't you have given me that much?"

"I've made my decision."

"Possession is nine-tenths of the law, they say. I lived in that house practically my whole life. I know this land inside and out. You haven't stepped foot on it in nearly twenty-seven years. More, probably. I'll take you to court."

"You'll only delay the inevitable," her father snapped. "It's a waste of time and money."

"Yes, it is," Sammy interrupted, taking the wood box from Dane and handing it to Bell. "No one needs to go to court. All you have to do, sweet thing, is look inside that box. You will have all the answers you need."

"Mr. Kendrick, you have no say in this matter," Dr. Warwick said.

"I don't. But my very good friend entrusted that box to me on his deathbed. I have kept it safe and delivered it into Bell's hands as promised." Sammy held Bell by the shoulders and told her, "Your grandfather instructed me to give you that box after your grandmother passed. I promised. I delivered." He tapped his index finger on top of the box. "This is what you deserve. What is rightfully yours."

Bell placed the box in Dane's hands. She opened the lid and pulled out the silver-framed photograph on top. The tears welled in her eyes and spilled over. She traced her finger over the glass and her grandfather's smiling face. Four years old, she sat on his lap in a chair on the porch, a book in her hand, smiling up at her grandfather with such love and delight on her face. She wished she remembered this captured moment and held on to the joy she saw on her tiny face.

She turned the picture so Dane could see.

"Damn, sweetheart, you look just like him."

"He had dark hair and blue eyes," she whispered, the tears cascading down her cheeks. "Grandmother filled the house with so many things, I haven't seen a picture of him in years. The picture of him in my mind is so vague now. But look, there he is."

"She hid the pictures and her grief with all that stuff," Dane guessed.

Sammy touched her shoulder. "He got such a kick out of hearing you read to him. You liked *The Count of Monte Cristo* and *The Three Musketeers*."

That made her smile. "I still love them. I read them at least once a year."

Bell put the photograph back in the box and pulled

out the large envelope with her name on it. She slit the opening with her index finger and pulled out the handwritten note and documents. She held the letter so Dane could read it with her.

My dearest Bell,

You are the light of my life. I have enjoyed every moment I have gotten to spend with you. I wish we could have shared many more. I wish I was there to see you grow and reach your full potential. I know you will do great things. You will be a woman with heart and smarts. You have exceptional strength, intellect, instincts, imagination, and kindness. Never let a few people who look at you through eyes fogged with their past and judgments, instead of with an open and loving heart, stop you from knowing inside that you are an incredible person. I hope you find peace and love and laughter. Those are the gifts you brought into my life.

I could have been and done more, but I loved my simple life on the ranch. Being there made me happy every day of my life, but never so much as when you came into my life and shared it with me. Do what makes you happy. Be whatever it is that makes you happy, but know that you will always have a home.

What they denied you, I give to you in total, because it is mine to give, not theirs to take away.

I love you, my sweet baby girl. I hope that brings you comfort when you need it, because your love filled me up. Find someone whose love

*fills you up and hold on to them forever. I held
on to you as long as I could.
   With all my love, I leave you my heart.
   Your grandfather,
   Thomas Warwick*

"You are loved, Bell," Dane said. "You always were. You will always be."

"I wish I remembered him better. My memories float in and out so fast, I can't really remember what they are or what they mean."

"Just take those words and those documents he left you. That's all you need to know and remember," Sammy said.

"What is in those documents?" her father asked.

"His dying request," Sammy answered.

"The one thing that was his to give, not yours to take away. Like you think you can do," Bell added. "The deed to this land."

"Which belongs to me. I am my mother's heir," her father argued.

"Not according to him," Sammy said. "He had a lawyer draw up the will, and Edna signed it."

"She always left things like that to him. She probably didn't even read it." Bell's father tried to snatch the paper from her.

Dane grabbed his wrist and held it. "Don't you dare fucking touch her."

"This is none of your concern."

"She's my concern," Dane shot back. "You will treat her with respect. You're so damn concerned with the land and having everything you want, but you're not worried about the madman asshole out there trying to kill Bell."

"The police are investigating the matter," Dr. Warwick said.

"That would be good enough for you. Let someone else do the work. Let someone else raise Bell. You think you can swoop in and tell her what to do. Who the fuck do you think you are? Certainly not a man who can call himself a father with a straight face. Not a man at all if you can turn your back on your own flesh and blood and disregard her existence, her hopes, her dreams, everything she is and has ever accomplished and will accomplish. Get the fuck off her land."

"Not until we settle this matter. Bell?"

"Grandfather settled it. This was his wish."

"I don't know why you are being so difficult about this. You don't even want the land," Dr. Warwick said.

"I don't? How do you know what I want? You don't know anything about me. You dumped me here, left, and went back to your perfect family and home and never looked back. You never cared about me or anything I did. I lost the one and only person who ever loved me in this family," Bell yelled. "I have a right to keep what Grandfather left to me."

"You live with him now." Dr. Warwick pointed to Dane.

Bell shook her head. He didn't get it. "That is Dane's home. His land. His business. His cattle and horses. What little possessions I had burned in the fire. This land is the only thing I've ever had that is all mine."

"Dane is rich. He can give you anything you want."

Bell turned to Dane, hoping he understood. Someone had to understand.

"I can buy Bell whatever she wants except the one thing she's never had," Dane told her father. "A family. A piece of her heritage. Acknowledgement that she is a piece of the Warwick history, despite how hard you try to erase her from your hearts and minds. That is what her grandfather left her. That is what he made her a part of. Not just a piece of land. Her place in the family as his beloved granddaughter."

"I'll buy the land from you," her father offered.

"You can't put a price on what this land means to her," Dane answered for her. "One day, she'll have a child of her own. She'll have a piece of her grandfather to pass on to them. She'll build onto the legacy her grandfather left to her."

Dane ran his hand down her hair and rested it on her neck, his fingers lightly brushing her skin. He comforted her with his touch, his words, his understanding of how deeply she felt about this. Now that she knew about her grandfather, how he felt about her, and what he'd left her, she wanted to hold on to it, his memory, and fulfill his wishes.

Dr. Warwick tried to say something, but Katherine stepped in between Bell and him. "Let it go, Dad. The house is gone, but Bell is right. This is her home."

Touched her big sister stood up for her, Bell took her hand. "Thank you, Katherine, for understanding this is all I have."

Katherine hugged her close.

"That's not exactly true, sweetheart. You have me," Dane pointed out.

"Yes, I do. You fill me up."

That earned her one of those smiles she liked so much.

"I want a copy of those papers," her father demanded.

"I'd send them to you, but I don't have your address," Bell responded.

"Give them to your sister this Sunday at the funeral. I expect you'll want to say goodbye to your grandmother. Come on, Katherine. It's time to go," her father ordered and walked back to Tony's truck without so much as a goodbye.

Tony held his wife's hand and stood beside her. Katherine's eyes glistened, but she didn't shed a tear. "This isn't how he usually is. I hear him speak to you with that neutral tone and it tears me apart. I don't recognize the man who raised me. I don't understand any of this."

"Let me put it to you plainly," Bell responded. "He has no love for me, Katherine. I am the result of a mistake he made and wishes he could take back. I am the living reminder that he is not as perfect as he thinks he is. My mother seduced him. He gave in to his baser needs and let his libido lead him straight into temptation. Despite his superior intellect, my mother showed him that he's no better than any other red-blooded man with a hard-on for a pretty woman. Every time he looks at me, all he sees is how stupid he was and that he got caught—by his colleagues and his wife. His pride and narcissism won't allow him to admit people make mistakes and he's only human. So he pretends I'm not his daughter. I don't exist. Because if I don't exist in his world, then he isn't a flawed human but the perfect PhD with the stellar reputation, the adoring husband to his pretty, doting wife, and the perfect father to the wonderful daughter he raised."

Katherine actually turned green and put a hand to her stomach. Her eyes filled with unshed tears. "I'm sorry, Bell. I don't know what to say besides this is so, so wrong." She placed her hand on Bell's shoulder. "Will you be okay at Dane's? Is there anything you need? I'm here for you. I want to help."

"Dane's sisters took care of my immediate needs." She swept her hand down to indicate her outfit.

"They've got great taste. You look fantastic."

"Thank you. He and his brothers, along with the sheriff's department, are seeing to my safety." She cocked her head toward the sheriff's vehicle parked thirty feet away.

"If you need anything, please call me. As for Dad, I don't know what to say."

"I'm used to being invisible to him, Katherine. Let it be. The more you try to fix it, the worse it will get. Don't ruin your relationship with him because of me. He doesn't want to be a part of my life. After today, I think that is actually a good thing. I don't want or need someone like him in my life."

Her grandmother's antipathy had been enough for one lifetime. She wanted more of what her grandfather spoke of. Peace and love and laughter. The man standing right beside her, his hand on her shoulder, his body pressed to hers, gave her all of that and more.

"Bell, when the timing is better, I'd like to talk to you about a business deal," Tony said. "Don't say no yet. Give me a chance to put something together to show you. When things settle down and that bastard is behind bars, I'd appreciate it if you'd at least hear me out."

"I will. When this is done."

"Thank you. I appreciate it." Tony held his hand out to Dane. "We'll catch up later. Glad to see you walking around without crutches."

"Me, too."

"You need any help securing your place, you let me know. I can lend a hand."

"Thanks. I think we're covered right now, but I'll let you know if that changes."

Bell hugged her sister one last time, then waited for them to drive away. She needed a minute to collect her thoughts and absorb all that happened.

"You okay, sweet thing?" Sammy asked.

"Why didn't you ever tell me?"

"What good would it do you to know this land belonged to you after your grandmother died? Wouldn't have changed your situation any. You're a good girl. You took care of that viper these past years. You earned this land, but more than that, you deserve this land because it's your birthright. Your father denied you that by not giving you his name. Your grandfather hated him for that alone. A man's name, his word, his integrity are what makes him a man. Your grandfather despised your father for turning his back on his family, on you. He loved you something fierce, sweet thing."

Bell went into Sammy's arms and held him close. "Thank you for keeping this for me."

"I wish I'd done more. I checked on you, sure, but I could have gotten that old bat to do better by you if I'd tried."

"Don't. You looked after me and did what you had to do for your family. I did okay on my own." Bell didn't begrudge Sammy for looking after his own at the time. Rory, Ford, and Colt's parents died on a treacherous road in a snowstorm when the hillside gave way and buried their car in an avalanche. They froze to death before help arrived. Sammy took over raising the young boys on his own.

"Aw, you turned out all right, I guess, sweet thing," he teased.

Rory laughed with his grandfather. She smiled, despite the difficult morning she'd had.

"Come on, Granddad. We need to head up and check on Ford and Colt."

"Got a surprise for you, sweet thing. You done here?"

"For now." She let her gaze fall on the wrecked

house. She thought of all she'd lost, and how much she'd gained with one letter from her grandfather. Even without Dane's love, she'd be full. She'd been accepted and loved by a kind and generous man. He'd seen past what she represented to who she was. It had taken twenty-six years, but she finally felt a part of her family.

"Bell?" Dane called her out of her thoughts.

"Yeah?"

"I'm sorry for your loss, sweetheart."

Not for her grandmother but for her grandfather. She hadn't really remembered him. Today, he came into her life and left it all at once. She mourned him. She wanted to celebrate him in some way. She'd have to think about it. Right now, she felt numb. Her mind didn't want to think anymore. Her heart couldn't take it either.

Dane took the papers from her hands and placed them gently back into the box. Something rattled when he closed the lid. He opened the box again. She peeked inside, pushing the papers aside to reveal her grandfather's ring. A simple, thick gold band for a man who loved his simple life. She slipped it on her thumb and held her hand to her chest over her heart. She let the tears fall.

She leaned into Dane's chest, and he wrapped his arm around her, holding the box under his other arm at his side. He kissed her on the head and let her cry all over him. Such a good man. How could she ever have thought he'd never be serious about anything or anyone?

It didn't take them long to get home. When they pulled into the driveway ahead of the sheriff's vehicle parked at the end of the drive to watch the road, she gasped.

"What are the Kendricks doing?"

"Building you a new chicken coop. Looks like they're just about done. Go see."

Bell handed the wood box into Dane's outstretched hands. She jumped down from the truck and rushed over to the men. She knelt next to the two crates of chickens and peeked inside. Seven full-grown Dorking chickens and eight Buckeye chicks.

"You'll have eggs in no time, sweet thing."

"You guys, this is too much. I don't know how to thank you."

"You just did," Rory said, handing Ford another piece of wood to trim out the door to clean out the coop.

"This will see you through a lot of years," Colt said, tapping in another staple to hold the chicken wire in place.

Ford stood back and surveyed their work. "I'll grab the nesting boxes out of my truck. Colt, you put up the perches. All you need to do, Bell, is lay in some straw along with the woodchip bedding we brought and put your birds in here. You're all set until the temperatures start to drop. You might need a heat source, but I think you've got good insulation and ventilation in this design."

"I love it."

Dane and Rodrigo came out of the stables with the straw and a stack of newspaper. They all worked together to finish the coop. She did the honors and let the chickens out of their crate. They scratched at the ground in the fenced-in area. A couple found their way up the ramp and into the coop to scope out the nesting boxes. She stared at them flitting about the pen as she let the day settle in her mind.

Rory, Ford, Colt, and Sammy stood behind her. She turned to face the men and smiled, despite the sheen of tears in her eyes. "Thank you for this. You don't know how much it means to me."

"Be safe, sweet thing. Listen to Dane. Stay close to

the house and always with someone." Sammy hugged her close. "I'll be by to check on you like I always do."

"I'd like that a lot."

"We'll be seeing you," Rory said, giving her a pat on the shoulder. Ford and Colt followed suit.

They drove away in their trucks. Dane held his hand out to her. She took it and walked with him back to the house.

"So, fried chicken for dinner," he teased.

She laughed. "No. Not tonight."

He held the door for her. "I'll make you some lunch. Why don't you sit in your new chaise and read for a while. After all you've been through this morning, you deserve a break."

Bell stared at the setup Dane had made for her when he brought the wood box into the house. Alongside the chaise, he'd put a small round table with the wood box, the silver framed photo of her with her grandfather, and two books stacked on top. She moved closer and read the titles. *The Count of Monte Cristo* and *The Three Musketeers*.

"How did you know?"

"When I went into your room, those were two of the titles beside your bed. I figured they had to be your favorites. I asked Ella and Gillian to include them in the books they bought you."

Bell turned and went up on tiptoe, hugging Dane close. "I don't deserve you."

"Yes, you do. I'm working on deserving you."

"Done. You have been the best first boyfriend ever."

"Good, then you'll never need another."

She cupped his strong, rough jaw in her hands and looked him in the eyes. "I only want you."

He kissed her gently, but the heat turned to a need

they both gave into, holding each other close and losing themselves in the moment. Dane pressed his forehead to hers, breathing deep.

She didn't want to lose this closeness. "How about I help you with lunch, and we watch one of those shows you're always talking about on TV?"

"I'm corrupting you with TV."

"We'll snuggle and maybe make out."

"Maybe?"

"Definitely." She smiled up at him.

He traced his finger over her forehead. "That's better."

She smirked. "You know we're going to make out."

"No. You smiling again is better. I hate it when you're sad."

Bell smoothed her hands over his chest. "You make me happy."

"I'm trying."

"We'll let it be for now." She went up on tiptoe and hugged him close again, his arms wrapped around her, all his strength and kindness easing her mind and heart. "I just want to be with you."

"Done."

They made lunch together and settled on the couch, paper plates with roast beef sandwiches and chips balanced on their laps. Dane found an action adventure movie.

"Lots of explosions, little story line, and mind-numbing fun."

"I'll take it."

She never did see the end of the movie. Instead, Dane pressed her into the couch cushions, laid down the length of her, and made her forget everything but her need and love for him.

CHAPTER 21

Dane sat on the patio at Wolf Ranch, watching Justin and Bell out in the field playing with Justin's dog, Charlie, and Ella's dog, Bentley. Justin and Bell threw balls, and the two dogs took off after them. Justin laughed when Bentley jumped up on him and tried to stuff the ball into his neck with his mouth. Bell pushed the dog off the boy, took the ball from Bentley, and handed it to Justin to throw again.

Blake and Gillian were inside with Gillian's grandparents, the Kendricks, and Dane's parents. Ella sat on the stone ledge watching the two play.

Gabe sat beside Dane, staring at him.

"What?" Dane finally asked, tired of the scrutiny.

"You're in love with her."

Dane raised one eyebrow. "Yeah. So?"

"So, is this a forever kind of thing, or I'll-let-it-ride-for-now kind of thing?"

"You ever seen me do the I'll-let-it-ride-for-now thing?"

Gabe narrowed his eyes. "No. So it's all or nothing?"

Dane stared at his love, standing in the field, and

couldn't think of spending a single day without her. "I'm all in."

"Huh." Gabe took a sip from his drink, a thoughtful look in his eyes.

"What is that supposed to mean?"

"I never thought you'd fall this fast and hard."

"Why? You did for Ella. Blake did for Gillian. Why can't I have that with her?"

"She's not the type of woman I ever thought you'd go for, but she is kind of perfect for you," Gabe said. Dane had said something similar to him about Ella.

"Because she doesn't let me get away with any BS?"

"That. You've changed these last weeks you've spent with her. You're more thoughtful. Settled."

"Aren't those good things?"

"I thought you'd have a hard time transitioning back to ranch life. The daily grind. But you seem . . . what's the word? Happy."

Dane smiled and shook his head. "I am happy. The ranch is a work in progress. I've got another week in this brace and a couple more of physical therapy after that. Bell took off the next two weeks of work. After the funeral on Sunday, I thought I'd take her away on a short vacation."

"Where do you want to go? I'll set it up," Ella offered.

"Ella, you are not the family travel planner. I can do it myself," Dane replied. When Ella frowned, he explained, "Thanks for offering, but I want to do it and surprise her."

"Taking her away from here won't solve the Rowdy problem," Gabe said.

"No, but if she's not here, he can't hurt her."

"How is she doing now that she met her father?" Ella asked.

"You tell me. How does it feel to know your own family hates you? How do you cope with that? The man acted like she's a complete stranger. It made me sick to hear the way he spoke to her without any compassion or . . . I don't know, feeling."

"Finding out about her grandfather must have helped," Ella said. "I had my sister. She had her grandfather."

"But Bell doesn't have any memories of him like you do of Lela. She drifts away on her sadness. I pull her back to me, but I'm afraid it's stronger than me sometimes."

Ella turned and stared at Bell, standing in the field looking off into the distance. Dane felt her loneliness and sadness from here.

"Give her time," Ella said. "It's a lot to reconcile. Hardships like this are even more difficult when it's family. Betrayal like that is never expected and so hard to get over."

"I think she might have an easier time getting over it. She expected her father to dismiss her. You never expected your uncle to come after you."

Gillian and Blake walked out on the patio. "Time to eat."

Gabe rose from his seat and grabbed Ella's wrist, pulling her up and over his shoulder. He stood tall, and she screamed and laughed at the same time, smacking him on the butt to put her down. "You can't carry me like this anymore."

"Why not? Now I've got you right where I want you." Gabe gave her a smack on the butt.

"Put me down." Ella's voice rose with concern. "I'm pregnant."

Gabe hurried to put her back on her feet gently. He stared down at her. "What?"

"I'm pregnant."

"You're sure? The last two months you didn't say anything . . ."

Ella pressed her fingers to his lips. "I'm sure."

Gabe confessed to Dane weeks ago that they'd been trying for the last six months to get pregnant but had only been disappointed. The smile on his brother's and Ella's faces told him how much they wanted this.

"You're pregnant," Gabe repeated. "We're having a baby."

"Yes and no."

"What?" Gabe's eyes narrowed with concern.

"Yes, I'm pregnant, but not with one baby. Two."

"Twins?"

"I'm about seven weeks along. I had an ultrasound yesterday when I went to town, and you thought I only went grocery shopping. The doctor confirmed."

"Twins." That single word held all the surprise and awe showing on Gabe's face.

"Genetically speaking, the odds are much higher for a twin to have twins," Bell said, stepping up beside Dane. "Congratulations."

The congratulations rang out from everyone.

Dane's mother joined them on the patio and hugged Ella close. "Just think, it won't be long before we'll have three new members of the Bowden family, between you and Gillian giving birth. They'll grow up together and play together."

"I'll be an uncle to three babies," Justin announced.

Bell looked up at Dane. "You're going to be an uncle to a lot of little ones soon."

Somewhere inside, a piece of him wanted her to tell

him he'd be a father soon. He hadn't known he'd wanted that at this point in his life, but seeing his family surrounding them, Gillian's belly growing, knowing Ella carried two more Bowden babies, he wanted it very much. He wondered how Bell felt about having a baby and starting a family. Did she want that for herself after the way she'd been raised and treated by her own family? He didn't know and wasn't sure how to ask her.

The thought of spending his life with her and never having kids made him feel unfulfilled. He wanted her to be his wife and the mother of his kids. He wanted to have it all with her. He hoped she wanted that, too.

"Come on, the table is set, the food is getting cold. Let's eat and celebrate all we have to be thankful for this Thanksgiving," his mother said.

Everyone went inside, but Bell held Dane's arm to make him wait.

"What is it, sweetheart?"

"I just wanted to tell you that I am the most thankful for having you in my life."

Her honesty melted his heart. "I'm the lucky one, Bell." He kissed her softly, remembering his whole family was inside watching them out the giant windows.

He took her hand to walk with her into dinner. Before they got to the door, she asked, "Does it make you nervous that all of your brothers either are or are about to be fathers?"

"No. Why would it?"

"This from the man who has a drawer full of condoms next to his bed."

"Any time you want me to keep that drawer shut, all you have to do is say so, sweetheart."

She cocked her head and stared up at him. "That surprises me. You're always so careful."

"Always have been. Doesn't mean I don't want to be a father someday." There, he'd said it out loud, but he still didn't know and couldn't read in her how she felt about having a baby. "What about you?" He held his breath waiting for her answer.

"What? Do I want to have kids?"

"Yes."

"Yes. I think about it a lot. Especially now," she confessed on a whisper and a soft smile.

"You mean now that we're sleeping together all the time. Living together. Getting closer every day."

"Yes."

The relief washed through him. "Then we're thinking the same thing."

She put her hands on his chest and stared up at him. "Are you serious?"

He squeezed her hips, pulled her snug against his body, and looked her right in the eye. "I'm dead serious about you."

Gabe whistled for them to come in.

Dane traced his finger along the side of her face and gave her the God's honest truth. "I love you. You're a part of my life now. You are my future. The one I have because of you. The one I look forward to because of you."

Bell's eyes shined with unshed tears.

He cupped her cheek in his palm. She leaned into his hand. "No more crying, sweetheart. It kills me when you cry."

"Then kiss me."

He didn't need to be told. Kissing her was his pleasure. He did so, keeping in mind they had an audience. She shivered in his arms.

"Let's go. It's getting colder every day," he complained.

Inside, Dane helped her off with her coat. He laid it over the back of the sofa, and they took their seats beside each other at the table. Dane kept her hand in his.

"It's about time you two stopping kissing, and we started eating," Colt said from across the table.

"Jealous?" Dane asked, egging Colt on.

"How did your bachelor dates go?" Ella asked all three of the Kendrick brothers.

"Don't ask," they said in unison.

Everyone around the table laughed.

Dane's father stood at the head of the table and raised his glass of wine. They all followed suit.

"I think we can all agree on the one thing we are thankful for this Thanksgiving. Family."

They all clinked glasses.

Dane leaned into Bell's side and whispered in her ear as she surveyed everyone around the table. He kissed her cheek and squeezed her hand. "Look around you, sweetheart. This is your family. This is where you belong."

CHAPTER 22

Bell stood next to the stall door, petting Dane's favorite horse, Demon. After the funeral service on Sunday, he'd brought her down here and introduced her to all of his beloved horses. He'd saddled Demon, plunked her in front of him, and taken her for a ride. Nervous and scared at first, she'd settled into Dane and the horse's gait. By the time they'd reached the river where they'd first met, she'd relaxed and discovered she loved riding. Dane promised to teach her.

"Hey, sweetheart," Dane called, walking out of a stall down the aisle. One of the horses was sick. Dr. Potts had come to tend to the animal. He walked out of the stall behind Dane. "Give Demon one of those candies on the table beside you," Dane told Bell. "He loves them."

She picked up the roll and peeled one off. "You give him cherry Life Savers."

"He likes them."

"Dr. Bell, looks like you've made a friend." Dr. Potts nodded to the huge horse leaning over the gate trying to get his candy.

"He may be big, but he's a pussycat."

"Dane knows how to tame the meanest of beasts. Demon was quite the biter when he got here."

"Really?"

"Oh yes. Dane's right up there with Blake when it comes to training horses. You have a nice day. I'm headed out, Dane," Dr. Potts called down the aisle.

"See you, Doc. Thanks for coming by and checking on Maggie."

"I'll be back around next week. Call if you need me sooner."

"Will do." Dane stopped beside Bell and gave Demon a pat down his long neck. "Alone at last."

She smiled. "We are never alone. Your guys are just out in the corral working with another horse."

"We're alone enough for me to do this." He leaned down and kissed her softly.

He tried to back her into the stall door, but she sidestepped when Demon nibbled at her hair. To play, she backed away from Dane, and he pursued her with long strides that closed the distance quickly, that wicked smile she loved on his face.

The smile disappeared, and Dane snaked out his hand and grabbed her by the neck to pull her close. "Damnit, I tell those guys every day." He reached behind her and pulled the sharp metal rake from the wall hanger, turned it around, and rehung it so the tines weren't sticking out. If she'd backed into it, she could have been seriously injured. "One of these days, someone is going to get hurt."

"Why don't you hang it down lower, or put it somewhere else?"

"I guess I should, but it's such a convenient place to keep all the tools hung up."

She surveyed the array of shovels and rakes. It made sense to keep them here within easy reach.

A loud whistle went up from one of the guys. Dane narrowed his eyes on her.

"Someone is here. Stay put."

"I'm not staying in here alone. I'm coming with you."

"I'm trying to keep you safe."

"I'm the safest when I'm with you."

He frowned and narrowed his eyes, but took her hand and led her out of the stables. A white van pulled into the driveway. The woman at the wheel got out, rounded the front, and opened the passenger door. She pulled out a blonde toddler from the front seat.

"Kaley," Dane whispered. "What is Mrs. Hubbard doing here?"

Nervous for no reason she could decipher, Bell said, "Let's go find out."

Kaley saw Dane coming and ran for him. Her little legs were still unsteady, but she made it the ten feet to him with a big smile and her arms stretched up to him.

Dane picked her up off her feet and held her to his chest. "Hello, beautiful, how's my girl."

"Da."

"That's right, baby. Almost there. Add a couple more letters to that, and you'll have my full name. You're still the prettiest girl I've ever seen." He glanced down at Bell. "Second prettiest to you, sweetheart."

"Such a charmer," she teased, rolling her eyes.

"Hello, Mrs. Hubbard. This is my girlfriend, Dr. Bell. Bell, Brandy's mother, Mrs. Hubbard."

"Patty, please."

"How are you, Patty?" Dane asked.

"Tired, but we made it. I'm sorry to show up out of the blue like this."

Bell eyed the back of the van, full of boxes and furniture. The alarm that went off upon their arrival went off again.

"That's okay," Dane said, kissing Kaley's cheek.

"We need to talk." The serious note in Patty's voice made Dane's smile falter.

"Okay. Come inside." He turned to the house with Kaley still in his arms.

The little girl tugged on his nose and pressed her forehead to his cheek. "Da."

Bell had to admit, they looked really cute together. She didn't have to wonder what he'd be like with his own children. He obviously adored the little girl.

Dane showed Patty into the family room. Dane set Kaley down by the coffee table. Patty pulled a container from the diaper bag. "Do you mind? She's hungry. We've been on the road for hours today."

"Not at all," Dane said.

Patty poured some crackers on the table for Kaley and set her sippy cup next to it. Kaley dug in, grabbing a handful and stuffing them into her mouth.

"One at a time, Kaley," Patty said, smiling at the girl's exuberance. The smile faltered and tears came into her eyes. "She looks so much like her mother."

"Yes, she does," Dane agreed. "I'm sorry for your loss, for what happened to Brandy. Everything. I wish I could have made her memorial service."

Patty waved her hand to brush that aside. "I understand. You've had enough to deal with here with that evil monster Rowdy making trouble. I hate him. I can't believe they haven't found him. He's the one who should be dead. Not my Brandy. He won't stop."

"What do you mean?"

"He's been calling. Making threats. He uses those . . . what do they call them? Burner phones, so the police can't trace the call."

"Is he threatening you?"

"Not me. Kaley. He wants her."

"No way he gets her. The police will lock him up for the rest of his life for killing Brandy and Mrs. Warwick, not to mention the attempted hit-and-run on Bell."

"I realize that, but I can't protect Kaley if he comes back. The police keep watch on our place and me when I'm able to leave my husband in order to run errands and things, but it's not enough. There's something else."

"What?"

She sucked in a deep breath and whispered out, "I'm dying."

"What?" Dane's surprise and concern showed on his face. He went to Patty, sat beside her on the couch, and took her hand. "Brandy never said anything to me."

"I told her the morning she died. She was upset. I can't help but think—" Tears clogged her throat and choked off her words. "That when she died she knew there'd be no one left to look after Kaley. I had no choice but to move her father into a care facility two days ago. That's when we drove here."

"Patty, I don't understand why you came to me. If Rowdy wants to take Kaley, this is the last place you should have brought her."

"I thought Brandy died believing no one would look out for Kaley, but I was wrong. She planned for this eventuality. Oh, it breaks my heart to know she believed that man would go too far one day and kill her. I wish I could have saved her from that man. But she found a way to save Kaley from him."

"How?" Dane asked.

Patty pulled a thick folder from the diaper bag. "Kaley is yours. I brought her here to live with her father. Soon you will be the only family she has left."

Dane's mouth dropped open. He pulled his racing thoughts together. "You can't leave her here with me."

Bell gasped. He glanced at her. The blood drained from her face. She turned on her heel and walked out the front door, slamming it shut behind her. Dane held back the curse burning on his tongue.

"Oh, dear. I'm sorry," Patty said.

"I'll be back in a minute." Dane ran for the door and flew through it.

Dane's footsteps crunched on the gravel as he ran up to Bell. He grabbed her jacket and stopped her in her tracks before she opened the truck door and ran away from him.

"Don't you dare get in that truck and leave without listening to what I have to say."

She turned to face him, her heart torn in two, making her chest ache so bad she could barely breathe. "What is there to say? You just told her that you don't want your daughter. She can't stay here."

Fury flashed in his eyes, but he reined in his temper and gently cupped Bell's cheek. "I cannot tell you how much it hurts me that you think I'd do that."

"You just said—"

"And now I'm going to explain, so shut up and listen. I will forget you could possibly think I'm that heartless because you're looking at this through your past-colored glasses. I'm asking you to look at me. Remember everything you know about me and tell me if you truly think I'd turn my back on my child." He bit out the words. She hated that she'd hurt his feelings, but she still didn't understand why he didn't want his child.

"No. No. But if she's yours, why wouldn't you want her to stay here?"

"Damnit Bell, she isn't mine."

"She calls you Da."

"She's not even two. She can't say Dane. I'm telling you the truth. I am not Kaley's father."

"But you told me you slept with Brandy that one time."

"Yes. I may not be a genius, but I can do the math. I slept with Brandy five months before she got pregnant with Kaley. I used a condom. I always use a condom. You know that.

"The reason I don't want Patty to leave her here with me is that Kaley belongs with her family. You better than anyone should understand that much. I can't take her away from them."

No, Dane would never do that. Family mattered. Friends mattered. Bell pressed her fingertips to her temples. "I'm still confused. Why does she want you to keep Kaley if she's not yours?"

"I was about to find that out when you ran out on me."

"I'm sorry." Her bottom lip trembled and tears welled in her eyes.

He pulled her close and hugged her tight to his body. She snuggled close, hoping she hadn't damaged this wonderful thing they shared and she couldn't live without.

"I know you are, sweetheart. Don't ever run away like that again. If you're upset or mad at me, then say so. I can take it. There's nothing we can't work out."

"I'm sorry I thought the worst."

"Next time ask me what I mean instead of just leaving."

"I will. I promise." She pressed her forehead to his chest and sniffled, holding onto him, afraid to let him go.

"Bell, everything is okay. I'm not mad at you."

"That was a really mean thing I thought about you."

"You had your reasons. I get that. With my reputation, it's not a far reach to think I might have fathered a dozen babies."

"Two dozen," she suggested, raising one eyebrow.

He laughed, knowing she was right. He'd been a complete dog in his day, but he'd changed his ways now that he'd become loyal to her.

"I don't know how you put up with me," she said.

"I'm still the lucky one," he replied, kissing her on top of her head.

She looked up, and he took advantage and kissed her softly. She'd forgotten to grab her jacket on her mad dash out the door. He held her closer to his body to keep her warm and made her burn by taking the kiss deeper, showing her how much he loved her. One misunderstanding wouldn't change that.

"Patty is waiting for us to come back. I am so embarrassed for running out like that."

"Don't be. Let's go find out what's really going on."

"Okay." They walked back up the path and took the stairs up to the porch. Before Dane opened the door she said one more time, "I'm really sorry."

He hugged her close to his side. "I love you, Bell."

"I love you, too."

Patty played with Kaley on the couch, holding her hands and letting her jump on the cushion. She looked over at them when they walked in.

"I'm so sorry I sprang that on you the way I did. Bell, what you must think."

"Why don't you explain why you want to leave Kaley with me," Dane suggested.

"Okay." She took a deep breath and hugged Kaley close. "I have stage four breast cancer. The doctors say I've only got weeks left. No matter what happens, I'd need to find someone to raise Kaley. Brandy made sure that if something happened to her, that person would be you. She never said anything to me. Probably so I wouldn't worry. But I found the papers, and she names you."

Patty handed the folder to Dane. Bell stood beside him and looked over the papers with him.

"Brandy put Dane's name on the birth certificate," Bell said on a gasp.

"I can only think she did that to ensure Rowdy never got custody of Kaley," Patty explained. "She kept a copy of every check Dane sent to her each month."

"To prove he'd been supporting his daughter," Bell guessed. "You've got text messages between you and Brandy where you ask about Kaley and demand she send you photos. Even if Rowdy demanded a DNA test, she's proven that you are the father of record and that you not only took an interest in Kaley but you also supported the child you believed is yours."

"But I know she's not."

"Yes, but she knew you'd keep Kaley from Rowdy. You'd go to court, and you'd say Kaley is yours. You'd fight for her to keep her safe."

"See, now that is the Bell who believes in me. The one who loves me and sees me for who I really am."

"I took those past-colored glasses off and smashed them underfoot."

Dane caressed Bell's cheek, then turned to Patty. "Still, Patty, I can't take Kaley from her family. If you're sick, don't you want to spend as much time with her as you can?"

"I want that more than anything, but I need to be sure she has a home and someone who will love her the way Brandy and I loved her. Dane, I'm asking you to fulfill my daughter's last wish. Take care of her daughter and make sure that man never sees her again."

Dane stared down at Kaley, hugging a stuffed rabbit to her chest, sucking her thumb, and dozing off with her head propped against her grandmother's arm. Such a sweet girl. Too young to have lost her mother and soon her grandmother. She deserved better. She deserved a loving home with family, but if she couldn't have that, how could he say no, when he could give her a good life?

Bell stood beside him, waiting for him to say something. He didn't want to do anything without talking with her first.

"Patty, please excuse us for a minute. I need to talk to Bell."

"Of course. When I came, I expected the decision to be yours alone. I understand that you'll need to make the decision together."

Dane took Bell's hand and dragged her after him to the kitchen. He stopped by the counter and tried to organize his thoughts.

"Why are you hesitating? Tell her you will keep Kaley and raise her as your daughter. You know that is what you want."

"Yes, damnit, it is what I want, but not if I lose you in the process."

Bell's head went back like he'd smacked her. "What?"

"We just started seeing each other . . . what, a month

ago. You've been nearly hit by a car, had your house burned to the ground, lost your grandmother, moved in with me, and now I'm asking you to raise another woman's child."

"So."

"So?"

"I don't understand why you think any of that is your fault, or why that would somehow make me want to leave you. I love you more for wanting to keep Kaley and raise her as your own."

"Not me raise her. Us. As a family." He held his breath, waiting for her answer. He'd ask her to marry him right now, this second, but he held the words back because he didn't want her to think he was asking her just because of Kaley. Too many things had happened all at once. He wanted to ask her the right way, at the right time, and for all the right reasons, which were true right now and would still be true when the timing didn't suck this bad.

"That was a statement, right? Because you can't seriously be asking me if I want to raise Kaley with you when you already know the answer."

"Just say it."

"Yes. I will raise Kaley with you."

He dragged her into his arms and hugged her close, kissing the top of her head. "You won't regret this. I swear, Bell, I'll make you happy the rest of your life."

"I never doubted that you would. I never thought we'd start this early on the kids," she teased. "We're gonna have to work on our communication skills."

He laughed. "Will Smith. *Independence Day*. Nice one, Bell."

She looked up at him, her brow scrunched in confusion. "What are you talking about?"

He laughed under his breath. He should have known better. She didn't get the reference at all. "It's a movie. The guy says that line."

"Oh."

"We'll watch it later tonight after Kaley goes to bed."

"You noticed the car was full of her stuff, too."

"I didn't think she was moving in here, that's for sure."

"Let's go talk to Patty. Which room should we put Kaley in upstairs?"

"I guess the one closest to ours."

"Makes sense. I hope she sleeps through the night," Bell said. "If not, you get the first shift."

"Why me?"

"I'm a doctor. I need my sleep."

"Oh, I see how this is going to be when we have a baby."

"Get used to it."

He didn't know how to tell her how much it meant to him that they could be like this. Have an argument, make up, make serious decisions, and go back to laughing all in the space of half an hour. Life with her would never be dull, but it would be easy.

"Patty," Bell said when they reentered the family room. "Dane and I will of course raise Kaley. With your blessing, when the time is right, I will adopt her."

Patty glanced at Dane, who nodded his agreement. He hadn't thought that far ahead, but it was exactly what he wanted.

"It's such a relief to know Kaley will have a mother and a father. You two seem really good together. I can see how much he loves you," she said to Bell. "You love him, too. A lot, to go along with this."

"Dane and I want the same things. Love and family.

You and Kaley are a part of that now. How long would you like to stay?"

"What?"

"I assume you'll stay at least a few days to get Kaley settled, teach us what we need to know about her, and make arrangements for your care here."

"What?"

"Dane led me to believe your husband's stroke left him incapacitated and mostly unaware of his surroundings."

"Unfortunately, that is the case. I hate to leave him."

"Well, I'm a doctor. I work at the hospital in Bozeman and the clinic in Crystal Creek. With your permission, I could make some calls, find out about a facility here for your husband. I can get you in contact with an oncologist at my hospital, who can review your case and make arrangements for your treatment and care. That way you will be close to Kaley during this difficult time. If you pass, I will continue to oversee your husband's care, and Dane and I will take Kaley to see her grandfather on a regular basis."

Silent tears fell down Patty's cheeks. She didn't say anything.

Bell sat beside her and took her hands. Kaley slept soundly next to them. "Kaley should be with her family for as long as she has you. You should be with your granddaughter and enjoy her while you can. Dane and I will not take her from you. We will do everything we can to show Kaley family sticks together in good times and bad."

Patty turned to Dane. "Hold on to her."

"I am, with both hands."

"I never expected it to go like this. I thought I'd bring her and go home and . . ."

And die, Dane thought what she couldn't bring herself to say. "That's not the way we want it. Bell's right. We're family now. We stick together. So, I'll get my guys and we'll unload Kaley's things and put them upstairs in her new room. I've got a room up there with your name on it. Second door on the right off the stairs. It's only got a double bed right now, but we can get you a table and whatever else you need while you stay here. There's a bathroom right across the hall. When the time comes, Bell will know how to help you with your final arrangements."

"I can't thank you both enough. This is more than I expected. It'll mean a lot of changes, but if I can stay with Kaley as long as possible . . ."

"I'll start unpacking the car. Bell, Patty might be hungry after her long trip."

"Right. Let's go into the kitchen. I'll make you some tea and something to eat. We'll discuss the details, and I'll make some calls."

"Just like that?" Patty asked, still trying to process everything.

"Yes, just like that," Bell confirmed.

God, he loved her so much.

"Ah, is Kaley okay on the couch?" Bell asked.

"She sleeps through just about anything. She'll be fine for at least an hour."

Dane winked at Bell, then headed out the door to get his guys to help unload. Maybe he'd send Rodrigo home with Patty in the next couple of days to help her pack their place and get her back here. It would leave him a man short, but Patty needed the help. On second thought, he'd keep Rodrigo here and call his friend Frank. He had a place on the Nevada-Arizona border. Maybe he and a few of his guys could help out Patty.

Frank knew Brandy from her days following Rowdy on the circuit. Yeah, Dane would call in a few favors.

He whistled for his guys. They walked out of the stables, and he waved them over to the back of the van. He opened the doors and stared at all the stuff.

"What's up, man?" Rodrigo asked.

"My daughter is coming to live with me and Bell." Might as well solidify the story with the people in his life just in case. He didn't think Rowdy would ever get to see Kaley again, but he didn't want Rowdy's family coming and taking her either. Someone like Rowdy didn't start off bad. Dane could only imagine the people he'd come from. "We need to move her into her new room upstairs. You guys mind helping me unload?"

"Sure thing, boss." Rodrigo took two big boxes.

The other three guys grabbed boxes and bags and headed for the house. Dane had good people working for him. Always ready to pitch in where help was needed, even when it fell outside their job. Like watching over Bell.

Dane grabbed a huge garbage bag that weighed a lot less than he expected. He felt the bag with his hand and smiled. Stuffed animals. "Looks like I'm going to have to get used to stepping over toys." He didn't mind. In fact, he couldn't wait. He'd loved hanging out with Kaley and Brandy in the past. This would be different. He'd be responsible for raising her. He'd be her father in every sense of the word but one. She might not have his blood, but she had his heart.

CHAPTER 23

Bell stood in the doorway, watching Patty change Kaley's diaper. After three days, she and Patty had become good friends. It hurt Bell's heart to watch Patty with Kaley, knowing these moments were precious. Soon, Patty would succumb to the cancer inside her. She'd waited too long to get treatment. Not her fault. Just a sad fact of life. Like many women, she'd had other priorities. She'd given herself to her husband, daughter, and granddaughter and forgotten to take care of herself first. A lesson Bell intended to take to heart so she'd be here for Kaley and whatever other children she and Dane had in the future.

Patty lifted Kaley's shirt and blew a zerbert on her belly. Kaley laughed and tried to push her shirt down, but Patty gave her another zerbert. Kaley's giggle filled the room. Bell would remember to do that in the future to help remind Kaley of her grandmother. They'd already taken several pictures. Bell emailed them to a shop in town to be printed and framed for Kaley's room. She included a few of the snapshots of Brandy and Kaley together that Brandy had sent to Dane's phone. They'd put them around the house, so that no matter where Kaley went, she'd be surrounded by family. Kaley would know that Bell and Dane considered Brandy and Patty family. Bell would have to get some pictures of Patty's husband.

The room turned out great. Dane had already painted it Cottage Cream. The pine furniture Patty brought suited the room perfectly. The rocking chair got to Bell the most. She imagined Brandy in that chair feeding her child late at night. Such touching and intimate moments mother and daughter shared, gone now that Rowdy had killed Kaley's mother. Bell vowed she'd try to fill that void by loving Kaley as her own.

Kaley's toy box overflowed with stuffed friends. She didn't go in for the baby dolls. No, she had a whole farm and zoo happening in the room. Dane sorted the animals between the toy box and another bin by the crib, Patty pointing out which were her favorites for nighttime and playtime.

Kaley's lavender blanket lay in the crib. The yellow one with the purple violets was probably on the couch where Kaley and Dane watched Looney Tunes this morning. So sweet, they'd shared a bowl of Oh's cereal. Kaley had sat on Dane's lap, mesmerized by Bugs Bunny.

"Look, Kaley. Mommy's here." Bell's heart melted when Kaley put her hands out to her. She'd been hesitant to allow Kaley to call her Mommy so soon after Brandy had disappeared from her life, but Patty insisted they teach Kaley now where she was going to live and who was going to be her mother and father.

Kaley continued to call Dane Da. Now they used Daddy, too, to indicate to her that *Da* meant "Daddy."

They put on happy smiles and played their new parts, hoping that as Kaley adjusted to her new home and new parents, she didn't notice their sadness for all she'd lost and would soon lose.

Bell didn't need time to adjust. She loved Kaley. Once she made the decision to be her mother, every time she looked at the bright-haired little girl she felt it inside. Kaley belonged to her. Even if things didn't work out with Dane, she'd never walk away from Kaley.

She'd assured Patty of that fact.

Patty smiled and shook her head, saying, "No way that man ever lets you go."

"Ma-ma," Kaley said, sitting up on the changing table.

Bell walked over, put her hands under Kaley's arms, and lifted her up, spinning her around in a circle with her legs stretched out in the air. Just like Brandy used to do with her, Patty said.

Kaley landed on her hip, and Bell touched her nose with her index finger. "How's my sweet baby girl."

"Andy. Orse."

"You want to give candy to the horse."

Kaley nodded and kicked her feet.

"Let's go find Daddy. Patty, how are you this morning? I didn't see you at breakfast."

"I slept in for the first time in I don't know how long. Thank you for getting up with this one at the crack of dawn." Patty poked Kaley in the ribs to make her giggle.

"Dane is an early riser to check on the horses and cattle. He brought me Kaley. She slept in our bed for another hour with me, then she shared some cereal with her dad."

"Thank you for doing this. Going along with being Mom and Dad so soon. I know it's not easy."

"I don't want her to ever think I took her mother's place."

"You are so good with her. She'll only know you as her mother. I'm okay with that, because you'll tell Kaley about Brandy."

"I wish I'd known her. I met her once, but I don't have the memories you do."

"I've thought about that. I think I'll get one of those recorders and leave Kaley some messages she can watch throughout her life. Dane suggested it."

"We can pick one up when I take you to your doctor appointment tomorrow."

"Andy. Orse."

"Okay, sweet baby, let's go give Demon some candy."

"Demon!" Kaley yelled.

"Great, the only word she gets right is that one."

Patty smiled and touched Kaley's shoulder. "Tell Dane and his guys to watch what they say around her. You never know which words will become her new favorites."

"Right. You sure you don't want to stay longer? We can move your flight from the day after next to sometime next week."

"Nana." Kaley held out her hands to Patty.

"Go ahead. Take her. She needs all the hugs she can get from you." Bell handed over Kaley, despite Patty's trying her best to let go little by little.

"She'll get lots of hugs from Dane's family today. What time are they coming?" Patty asked.

"In about half an hour. I'm kind of nervous having them all here at the same time. Dane's got such a large family."

"It's growing even larger with his two sisters pregnant."

"Kaley will have cousins to play with for sure. It won't be easy for Kaley no matter what you do, so fill in this time with as much love as you can."

They stepped out onto the porch and found Dane standing in the middle of the chicken coop with a hammer and some extra wire.

"Da," Kaley called, pointing at Dane.

"Let's go see what Daddy is doing with Mommy's chickens."

Lacking the energy and strength she needed to carry Kaley, Patty set her down and took her hand. Kaley tugged on Patty's hand to get free.

"Da."

"Go get him," Patty said, releasing Kaley's hand. She ran for Dane, calling Da, but Dane couldn't hear her this far away.

Bell whistled like Dane and his guys did all the time to get their attention when they were far away. Dane's head shot up, concerned she'd alerted him to some threat. Instead, she pointed to Kaley on the run toward him. His smile spread across his face and warmed Bell's heart. His delight in the little girl touched a place deep in her heart. Here was a man who knew how to love and love well.

She and Patty stopped several yards away from the chicken coop and rescued a wayward chick that had escaped through a hole in the fencing. Funny, it looked like someone had kicked it in, intent on destroying it. Bell studied the coop. One of the doors had been ripped off, the hinges broken. One of the Dorkings lay dead in the corner.

Bell didn't want to frighten Patty. Her suspicions that it wasn't an animal who'd gotten into the pen and coop were unfounded. She was jumping to conclusions because of the threat Rowdy posed every second of every day. Right?

"They are so cute. My grandmother raised her own

chickens in Kansas. I used to love to visit the farm," Patty said.

Bell patted the soft little chick in her hands with her thumbs to calm it. As she held her hands out so Patty could take the chick, a movement past Patty's shoulder caught her attention. The barrel of a rifle pointed right at Patty's back. The dark silhouette of a man standing just inside the stables shifted and stilled.

With only seconds to decide what to do, Bell shifted so the person in the stables couldn't see her speak to Patty.

Bell reached out and held Patty's arm to keep her from bolting. "Take the chick. Walk over to Dane. Act like nothing is wrong. Give him the chick and tell him that Rowdy is in the stables with a rifle pointed right at you. Get Kaley and yourself to safety."

"What are you going to do?"

Bell snuck a peek around Patty. Sure enough, Rowdy held up his hand and crooked his finger for her to come to him.

"Go now. Take Kaley up to the road where the sheriff's vehicle is parked."

Bell stepped around Patty and walked toward Rowdy and certain death. Fear washed through her but turned to a determination she'd never felt when Kaley called out, "Ma-ma."

"Bell," Dane called when she didn't turn their way.

Instead, she walked right into the hands of a killer, knowing only one of them would leave the stables. She'd do anything and everything to keep her promise to raise and love Kaley. She'd do anything to keep the life and love she'd found with Dane.

She stepped into the stables, her eyesight off due to the darker interior. To give herself a moment to adjust, she went on the defensive.

"You killed Brandy and my grandmother. Why the hell would you be so stupid as to show up here?"

"Don't call me stupid, you fucking bitch." Rowdy stepped out from behind a feed bin.

The smell hit her all at once. Stale beer, cigarettes, acrid body odor, musty earth, and the unmistakable smell of rotting flesh. He held the rifle pointed at her chest, his left hand holding the barrel. His right hand, at the trigger, was completely covered in third-degree burns. Red and raw like meat, blackened at the edges and scabbed. He could barely close his hand around the gun. Infected, pussy blisters formed at his wrist and on some of his fingers. The burns went so deep that a few of his bones were exposed.

"That looks bad. Turn yourself in now, and maybe you'll keep your hand. If not, it'll rot off, and you'll die from sepsis. You need to go to a hospital."

"And end up in a fucking cell. No way. I'm here to tie up loose ends and see that fuck gets what's his. He thinks he can take my woman, my child, and get away with it."

"Dane and Brandy were friends. Can you say the same? Did you care for her, keep her safe, love her the way she deserved to be loved?"

"She was mine!" His warped mind only saw Brandy as a possession. Not a person to be respected and loved. Something to hold on to and show the world, *Look what I have*.

"You made her afraid of you. You made her want to stay as far away from you as possible."

"I loved her."

Angry he couldn't see the truth, she let her fury fly with her words. "You hit her. That's not love. That's abuse. That's you trying to be in control when you are not. That gun doesn't put you in control. You're sweating like crazy because you've spiked a fever. I'll bet you're suffering from dizziness. Soon, you'll pass out. Right now, the only thing keeping you going is your lust for revenge against someone who did nothing to you."

"How about I just shoot you now, bitch, and get it over with?" His finger contracted on the trigger.

She held her breath, trying to think past the fear clouding her mind. "Because we both know you're waiting for Dane to come in here. What fun would it be to kill me without him being here to see it?" She hoped that made him wait.

"Exactly."

She tried not to show her relief that she'd bought herself a few more moments.

Rowdy's hands shook. He swayed side to side, his feet wide to steady himself. Desperate, Rowdy had chosen this place and time to make his last stand, because he didn't have much time left if he didn't get medical help.

"We both know one other thing."

"What the fuck is that?"

"Dane will never let you get away with this."

Patty walked up to Dane at the fence. She dropped the chick at his feet and took Kaley from his arms.

"Where is Bell going?"

"Rowdy is in the stables with a rifle pointed this way. I'm taking Kaley to the sheriff's car up on the road."

"Shit."

"Sit," Kaley repeated.

He almost swore again. "Get moving. I'll get Bell."

"Be careful."

Dane didn't know if Rowdy could see him or not. He took a chance and went the opposite way, along the back of the toolshed, to come around the stables from the other side. Rodrigo had been working with the horses in the stables. Dane wondered how Rowdy had gotten onto the property without being seen by one of his guys. They'd been so vigilant these last days, especially with Kaley on the property. Gabe had even sent Dane a couple more guys. He checked the house and saw them keeping watch from the front and back porch. They wouldn't have been able to see the stable doors from their vantage point.

Fuck. He should have put a man in the hayloft.

No sense beating himself up about it now. He needed to think and figure out the best way to take Rowdy down.

He whistled to the guys up at the house and pointed to the stables. He put his index finger to his lips to indicate they should be silent. He pointed two fingers at his eyes, then back at them, letting them know if they moved down toward the stables, Rowdy would see them. He pointed toward the road, indicating they should walk away from the stables and come around the way he'd gone, in order to stay out of Rowdy's sight.

Rodrigo lay sprawled in the dirt at the back of the building. Blood seeped out of a nasty wound on his forehead. Dane checked his pulse, relieved the man was still alive.

Bell's calm voice drifted out to him. He needed to get to her, so he reluctantly left his friend.

With his back pressed to the stable wall, he poked his head around the side and caught a glimpse of Bell standing in front of Rowdy, the rifle trained on her chest. Rowdy looked like shit.

They stood in the center aisle, past the stalls. No way for him to get inside without being seen.

With nothing but bad options to choose from, he went with the one thing that always got him through. Attitude. Sometimes you had to fake your way through a situation to come out on top. When you rode a hulking beast of a bull, you got on, gritted your teeth, and hoped for the best. Right now, he'd set his fear for Bell aside and do what he had to do to keep her safe.

Dane walked into the stables with languid strides, like he had all the time in the world. Rowdy's gaze shot to him. Bell tried to step away, but Rowdy dropped the gun and grasped Bell's arm, pulling her to his chest. He caught her by the throat, his fingers digging into her skin just under her jaw. She grabbed his arm with both of hers, trying to pull it away. Rowdy pulled a wicked hunting knife from his belt with his mangled hand. He pressed it to her side and winced in pain. His hand looked bad.

"Come on, man, you don't want to do that." Dane took his time closing the distance between them. "Let her go before this goes too far."

"It's already gone too far. They're going to put me in jail. Well, I'm not going. It's time someone showed you. I'm going to make you pay. You can't take what's not yours."

"Come on, man, we used to be good friends. I'd never take anything from you."

"You took every bull riding prize. You took Brandy. You took my daughter. I saw the phone messages. I saw the way you talked to her, telling her you'd take care of her. She was mine. Not yours."

"She was yours, man. One hundred percent. Brandy loved you, but you pushed her away. You hurt her. All I did was help a friend."

"That's not true. You were fucking her behind my back. You had a dozen women at a time and still you had to have her."

"No, Rowdy. Brandy was my friend. You accused her of sleeping with every cowboy who crossed her path. Half the time she didn't even know the guy. Instead of spending time with her, you went to the bar and drank yourself stupid, flirting with waitresses instead of the woman you had at home."

"That's not true," he whined, like a child who'd gotten caught in a lie.

"You know it is. Why the hell did you take this so far? Why didn't you sober up and talk to her? Why the hell did you kill her?"

"She didn't want me. I didn't mean to hit her that hard. All I wanted is my family."

Dane shook his head and tried to keep Rowdy's focus on him. "Now that's never going to happen. You threw it all away the second you hit Brandy the first time, the tenth time, the hundredth time, until the last time, when you killed her. Over and over again you showed her she could never be with you and be safe."

"I tried to talk to her. She wouldn't listen. I told her I'd changed."

"Right. Then you hit her again."

"She pissed me off. It's her fault for not keeping her damn mouth shut and doing what she's told."

"Women are like that. They've got their own minds. They do what they want to do." Dane rolled his eyes, letting the sarcasm in his words show on his face.

"All I wanted is to be with her. I wanted to see Kaley." Rowdy pressed the knife into Bell's side. Bell screamed and struggled, but Rowdy held her tighter and made her stop.

Dane held up his hand. "I can make that happen. Here's the thing, man, you're holding the woman I love. I want her back. In one piece. So drop the knife. You and me, we'll go get a beer, and you can see Kaley. She's here."

Too late. Rowdy's eyes searched both exits. Two deputies on both sides of the stables moved in and held their guns trained on Rowdy and Bell. Rowdy eyed the cops, his skin turning a sickly, pasty white. Sweat glistened on his skin. His scorched hand trembled with the knife at Bell's side.

"They'll never let me go. They'll put me in a cell to rot."

"Arrested is a hell of a lot better than dead," Dane pointed out.

"Right, I'll be in a cell, and you'll have her, my kid, a fucking happy life. The one I should have had with my girl and my kid. You took her. I want her back."

"I can't bring Brandy back, but you can see Kaley. Put the knife down, and we'll go see her. You don't want to frighten her, right?"

"You fucking lie. You won't let me see Kaley. I'll fucking kill this bitch, then you."

Unreasonable asshole. Didn't he see there was no way out of this? No, Rowdy meant to take this all the way. He pressed the knife into Bell's side again. She gasped and flinched.

"You'll finally fucking pay," Rowdy yelled.

The rage consumed Dane. "If that's how you want it, then come on," Dane yelled. "You want a piece of me, then you come here and take it from me like a man. Not some fucking pansy-ass who preys on women. Bell never did anything to you."

Rowdy dug the knife into Bell's side again. Dane's

stomach tightened with dread. His heart slammed into his ribs, but he held it together. He had to for Bell's sake.

He hoped the deputies didn't do anything stupid, like shoot with Bell in the way.

"I'll gut her and drop her at your feet like women do every time you give them that damn smile."

Dane held Rowdy's gaze and smiled with enough venom behind it to make Rowdy's eyes go wide and fill with fear. "You draw one drop of blood from her, asshole, and you'll be dead before you take your next breath."

"That's what you think," Rowdy warned, but his voice trembled. "Fuck you!" Rowdy cried as he swiped the knife along Bell's side. Blood bloomed over her white sweater like a crimson flower as she pushed away and fell to the ground.

Dane threw a right hook into Rowdy's nose, breaking it with a sickening snap, just like Gabe taught him. Rowdy tried to swing the knife again, but Dane planted both hands on his shoulders and shoved him up against the wall as far from Bell as possible . . . right into the metal rake the guys kept hanging spike-side out. Several tines punctured Rowdy's neck. His eyes grew huge as blood spurted out of his mouth and trickled to his chest while he gasped for breath.

Stunned, Dane released him. The rake came unhooked from the wall. Rowdy's legs gave out, and he fell on his ass on the floor, his head bowed forward. The knife slipped from his hand and clinked on the concrete.

Dane knelt next to him and whispered, "I warned you, motherfucker."

The two deputies shoved Dane aside. Bell grabbed

him from behind and pulled him back. He turned and took her in his arms, hugging her close, with Rowdy dead at his back.

"Are you okay? How bad are you hurt?" He held her away and peeled her sweater up to look at the gash on her side just above her hip.

Bell stared down and touched the nasty cut with her fingertips, prying it apart and hissing in pain. "It's not that bad. Maybe needs a few stitches. That's all. I'm fine."

"You're not fucking fine. You're bleeding."

"First, stop swearing. Second, face it, I'm better than him." She cocked her head in Rowdy's direction.

One of the sheriff's deputies checked out Bell. A second bent and checked Rowdy's pulse, then shook his head no to the other officers.

Dane wanted to feel remorse, but all he felt was relieved the asshole was dead and would never harm anyone again. So relieved to have Bell in his arms safe and relatively unharmed, he hugged her close again and kissed her on the head, despite the paramedics who'd arrived seconds ago and were trying to staunch the bleeding with bandages.

"You need to go to the hospital," he said, wincing when she hissed in pain.

"Uh, I'm a doctor. I can sew myself up."

"Oh God, please don't do that."

"We'll walk you out to the ambulance and clean that out, Dr. Bell. If you'd like, we can drive you in to the clinic."

"I'll take her," Dane said.

"Mr. Bowden, there are a lot of people outside who'd like to see you and Dr. Bell," one of the officers said.

"My family is here to meet Kaley," Dane said, running a hand over his head, remembering the party they'd planned to welcome Kaley to the family.

"Go get Kaley. She's probably scared. See your family. I'll get this cleaned up and be back soon."

"I'm not letting you out of my sight. They can stick around and get to know Patty and Kaley until we get back."

She kissed him. Long and soft and laced with all her love. He took it in and let it fill him up. She kissed her way up his jaw to his ear and whispered, "Thank you for what you did. Are you okay?"

"I'm fine."

She cupped his face and stared into his eyes. "Are you sure?"

"I'm better than great. I have you."

CHAPTER 24

Bell stood in the midst of the Christmas morning melee and wondered why she'd ever agreed to host Christmas for Dane's entire family, when she'd never had a family gathering of this size and scope. Gifts covered half the room. Torn wrapping paper covered the other half. Kaley opened all her gifts and tossed them aside, finding it more fun to toss the paper and ribbons than to actually play with any of her new toys. In fact, she sat inside a huge box filled with Styrofoam popcorn, covering herself up and tossing it in the air like snow.

Gabe, Blake, and their father sat on the sofa, watching a football game, which Dane had recorded. Their gifts were stacked on the floor. Gillian, five months into her pregnancy, held one hand to her round belly and the other on Justin's back, looking over his shoulder as he played with his new tablet.

Joan and Patty sat in chairs by the window, quietly drinking tea and talking. Bell, Dane, Kaley, and Patty visited with Patty's husband at the care facility in Bozeman yesterday. Patty's hair had all fallen out due to the chemotherapy that might prolong her life a few more precious months but wouldn't save it. She wore her new purple cap with the white flower Kaley picked out with Bell. Patty smiled down at Kaley with a mix of joy and sadness. Patty caught Bell's eye. Bell read the look. This would be her last Christmas with Kaley, but Kaley would be in good hands and surrounded by family.

A family that kept growing. Ella walked out of the kitchen with a mug of hot chocolate, her newest craving now that she was a few months into her pregnancy. She went to Gabe and sat on his lap. He hugged her close and slid his hand over her small baby bump. Ella turned her head and kissed his forehead. So sweet.

Dane sat on the hearth, his stack of opened presents and hers next to him. He loved the new Black Stetson she'd gotten him, since his had gotten ruined during the bull riding championships. He didn't have the brace anymore. He walked with a slight limp, but his leg had completely healed. He loved being back to work on the ranch and riding. He loved it even more when she and Kaley went with him. He'd even bought Bell a horse, a gentle mare she loved and named Daisy. When Dane mocked the name, she told him she'd always wanted a horse named Daisy. He just smiled and kissed her.

Dane rose, snagged the TV remote from the table, and paused the game.

"Hey, we're watching that," Blake grumbled.

"Hold on a second. I need to do something." Dane closed the distance between him and Bell and took her hand. "Did you enjoy Christmas?"

"It's like nothing I've ever seen." She scanned the chaos in the room. She loved it that everyone around her smiled with warm eyes on her, knowing growing up, Christmas had never been like this.

"I bet you're wondering why I didn't give you your gift yet."

"Oh, you didn't have to get me anything. I loved all my presents from your family. Really, thank you everyone. I got more gifts today than I did my whole life." Tears stung the backs of her eyes. She'd never known such kind and loving families existed. "Your generosity is truly overwhelming."

"We love you, Bell," Dane's mother said. "You're family."

Bell smiled through the overwhelming emotions roiling inside her. She blinked back the tears.

Dane squeezed her hand to pull her attention back to him. He brushed away the tear that escaped her lashes and fell down her cheek.

"My family gave you a lot of really nice things. My gift to you is a little bit different. It's something you always wanted but never got. Something I will only ever give once, and only to you, but you can use it every day for the rest of your life."

"What?" she asked, confused.

"My last name." Dane knelt on one knee and held a black velvet box up to her with a huge diamond engagement ring inside.

Silent tears spilled down her cheeks. She pressed her fingers to her mouth, holding back the sob, and time stopped.

"I love you. I want you to be my wife. Your mother never got past the B names, and I'm hoping you'll do the same and say you'll marry me and be Dr. Bell Brittany *Bowden*. Will you marry me?"

"Yes," she gasped out. Her knees buckled, and she fell into him, hugging him close and crying all over his shoulder. He kissed the side of her head a hundred times and brushed his big hand over her hair to soothe her. She couldn't help it. This man loved her, wanted to make a life with her. He wasn't giving her just his name but also the love and family she never thought she'd have.

Dane set her back on her heels in the middle of all the Christmas paper and bows and slid the ring on her shaking hand. He kissed her fingers, then cupped her face, leaned in, and kissed her socks off.

The room exploded with a round of clapping. Congratulations went on for five minutes, interrupted by the doorbell.

The Kendricks came calling to deliver presents to Bell, Dane, and Kaley. Sammy flirted outrageously with Patty and Joan. Rory, Ford, and Colt grabbed chairs from the dining room table Bell and Dane picked out weeks ago. The brothers set the chairs up behind the sofa to catch the last half of the football game with Dane's brothers.

Katherine and Tony showed up a half hour later, their hands filled with gifts, too.

Shopping for all these people had been exhausting, but seeing their faces and watching the joy come over everyone made it all worth it.

Bell fell into bed that night and held her hand up to the moonlight streaming in through the windows. The soft light caught the brilliant diamond and made it sparkle.

"Put that thing down before you blind someone."

Dane jumped onto the bed beside her, landing on his stomach and making her bounce. She giggled and smiled over at him. He wrapped his arm over her belly and propped himself up on his other elbow, his cheek planted in his palm. The happiness in his eyes and smile made her insides flutter with excitement.

"When are you going to marry me?" Dane asked.

"Until today, I might have said let's go to Vegas and get married tomorrow."

"I like that plan. It's where we met. Again."

"After having everyone over today, our family and friends surrounding us, I want to get married here with all of them."

"That's an even better plan, even if I do have to wait longer for you to be my wife."

"I love you."

"Oh yeah? Show me." He shifted over and lay down the length of her. She spread her legs wide to accommodate his big frame. He held himself off her chest on his forearms and stared down at her. "I love you so much."

His head dipped, and he kissed her softly on the lips. So much tenderness in the simple touch, but it sent a wave of heat through her body. With every new kiss and caress, he sparked her nerves like a flame to fuse. All that heat traveled through her body and pooled low in her belly, gathering energy like a storm ready to shoot a bolt of lightning.

Dane took his time, building that ball of energy into a crackling, living thing inside of her with soft strokes and hot, wet kisses. The storm moved through her. When he finally sank into her, she welcomed him with a soft moan.

The end came like the storm surge. It washed over her all at once, like crashing waves that pulsed through his body into hers. When they subsided, Dane relaxed in her arms, his warm breath in her hair and at her neck. His weight sank into her, and she soaked up his warmth. He rolled to her side, gathered her close to his chest, and kissed the top of her head.

"I love you, sweetheart."

"Thank you, Dane, for a wonderful day and this amazing life we're building together. I am so lucky. You, Kaley, and your family are such a gift in my life. My grandfather hoped I'd find love and hold on to it and those things would fill me up. I am so full, my heart overflows with love for you and all the blessings in my life."

"You have filled up my heart and my life with everything I never knew I was missing until I found you. I'm the lucky one."

EPILOGUE

Bell could barely contain her excitement, watching Kaley blow the candles out on her birthday cake. Two years old. The time had gone so fast over the last four months since Christmas. She and Dane were married last month on the ranch. They'd used the snowplow and cleared a piece of land out back, where they'd erected a huge tent with a wood floor. She'd loved the round tables, with their white tablecloths and roses in antique silver ice buckets. Dozens of votive candles filled the tables, and spotlights pointed at the tent walls cast a soft glow over the room. Heaters kept their family and close friends warm in the chilly early spring temperatures, but all she'd needed was the smile Dane sent her when he stared at her walking down the aisle on Sammy's arm. So sweet, Sammy stood in for his good friend, her grandfather, and had given her away. Katherine, round with her pregnancy, stood beside her at the altar as her matron of honor. Tony struck a deal with her to lease part of her land and Dane's that connected to the smaller property they owned. It would allow Tony to expand his business. Bell and her sister had grown closer, visiting each other often, especially now that Bell had taken Ella's offer of a full-time job at the new clinic. She loved it there, and she loved getting home early to spend time with Dane and Kaley. She'd given up filling her days with work. Now she couldn't wait to get home to her husband and daughter.

Dane smiled at her from across the table as everyone sang "Happy Birthday" to Kaley. That smile never failed to warm her heart. He'd set her ablaze with a searing kiss when the preacher announced them husband and wife. He'd held her so tightly that she hadn't been able to breathe. After the kiss, he'd pressed his forehead to hers, stared into her eyes, and said for the first time, "I love you, Dr. Bowden." The name he'd given her. The name she'd always been waiting for.

Gabe, Blake, and Caleb had given Dane a slap on the back and a hug before they'd walked back down the aisle past Dane's parents and Ella, late in her pregnancy and anxious for her twin daughters, Lela and Amanda, to be born. Gillian had been there, too, holding her newborn son, Casey.

Bell and Dane shared a magical wedding day and night, which resulted in the gift she had for both Dane and Kaley today. She'd held off telling Dane, waiting for this time, when the whole family was together again. A family that had welcomed not only her but Kaley, too, with open arms.

Cheers went up from everyone gathered when Kaley blew out both candles. Kaley and Justin both pulled a candle from the cake and licked the frosting. Justin's dog, Charlie, barked at the boy, wanting a taste of whatever he had.

Kaley bounced on Patty's lap. The treatment Patty received had given her these few precious months. They hoped for a few more. Patty's body grew weaker, but her spirit got stronger every day she got to watch her granddaughter grow happy and healthy.

Kaley accepted Bell and Dane as her mother and father. The transition hadn't been easy. Kaley missed her mother, but they kept reminders of Brandy throughout the house in pictures and a few of Brandy's things. Others, like jewelry, diaries, and other special family items, were tucked away for when Kaley got older.

"Now, Mommy?"

"Yes, sweet baby. Now."

Kaley stood on the chair and pulled the zipper down on her jacket. "See, Daddy. Mommy got new shirt." Kaley pointed to her pink top, which had a picture of a blonde princess that looked an awful lot like Kaley and the words "I'm the big sister!"

Dane stared up at Bell, his arm already around her waist as she stood beside him, watching Kaley. His hand contracted on her hip and his other came up to cover her belly. "Are you kidding me?"

"You're going to be a father. Again."

"We're pregnant?"

"Yes."

The whole family sent up another round of cheers. Dane hugged her close and lifted her right off her feet. He kissed her with so much love that her heart overflowed.

Bell saw that same love in his eyes every day, but it sparkled exceptionally bright when they welcomed their son, Thomas Charles Bowden, into the world. He was named for her grandfather and Dane's father. On that day, she reflected on her life and all the gifts that had come into it since the day she met Dane. Until then, she'd lived an anything but charmed life. Now she had Dane, Kaley, Thomas, their whole family. She truly was lucky in love.

This winter, join Jennifer Ryan as she returns to her *New York Times* bestselling The Hunted Series

EVERYTHING SHE WANTED

Ben Knight is back . . .

Ben Knight has dedicated his life to the law and to protecting those in need. As a child, Ben couldn't save his mother from his abusive father, but he will stop at nothing to save his clients, including the hauntingly beautiful Kate Morrison, who's running from a man who thinks his wealth will let him get away with anything—including murder.

Kate and Ben have crossed paths but have never crossed that professional line. Now that he's agreed to help her put Evan Faraday behind bars where he belongs, she'll have to do the one thing that's never come easy—trust the sexy lawyer with her life and the life of her precious son.

Will Kate learn to trust Ben in time to save herself, and will they have a chance to explore the feelings blossoming between them before it's too late?

**Coming January 2016
from Avon Impulse
Keep reading for a sneak peek!**

"He did it, Kate."

Kate stared at her sister Margo, trying to understand her enthusiasm. Nothing ever went this right in their world, so Kate waited for the hammer to drop.

"He left her. We're going to finally be together like we've wanted for all these months."

"Donald said he'd leave her when you met and practically every month since then. He swore it when Alex was born. What makes this time any different?"

"You're such a pessimist."

"No, I'm a realist."

"The proof is in the safe downstairs. He had his lawyer draw up all these new papers. He told her today. It's done. He isn't going back there. He's staying with Alex and me."

She'd seen Donald downstairs sitting on the sofa, a drink in hand, balanced on the armrest. The solemn look on his face piqued her interest. She'd thought he'd had a bad day at work. Instead his two worlds had collided and he'd had to pick a side. The miserable life he'd been living with a woman he didn't love, and in fact despised, or the woman he adored, who made him happy.

Kate hadn't always been on board with her sister dating a married man. In fact, Kate didn't find out Donald was married until after Alex was conceived. She didn't like Margo keeping secrets from her. It still irritated her. Margo wanted this family so bad that Kate overlooked the imperfections in the relationship and focused on her sister's happiness.

"Why now? Why'd he finally do it?"

"For me and Alex. He wants to be with us."

"There's never been any doubt of that, except for the fact he didn't ask her for the divorce."

"It's complicated."

"That's an excuse, Margo. You have a son."

"So does she."

"Their son is twenty-five. Yours is four months old."

"Donald had to think about the company, the money, everything else they share. It's not a simple thing to divorce when there is so much at stake. Breaking up the company like that, giving her a huge piece and a say in what he spent his life building makes it hard for him. I don't know what happened. We haven't had time to discuss it, but something changed and he gets to keep everything."

"How is that possible? This is California. A community property state. She's entitled to half."

"She signed a prenup. Whatever stipulations are in there, she violated them and only gets a million dollars."

"I'd take the million and be happy."

"Would you? After nearly thirty years of marriage and living with the means to do and buy anything you want, you'd take a million and be happy? A house in most areas around here costs at least half that, if not all of it."

Kate tipped her head, acknowledging that truth. "So what did she have to say about all of this?"

"As you can imagine, she's pissed. I don't know all the details. Donald and I want to sit down and talk about it and what comes next."

"Which is why I'm here. You want me to babysit."

"Please. It's only for a few days."

"Days? Margo—"

"He's nervous about what she'll do now that she knows about the divorce. He wants Alex away from here in case she does something."

"What does he think she'll do?"

"Oh, mostly just throw a fit. Maybe come here to cuss him out and demand he give her what she wants. He doesn't want Alex here if that happens."

"Does she know about you and Alex?"

"About me, yes. Not Alex. At least Donald and I don't think so."

"And you want to keep Alex a secret a while longer."

"At least until Donald and I can be married. Please, Kate, will you take him for a few days? Four tops."

"I told you I needed time. I'm just settling in to seeing him with you when I visit."

"You never expected it to be this hard, did you?"

"No. But nothing is ever easy, is it?"

"Not for you and me." Margo put her hand over Kate's and squeezed. "If something happens, go to the safe deposit box. Everything you need is there. I set it up just like you taught me."

"Always have an escape plan."

"Everything is going to work out this time. I'll have Donald, Alex, the happy life we're building. Everything you and I dreamed of having for ourselves one day."

"If you believed that, you wouldn't ask me to take Alex and remind me that even now we need a way out."

"I know everything will be okay. I'm being cautious and protective of what I have. When we had nothing, it was easy to walk away. Now I have too much to lose to leave it to chance. Please, Kate. Do this for me, so I'll have peace of mind and can see Donald through this rough patch."

Kate gave in to need and picked up Alex from his crib, holding him to her chest. She stared down into his beautiful silver-blue eyes and frowned. "Your mother knows exactly how to get me to do her bidding."

"I know it's a lot to ask . . ."

Kate brushed her lips against Alex's forehead and smelled his sweet baby scent. Her heart softened, threatening to melt in her chest and reduce her to a teary-eyed mess. "I got this, Margo."

"You always do."

"Is everything okay?" Donald asked from the door.

"She said yes," Margo answered.

"Thank you, Kate. It's a lot to ask . . ."

"Both of you stop. I'm the aunt. I'm the perfect person to ask. You two enjoy a few days alone. Alex and I will hang at the bar, go dancing, you know, have some fun."

Margo laughed and touched Kate's shoulder. "You know he doesn't have ID to get into the bar."

Kate shrugged that off. "I could probably call some old contacts and get him a fake one."

"Okay, but cut him off after one bottle," Donald teased, holding up the baby bottle in his hand.

Kate took it and stuffed the nipple into Alex's mouth. He sucked greedily.

"You hear that, little man," Margo said, "One bottle and you're done. Aunt Kate will take care of you. Maybe you can teach her to smile more often." Margo kissed Alex's head and gave Kate a look that clearly said, "You're too serious."

"I'll take the bags down to the car," Donald volunteered, grabbing the diaper bag and a small suitcase.

"I put two cans of formula and extra bottles in the suitcase. More than enough for the few days you'll have him." Margo picked up the blanket from Alex's crib and a soft teddy. "These are his favorite. Donald will also put the play pen I left downstairs in your car. He can sleep in that." Margo scanned the room. "His pacifier is pinned to his shirt, but let me run downstairs and grab a spare just in case."

Kate sat with Alex in her arms in the rocking chair and let him finish his bottle. "Go. We're good here."

Margo stopped at the door and turned back. "You're going to be a wonderful mother someday."

Kate plastered on a fake smile for Margo's benefit. "You were always the sweeter, kinder, gentler one of us. Alex is in the best hands. I'm better by myself."

"Anything is possible, Kate. Just look at what I have with Donald."

"You two seem happy together. I'm happy for you."

"I hope you have something even better than what I've found. You just have to learn to trust and have a little faith."

This from the woman who fell in love with a married man and went to extreme lengths to have his child and the family they never had growing up at all costs, including sharing him with his wife—though he swore he hadn't slept with her in the last few years, especially since he met Margo. Kate dropped her cynicism and admitted the couple seemed happy. Kate wanted them to get past the impending divorce, marry, and be a family. They deserved it. Alex deserved to have his two loving parents together and happy without all the hiding their relationship and the drama.

"Come downstairs when he's finished."

Margo left the room. Kate sat in the waning sunlight and rocked Alex back and forth. She studied his sweet face from his wide forehead to his softly rounded cheeks. He caught her watching him and took time out of gorging on his milk to smile at her with his mouth still wrapped around the nipple.

"Charmer. You know I can't resist you. Don't tell your mother, but I really am looking forward to having you all to myself for a few days."

Dangerous, dangerous ground. Her heart might not be able to take letting him go again. She loved the little boy. He almost made her think dreams do actually come true and don't always turn into nightmares. Almost.

Kate put Alex up to her shoulder to pat his back. He let out a huge belch and settled his cheek back on her shoulder. "That's my big boy. You sound like every guy I've ever met in a bar."

Actually, it had been a long time since she'd been a part of that scene. She'd given up playing the party girl, the tough girl who liked even tougher guys, the girl who didn't care about anyone or anything, who only wanted to have a good time. Nothing about that scene or that girl seemed fun anymore.

At twenty-two, she turned a corner and got serious about herself and her life. For all her negativity about what happened to her in the past and the rotten way she'd been raised and treated, she'd never done a damn thing to change things for the better. A hard realization to wake up to on her birthday, to look back at her life and realize all she'd been doing is surviving. She wanted more. So she went back to school and got her degree in social work, using the supervised hours she worked in the field to gain experience and hone her skills to help with teenagers. She worked during the day and attended school at night to finish her masters this past year. Twenty-eight now, she finally had a job and a purpose in life that filled her up most days, even as the daunting task of helping others who sometimes didn't necessarily want it dragged her down but never knocked her out. She loved her clients. Most of them anyway. Teenagers had a way of making you earn every small achievement. They made her think and come up with creative ways to connect with them so she could get them to trust her and eventually try to change their lives.

Like she'd done.

"Come on, let's go find your mom and dad. It's time to blow this joint and get you settled at my place. Don't get me wrong, kiddo, I'm happy to have you for a few days, but that's it. You're not staying."

She tickled Alex's belly, making him laugh, before rising and carrying him out the bedroom door and across the landing to the stairs.

"It's going to be all right," Donald assured her sister. He reached up and cupped Margo's face in his hands, sweeping his thumbs over her cheeks and looking her right in the eye with so much love and devotion that Kate looked away. The tenderness in his affection for Margo stunned her every time. She'd rarely seen that kind of kindness and love between two people. She envied her sister that connection to Donald. It's why she'd agreed to help them, why she believed in them even if she didn't admit as much to her sister.

"What's wrong?" she asked, stepping down the last few stair treads. "Did something else happen?"

"Evan called. He's upset about the divorce and what that means for him as well as his mother," Donald said in his usual diplomatic way.

"Donald is cutting off his unlimited supply of funds and putting him on a reasonable budget," Margo added, rolling her eyes. Although Margo lived in a big, fancy house, she still clipped coupons and bought items on sale. She didn't take what she had for granted.

Something about the worry clouding Donald's eyes about the call triggered Kate's inner voice to warn her of danger. Her gut went tight. As easygoing as Donald was, his son Evan's personality swung the other way. All the way to volatile. Rage mixed with antipathy and entitlement. Not a good combination when you just told a rich kid he'd been essentially cut off.

"How did you leave things with him?"

"I told him to speak to his mother to get the real truth of why I'm doing all of this. He deserves to know, then he'll understand that what I'm offering is generous under the circumstances."

"He's been in trouble in the past. Do you think he'll come here and cause trouble for the two of you? Is that why you want Alex out of the house?"

"No," Donald said definitively. "No." This time the word held a lot less certainty. "My concern is that these types of calls will go on for the next few days, especially when my lawyer contacts Christina to serve her the papers. It's going to be a stressful time, and I don't want my emotions and Margo's worry to upset Alex. It's better this way."

Kate read between the lines. Donald didn't want to upset Margo, but he expected trouble in some form from his wife and son. At the very least, he knew they wouldn't go away quietly.

"I promise, Kate, I'll take care of everything. I won't let anything happen to Margo."

"I hold you to that promise."

He smiled, released her sister, and came to stand in front of Kate. He put his hand on Alex's back and the other on her shoulder. "I know you will. Margo, Alex, *and you* are my family. This will all blow over and we'll move on together and watch Alex grow into a wonderful and loved man. He is the gift we share. Nothing will make me happier than to have this business behind us. I want to spend the rest of my life making Margo happy and raise our son. All of us together and happy."

Kate's inner pessimist shouted, "Yeah, right." But holding Alex in her arms, seeing his happy face and the innocence in his eyes sparked the belief that maybe the life Donald described wasn't out of reach. They needed to work for it, and that included taking care of old business.

"Call me if anything more happens. Keep me in the loop."

"We will. I promise," Donald agreed.

Her sister and Donald walked her out to the car. Margo took Alex, hugged him close, and put him in the car seat in the back. Margo settled Alex, then kissed him on the head. "Be good for Auntie. I'll miss you, sweetheart. I love you."

"I promise, I'll take good care of him."

"I know you will. It's just I've never been away from him since he came home."

"Go with her," Donald suggested at the last minute.

"No. I'm staying with you and seeing you through this ordeal."

"That's just it, it is an ordeal. I'll handle it. It's not for you to work out, but for me to do."

"We're a couple. Partners. We do things together. The fun things and the tedious."

Donald hugged Margo close. "I much prefer the fun we have together."

"Then Kate will take Alex, and you and I will have some fun." The sparkle in her sister's eyes when she said those words made Kate blush. These two were good together. Margo's fun nature balanced Donald's seriousness.

Donald set her sister aside, leaned in and kissed Alex goodbye, closed the door, and opened Kate's door for her. Before Kate took her seat, he reached for her hand and held it tight. "Thank you for doing this." He pressed hard on the key he'd placed in her hand and whispered, "Just in case."

*G*ive in to your Impulses!

These unforgettable stories only take a second to buy and give you hours of reading pleasure!

Go to *www.AvonImpulse.com* and see what we have to offer.

Available wherever e-books are sold.

*Next month, don't miss these exciting
new love stories only from
Avon Books*

Facing Fire by HelenKay Dimon
When his uncle is brutally murdered, Josiah King knows that he and his black ops team are targets, along with everyone they love. Josiah is determined to unravel the plot—until long-legged redhead Sutton Dahl becomes a dangerous distraction. Josiah and Sutton become unlikely partners, fighting for their lives even as the attraction between them flares into real passion.

The Legend of Lyon Redmond by Julie Anne Long
Rumor has it she broke Lyon Redmond's heart. But while many a man has since wooed the dazzling Olivia Eversea, none has ever won her—which is why jaws drop when she suddenly accepts a viscount's proposal. As the day of her wedding approaches, Lyon—now a driven, dangerous, infinitely devastating man—decides it's time for a reckoning.

Forever Your Earl by Eva Leigh
Eleanor Hawke loves a good scandal. And readers of her successful gossip rag live for the exploits of her favorite subject: Daniel Balfour, the Earl of Ashford. Daniel has secrets, and he knows if Eleanor gets wind of them, a man's life could be at stake. What better way to distract a gossip than by inviting her to experience his debauchery first-hand?

Available wherever books are sold
or please call 1-800-331-3761 to order.